Terry Wright

2016, TWB Press
https://www.twbpress.com

The 13th Power War
Book 3 in "The 13th Power Trilogy"
Copyright 2016 by Terry Wright

Published by TWB Press, https://www.twbpress.com

Cover Art by Terry Wright

ISBN: 978-1-944045-25-8

Then came man, about 20,000 years ago, and from that point on he destroyed his enemies without compassion, enslaved other races, and murdered for sport all manner of men and beasts.

Chapter One

ON THE OTHER SIDE OF THE GALAXY:

High in orbit above the green planet, *Questnar's* flight deck bristled with activity. *"Turn to heading five...twenty-four...nine,"* came the controller's voice over the intercom. Luthes Rez configured his Orbital Patrol Ship for docking.

He gripped the helmswheel, specially molded to fit his long fingers, and swung *Questnar's* bow to port. A million stars swept across his scope screen as the digital bearing indicator scrolled through the turn. With the twin suns of Beltzee now aft, the ship's shadow fell on *Latearian*, a spherical spaceport gleaming silver and red against the star-studded backdrop of space. Blue and green lights twinkled on its out-masts, and internally lit viewports glowed like a thousand eyes in the night.

Luthes' heart beat wildly. This wasn't just a routine supply run to restock the ship's stores. This time his wife and daughter were on-station, awaiting his arrival.

He pulled back on the throttles. Sixteen roaddium thrusters retracted. The huge Orbital Patrol Ship eased into a glide slope toward the remote outpost orbiting beyond the planet's ring-plane.

"Clear to dock," the controller said.

ComCap Kerillan sat upright in his observation chair. Crystalline bars gleamed from the shoulder pads of his white jacket. "Take us in, Trantenant Rez."

"Yes, sir." Luthes aligned his tracking beam with the

locator beacon on Dock Two. Though he'd executed this maneuver many times and never once put a dent in his ship, the procedure always made his fingers tingle, especially now that he had an audience. He imagined Verrilla holding Sashi's small hand as they waited on the receiving deck, probably at a viewport, in awe of *Questnar's* majestic approach. After a year's tour of duty in orbit, Luthes struggled to contain his excitement over seeing them again.

An alarm sounded a shrill wail that sent a chill up his spine. Countless training exercises had conditioned him to immediately recognize the alert: *Repulsor Stations.*

"Tarreeda Cruiser at three...forty-four...four," Operations reported.

ComCap Kerillan leaned forward, his eyes fixed on the interceptor strobe where a red blip had come out of deep space. Disbelief etched deep lines in his weathered face. "How do you know it's the Tarreeda?"

"Who else could it be?"

"Abort the docking," Kerrillan shouted.

Luthes executed full power. *Questnar* shuddered as the thrusters reengaged. He spun the helmswheel to starboard, pitched the bow up, and watched *Latearian* disappear from his scope screen along with all hope of seeing his family any time soon.

"Navigator to helm. Set course, seven...twenty-two...zero."

"No," Kerillan bellowed. "We will not run from these murderers."

"But, sir. A direct frontal repel on a Tarreeda cruiser? We'll be slaughtered."

"We must protect *Latearian*," Kerillan ordered. "Trantenant Rez, turn about, three...forty-four...four."

"As you wish, sir."

Operations' protocol mandated evasive action should a lone Orbital Patrol Ship encounter a Tarreeda cruiser. The ComCap should fall back, await the Beltzan Fleet, and then join the armada to repel the invaders. But now, with the other ships patrolling thousands of decks away, Luthes feared his wife and daughter might witness the total destruction of *Questnar* and his untimely death.

"Repulsors on full."

A lump formed in Luthes' throat. *Latearian* could be caught in the crossfire. Verrilla and Sashi could be killed, or worse: captured, enslaved, and tortured for no better reason than their long fingers. The Beltzans were different from the Tarreeda and thus scorned throughout history.

Strapped in his helmschair, Luthes felt powerless to help his young family.

Navigation announced, "It's traveling too fast, sir. New heading, two...thirty-five...one."

The red blip streaked across *Questnar's* flight path, far out of repulsor range.

"Give chase."

"Navigator to helm, new heading, two...thirty-five...two."

Luthes gave the helmswheel a hard spin to port. The Tarreeda cruiser fell dead-center in his scope screen. Though the killers appeared to be running, he knew they could turn and fight at any time. At least now, *Questnar* would draw fire away from *Latearian*, which made him breathe a little easier, however short-lived, as the Tarreeda cruiser just entered low orbit around his green home planet of Beltzee. A new fear knifed his chest. The Tarreeda might be here to attack the planet. Luthes could only imagine the horrors awaiting the citizens below: burning cities, charred bodies—

"Communications," ComCap Kerillan shouted. "Alert the fleet, and get a z-visual up here now."

Outside scanner images came up on the scope screens with resolution set to maximum zoom. Luthes made out the silver form of a swept-winged craft, smaller than a Beltzan cruiser and tiny compared to his Orbital Patrol Ship.

Brilliant beams of light emanated from eight stern ports on the cruiser, driving it forward, a propulsion system he'd never seen before.

"Range, four-four-seven decks," navigation announced.

Had the Tarreeda developed a new kind of cruiser, one that could takeoff and land, operate in space, and still deliver enough firepower to destroy the Beltzan fleet?

Another thought jarred his brain. What if this cruiser wasn't alone? Perhaps it was a scout with an approaching armada behind it. After all, the Tarreeda had twenty thousand years to prepare for this invasion. And they had every reason to seek revenge against the Beltzans who had banished them to the Ice Planet. Now *Questnar* could be Beltzee's only hope for survival. She was the most powerful Orbital Patrol Ship in the fleet, equipped with the fastest engines and the heaviest repulsors. And it would be up to his piloting skills to repel the invaders.

With renewed concentration on his scope screen, he gritted his teeth and hummed a hymn to *Cada*, God of the Universe. However, even at full throttle, the gap between *Questnar* and the Tarreeda was not closing fast enough. Already the cruiser had reached Beltzee's horizon and disappeared into the dark side.

"Navigator to helm, turn hard, four...sixty-four...ten."

Luthes swallowed. That was ninety degrees off course. "But why?" he shouted. "I can still catch them."

Kerillan stabbed him with a sharp glare. "Slow to five decks and prepare to rendezvous with the fleet."

Disappointment smothered the cold dread in Luthes' bloodstream. He worked the helmswheel to starboard. ComCap Kerrillan was right to give the order. Their odds of survival would be much greater if the fleet were behind them.

The ComCap addressed his Operations officers. "Prepare to repel the invaders on their next orbital pass.

Has Fleet Base been notified?"

"Reinforcements are on the way up, sir."

"Pray to Cada they arrive in time."

Pride swelled in Luthes' chest as he steered *Questnar* toward the fleet, which had assembled atop the color-streaked Beltzee ring-plane. Thirty or more Orbital Patrol Ships pitched and yawed on invisible waves of energy reflecting off the rings.

As ComCap Kerillan conferred with Operations about tactics and protocol, Luthes watched Beltzee slowly turn beneath *Questnar's* keel. Green fertile lands dotted with blue seas and crisscrossed by red river basins stretched to the horizon. White bands of clouds drifted in the atmosphere, which changed colors from green, to yellow, to orange and red, and then to the black velvet of space. He had seen this sight so often that he'd become numb to its splendor, but now he feared his beautiful world was doomed.

A squadron of Orbital Patrol Ships materialized below the ring-plane. The Kedrikan division, fresh from the teleport at Kedrikee, now formed a line of defense along grid thirty-three, the last known orbital track of the invaders. Luthes felt emboldened but checked any sense of relief. More ships merely gave the Tarreeda more targets to destroy.

"Twenty seconds to apogee," Operations announced. "Repulsors on ready, sir."

Kerillan gave the order. "Trantenant Rez, bring *Questnar* forward of the fleet. We shall draw the first volley. Evade if you can."

"Fifteen seconds."

Sweat beaded on Luthes' forehead. Nudging power to the thrusters, he understood the ComCap's strategy. *Questnar* could withstand more cannon fire than the smaller Orbital Patrol Ships, but how much more remained to be seen.

Operations officers huddled around the strategy dome and chattered over tactics and probabilities, this being the first time their training had been put to the test. And for the first time Luthes contemplated dying from a Tarreeda plasma cannon blast: a flash of light, crushing pressure, and then nothing.

"Ten seconds."

What would become of his wife and daughter? Would the Tarreeda use them as they pleased, for their pleasures or their toils? He wished the ugly race of hairy-faced, short-fingered barbarians had stayed on the Ice Planet. Now he feared he'd witness what all of Beltzee had dreaded for generations, the Tarreeda's return to power.

"Five seconds."

An eerie silence came over the flight deck. Luthes' heart pounded behind his eardrums. He pinched himself, hoping to awaken from a nightmare.

The cruiser reappeared from the dark side.

"Range, two-two-zero decks," navigation shouted.

"Fire."

A ball of brilliant energy boomed from *Questnar's* bow-mounted repulsor cannon, flashed across space, and slammed into the Tarreeda cruiser. It veered off to port, spun in a circle, and stopped.

"Advance," Kerillan ordered.

Luthes shoved the throttle bars full forward. "Engaged."

Questnar accelerated with the fleet and began closing in on the invaders. He'd never seen battle. None of them had. They'd never killed anyone. The thought of taking a life, even in self-defense, made his stomach sick. The blood of another living soul on his hands could never be washed off. But he would do what he had to do, as they all would, to protect their home planet.

"Range, four-zero-five decks."

"Hold fire! Wait for my command!"

The Tarreeda were probably recovering from the surprise repel and preparing to unleash a volley from their deadly cannons. If so, the entire Beltzan Fleet could be wiped out. Since the Tarreeda Wars, lethal weapons had been banned on Beltzee, but considering the violent nature of the Tarreeda, no such ban had been put into place on the Ice Planet. These warmongers believed the deadlier the weapon the better.

The League of Beltzee may have left itself gravely under-defended. However, the cruiser was so small its hull could easily be shattered by multiple repulsor blasts. The fleet wasn't defeated yet.

"Range, three-zero-zero decks."

Luthes looked at his hand and cringed at the thought of being persecuted because of his four-jointed fingers. He cast a solemn glance at the ComCap and down the polished flight deck to the other stone-faced Beltzan crewmen at their stations. If the fleet failed to stop the Tarreeda now, their futures would be fraught with unthinkable acts of torture and death, their bodies impaled on stakes, nailed to crosses—

"Range, two-five-zero decks," Navigation announced.

The cruiser just floated in place. Why hadn't the Tarreeda unleashed their arsenal of cannons?

"Range, two-three-zero."

What were they waiting for?

"On my mark..."

The Tarreeda cruiser's light thrusters dimmed out.

Something wasn't right about this...

"Wait," Operations ordered.

An alarm sounded. *Repulsors Locked Out.*

"What's the meaning of this?" ComCap Kerillan bellowed.

"It's unarmed, sir,"

"How do you know that for sure?"

"They would have fired by now. We recommend

capture and interrogation at Fleet Base."

"And allow those murderers back on our planet?" Kerillan grumped. "Not on my watch."

"This could be the beginning of something bigger, sir."

"We cannot forget what they did to our ancestors."

"But we need to know what they have planned for us."

Rubbing his smooth chin, Kerillan said, "Very well. All ships close in. Be careful. It might be a trap."

Additional Orbital Patrol Ships appeared in the distance, some from Retakan, and others from Berakatee. Together, they swarmed around the Tarreeda cruiser, closing in, blocking every escape route.

"Navigator to helm," Operations called. "Proceed on visual for capture."

Uneasiness wormed in Luthes' stomach. He worked the helmswheel and throttles, maneuvering the gigantic *Questnar* into position, bow-to-bow with the small cruiser. Trepidation gripped him fiercely, caused his palms to sweat. The Tarreeda crewmen were up to something. He was sure of it. They were giving up without a fight, totally unlike any Tarreeda tactics he'd ever read about.

With nerves on full alert, each muscle ready to command *Questnar* to evade, he retracted the thrusters to full stop and hoped they hadn't fallen into a trap.

With intensified curiosity, he studied the cruiser on his scope screen in hopes of getting a glimpse of the Tarreeda through the craft's front viewports.

"Magnetabeam engaged," Operations reported. "We've got them."

"Boarding teams report to the docking bay," Kerillan said. "With stun-wands and headgear. I don't want any mistakes."

"Right away, sir."

As the magnetabeam drew the Tarreeda cruiser

toward the docking bay, huge doors opened on *Questnar's* bow. Already, the shield had been deployed to hold back the vacuum of space.

Luthes focused on the cruiser's viewports. The silhouettes of three figures appeared, backlit by interior lighting. A little closer and he'd get a glimpse of their faces, faces that Beltzan eyes had not seen for a thousand generations.

Bow-mounted lamps flared on, illuminating the Tarreeda cruiser and its occupants as they stared out their viewports at *Questnar*. Luthes' jaw dropped at the sight of their light-skin and hairless faces with white-rimmed eyeballs. One was a square-jawed male with a patch of black hair under his nose. The other two were soft-faced females, one with short black hair and one with long yellow hair, stunningly similar to his wife, Verrilla. Beautiful. But how could that be? The Tarreeda were ugly.

The cruiser executed a hard turn to starboard, exposing its flank to the fleet, as if to turn and flee. Luthes expected to see a black cross painted prominently on the fuselage, the sign of the Tarreeda. Instead he saw symbols he didn't recognize: *NASA - USA*

A chill shuddered through his body. "Sir," he shouted to Kerillan. "These are not the Tarreeda."

The cruiser suddenly disappeared from the scope screen as if it were sucked away by some invisible force.

"Docking bay, report."

"They're gone, sir."

Luthes couldn't believe what he had just seen.

Aliens.

Chapter Two

At 37,000 feet and somewhere over Georgia, roaring Hawker jet engines were but a soft drone inside the luxurious passenger cabin. Dr. Janis Mackey fidgeted in his plush seat, annoyed at his wife, Tracy, as she flipped through the pages of a Cosmopolitan magazine. She sat next to him, legs crossed at the knees, not the least bit apprehensive about this impromptu flight to NASA.

Janis loosened his tie. He couldn't get Stan Burton's message out of his mind, the one he'd left on his phone while he and Tracy vacationed in Steamboat Springs, celebrating their first wedding anniversary.

"Janis, I need your help. Bring Tracy."

Stan's voice had sounded urgent and raw with worry. What kind of trouble had he gotten himself into this time? Janis looked at his watch and exhaled loud enough to draw Tracy's attention away from her browsing. "Thirty minutes."

"Relax," she muttered.

The forty-four-year-old laser physicist wasn't easily shaken. It was the redhead in her.

His gaze traced the sleek lines of her gray pantsuit, her white lace collar, and on to her flowing red hair that glistened with sunlight beaming in through the oval window. Some people had said she was his trophy wife. Not so. She was his rock. "I don't know how you can be so relaxed."

She scanned another magazine page. "You worry too much."

Somebody had to. "Stan didn't say what this meeting

was about."

Tracy closed the magazine. "It must be some math problem."

"He's an engineer, quite familiar with mathematics. But why us?"

"Who else can he trust?"

"He should've called Ray Crawford."

The Hawker hit a bump of air. Janis's stomach jumped and settled.

Tracy's eyebrows tightened. She put down the magazine. "Ray's been drinking again."

"Kate's death hit him hard, I know, but—"

"She meant the world to him."

"But that's no reason to drink himself stupid. I think there's more to his depression than mourning over his dead wife."

"Like what?"

"Something's been on his mind since he came back from the 13th Power."

"You should ask him about it."

"I have no desire to talk to him. Look what happened the last time I got involved with him. We both damn near got killed."

"He's your best friend."

"Was—"

Ding. The fasten seatbelt light blinked on, and the jet began to sink in the air.

Tracy gazed out the oval window. "He took a big risk."

"It wasn't like he went to the ends of the earth. No. He travelled across the galaxy to get his family back. And it almost worked."

"Lisa's taking care of him now."

Ray's daughter, Lisa, the California girl: blonde, tanned, and crazy like a fox. "It's been a year since Kate died. About time Ray got on with his life. Lisa has better things to do than babysit him all day."

"Some people take a long time to recover from grief." Tracy turned from the window. "Would you get over losing me in a year?"

She had him on that point. "Eternity, babe. Eternity."

As the Hawker banked left, the captain announced, "We've been cleared to land at Kennedy Space Center. It's a balmy eighty-three degrees under partly cloudy skies."

Janis took Tracy's hand. "I've got a bad feeling about this."

"Florida can't be worse than California."

"I mean...why the private jet...and the escort?" He indicated the scar-faced man in the black suit, sitting back by the lavatory door. He'd been whittling on a piece of wood the entire trip. Tiny shavings littered his slacks and the area around his seat.

"I like the royal treatment," Tracy said. "Makes me feel important."

"It makes me feel indebted."

Smiling, she gave him a reassuring tap on the knee. "Maybe they'll take us to Disney World."

Janis smirked. How typical it was of her, always making honey out of horseshit. "Stan didn't invite us to NASA for a vacation. Something big is going down."

"Let's hear him out, decide then."

He watched out the window as the Hawker touched down at the Shuttle Landing Facility and taxied toward the parking tarmac. A black limousine and a line of dark blue Air Force staff cars awaited them. Military brass and men in black suits stood around, their eyes on the jet as it whined to a stop.

Tracy looked out the window. "I don't see Stan."

Janis took a look for himself. "Who the hell are all those guys?"

The scar-faced man folded his jackknife. "Your welcoming committee." His gruff voice matched his rough complexion. He stashed his whittling project into his suit coat pocket. "Show them your best behavior, kids."

Tracy said, "They look like car salesmen."

A chill tingled Janis's neck hairs. He unfastened his seatbelt and stood. "I hope you're right about Disney World."

Stooping to clear the ceiling, their scar-faced escort moved up the aisle. "Let's go."

The cabin door popped open. Sunshine burst in. He followed Tracy out. The humidity hit him first, and then the heat. The smell of sea brine tainted the air along with the buzz of dragonflies. Turkey vultures circled on thermals above. The entire area was infested with the big birds, some perched on power poles and communications towers while others strutted about the runway drainage canals, wings spread to cool themselves. They looked like a bad omen straight out of a horror movie.

"Welcome to Florida," Janis muttered to Tracy under his breath.

"Will you stop it?"

Several yards away, the military brass stood at attention. Black-suited men stepped forward flanking a four-star general. A brick wall of a man, he wore a pressed khaki Army uniform, the buttons reflecting sharp spines of sunshine. From this distance, the slab of ribbons pinned to his chest resembled a fruit salad. The smile on his weathered face seemed genuine.

Walking toward the general, Tracy clutched Janis's arm. "What's he doing here?"

Janis had seen that face before, on the news and in the papers and on the Internet. General Brigham. He was a worse omen than the vultures. The Star Wars fiasco. General Brigham's testimony had taken down the President along with his chief advisors. Terrorism escalated around the world. He'd shown how America couldn't be trusted with its own weapons of mass destruction.

"Welcome to Kennedy Space Center." General Brigham outstretched a beefy hand.

Anxiety pulsed through Janis's veins, lethal as snake venom. He ignored Brigham's offered hand, not wanting to appear the least bit friendly. "What's this all about?"

"Where's Stan?" Tracy asked.

Brigham retracted his hand. "Let's get out of this sun, shall we?"

He ushered them to a black limousine where an airman wearing dress blues opened the rear door.

Janis looked at Tracy. She got in without hesitating. He took a deep breath and ducked inside. The air conditioning felt good. He sat next to her on a seat directly across from the bar. Once the general was seated, the door slammed shut, and the limo sped off. Out the rear window, Janis saw the staff cars swing around and fall in line behind them.

Janis blinked. *What's so goddamned important that we require an escort?*

Brigham offered up a bottle of scotch. "Care for a shot?"

Tracy shook her head.

The general may have thought he had everything under control enough to relax with a drink, but Janis didn't share his confidence and waved him off.

"Very well." Brigham poured himself a double. "Our first stop is the briefing room."

"Will Stan be meeting us there?" Tracy asked.

"We have an interesting program in store for you."

Janis frowned. *All this hoopla and no urgency? An interesting program?* And Brigham was deliberately dodging questions about Stan's whereabouts. "Why didn't Stan meet us when we arrived?"

The limo turned off the flight line and picked up speed.

Brigham eyed the amber drink in his glass. "Stan

Burton is a little busy right now."

"Too busy for his friends?" Tracy leaned forward. "Then why did he ask us here? What's the matter with him?"

Brigham showed a bulldog scowl. "Are you people always this paranoid?"

"If you knew what we've been through—"

"Stan told me all about it," Brigham cut in. "The 13th Power experiment, Simi Valley, the Higgs boson, the transporter—"

"So you see why we have to be careful."

"Can't be too careful with the Higgs, now can we?" Brigham grinned and downed the scotch.

"The Higgs boson is nothing to fool around with, General," Janis chimed in. "It's the particle that gives matter mass. We call it the *God* particle for a reason. Screw around with the Higgs, get it wrong just once, and the earth could be reduced to a cloud of dust drifting in the proverbial firmament."

Brigham huffed. "Bullshit."

Idiot.

The limo careened across a parking lot, turned into a garage, and squealed down a concrete ramp, finally grinding to a stop in front of an entrance marked *SECURITY*.

Car doors slammed. An entourage of officers and suits gathered around the limo while the driver marched around and let Janis and Tracy out.

The general addressed his men. "Wait here."

With Tracy on his arm, Janis followed Brigham through the doors and down a long corridor to a door marked *Briefing Room*. The area was roped off with yellow tape and guarded by armed soldiers.

"Right in here." Brigham led them into a dimly lit room where rows of chairs stood before a raised platform. A counter stretched across the back of the platform, cluttered with computer monitors, digital clocks, and models of the space shuttle, communication satellites, and the International Space Station. On the wall hung a map of the earth with several orbital tracks drawn on it. A giant flat screen TV began to drop from the ceiling.

Brigham stood in front of the descending screen. "This is the room NASA uses to update the media on the progress of their missions. For this briefing, of course, the media is not invited. Have a seat."

The flat screen clacked to a stop.

Janis gritted his teeth. "We came all this way to see a movie?"

"Where's the popcorn?" Tracy asked.

"Are you brainards always this difficult?" Brigham shot back.

"We'll show you how difficult we can be," Janis shouted. "Get Stan Burton in here right now."

"Shut up and take a seat." Brigham's voice had dropped an octave, giving Janis cause for alarm. The man meant business.

Janis didn't care to experience Brigham's ruthless reputation firsthand, so he swallowed his disdain and sat with Tracy in the middle of the front row.

Brigham growled out, "That's more like it."

The briefing room door closed with a bang. A dead bolt clicked. Janis felt trapped. Were they locked in, or was everyone else locked out?

Holding up a remote control device, Brigham began, "What you are about to see here is top secret. In other words, Janis, you tell no one."

"And if I do?" Janis asked, intent on defiance.

"If this gets out, I'll know who talked. Your lives won't be worth a nickel."

Janis clenched his fists.

Tracy squeezed his arm. "Just go with the flow, dear."

He slouched in his chair. "Bastard," he muttered.

Brigham cleared his throat. "Stan was interlinking a new calibration program in the space transporter. You know the one, Janis, the one Ray stole from NASA and flew into the 13th Power."

"He borrowed it," Janis said.

"Stan came across a recording of that flight."

Tracy said, "Ray destroyed the data disc."

"The space probe made a digital backup in the computer. When we asked Ray about it, he wouldn't talk to us."

"So you're going to show it to us?" Janis asked. "What for?"

Brigham raised an eyebrow. "Have a little patience, will you?"

Janis groaned, but his curiosity was a bursting dam. What had the space probe recorded?

The lights went out.

Brigham went on with his narration. "We dubbed the cockpit voice recorder over the space probe video of what Ray and his wife and daughter would have seen out the windows. They'd travelled a hundred-thousand light years from earth in about seven seconds. The Higgs Field made it possible, an interstellar highway discovered during the 13th Power experiments in Simi Valley."

"Old news," Janis said.

"Well, here's something new for you, Janis." Brigham activated the remote.

A beeping alarm sounded. The screen brightened as a white waveform pattern oscillated on a black background.

Kate's voice on the cockpit recorder: *"What's that?"*

"The space probe." Ray's voice. *"It's detected something."*

Switches clicked. The beeping stopped, but the pattern continued wavering on the screen.

"It's a radio frequency," Ray said. *"Coming from..."* Keyboard clatter.

The space probe switched to video mode. Two yellow suns appeared on the screen, bright enough to make Janis squint.

"A binary star," Tracy said. "That's not uncommon."

Janis muttered, "So what's all the fuss about?"

The twin stars swept from the screen. Star-studded space streaked by until a planet appeared. Colorful rings encircled its green and blue surface. The space probe started beeping like crazy. A message scrolled across the screen: *MULTIPLE LIFE FORMS DETECTED.*

"There," Ray said on the recording. *"Coming from that green planet."*

Janis sat up straight, his heart beat rising.

Ray's voice: *"We're not alone."*

"Why didn't he tell us this?" Tracy asked.

Janis couldn't breathe. He felt numb. Ray had been keeping the ultimate secret. No wonder he'd turned to the bottle.

The transporter streaked toward the green planet at breathtaking speed. Flight control computers initiated a low altitude orbit, just inside the wide, rainbow-like ring-plane.

Lisa's voice: *"I hope you know what you're doing, Dad."*

"Ray doesn't have a clue what he's doing," Janis managed to whisper to Tracy, his tongue dry as pencil lead.

Brigham snickered. "I bet you're glad you came now."

Janis set his jaw. What did Brigham intend to do with this information?

The space probe recorded the transporter's passage into darkness. Lights appeared on the planet's surface now, some in huge clusters, some smaller, each with a network of luminous arms radiating outward and connecting with the other bright clusters. Some areas were pitch-black. Some flickered with lightning.

"My God," Tracy said. "Are those cities and

highways."

"An entire civilization," Brigham said.

Anger and betrayal made a hot stew in Janis's stomach. "Why the hell didn't Ray tell us about this?"

The scene returned to daylight, revealing an armada of wedge-shaped spaceships that seemed to have come out of nowhere. Janis's heart lurched. The closest ship was a massive gray and white fortress with lighted towers and flashing perimeter lights. Behind it, thirty or more smaller ships lined up above the planet's ring-plane. The fleet pitched and rolled like boats riding the swells of an invisible sea.

Ray's voice: *"Oh, shit!"*

A blast of light came at the transporter.

"Hold on!" Ray shouted.

Boom.

Rattling alarms went off. The space probe view shuddered. The transporter stopped.

"Hold together, baby." Ray's voice.

Tracy gasped. "They're under attack."

"Ray should have told us about this," Janis said. "I'll kill him."

Another armada of alien ships materialized out of nowhere.

"They're surrounded," Janis said, trying to remember this wasn't a Hollywood movie. This was the real deal.

"Dad?" Lisa's voice, squeaky with terror.

Kate's voice. *"Get us out of here, Ray."*

Tracy clutched Janis's arm. "They're trapped."

"They're going to kill us!" Kate's voice.

Ray: *"They could have done that by now...if they wanted."*

"They're going to take us alive, Dad...experiment on us—"

"Not if I can help it."

Keyboard clicks. A moment passed before a

computerized female voice announced: *Regeneration in one minute.*

"He's activated the regenerator," Tracy said. "Now we know why they came back early."

Janis's fingers tingled. A hum filled the briefing room. On the bow of the massive spaceship, a huge opening appeared, like some kind of door.

Regeneration in thirty seconds.

The space probe recorded the alien ship's brightly lit interior, a landing dock, Janis assumed, with yellow and red markings on the floor. Figures moved upright like humans. They wore maroon uniforms and yellow helmets with silver face shields. Black-gloved hands with extremely long fingers brandished sticks or clubs...or some kind of unimaginable weapons.

"Aliens," Tracy croaked.

Janis couldn't believe his eyes.

Ray said, *"They're going to pull us into that ship."*

Regeneration in five seconds, four, three...

The view turned liquid, blurring and distorting the spaceship and the waiting aliens with weapons extended.

...two, one...

Janis held his breath.

...zero!

In a flash of light, the alien spaceship shrunk to a pinpoint and vanished. The green planet disappeared. The space probe seemed to be in freefall through a spinning tunnel of starlight, bending and twisting in space like a cosmic amusement park ride until the screen went black.

Janis sat, mouth agape, blinking, his mind reeling in disbelief. "Ray has got a lot of explaining to do."

The room lights flickered on.

Tracy sighed. "There goes our trip to Disney World."

Chapter Three

O n the outpost *Latearian*, Docking Bay Two's massive chamber echoed the sounds of ceremony and commotion. Luthes disembarked *Questnar* through port-gate seven to meet his wife and daughter. They were supposed to be around here somewhere.

Heavily ionized air tasted like copper. From every direction, cart trains laden with supplies and equipment wormed toward upload lifts under *Questnar's* keel, a massive expanse twice the length of the other Orbital Patrol Ships. Maintenance men rolled scaffolds to access panels and put rattle wrenches to fasteners. Tanker crews attached hoses to outboard terminals and began recharging the thrusters with roaddium fuel. In the front reception area, personnel dressed in blue uniforms greeted new arrivals and distributed information drafts, ricca juice, and wedges of sweet lara.

Luthes scanned the triple-decker banks of windows above, hoping to see Verrilla and Sashi with their faces pressed to the glass and their eyes beaming wide, but the receiving deck was crammed with spectators and crewmen's families, everyone vying for a view of the goings-on below. After a year of orbital patrols and constant battle station drills since the Tarreeda alert, *Questnar* had finally come to port, victorious, or so it seemed, as the invaders had not returned.

"Trantenant Rez."

Luthes whirled about and faced his ComCap. "Yes, sir."

"Fine job," Kerillan said. "One day you shall have

your own command."

"Like my father, yes, thank you for your confidence in me, sir, but today I must find Verrilla and Sashi."

Kerillan looked around at the crowd. "Good luck with that."

There must've been a thousand Beltzans milling about.

"Verrilla's not answering her PCD." Luthes unsnapped his Personal Communications Device from his belt and showed him the display. "Goes directly to message box."

"Maybe she's not on-station."

That would account for her not answering his call. The last time he talked with her over *Questnar's* com-channel, she'd said she wanted to go home. However, teleportation had suspended operations during the Tarreeda alert, a kneejerk reaction so common in the name of security; no one got on or off the outpost until the threat had passed. "You're probably right," Luthes said to Kerillan. "Now that teleportation is operational, she may have gone home."

He knuckled Luthes' shoulder. "Check the message terminal. She probably left you a note. If not, see the teleport officers. They will have a record of her departure."

"If I can get through this crowd."

Wagging a long finger, Kerillan said, "Just don't be late for debriefing."

"No, sir."

Kerillan turned and disappeared into the masses.

Feeling abandoned, Luthes made his way to the message board terminal along the starboard bulkhead, a vast screen of scrolling names. Flashing green lights next to the names indicated messages awaiting crewmen or officers. They stood the length of the terminal, shoulder to shoulder, headsets in place, listening to their messages.

He found his name. No green light. Why would she

have left without leaving him word? A simple PCD call. A message. A com-channel text. But nothing?

Disappointment and frustration waged war in his chest. Now he'd have to go up to *Teleportation* to see what they knew of her whereabouts.

He muscled through the crowd toward lifts in the front atrium. On level C, he rode the stand-way to a maze of dimly lit corridors that reverberated voices and footsteps. The filtered and moisturized air smelled like wet boots and pulsed with vibrations emitted from the riddium power plant deep within *Latearian's* core. He followed the signs to *Teleportation*.

Fleet crewmen stood in long lines for their turns in the recently reactivated TelePods. Sure that his rank would give him priority, Luthes strode directly to the counter.

A plump clerk cast him a questioning glance.

"I only want information," he said. "How long must I wait for a teleport officer?"

"They are on the receiving deck." She twitched her nose. "It's not often an Orbital Patrol Ship arrives with such fanfare. You must be proud."

"I'm looking for my wife and daughter...Rez. Can you help me?"

"Let's see." She engaged a virtual log scanner and spoke to it. "Rez...Report...Please."

A bleeping sound then: "Ah, here we are. Verrilla and Sashi Rez. TTP 883. Tele-to-port on station."

"But did she leave?"

"Tele-from-port has not been activated. They must be here somewhere."

"She's not answering her PCD. Maybe you can call her quarters."

After a quick glance at her control panel, she shook her head. "All the conduits are busy. Once the fleet is in and all personnel are taken care of, I'm sure things will settle down. In the meantime, she may find you."

"Thanks."

Her encouraging words didn't make him feel any better. The thought of his wife searching for him in the midst of all this chaos settled in his stomach like a hunk of granitite. As he turned from the counter, he checked his PCD display once more.

Nothing.

Worse, the reminder flashed *URGENT*. He had to hurry to debriefing.

***

On her hands and knees, Verrilla worked a scrubber on the galley floor. Sweat soaked her blouse, and her fingers and knees ached. Steam from massive pots swirled through the air and carried with it the aroma of cavou stew, a concoction of whitefish and cavou roots smothered in yampamam broth, aromatic and spicy. Dunking the scrubber into a soapy bucket, she moaned and swiped the floor once more. Soon, the first-shift personnel on *Latearian* would break for midmeal, jam the serving lines, and fill the cafeteria with chatter about *Questnar* and the Tarreeda. Duty first, always duty first, but this was no life fit for an officer's wife.

"Mom." Sashi lugged in a fresh bucket of water. Her sopping dress hung on her dainty frame. "We have to hurry."

Sitting back on her heels, Verrilla hooked a loose lock of yellow hair behind her ear. "We cannot go until after everyone is fed and this mess is cleaned up."

"But Daddy is probably looking for us."

"He's worried sick, I'm sure." She would have called him if Sashi hadn't dropped the PCD in the water bucket. Cada had a weird sense of humor.

Working the scrubber again, Verrilla shared her daughter's impatience. This had been a trying journey for both of them, especially after the Tarreeda alert. Their guest quarters had expired two days later, forcing her to seek a berth on Level T for transients. Officers' wives carried no more weight on this remote outpost than any other refugee. Luxury accommodations were as impossible to come by as new dresses.

She remembered that day as if it were yesterday. On the lift to Level T, Sashi had started crying.

"I want to see Daddy."

Verrilla smoothed Sashi's tangled white hair. "When he gets back, honey. I promise."

The lift stopped at Level L. A stocky man got on. He wore a white shirt and baggy gray pants which he'd tucked into the top of his boots. A Beltzan Fleet Service emblem adorned his left arm sleeve, a picture of the ringed planet resting in Cada's upturned palms. *The Shield of Beltzee*, it read.

"My husband is in the Fleet's service," she told him.

He nodded but didn't look at her.

Tears streamed down Sashi's face. "Why did he have to leave?"

The man stood facing the door as if he were trying to ignore the wailing child.

"She's cranky," Verrilla said. "I'm sorry."

He cleared his throat. "It's a trying time for us all."

"My husband was to meet us here, but the Tarreeda alert called him away."

The man's eyes widened. "Is he on *Questnar?*"

"Yes. The helmsman."

The man bent down to crying Sashi. "I have always wanted to serve on *Questnar*. She is a fine Orbital Patrol Ship. You must be proud of your daddy."

"When will he be back?"

"The Tarreeda alert will end soon." The man smiled. "Meanwhile, my name's Master Dargantan, but you can call me Master D, if you like."

She whimpered. "I am Sashi."

"And I'm Verrilla. Verrilla Rez." She bowed to him slightly.

"I'm proud to meet you both, and I'd be honored to be of service to the helmsman's family."

He'd offered her a contract, complete with meals and a very nice suite until *Questnar* returned. The work would be hard, he'd promised, but important work aboard *Latearian*, in the kitchens. Verrilla liked to cook, and Sashi could help out, so she'd accepted his offer. After all, how long could Luthes be gone?

Days went by: thirty, sixty, one hundred then two hundred. After three hundred she stopped counting. An entire year passed without celebration, no birthdays or Cada retreats. Just work, eat, and sleep. Thoughts of Luthes kept her going. Her daughter gave her strength...

"Mom? Are you all right? Mom?"

Verrilla flinched. "Oh dear." She found herself sitting in a puddle of soapy water, scrubber in hand, dress soaked.

A deep voice groaned. "Day dreaming again, V. Rez?"

She looked up at her towering employer. "Master D. I'm sorry. It's just that...well...my husband is here and I wish to look for him after midmeal."

"Please, Master D," Sashi said with teary eyes.

"Of course." He inhaled. "But your husband has been called to debriefing. I came to tell you."

"Debriefing?"

"They must decide what to do...you know...about the Tarreeda."

"But the alert is passed."

His expression turned glum. "Not for the fleet. Not ever."

Her heart pumped dread. "Are you saying we might not see him for *another* year?"

"I hope that is not the case."

She dropped the scrubber into the water bucket. "Then we will go home."

"No, Mom, please. I want to see Daddy."

Verrilla's heart panged. At this rate they'd never see him again.

***

The debriefing room on *Latearian's* Level K filled quickly. ComCap Kerillan took a seat in front of the podium and set his hat on the chair next to his, saving it for Luthes, and offered his Operations officers seats on either side. From the intensity of the chatter around the room, this debriefing would be charged with many emotions: fear and desperation mostly.

Dignitaries and specialists from Beltzee had been teleported up, as well as reporters from several jurisdictions. Fleet Base officers sat in the front row, reports on their laps. The room buzzed with their conversations, mostly gibberish until Kerillan switched on his collar-mounted translator, which interpreted all seven languages spoken within the League of Beltzee.

Though apprehension tightened his chest, he felt confident his Operations experts, and those who'd gathered here, could sort out the Tarreeda question and come up with an explanation for what they had witnessed aboard *Questnar*.

Luthes entered the room. His brows looked heavy with frustration, his eyes hurried as they scanned the assembly.

"Trantenant Rez, over here."

Winded, he rushed to Kerrillan. "I couldn't find them, sir."

"There will be time later. Sit." He picked up his hat from the chair next to him.

Luthes sat and enabled the translator on his collar.

Fleet Base Commander Sangrean came in, followed by an entourage of aides. One of them announced, "Commander on deck."

Kerrillan and the others stood and greeted him with the customary stiff-handed salute from the chin.

"You may be seated."

A rustle as Kerrillan sat, and then silence.

Sangrean stood taller than most Beltzans and wore his blue crystal-studded uniform with statuesque pride. Dark glasses hid his eyes. Removing his broad-billed commander's hat, he stepped to the podium and called the assembly to order. "The matter before us is of grave importance." His voice was laced with anxiety. "Did a Tarreeda cruiser return to Beltzee? According to *Questnar's* expert on the Tarreeda, Trantenant Rez has testified to his Operations officers that the creatures he saw in the viewports were not the Tarreeda, but aliens who looked very similar to ourselves."

Voices stirred.

"However, we are all in agreement on one point. This craft was not one of ours."

"Then where did it come from?" a reporter asked. "Where did it go?"

Sangrean held up a hand. "If these were not the Tarreeda, then aliens have found us."

"There is no proof that any other beings exist," a specialist said. "We are alone in the universe. Cada is specific about that."

"Except for the Ice Planet," someone put in. "The Tarreeda."

Commander Sangrean removed his dark glasses. "And that is why I have invited Specialist Regarius to testify on the matter. He holds many degrees and awards for his work in molecular biology and the evolution of the gene chain. Sir, please come forward."

A Beltzan specialist stood, and with brisk steps, he

approached the podium. He wore a long-sleeved white tunic denoting his high status among the scientific brethren. Kerillan's first impression of him was *old*, but by the way his gray hair stuck out over his big ears and his thin glasses teetered on his bulbous nose, Kerillan's second impression was *smart*.

After clearing his throat, Specialist Regarius spoke into the microphone. "I have done many studies of evolution on Beltzee, and from the old books I have found evidence of the Tarreeda's microbiology. Through intensive experimentation, my colleagues and I have discovered the Tarreeda possess a gene that predisposes their race to violence."

Agreement whispered through the assembly.

"Eons ago, we Beltzans evolved in the temperate regions of our planet. We fed on fish, grains, and fruits. However, in the hot equatorial regions, the Tarreeda arose. They roamed the jungles and plains, killing animals and eating their flesh."

A spontaneous gasp swept across the room.

Kerillan's stomach lurched at the thought of eating an animal.

"Their dark skin protected them from intense sunshine, and the males grew hair on their faces. They wore robes made of animal skin."

Kerillan nodded, impressed with the Specialist's knowledge.

"Because of their lust for the taste of meat, they didn't develop agriculture, and as time passed, the killing of animals led to the killing of each other over hunting territory, and then the killing of Beltzan missionaries sent in to civilize the roving hordes. It wasn't long before they attacked our citizens, raided and looted our cities. Their defective gene became a curse upon our planet."

Muffled agreement stirred the air.

"After the battle of Zarakatan, our forefathers showed

the defeated Tarreeda mercy and herded the survivors onto seven huge transports and launched them to the Ice Planet, a totally different environment than they were accustomed to on Beltzee. They had to adapt or die. Over a thousand generations, the cold climate and diffused sunlight would have mutated their gene chain, lightened their skin and hair. Eventually they would evolve to look more like us."

Kerrillan blinked. Made perfect sense.

Regarius turned to Luthes. "Young Rez, tell us about the male you saw in the viewport. Did he wear hair on his face?"

Luthes straightened in his chair, obviously proud for having been called on to testify. "Only a patch under his nose, sir."

"But hair just the same?"

"Yes, but only a little—"

"Black hair?"

"Yes. But the yellow-haired female was not a Tarreeda. She was beautiful."

"Your report is clear on that, but one's hair can be dyed. You also stated the other female was beautiful. Please tell us then, young Rez...what color was *her* hair?"

"But the Tarreeda are ugly, sir."

"Her hair, Trantenant Rez. What color was her hair?"

Luthes sighed. "Black hair, sir."

A buzz ripped through the assembly.

Kerillan saw the specialist's logic clearly. The Tarreeda were dark-skinned, black-haired beasts draped in animal fur. Their physiology changed some since then, but not entirely.

Regarius raised his voice. "I'm here to tell you, it is scientifically possible that the creatures in the cruiser were in fact the Tarreeda. And I assure you, they will be back."

The assembly erupted in loud conversation. Reporters rushed from the room.

Looking at Luthes slumped in his chair, Kerillan said,

"You made an honest mistake."

"But they could not have been the Tarreeda."

"The alternative is too improbable," Kerillan said. "Aliens? Our scanners would have picked up some evidence of their existence."

"You saw the interceptor strobe on *Questnar*. The red blip came out of deep space."

"The Ice Planet is in its orbital vertex," Kerillan explained. "Farthest from our suns. That incoming trajectory could have made it look like the cruiser came from deep space."

"Then what about the missing cross? The Tarreeda cross."

"It may have been abandoned as their symbol," Kerillan replied. "Lost to younger generations. I believe the specialist. They were the Tarreeda."

Luthes stood. "They were not." He stormed out.

Kerillan let him go. The young trantenant would soon realize his error. A bigger question still loomed over the assembly. What were they going to do about the Tarreeda?

Sangrean took the podium and banged his gavel. "We must prepare for battle."

An Operations officer stood and waved off the chatter. "If the Tarreeda launch a full-scale assault, we may not be able to repel them with our repulsor cannons."

"What defense do we have?" someone shouted.

"We have no lethal weapons," someone chimed in. "After the carnage at Zarakatan, Beltzan Judicials had seen the true horrors of war and banned lethal weapons from this planet. Now we are doomed."

"We need plasma cannons," someone put in. "Scatter blasters."

"Reproducing deadly weapons from our past is not the answer," Sangrean said. "We will not reduce ourselves to the Tarreeda's level. We shall fight with honor, and if Cada wishes, we shall die with honor."

"There is no honor in defeat." This came from an Orbital Patrol Ship ComCap of the Kedrikan fleet who sat in the front row. "We must arm ourselves."

"And become murderers like them," another called out. "I'd rather die."

Holding up his hand, Sangrean shouted, "Silence!"

Kerillan feigned calm and waited for the melee to subside, then: "Do you have a plan, sir?"

"It is a long shot, but yes."

"May we hear it?"

"First rule of engagement," Sangrean displayed one long finger, "know your enemy. The Judicials have beseeched me to use restraint. Therefore, I shall need a volunteer."

A murmur rose from the ranks.

"I need one Orbital Patrol Ship for a dangerous mission."

Kerillan sat forward. "May I request specifics, sir?"

The room fell silent.

"We must learn of the Tarreeda's strength," Sangrean said. "On the Ice Planet."

Someone gasped. "Reconnaissance?"

An officer said, "It will take the entire fleet to ensure even a minimum of safety."

"We cannot leave Beltzee undefended," Sangrean responded. "One ship, gentlemen. Whose will it be?"

"It's suicide, sir," a Kedrikan put in.

"Whose will it be?" Sangrean growled out.

"One ship against the Tarreeda?" Someone questioned. "What if we are discovered snooping about? We will not stand a chance."

Kerillan had heard enough. The League of Beltzee's future rested on this mission. He knew his officers and crewmen would agree. "*Questnar* is at your service, sir." He stood. "We shall leave at once."

As if he knew all along that Kerillan would volunteer,

Sangrean smiled. "Very well. And take Specialist Regarius with you. He may be of help."

"Yes, sir."

"Relay your findings to Fleet Base Command."

The Kedrikan ComCap got to his feet and chin-saluted Kerillan. "Cada be with you."

The assembly stood and chanted. "To Cada, to Cada."

"Good luck, men." Sangrean donned his hat and dark glasses. "Dismissed."

A knot squeezed Kerillan's stomach, not because he'd have to fly to the Ice Planet, not because he'd have to recall his crew or fight the Tarreeda, but because he'd have to tell Luthes he wouldn't have time to find his wife and daughter.

Chapter Four

With shock buzzing in his brain like summer cicadas, Janis followed Tracy out toward the waiting limousine. Finally Brigham was taking him to meet with Stan, who would hopefully lend some insight into what NASA expected from him and Tracy. Undoubtedly, Ray and his long-fingered aliens would be the death of them both.

Tracy held Janis's arm. "Ray should have told us about the aliens."

"I've wasted enough time trying to understand him, but I'm sure he had good reason for keeping the encounter to himself."

"Lisa knows too."

"And she hasn't said anything either."

"We're not alone in the universe, Janis. That's going to change everything. Religion, philosophy, science..."

"Maybe that's why they kept quiet."

"Lot of good it did them."

As they approached the limo, the airman swung the door open. Once inside, Janis sat across from Brigham and stared at him. Aliens and NASA, what was the connection to the Department of Defense? Why did they want him involved...and Tracy? What did Stan have to do with it? Why should anyone care? The aliens were a hundred thousand light years from earth. No threat to anybody. And since the equipment in Simi Valley had been dismantled, there was no way to go back. What the hell was going on around here?

Engine roaring and tires squealing, the limo sped

away from the curb. Janis gripped the bar rail. "Ray kept these aliens a secret for a reason, General. I think it should remain that way."

"Don't worry." Brigham's jaw protruded in smug confidence. "We're not letting this out. It's classified Top Secret all the way, the Department of Defense, the National Security Agency. A need to know basis only."

"So why did you let us in on it? Tracy and I don't have a need to know."

"On the contrary, you must know if we are to succeed."

Janis didn't like the sound of that. "Succeed at what?"

The general reached for the scotch bottle. "That space probe recording..." He poured a splash of scotch into a glass, offered it to Janis momentarily, and then pulled it back. "Did you watch it closely?"

"I slept through it." Janis lied.

Turning left, the limo accelerated toward a huge hanger on the other side of the haze-shrouded wetlands.

"The spaceships, Janis...they appeared like magic."

"I noticed that," Tracy said. "But I was too shocked to give it a second thought."

"Teleportation," Brigham said. "You saw it with your own eyes and still you didn't see it." Brigham threw down the scotch and wheezed. "Those aliens possess teleportation technology."

Janis didn't get the significance. "So what?"

"NASA wants it."

"What for?"

"Do you have any idea how much it costs to launch a shuttle?" Brigham set the shot glass on the bar. "Millions, Janis, an incredible use of resources. Teleportation is the answer."

"And you plan to...what?"

"Take it from them, of course."

"How the hell are you going to do that?"

"You'll see."

Janis's stomach felt sick. A shot of that scotch would probably go down good right now.

In the shadow of the huge hanger, the limo sped through an open garage door flanked by heavily armed security personnel. The door closed immediately. Janis spotted Stan standing with a group of men in black suits. He looked more like a hippie than a mechanical engineer, his long brown hair hanging down past the shoulders of a nicely pressed white lab coat.

The limo pulled up in front of the men. Janis fought mixed emotions over seeing his old friend again. He wanted to get directly to the matter.

"Let me handle this," he said to Tracy and bolted from the car and planted himself in front of Stan. "What's this all about?"

"Good to see you, Janis." Stan offered his hand.

Janis batted it away. "Aliens? Teleportation? Brigham's talking nonsense...right?"

Stan glared at the general. "Couldn't wait, could you? Just had to open your mouth."

Brigham grunted. "I wanted to see him flip out."

Tracy ran up beside Janis. "Let's hear what he's got to say, dear."

"Hello, Tracy." Stan's smile was warm and welcoming. "You're looking lovely as ever."

"Why didn't you meet us at the plane?" she asked.

Stan smoothed his lab coat. "I wanted everything to be just right for your arrival...when you take a look at what we're doing here."

"It stinks already," Janis said.

"Beyond those doors..." Stan indicated a massive set of overheads that led to the innards of the huge hanger, "we have assembled the most technologically advanced project that science has ever undertaken in the history of the world. It dwarfs Fermilab and CERN combined. Solartech Labs was kindergarten stuff. Don't be too quick to judge us until you've had a look for yourself."

"I'm not interested in any more projects, Stan, especially ones that involve General Brigham and intergalactic larceny."

Tracy tugged on Janis's arm. "Let him show off his new toys so we can go home."

Janis looked into Tracy's hazel eyes. She'd become his rock, his reason for persevering under the worst conditions and against the toughest odds. Even in defeat, she was his strength, his inspiration, and his hope for the future. Now everything about Stan's great project lurking just beyond those huge doors made his stomach hurt. Scientific experiments were never easy, and the men behind the scenes were often motivated by their own agendas, making them unpredictable and dangerous. The stakes were always high. No good could come from dealing with Brigham and the men in black suits. Janis wasn't about to put Tracy in harm's way again. "No thanks, Stan. We're going home."

General Brigham signaled to the suited men. They gathered around quickly. "This is our party," Brigham said straight-faced, his dark eyes glaring, his voice as demanding as it had been in the briefing room. "We're prepared to do this the hard way, if you prefer."

Janis wasn't surprised it had come down to coercion, and having dealt with government bullies before, it would be in his best interest to go along with them...for now. "And if I still think it stinks, what then, are we free to go?"

"You're going to love it," Stan said.

"And if we don't?"

Brigham glared at Janis. "You *will*."

Tracy pulled on his coat sleeve. "Let's give them their money's worth, Janis."

"Keep an open mind," Stan put in. "If you don't like what we have to offer you, then yes, you can go home."

"I'm supposed to believe that?"

"You have my word."

Janis mulled that over. He'd always trusted Stan, had no reason not to trust him now, but the whole thing made him want to sniff a skunk's butt for relief. "Let's get it over with."

Stan stepped back. "Right this way."

The massive overhead door rattled up about ten feet and stopped. Janis looked in. His heart stopped, stuttered, and lurched. "Fuck." A lump the size of Texas lodged in his throat.

Tracy gasped. "My God."

Wingtip-to-wingtip, nine space shuttles lined the left side of the hanger parked tails to the wall, and seven more were similarly parked on the right side. Each sat atop three massive landing struts with eight giant tires. Bone-white fuselages glistened under a million ceiling lights where vertical stabilizers adorned with NASA emblems reached up to the rafters.

"Welcome to NASA Aerospace," Stan announced, beaming like a proud father. "Sixteen of the finest flying machines ever made. Pulse light engines. Hypergolic thrusters. Fast. Maneuverable."

"Are you out of your mind?"

It didn't take a rocket scientist to see they'd removed the Pratt & Whitney RS-24 engines, meaning the shuttles couldn't be launched from Kennedy in the usual way... "Oh, Shit." A strangling fear gripped Janis's lump-clogged throat. "Stan..." Janis swallowed hard. "Don't tell me you're planning to degenerate these things into the 13th Power."

Stan smiled. "Come with me."

"Stan?" Janis followed him across the hanger, remembering the reference to CERN and Fermilabs and the most technologically advanced project in the world. It didn't take a second to figure out what they had in mind, a return trip to the 13th Power. To the aliens. To rob them of their teleportation technology. And it was a sure bet those aliens wouldn't stand by and let that happen without a fight. It would mean intergalactic war. "This isn't a good idea, Stan."

Tracy asked, "What's not a good idea?"

Janis decided not to tell her, let her figure it out on her own.

Stan led the way to an area of the floor marked off with yellow warning stripes. General Brigham and the suits stood close behind him. A clunking sound. The floor began to move.

Down.

"We patterned this lift after the ones used on aircraft carriers," Stan explained as the platform creaked downward, "to move jets between the flight deck and lower levels. Of course, this one is much larger."

Janis wanted to be impressed, but it was tough to beat sixteen shuttles. "What are you guys doing down there?"

Brigham said, "Shut up and enjoy the ride."

Janis glanced at Tracy. Her face had turned ghostly white. The hanger floor disappeared above them as the lift traveled down a dimly lit shaft of steel girders and concrete walls painted in red and yellow stripes. Water trickled from seams in the walls and cascaded down the shaft. The acrid smell of metal slag permeated the air, which got colder the farther down they went. A chill leached into his bones.

The lift descended into a steel chamber eight stories high, octagonal in shape, and reinforced with thick I-beam ribs. Halogen floodlights illuminated rust-red walls laced with black piping. From the ceiling hung mechanical arms, Janis counted sixteen of them, some short, some long, with hydraulic muscles and claw-like hands. Sixteen arms, sixteen shuttles, the correlation hadn't escaped him.

"We're a hundred fifty feet into the water table," Stan explained as the elevator continued down to the chamber's grated floor. "That presented us with some difficult construction problems. Ground water, specifically. We built a grid of porous piping around the site, which draws in the water and directs it into the MIGGS' cooling system." He pointed to his right. "Over there."

MIGGS? Slowly, Janis turned to look toward the far end of the chamber. Sixteen Proton Laser Resonators protruded from the wall, their black particle-beam barrels ringed with red Xenon proton emitters. Each PLR was positioned in direct relation to the staggered claws on the hydraulic arms.

"What do you think of our SuperMIGGS?" Stan asked Janis.

"I think I'm going to be sick."

"You got the picture now, Dr. Mackey?" Brigham asked. The suits stood behind him at parade rest.

Tracy said, "He's joking, right, Janis, he's joking."

"They're going back, but this time they'll land on the green planet."

"Oh my God." Tracy glared at Brigham. "What are you guys going to do to the aliens?"

Stan turned toward her, shoved his hands in his lab coat pockets. "I can't believe you, Tracy ... Janis. We're on the verge of the greatest scientific expedition the world has ever seen and you're acting like it's a witch hunt. We're not going to do anything to the aliens."

"No good can come of this." Janis felt small as David standing against Goliath. "Especially with Brigham and the Department of Defense involved. Why are you in cahoots with these rats?"

"The aliens can teleport their vehicles into orbit, Janis."

"You can teleport shuttles across the galaxy. That trumps their technology."

"The Higgs isn't practical. We have to go 100,000 light years away and then come back just to attain orbit.

Ground-to-orbit is better. Besides, with the Higgs Field, who knows what star system or asteroid field might be in the way. I'm hoping the teleportation system will not only be safer, but cost less to construct and maintain."

Janis spun around, arms outstretched, palms up. "This couldn't have been cheap to build."

"Compliments of Solartech Labs in Simi Valley," Brigham said. "We seized all its assets along with Dr. Curtis's estate, and blew the whole wad on this project."

Janis winced at the mention of Curtis's name, aka Melvin Anderson, richer than God thanks to his stolen antiquities and black marketeering.

"We need the alien's teleportation technology for NASA Aerospace," Stan added. "We're hoping this initial expense will pay off with cheaper transport costs. Maybe then, Congress won't mothball the shuttles."

"They already did..." As soon as Janis said it, he knew he'd wasted his breath. "Congress doesn't know about this project, do they?"

Stan and Brigham shared a conspiratorial look.

"Oh my God," Tracy said.

"I get it." Janis wagged a finger at Stan. "Once you show them a better mouse trap, they'll reinstate the shuttle program. But to do it, you've got to burglarize aliens on another planet."

"Mark my word, Dr. Mackey," Brigham said. "Without those shuttles, we'll have to hitch rides to the space station from the Russians, the Hubble telescope will fall in disrepair, as well as our Star Wars defense system. America will be forever vulnerable to ballistic missile nuclear attack from Iran or North Korea. That's not going to happen on my watch, because if it does, my career will go down the toilet."

"Everything we've worked for since 1961 will be lost," Stan said.

"And all these people will be out of work," Tracy

Terry Wright

added.

Janis palm-banged the side of his head. "Not you too, Tracy?"

"They've got some good points, Janis."

"They're talking about invading another planet, for Christ sake."

"We're going to hit them hard and fast," Brigham said.

"You're a regular Attila the Hun," Janis shot back. "Stan, why are you in on this?"

"I'm an engineer, Janis. That's what I do best. I believe this project will benefit humanity, but it's all for naught without you. You're a mathematician. That's what you do best. In order for all my marvels of engineering to work, I need you and Tracy...and Lo Chin."

"No, not Lo Chin. Don't drag him into this too."

"He's the best computer programmer in the business. Don't you see? You're looking at a bunch of hardware here." Stan spread his arms. "Without the math and the programs and the laser technology, it's nothing but scrap iron." He pointed to a rectangular window four stories up, a window made of thick glass with rounded corners mounted in a rubber seal. "Up there, in the control room, our supercomputers are useless without you guys. You've done this before, in Simi Valley. With your help we can return to the 13th Power and get the technology we need to keep NASA Aerospace flying."

"And our country secure," Brigham put in.

"So what do you say?" Stan asked.

Janis took a step back, glanced at Tracy, saw the same concern in her eyes as his: What price would humanity pay? "We don't want anything to do with this, Stan."

"But..."

"It's insanity, Stan. Don't you get it?"

"Think, Janis. We're going to make history here, mankind's first intergalactic mission."

"You mean conquest."

"It's a mission," Stan insisted.

Clearly, Janis understood Ray's reason for keeping his discovery a secret. "Ray didn't tell us about the green planet for this very reason. He didn't want anyone to go back there."

"He's an idiot," Brigham said.

"The aliens didn't destroy his transporter. They didn't try to kill him ... or his family. I think he was returning the favor by keeping their existence a secret."

"Let's go home, Janis," Tracy said. "I believe Ray did the right thing." She turned to Brigham. "Take us back to the plane."

Brigham stood with his feet spread apart, his hands behind his back. "Is that your final answer?"

"You've got the picture," Janis said with every bit of sarcasm he could muster.

The general nodded and rocked forward on the balls of his feet. "Very well, Dr. Mackey." He turned to his men wearing black suits. "Arrest her, boys."

They rushed forward and grabbed Tracy's arms.

Shock froze Janis in stark bewilderment.

"What are you talking about?" Tracy shouted as handcuffs clicked on her wrists. "Let me go."

Janis lunged at the general. "Brigham—" A black-suited thug stepped in and punched Janis in the stomach. He collapsed to the grated floor, gasping. It was the same man who'd escorted them to NASA in the jet, the whittler with the scarred face. "You bastard."

The suit came at him again, fists balled, but Brigham shouted, "Agent Peterson. That's enough." He looked down at Janis. "I was hoping you wouldn't cooperate." He cackled.

"Go to hell."

Brigham stepped up to Tracy with his shoulders back and loomed over her delicate frame. "Tracy McClarence

Mackey, you have the right to remain silent."

"You can't be serious."

"Anything you say can, and *will*, be used against you in a court of law."

"Janis, help me."

"You have the right to an attorney..."

Struggling to his feet, Janis hardened himself against the pain in his stomach and ignored the suits standing close by, their teeth clenched. "On what charge?"

"If you can't afford an attorney, one will be appointed to you by the court."

"Janis?"

"Damn you, Brigham. What are you doing?"

"Do you understand your rights as I have stated them?"

Tracy spit in his face.

Brigham stood stoic, removed a handkerchief from his pocket, and wiped spittle from his cheek with strained dignity. "I take that as a yes."

Stan pushed past the suits. "You never said anything about arresting her." He looked at Janis. "I swear...I didn't know—"

"Stay out of this, Stan," Brigham barked.

Tracy scowled at the general. "What's the charge?"

"Treason." Brigham said the word as if it were gospel.

Janis staggered. He couldn't believe it. "What are you trying to pull, Brigham?"

"You're crazy." Tracy's voiced dripped contempt.

The general's eyes narrowed on Tracy. "During your experiments at Solartech Labs, you were working undercover for the CIA. Is that right?"

"So?"

"That makes you a willing participant in the 13th Power conspiracy, does it not?"

"But the President asked me to help him with Star Wars."

"The President?" Brigham huffed. "We all know how corrupt he was. Landed him in prison. You were in on it too. I rest my case."

"I didn't know they were doing anything illegal."

"Fly with crows, expect to get shot at, Tracy, or in this case, executed." He said it with a grin.

Janis couldn't get his next breath. This couldn't be happening. "Executed?"

"Treason is still a capital offense," Brigham said in a sing-song voice.

"She was serving her country. You'll never make it stick."

The general's eyebrows arched. "Want to bet?"

The air wheezed from Janis's lungs. Brigham could roundup the support he needed to get a conviction. And after what he'd done to the President, a little redheaded scientist would be easy to put away. Janis wasn't about to bet with Tracy's life. "We'll do what you want us to do."

Brigham smiled. "Now that's more like it."

"Let her go."

"I think not."

The suits started dragging her away.

"Janis," she cried.

He clutched his sore ribs and watched her disappear into the bowels of NASA Aerospace. Life on earth would never be the same.

Chapter Five

In Santa Barbara, California, terror welcomed Ray Crawford to another day. Cold sweats. A chill. Sunshine knifed through a chink in the blinds, illuminating the disheveled room in his beachside bungalow. And so another morning began, poisoned with memories: the chitter of wild rats, gunfire, and screams of the damned and dying. His head ached and he yearned for alcohol's blessed release.

He rubbed his eyes to clear the fuzz and reveal where he'd left that whiskey bottle, somewhere in his self-imposed hell on earth, a smelly, fly-infested exile from life itself, complete with all the garbage: greasy pizza boxes, crumpled burger wrappers, and squashed Chinese food cartons. A dozen empty Jack Daniels and Johnny Walker bottles lay scattered about like dead soldiers on the battlefield of grief.

"Kate." He muttered her name and felt helpless all over again, unable to save her. His wife's memory would haunt him today, as it had all the days before. Weeks had blurred into months. A year had passed. It seemed like only yesterday she'd died in his arms. The hole that loss left in his heart could never be refilled, not with concrete, not with ice, not even with his new love, alcohol.

He kicked off his blanket and sat upright on the couch. The dark television screen in the far corner reflected a shell of a man wearing underwear, unkempt black hair, and soulless staring eyes. His fall was a long drop from world-renowned nuclear physicist to pond scum at the bottom of the proverbial pit.

Only two things mattered now. The bottle. And his bladder. He had to pee.

Rising from the couch, he felt lightheaded, managed a step or two, wavered and paused to get his equilibrium. The bathroom seemed as far away as the moon. He stumbled forward. Cockroaches scattered. He kicked an empty bottle, tromped through trash any hoarder would be proud to own, and staggered to the toilet, sat to pee because he could hardly stand. Maybe he'd take a shower, throw himself under an ice-cold spray and scrub his skin until he bled. Maybe this time he'd come out clean. Free of guilt. Free of shame. Kate was dead because of him. Because of his obsessions. A drink would serve her memory better, maybe silence her screams and medicate his sorry soul.

But where did he leave that bottle?

Sudden pounding...from the front room. "Ray."

Someone at the door. "What the hell?"

"Ray."

Who had the nerve to crash his pity-party? Probably those government bastards from NASA again.

Anger churned in his stomach like rotgut moonshine. He staggered back to the couch and discovered the errant bottle of his quest wedged between the cushions. It was time to get back to work on drinking himself to death. Bottle to his lips, he drank hardily, content in the knowledge that the fire screaming down his throat would get him passed-out drunk by noon.

"Ray." More pounding.

He took another drink, felt the blissful buzz return like a security blanket.

"Ray. Open up. It's Janis."

Whiskey backed up in Ray's throat. Janis Mackey? Why the hell was a mathematician from Colorado banging on his front door?

"I know you're in there."

More pounding.

"Go away."

"Dad, please."

Lisa? What the hell was his daughter doing here? A conspiracy. That was it. They were ganging up on him again. No doubt to make him quit drinking. Fat chance. He took another swallow and welcomed the burn.

"Open the door, Ray."

He hadn't seen Janis since Kate's funeral, and he never expected to see him again. Ever. And judging from the frantic tone in Janis's voice, Ray was sure he didn't want to see him now.

"Ray."

"Dad."

Jesus. They were making enough noise. The whole neighborhood would rush over in a panic, thinking the old drunk had finally blown his brains out. "What the hell do you want?"

"Let us in," Janis said. "We have to talk."

"Come on, Dad."

Janis said, "Do you know what they're doing at NASA?"

"I don't give a damn."

"You gotta help us."

Ray didn't have to help anyone. Hell, he couldn't even help himself.

"It's General Brigham," Janis shouted through the closed door. "He's arrested Tracy for treason."

Ray felt a jolt, as if lightning had shot down his spine. Tracy? Arrested? Treason? He didn't want any part of Brigham and the Department of Defense, but... "Can't you people stay out of trouble?"

"You started this."

"It's not my problem. Go away." He swallowed another mouthful of whiskey. The burn made his eyes water. Heaven awaited his pickled brain.

"Dad, these are your friends. They need you."

The pounding went on until Ray thought his head would explode. "All right." Bottle in hand, he stalked through the trash. "Enough." He threw open the door and squinted against bright daylight. Lisa stood on the porch with her hands on her hips. She wore blue shorts, a yellow blouse, and a necklace with a gold crucifix. Sunlight radiated through her blond hair. "Don't lay their problems on me." He pointed a finger at her. "I told you, I'm through with them."

"Jesus, Ray." Janis scowled like he'd just found dog shit on his shoe. "You look like hell."

"I wasn't expecting company." Ray glared at Janis. The mathematician was all gussied up in black slacks and a white polo shirt. "What do you want from me?"

"For Christ's sake, Ray, put some pants on."

He glanced down at his yellow-stained underwear, felt no shame, and took another swig from the bottle. "As long as you're working for the Feds, I'm not talking to you, so get out before I—"

"Why didn't you tell us what you found in the 13th Power?"

"I don't have to explain anything to you." He shoved the door to shut it in their faces.

Janis stopped it from closing with his shoe and pushed his way inside. "The aliens, Ray. Why didn't you tell us about the aliens?"

"Damn you." Ray blinked. The aliens were safe, a hundred thousand light years from earth. And that's where they were going to remain, out of man's reach. "Get the hell out of my house."

Lisa walked in like it was Sunday morning. "Stop it, Dad."

"You can't come barging in here—"

"Whew!" She threw open the front curtains. "You promised me you'd stop drinking." She opened the sliding window. "Look at this mess."

Ray stormed to the window and slammed it closed. "I'll call the cops."

Janis pushed Ray up against the wall. "I want answers right now."

"Fuck you."

Janis slapped him across the face, a cheek-stinging rebuttal. "The aliens, Ray."

"They're none of your business...nobody's—"

"Dad! Our secret is out. It's over. Tell him."

"I didn't want anyone to know about them." Ray lifted the bottle to his lips, but before he could take a swig, Janis grabbed the bottle away.

"It wasn't your call."

"Everything mankind touches turns to shit, Janis. I wanted the aliens left alone." Ray reached for the bottle.

Janis held it out of Ray's grasping range. "But NASA is going to return to the 13th Power."

"Not if we don't help them. Give me the bottle."

"I don't want to help them. I want to stop them. If we don't step in, they'll get someone else who doesn't understand what they're dealing with. Other mathematicians. Other nuclear physicists. They'll do it without us, and your aliens will be doomed."

"It's not my problem."

"And Tracy's not your problem either, like Kate wasn't your problem."

If Ray didn't feel so weak and sick he'd have beat Janis's ass for that remark. Back then Kate was a doper and a whore, before they'd reconciled. Janis had no right to rub that welt, but he'd managed to give Ray pause to think about someone other than himself. "I'm sorry about Tracy, but I can't help her."

"Can't or won't?" Janis shouted, the desperation in his voice rising like a tidal wave. "I can't stop them by myself."

"Christ! I have my own problems."

"*You* are the problem, Ray. Look at you...wallowing in pity. You're not the only one who's ever lost a loved one. What about the books you were going to write...the Nobel Prize? Your fame? You're throwing it all away."

"He's right, Dad." Lisa slogged through the room, picking up garbage. "Listen to him."

Ray watched her for a moment then looked at Janis. There was a time the mathematician didn't believe in the possibilities of the 13th Power, the Higgs boson, not at first, but in the end, he'd profited the most. He'd found Tracy. He'd found love and happiness. All Ray got was a life of misery and loneliness when Kate's seedy past caught up with her. A bullet had ended their future. Now he couldn't get on without her. Wouldn't. "I-I miss Kate," he managed. Hot tears filled his eyes. "Why did she have to die?"

"I'm sorry, Ray." Janis put his hand on Ray's shoulder. "We miss her too, but right now we need to save Tracy *and* the aliens from General Brigham."

Ray looked Janis in the eyes, swallowed dryly, and decided to confide in him his worst fears. "I don't think the aliens have any lethal weapons, Janis, or they'd have killed us. Instead they tried to capture us alive. We need to leave them be, in peace."

"Brigham wants to steal their teleportation technology. He'll land on their planet with a ground invasion force, I suppose, in sixteen shuttles."

"Those shuttles are his weapons of mass destruction."

"They're just heavy transports."

Ray huffed. "I guess Stan didn't show you the upgrades, did he?"

"The pulse-light engines? Sure."

"There's more, Janis."

"More?"

"Each shuttle is equipped with Proton Laser Resonators mounted in the wings. Particle beams. Star Wars stuff, like in the movie, damn it. The aliens are going to be wiped out."

Janis's mouth fell open.

Ray jumped on the opportunity to grab the bottle out of Janis's hand. "They can't succeed without us, so I'm not going." He took a long pull on the bottle. "Now get the hell out of here."

Chapter Six

Luthes strapped himself into his helmswheel chair and listened to Commander Sangrean's voice come over *Questnar's* communications link. *"Position the remaining fleet around* Latearian. *Protect it at all cost. Our ground forces are on alert. If the Tarreeda return before you get back, we'll take care of ourselves."*

The docking controller said, *"Questnar,* you are cleared for departure."

Luthes' stomach tightened into knots of dread. He held the throttles in both hands, his long fingers taut with anxiety. Again the Tarreeda had interfered with his plans to see his wife and daughter. Again they'd be left alone on this remote orbiting outpost because of his duty to the fleet.

Settling into his high-back chair, Kerillan pointed a long finger at the scanner screen. "Take us out, Trantenant Rez."

"Yes, sir." Luthes lifted *Questnar* off her mooring irons, gave the helmswheel a spin to port, and throttled-up the thrusters. On the scope screens, *Latearian's* bright docking bay gave way to the star-studded backdrop of space.

"Navigator to helm. Set coarse, ten...forty-two...eight. Execute full power."

"Confirmed." Luthes shoved the throttles to maximum drive, hoping he'd live to see *Latearian* again and get another chance to find his wife and daughter.

Questnar shuddered in acceleration. Beltzee's twin suns began to shrink in the distance. Never before had an Orbital Patrol Ship been given a mission of this peril, to leave the relative safety of the fleet and venture into deep space alone. But someone had to do it, though why it had to be him, only Cada could know. He'd been so close to finding his family. Why couldn't *Questnar's* departure from *Latearian* have waited another ninety minutes, or even another day? He was jinxed.

"Trantenant Rez." The unexpected voice came from behind him.

Luthes turned to Specialist Regarius. He wore a white robe and sandals. His gray hair was mussed like he'd slept on it wrong. A wave of trepidation came over Luthes. He was still unhappy with Regarius for making a fool of him at the debriefing. "You should be in your seat, sir."

"I am curious, young Rez—"

"Please, call me Luthes." The Specialist's formal tone felt patronizing.

"Yes, of course. Luthes then it is. I was wondering how you have become such an expert on the Tarreeda."

"Obviously I'm not as proficient as you."

"We have differing opinions, yes. How did you come by yours?"

Luthes didn't answer. For all he knew it was another verbal trap.

"It is a long voyage," Regarius said softly. "We should come to understand each other."

"Why is that important?"

"It is my nature. I am curious about everything, including the Tarreeda. We have a common interest, I would say."

Luthes thought the old man was being sincere and decided to oblige him. "When I was young, my father told me the stories. He's ComCap of *Ditherium*, you know."

"Yes. You must be proud."

"Someday I'll have my own Orbital Patrol Ship."

"The Tarreeda, Luthes?"

"Of course." He realized how uncertain his future had

become. "The tyranny our ancestors endured at the hands of our enemies intrigued me. I read everything I could find about the Tarreeda. It was a horrible time to be a Beltzan, to be persecuted because we were different." He flexed his long fingers as evidence.

"Adversity brings out the best in us. It has been a long tradition."

"My wife and daughter were on *Latearian*," Luthes said. "I was trying to find them. The Tarreeda ruined our reunion. Right now, I can do without tradition."

"Come a time," Regarius replied, "tradition might be all you will have to hold on to."

"If we live through this suicide mission."

Regarius chuckled. "I have every confidence in ComCap Kerillan. *Questnar* is a grand Orbital Patrol Ship. We are in safe hands."

"I hope your Tarreeda don't prove you wrong."

"Keep an open mind, young Rez."

Luthes made a quick visual sweep of his instruments, ensuring the navigation equipment held them on course for the Ice Planet. "What do you expect to find when we get there?"

"Perhaps I will see a Tarreeda up close...like you did."

"They were not Tarreeda. I am not wrong."

"Worse things have happened." Regarius patted Luthes' shoulder. "However, you hold firm to your certainty, an admirable quality for a future ComCap."

"I know what I saw."

"Things are not always as they appear."

"Navigation to helm," the com-link interrupted. *"Flight data program is activated."*

"Confirmed," Luthes replied. Then to Regarius, "I have work to do." He hoped the Specialist would return to his seat.

Luthes switched his NAV screen to the new flight plan display. The three-dimensional stellar grid of planetary orbital tracks showed the navigational waypoints. An arcing blue line represented the prescribed flight path that would take *Questnar* into orbit around the Ice Planet. Luthes held a steady course.

Regarius said, "That trajectory on your screen there, it reminds me of a document I have here." Reaching into his pocket, he pulled out a folded paper. "Have a look."

"I'm a little busy right now, sir. You should sit down."

"This will interest you, I am sure."

Perhaps appeasing him would get him back to his seat sooner. Luthes examined the document and recognized the flight plan, an unusual item for the Specialist to possess. "Where did you get this?"

"Transport Launch Control archives. Mission J-T-146."

Luthes recognized the number. "The Tarreeda's flight to the Ice Planet."

"Looks just like your screen there, except for one thing."

The flight plan showed an arcing path from Beltzee to the far reaches of the solar system, out to the farthest planet from the twin suns, the white planet covered in ice. Nothing looked unusual to Luthes. He eyed Regarius, puzzled.

"Look closer," he said. "Above the Ice Planet's horizon."

Squinting, Luthes finally saw something strange. Mere decks from the planet's atmosphere, the flight path oscillated and ended.

"What do you make of it?" Regarius asked.

"They stopped transmitting," Luthes replied, thinking it obvious that their telemetry was missing.

"How could that have happened?"

"Is there an official report?"

"Nothing that I found, but there must be an explanation. What do you think could have caused them to stop transmitting? An equipment failure?"

Luthes rubbed his chin. Not long ago, Regarius had been at odds with him on the Tarreeda question, so why would the Specialist ask for his opinion now? Luthes regarded the old man cautiously. "Why not ask ComCap Kerillan or Fleet Base?"

"You deal with these things all the time, young Luthes. I am an expert in my field, as you are in yours."

"Sure." The compliment deserved a proper response. Regarius was wrong about the Tarreeda, of course, but he was sincere in his mistake. Luthes formulated a theory about the flight path. "Equipment failure is rare. Backup systems have backups. I would say the transmission probably experienced interference from the Ice Planet's magnetic field, or possibly an ozone-saturated ionosphere."

Regarius frowned. "Why do I fear it is not that simple?"

"Certainly you don't think they could've just disappeared." Luthes looked up at Regarius. "Do you?"

"That Tarreeda cruiser you saw certainly did."

Terry Wright

Chapter Seven

When Professor Milton Spears thought of Ethiopia, *Feed the World* came to mind. The horrific famines of the 1980s had dumped this poorest of African nations on the world's center stage. However, he knew there was more to Ethiopia than starving children and foreign aid. There was ancient history, and he was holding a piece of it in his hand.

On his knees and feeling dumbstruck, he scanned the landscape of his dusty dig. The excavated area was roughly sixty feet long by thirty feet wide and went twenty feet into Choke Mountain. Blue Nile Falls rumbled in the distance. Birds cawed, and the buzz of tsetse flies made the dry air seem alive. Upslope, safari tents flapped in the hot wind, and hundreds of boulders lay about like giant warts on the mountainside, boulders that had long ago broken away from the rocky cliffs looming majestically over the dig site three thousand feet up the mountain.

Down slope, the university's Land Rover sat at the narrow trailhead and reflected sunlight from its windscreen. The heat was suffocating this time of morning, but at this moment, it didn't matter to Milton, for time had become jumbled in his mind, archeological history turned upside down by what he had found.

He glanced again at the object he'd unearthed as it dangled from the tip of his magnetized screwdriver. To the untrained eye, the object looked like a hardened disc of clay the size of a silver dollar. However, Milton had spotted an exposed edge of the artifact when it too had reflected a sharp shard of sunlight, which only metal or glass could do.

When he attempted to scrape clay from its surface with the magnetized screwdriver, the piece stuck. His excitement mushroomed as he suddenly realized the artifact was made of iron...which was impossible 20,000 years ago.

Gayle Weatherbee knelt next to him. His student assistant wore khaki shorts and dusty kneepads, a sleeveless white t-shirt, brown hiking boots, and she smelled of insect repellant. "What's that, doctor?"

Speechless, he looked up and squinted against the African sun bearing down behind Miss Weatherbee. Her face was in shadow, her masculine shape a silhouette against the bright sky.

"Dr. Spears, are you all right?"

Struggling to his feet, stiff knees aching, he showed her the clay-encrusted object. "This site is over twenty thousand years old," he said hoarsely, his heart beating wildly. "The bone fragments...the carbon dating...we couldn't be mistaken about that. Twenty thousand years old..."

He mentally sorted through man's evolutionary timeline. Never before had Paleolithic bones and iron artifacts been unearthed in the same place. Yet here he was, sweating under the African sun and holding something that could not possibly have been made 20,000 years ago. "I don't know how to explain this."

Gayle moved around him, carefully placing her feet between stringed-off sectors in the dirt until sunlight shined on her curious face. Her brown eyes focused on Dr. Spears' find. "The Iron Age isn't due for another seventeen thousand years. Ten thousand years ago, Upper Paleolithic and Neolithic man made tools from stones, bones, and antlers. The Bronze Age came about 4,000 years later and then the Iron Age."

"I know. I know." Milton tried to make sense of this anomaly. "Steel tools and weapons came along around 1400 BC, with the Hittites first, and then the Romans around 900 BC."

"We've obviously made a mistake here," Gayle said. "This site can't be twenty thousand years old. There's no such thing as Paleolithic iron. Besides—"

"Give me a chance to think." God, she could go on and on. He grasped the artifact dangling from the magnetic screwdriver and examined it closely, but due to the thick clay coating, he could only determine that it was not perfectly round. Scraping the hard clay with the screwdriver tip alarmed him to the possibility that a slip could damage the object. He had to quell his curiosity for the sake of conserving his find.

Knowing the university's lab would be a safer place to clean the artifact, he dropped it into a plastic specimen bag, tucked it into his shirt pocket, and buttoned the flap. There had to be a reasonable explanation for it being here.

He removed his bushman hat and wiped sweat from his brow. Sunshine quickly heated the exposed skin of his balding crown. As his heartbeat returned to normal, he looked up the hillside where the ground had broken away eons ago when a landslide buried these ancient people under tons of earth. "They were living here, a settlement of some kind," he said to Gayle.

"Paleolithic man was nomadic," she reminded him.

"Look around you," Milton said with a sweep of his hat. "This was paradise 20,000 years ago, a jungle full of animals and birds, fresh water everywhere. Fish ... If I had wandered up here 20,000 years ago and looked out over the Blue Nile Valley, I'd have stayed."

"We haven't found any indication of anyone living here, no dwellings, no hearths." Gayle put her hands on her hips in a show of authority. "Man didn't settle in one place until the Neolithic period, not until agriculture came along. Up until then, he was a hunter-gatherer, even in East Africa when—"

Milton raised an index finger, not wanting her to get

started again. "These people smelted ore into iron which means they had the technology to build a carbon furnace." He patted the artifact in his pocket. "They could have lived here."

"It's probably just a burial ground."

"Open your mind, Miss Weatherbee. Could it be that the landslide didn't cover a burial ground, but produced one? Remember, a good paleoanthropologist does not assume answers, but poses questions."

"There's no evidence of terraces. How did they plant crops on this steep slope?"

"Maybe they didn't need to, or perhaps they didn't want to."

"That goes against everything we know," Gayle rebutted. "Agriculture made it possible for nomadic tribes to settle down, build cities and grow civilizations. Where is there any evidence of that on this site?"

"It's got to be around here somewhere," Milton replied somewhat stupefied.

"I say there has to be another explanation for this thing you've found."

Milton placed his hat on his head and moved toward the row of tents and his lifeline to civilization, the radio. "I'll have it flown back to the lab by helicopter. You take the Land Rover into Bahar Dar and find Jainaba. Tell him to roundup a hundred men and enough equipment for a major dig. Be back here tomorrow."

Hurrying after him, Gayle pulled a handkerchief from her back pocket and wiped sweat from her neck. "And what are you going to do?"

"Dig."

"By yourself?"

"There's something here, Miss Weatherbee." He kicked at the dirt. "Something big. Maybe an ancient city. Now go on, at once. And bring back a bulldozer."

"You've got to be kidding."

"The trail has to be widened for trucks and equipment, and there's the matter of these huge boulders that must be moved."

"But where am I going to find a bulldozer?"

"That's your problem."

***

Milton paced across section 42 of his dig, which ran a full sixty feet in length. This first cut along the fall line had produced a few bone fragments and told him he was digging in the right place. Now standing at the west end of section 42, he looked up the hillside and tried to imagine the original slope of the mountain before the landslide defaced it some 20,000 years ago. The debris field extended about a thousand feet to the east. He'd only excavated a fraction of the west escarpment. Gauging the depth of the landslide, he determined he'd have to dig another sixty feet into the slope to reach the original hillside. In addition, he'd have to remove an equal amount of earth piled on top of it. He was sure there was plenty of area for an ancient settlement to be buried here, if his theory was correct.

He climbed out of the site, and after working his way uphill through a clump of boulders, he looked down on the area and made a visual assessment of the task ahead of him. Sixty feet down, sixty feet into the slope, and one thousand feet along the fall line, he did the math in his head. He'd have to move one hundred thirty five thousand cubic yards of rock to completely excavate the site, an unenviable task by any measure. Also, tons of vegetation would have to be stripped from the hillside: a vast thicket of thorny scrubs now inhabited by a troop of chattering Vervet monkeys, several stands of jutting palms, and a carpet of thick-bladed grass with razor-sharp fronds. A million boulders would have to be removed. His back hurt just thinking about it.

In the distance, helicopter blades beat the air. He'd radioed the university two hours ago, right after Gayle left for Bahar Dar, which meant the Board wasted no time filling his request to transport the artifact he had found. A Bell 407 came into view, flying up from the valley, its white-tipped rotor blades whirling circles in the sky. Milton climbed down from the dig site to await its arrival. He'd already prepared the artifact transportation papers, which identified his find and documented the change of possession as required under the informed consent agreements on file with the Department of Antiquities. The paperwork trail would protect the credibility of his find.

The blue and white helicopter landed on a flat of dirt at the trailhead, swirling a cloud of dust into the air. As the turbine engine wound down, the side door opened, revealing a middle-aged man dressed in an unbuttoned white suit coat, sharply pressed white slacks, white loafers, and dark glasses. The sight of Emmett Collins produced a sharp pain in Milton's chest, as if a knife blade had severed an artery. Emmett was on the university Board of Trustees, the antiquities committee chairman, an all-around lying son of a bitch. Thick black eyebrows spaced unusually close together dominated his facial features and contrasted sharply with his strawberry-blond bangs.

Rotor blades chopped overhead as Emmett got off the helicopter, and stooping, he ran toward the dig site, a silver briefcase clutched in his left hand. "Dr. Spears, it's been a long time."

Milton couldn't believe Emmett's casual attitude. "What are you doing here?"

"So you've found something big, huh?"

"Why did the Board send you of all people?"

He looked up and shaded his sunglasses with his free hand. "Can we get out of the sun?"

"I'd rather you get back in that helicopter."

"That's not going to happen." Emmett pulled a

Terry Wright

handkerchief from his lapel pocket and dabbed sweat from his brow. "So let's get down to business, shall we?"

Milton gave him a cross look, then relented with a growl and led him to a table under the awning of the communications tent, which was crammed full of computer equipment and office fixtures powered by a humming Honda generator.

"It must be a hundred degrees in the shade." Emmett wiped his neck with his handkerchief, set the briefcase on the table, and popped the clasps. Inside, a loaded Beretta nestled menacingly in the folds of a blue velvet lining. "What have you got that's going to change human history?"

"Why all the cloak and dagger stuff?" Milton asked, indicating the open briefcase and the gun.

Emmett's left cheek twitched. "Your radio transmission may have been intercepted by *Shifta*."

"What makes you think that?"

"They've been reported operating in this area."

"I haven't seen any bandits." Milton had been working here for six months and hadn't encountered anyone.

"The Board has decided not to take any chances. Now then, let's see what you've got."

Milton regarded Emmett a moment, the business about bandits stuck in his brain. Between the phony story, dark glasses, and the Beretta, Milton felt a stranglehold of trepidation.

"Come on," Emmett said. "I don't have all day. That helicopter pilot charges by the hour."

Glancing at the Bell 407, Milton wondered why the pilot had kept the engine running. "What are you up to, Emmett?"

"Still don't trust your old buddy, huh?"

"Not after that stunt you pulled on the Rift Valley dig."

"We needed the funding, besides, that was a long time ago."

"Seems like yesterday to me."

Emmett's upper lip curled. "The whole thing backfired. It wasn't my fault."

"You outright lied to the Department of Antiquities. While I was cleaning up your mess, Don Johnson dug up the prize." Milton pinched a finger and thumb together. "I was that close to *Lucy*."

"Unfortunate, yes, but this time, I'm on top of things." He stuck out his chin. "This one's not going to get away. So let's see it."

Stepping back, Milton planted his boots firmly apart and folded his arms across his chest. "Forget it."

"Now wait a minute—"

"Just get the hell out of here, Emmett."

"I'm not going anywhere without that artifact."

"You're wasting the university's money." Milton nodded toward the idling helicopter as proof. "The Board will have to send someone else to get this artifact."

"You know the rules, Milton. You're obligated to turn over whatever you find. It's specified in the informed consent agreement. Addis Ababa University is the legal liaison, and I represent the university. I am the conservator, so give it up."

"What assurances do I have that you won't pilfer the piece?"

"None."

"Then you're not getting it."

Emmett retrieved the Berretta from the briefcase. "Don't make me use this thing."

A shot of adrenaline hit Milton's bloodstream. He'd never had a gun pointed at him before, and he found the experience infuriating. "You'd shoot me?"

"I'm just doing my job."

Milton wanted to slug the son of a bitch, but after

regarding the gun once more, he elected to retrieve the plastic specimen bag from his buttoned shirt pocket instead. "You'd rob your own mother."

"Compliments will get you nowhere. Now give me the artifact."

With teeth clenched, Milton handed it to Emmett.

He grinned. "There, that didn't hurt a bit now, did it?"

"Like getting a tooth pulled."

Emmett returned the Berretta to his briefcase and eyed the artifact. "What is it?"

"I wish I knew. Everything we've carbon-dated from this site is over 20,000 years old, but this piece is made of iron."

"That's not possible. Are you trying to pull something on me?"

"If the artifact was smelted in a charcoal furnace, six percent of it should be carbon, enough to carbon-date it."

Emmett removed the piece from the plastic bag, and holding it in his open palm, he lifted the sunglasses from his granite-gray eyes and examined it closely. "Hmm."

"Most of the artifact is coated with cement-hard clay," Milton said. "But a shiny edge caught my eye. It's made of some kind of iron."

Tossing it up as if testing its weight, Emmett said, "We'll need to destroy a piece of this to carbon-date it."

"It'll be worth it to find out what it is."

"A medallion, probably, but after 20,000 years, iron should have rusted away by now."

"I wondered about that too. There's something strange about the metal." Milton handed Emmett the transportation papers and the provenience card, which documented the artifact's origin. "You'll find these in order. Don't forget I'm the one who found it."

Examining the documents, Emmett smiled. "Good job, doctor." He signed the lines that confirmed transfer of the artifact, placed it and the papers into the briefcase, and took out the Beretta again. "Don't worry. I'll get it there safely." He thrust the gun behind his belt.

"You better not screw me around this time."

"Will you relax?" His left cheek twitched.

"I don't trust you as far as I can throw you."

"I'll get back to you with the test results." Emmett snapped the briefcase lid closed and spun the lock dials. "It's in the university's hands now. No longer your problem."

"Why don't I feel good about that?"

Sunglasses in place, Emmett looked out across the dig. "What are you planning next?"

"I've sent Gayle to get Jainaba. We're going to move this mountain if we have to."

"What do you think is buried here?"

"A settlement of some kind...more sophisticated than anything we've seen before."

"Good luck with that." Emmett headed toward the waiting helicopter. "I'm glad it's you and not me out here in the middle of nowhere."

"Be careful with my artifact."

Emmett waved him off and climbed into the helicopter, which quickly throttled up and rose, throwing dust everywhere. As it hammered down toward the valley, a horrible foreboding came over Milton. His intuition told him he'd never see his artifact again.

Chapter Eight

Gayle Weatherbee had been driving for more than three hours, and seeing Bahar Dar up ahead, she longed for a sandwich and a cold beer. The Land Rover clanged and popped as she negotiated her way around a throng of pedestrians, mostly stooped black women with bundled firewood strapped to their backs and men coaxing overloaded donkeys along. They paid her little mind as she passed and lumbered on down the gut-wrenching dirt road into the city.

Bahar Dar sat along the southern shore of Lake Tana, six thousand feet above sea level. The scent of jacarandas flowers and imported Australian eucalyptus trees filled the air. Unlike other dusty lakeside villages, Bahar Dar was a modern community with broad, tree-lined streets and many fine hotels. She imagined a shower and a soft bed. However, she had work to do and went right to her task, quickly passing the tourist havens and plunging into the business side of Bahar Dar.

Screeching to a stop in front of Atambo Mercantile, a weathered wood-plank storefront in the commercial district, she shut off the engine, yanked on the parking brake, and bounded out of the Rover with as much authority as any man.

Her bold arrival drew the attention of passing women wearing colorful long dresses and headscarves. On the shaded boardwalk, a group of black men dressed in waist-length tunics sat together chewing *khat*, a bitter leaf with the stimulating quality of a mild amphetamine. Cheeks bulging, they hushed their Amharic chatter and eyed her curiously.

"*Yik'ërta*...excuse me," she called out. "*Yeat nô, Jainaba?*"

"*Atambo*," one man said, pointing to the storefront.

"*Amesegënallo*...thank you." She entered the shadowy mercantile, her boots clunking on creaky wood flooring. Crates and lumpy burlap bags cluttered the place, leaving barely enough room for her to walk from front to rear. A fluorescent ceiling light blinked spastically, and the musty air stunk of rat dung and lye. "Anybody here?"

"*Selam*." Kebede, the chubby storekeeper, appeared from the backroom. Bald as an ostrich egg, he wore a white shirt, goatskin vest, and baggy black trousers. A bit shorter than her and skin black as ebony agate, his white eyes glowed across the dim room. "Welcome...ah...Miss Gayle it is, from the university. Come. You look like you have journeyed far."

She swallowed dryly. "I could use a beer."

"My compliments. You have arrived just in time for lunch."

"I'm looking for Jainaba."

"Yes, he is here. Please, won't you join us?" He indicated the backroom with a stubby finger. "This way." His broad smile displayed a mouthful of white teeth. This gave away the fact that he was a Woyta, a tribe of natives who ate raw hippo meat, giving them the whitest teeth in Africa. Holding that morbid thought, she wondered what was for lunch and followed Kebede into the backroom. The place was much homier than the messy storeroom out front, the walls adorned with colorful African tapestries and the lighting soft but adequate. Recorded harp music drifted through the air.

She spotted Jainaba, a lanky Amharan seated on a small stool in front of a *mesob*, a woven basket-like table. He wore a white polo shirt and blue shorts. Two black men she didn't know sat with him, and also the storekeeper's wife, mulu Alem. She wore a flower-pattern dress and gracious smile.

A large communal plate rested on the *mesob*. On the plate she saw heaps of *doro wot*, a spicy chicken stew that always gave her heartburn, *injera*, a bouncy flat bread, lamb, and vegetable *wot* made of chickpeas, bell peppers, and collard greens. The diners ate with their fingers. "Whatever happened to a good-old cheeseburger," she said and accepted from Kebede a cold *T'ella*, a locally brewed beer. "*Emesegënallo.*" She held up the bottle in a salute to Jainaba.

"Eee, Miss Gayle Weatherbee," he said in a squeaky voice. "I cannot believe my eyes have seen you. Sit. Join us."

Kebede offered her his stool. "Please, I am finished."

She sat with the others, downed half her beer, and after washing her hands with a moist towel, tore into the *injera*.

"You have business to bring you this far?" Jainaba asked. "Or does Dr. Spears find an end to his digging?"

"He needs you, Jainaba, and men and equipment for a major dig on Choke Mountain."

Jainaba's eyes grew big around. "Eee, it is expensive what you ask."

"The university can afford it."

Kebede rubbed his chubby palms together. "The doctor's credit is excellent. What does he require?"

"A hundred men with shovels and gear...and a bulldozer." She'd said it calmly, as if every one of those items would be easy to procure. She threw back a gulp of beer and scooped up some *doro wot* with a tatter of *injera*. To hell with the heartburn. As she was about to pop the food into her mouth, she caught a look of concern on Jainaba's face and hesitated. "What is it?"

He nodded to Kebede, who seemed to understand some unspoken language. "Come," he said to his wife and guests. "We shall begin preparations at once."

"Please don't rush off," Gayle said. "Finish your meal."

Rising, mulu Alem and the two black men followed Kebede out of the backroom.

"Jainaba, why—"

"I must tell you the story of Choke Mountain."

She chucked the food into her mouth and chewed, all the while scowling at Jainaba. "Come on." She swallowed. "You know I don't believe in stories."

"Albeit, you will listen."

"Fine. Lunch and a fairytale."

"At one time," Jainaba began, "our ancestors and the animals lived under Choke Mountain with Kaang, the Great Master of All Life. They all understood each other, and it was always light, even without the sun."

Gayle rolled her eyeballs.

"During this time of great harmony, Kaang activated his plan to build the world above. He first created a wondrous tree on Choke Mountain and gave it many branches that spread out over the land, and after he finished, he dug a hole at the base of his tree that reached all the way down to a door to the world below. First, a man came out the door and sat under the tree. Then a woman came out and sat next to him, followed soon by the rest of the people, and then all the animals emerged onto the land. Kaang gathered them together under his wondrous tree and instructed them to live together peacefully."

"Like that ever happened." Gayle swigged beer.

Jainaba didn't waver. "It was then that he told the people they could not chop his tree and build a fire or a great evil will befall them. They all agreed, so Kaang left them to live in their new world on Choke Mountain."

"Big mistake." Knowing where this story was headed, she dug into the *doro wot* again.

"As evening came, the sun began to sink, and the

people and animals watched this sight that none had ever seen before. But when the sun sank beneath the earth and darkness fell, fear entered the hearts of the people. They could no longer see each other, not having the eyes of the animals, and not covered in fur like the animals, the people became very cold. Forgetting their promise to Kaang, they chopped the tree and built a fire. Soon they were warm and they could see each other, but the animals were afraid of the fire and ran away. The next day, the people looked for the animals and came down from Choke Mountain and spread across the land. They divided into tribes, some moving to the Rift Valley and south into Kenya, and others going north up the Nile Valley and into Egypt, the Mediterranean, and soon they covered the earth and began killing each other for land and wealth and power."

"That's malarkey, Jainaba."

"Choke Mountain is the root of this evil," he replied.

"And this comes from a college educated Amharan?"

"So...maybe I do not believe it, sure, but the men I must hire to dig, they believe it is true, and their fear will greatly deter their willingness to work there."

"Offer them more money than they're worth." She felt powerful wielding Dr. Spears' checkbook. "I need a hundred men."

"I will see who I can find." Jainaba offered up a salute with his beer bottle. "*Nege*."

"Not tomorrow. Today."

He frowned. "What is the great hurry?"

"It's Dr. Spears. He's found something important."

***

Two hours later, Atombo Mercantile bustled with activity: growling truck engines, grinding gears, and men lined up, grunting as they loaded supply crates onto four-wheel-drive flatbeds, Dodge Power Wagon pickups, and onto the backs of mules and camels, anything that could carry a load. Gayle watched them load tents and blankets and tables and chairs and ropes and shovels and fuel and food and every imaginable article needed for an expedition into the African bush.

Jainaba had enlisted the aid of ninety men who brought with them goats for milk and cattle for slaughter and pigs and chickens and dogs to warn the camp of lions that stalked the night. Sandal-clad feet and animal hooves stirred dust from the road, which hung in the breezeless air like a murky morning fog over Lake Tana. Cumulus clouds were building above the mountainous horizon, and from the shaded boardwalk, Gayle watched the weather. Afternoon rains would soon drench her expedition, a welcome relief from the heat, but a muddy respite, at best.

"Here is the tally," the shopkeeper Kebede announced, approaching with a clipboard of papers. His hippo white smile told her he was pleased with the day's sales.

She thumbed through the invoices. "We are ten men short, and I don't see anything here for a bulldozer."

"But, Miss Gayle—"

"I specifically told Jainaba, a bulldozer."

"It is just that the price is too high."

"Jainaba." She stepped off the boardwalk and into the dusty soup of men and equipment. "Jainaba." Muscling her way through a line of men passing supplies toward the waiting trucks, she searched the mayhem expectantly. The sun was bright, and she shielded her eyes under a cupped hand. "Jainaba."

"Yes, Miss Gayle," he called out as he rounded the back of a truck loaded with crates. "I am coming."

"Jainaba," she shouted over all the noise. "What about the bulldozer?"

He came to her breathlessly, wincing as if poked with a sharp stick. "Eee, it is too much money."

"I'll be the judge of that."

"We should clear the way with back-breaking work instead of—"

"That will take weeks. If Dr. Spears wants a bulldozer, he gets a bulldozer. *Gebbawot?*"

"Eee, I understand, but you see..." His eyes widened as if a light bulb had blinked on in his brain. "No, I see you don't understand, so I will show you. Please, come with me. When you see, you will change your mind."

She followed him through throngs of dusty men and smelly animals to the end of an alley far removed from the commotion. There, he pointed to a rusted truck-tractor and trailer parked in the gutter. Tethered to the bent front bumper, a squealing pig, not much older than a piglet, struggled to get free of the rope around its neck. On the trailer, half a dozen men wearing headscarves and white tunics squatted atop a green Mitsubishi bulldozer, one that might have seen duty during World War II.

"There," she said. "That one will do."

A black man wearing a long robe of goatskin got to his sandaled feet and stood spread-legged on top of the bulldozer's mud-encrusted tracks. A long-blade Masai knife tucked behind a camel hair rope tied around his waist gave her reason for immediate concern. Multicolored beads and an amulet hung around his neck. Slowly, he dropped his hooded headdress to his shoulders, revealing scraggly black hair that hung in tangles. The irises of his eyes glowed albino white.

Gayle's skin felt crawly. "Who is that creep, Jainaba?"

"You see, it is not the machine we don't want for the dig. It is the one who owns it. His name is Maki, an Oromo farmer, and his brothers. They are trouble, Miss Gayle."

"How much do they want?"

Maki leaped from the bulldozer like a flying squirrel and landed in the dirt with barely a puff. His face was

African hard, his hands like leather, his upturned palms as white as her behind. "I have brought what you need," he said in an Africanized English accent. He approached within inches of her face. "But the price is high." Most of his front teeth were missing, and his breath stunk of *khat*. Behind him, the tethered piglet oinked and squealed.

Gayle choked down her instant dislike for the Oromo man and held her ground. She had to have that bulldozer. "Why do you ask a high price?"

"It is the curse of the mountain that dictates my fee," Maki said, his milky eyes glaring.

"There is no curse."

Maki pointed a gnarly-nailed finger toward Choke Mountain. "You know of Kaang, the Great Master of All Life?"

"I've heard of him." Twice today.

"Then you should know that Kaang never forgave the people for chopping his tree and setting it afire." Behind Maki, his brothers squatted vulture-like on the bulldozer's cowl and tanks, their hard black faces revealing no emotion. The pig squealed in defiance of its tether and its unenviable situation.

Gayle felt an urgent need to take the young animal away from its hideous master. Though she had great respect for the African people, she had little patience when it came to their superstitions. "There was no tree, Maki, no fire. It's only an excuse to jack up your rates."

Maki rambled on. "Kaang returned to his empty place inside the mountain and closed the door between the two worlds, forbidding the people to ever return under threat of a great curse."

She angled a sideways glance at Jainaba. "Tell him there's no curse, will you?"

"Eee. He won't believe me."

She glared at Maki. "It's just a story."

The pig's incessant squealing distracted her. She

thought to walk over and release it from its tether, but steeled herself and returned to the problem at hand. "There's no door on Choke Mountain."

Maki showed her a slanted smile, wide nostrils flaring. "It is a simple curse," he pressed. "If the door is opened, Kaang promised to destroy all the people with the utterance of a single word."

"No fire and brimstone?" Gayle taunted him. "Will a crack in the earth swallow us all? Because of a word? And what word would that be?"

"It is not known." Maki stepped back and grasped the pouch that hung around his neck on a leather cord, clutching it as if it were his link to eternity. "When the people learn the word, the knowledge this brings will be like a plague on the land to destroy everything mankind has ever believed about his history, his religions, his place on the earth with the animals."

"And you believe that?"

"Agree to my price, it will not matter."

"You're not afraid," she said with a 'gotcha' tone in her voice.

"My brothers, there." He pointed back at the bulldozer. "They are afraid of the word. I am not afraid because I have brought protection."

The piglet squealed as if possessed.

Gayle could hardly think with all the noise. She refused to believe the story, the curse, or Maki's protection from his god. She didn't believe in gods and churches and preachers. Especially preachers. Her disdain for one had torn her away from her family farm in Kansas and driven her into the heart of Africa in search of the true origin of man and proof that God and his garden was a myth. Now that she had a position with Dr. Spears, she wasn't about to cave in to any barbaric notions of Kaang and curses. She needed that bulldozer. She wasn't leaving without it. "How much?"

Maki grinned toothily. "Four hundred thousand birr."

She did the math and almost choked. "Fifty thousand dollars? I could buy one for that much, and probably a better looking one, at that."

"Eee. It is a good idea," Jainaba jumped in. "We should go to buy our own."

The pig squealed.

"But it would not come with my brothers," Maki added, as if that alone somehow sweetened the pot. "They are good diggers."

"*Betam wëdd nô*," Jainaba said. "It is too expensive."

Gayle elbowed him in the ribs. She still needed ten more men, and Maki's brothers would do. "Let me take care of this." Glaring at Maki, she countered, "Thirty thousand dollars."

Moving to the truck bumper, Maki grabbed the pig's scruff and lifted the little squealer then drew the Masai knife—

"Hey." Gayle's breath hitched with fear for the piglet's fate. "What are you doing?"

With a slash, he cut the pig loose from the rope.

She put her hand on her heart. "For a second I thought—"

"Forty-two thousand." He held up the pig as if he were selling it.

"You're robbing me blind, Maki," she shouted.

He shrugged. "It is our way."

The pig kicked franticly.

"Thirty-eight thousand," she said. "That is all. Not a penny more."

Maki plunged the Masai knife into the pig's ribcage. All twelve inches of the blade disappeared into flesh, the bloody tip coming out the backbone side. "We have a deal."

Gayle stifled a scream. Backing away, her hand over her open mouth, she didn't know whether to run or vomit.

The sight of that poor wriggling piglet with its wide-open eyes ringed in white, the sudden spray of blood from its snout, the horrible noises coming from its throat, and its little feet flailing, horrified her beyond belief. "Are you crazy?"

On the bulldozer, the brothers' eyes came to life, and wide smiles shone in the African sun. They began chanting, "Kaang! Kaang! Kaang!"

Mouth agape, Jainaba stepped backward. "Eee, they are all crazy."

Again and again, Maki stabbed the convulsing pig until blood came out of it like a canvas water bag shot full of holes. "It is our salvation." Maki tossed the pig up to his brothers on the bulldozer. They quickly went to bleeding out the pig on the engine cowl, the seat, the tanks, and the blade, smearing blood everywhere and chanting, "Kaang! Kaang! Kaang!"

Gayle watched the gruesome ritual through tunneled vision. "You're heathens."

Maki rushed up to her with long strides, his blood-soaked hands extended, his black and tangled hair flailing about. "Take my hands," he demanded. The devil now raged in his albino eyes. "We must make this pact between you and I and Kaang's pig, or the expedition on Choke Mountain will fall to the curse."

"Get away from me."

"Take my hands before the blood cools."

"I don't believe in that nonsense. Get away from me." She shoved him back, but with the swiftness of a cobra, he grabbed her hands and bent her palms up and backward, painfully forcing her to her knees. His touch set off fires in her stomach. He put his nose to hers and glared into her eyes. The stink of his body and the pig's blood forced hot bile up to the back of her throat.

"It is time you believed in something, Miss Gayle Weatherbee." Maki smeared the pig's blood all over her hands and threw her to the dirt. "We will accept a check." With that, he climbed into the truck-tractor and fired up the diesel engine.

"Jainaba." She looked up through swirling dust at his dumbstruck face. "Why didn't you stop him?"

"He is trouble, I told you already. You should not have bartered with him." Stooping, he grabbed her arm and pulled her to her feet. "I fear you have made a big mistake."

Gayle staggered at the sight of her hands smeared with sticky pig's blood and clumped with dirt. She would have vomited if her throat wasn't closed up. Sucking in a breath, she heard the truck grind into gear. "Maki," she grated out. "Where are you going with my bulldozer?"

"We will return at dawn for the journey to Choke Mountain." His barefoot brothers stood all over the bulldozer, fists pumping the air and chanting "Kaang, Kaang, Kaang," as they rode away in a cloud of dust. All that remained was the drained pig carcass, a silent heap in the dirt. Thunder rumbled in the distance.

Gayle fought to breathe. "What have I done?"

***

The next morning, as the sun's first rays reflected off Lake Tana, Gayle walked beside Jainaba along the line of loaded trucks, their engines rumbling. He wore a blue and white shirt, cutoff Levis, and leather sandals. Tugging on tie downs, he kicked tires and chatted with men who'd found suitable seating atop the crates. "Be safe," he told them in Amharic.

Moving to the next truck, she rubbed her neck, having spent a restless night on the front seat of the Land Rover. Visions of Maki, bleeding pigs, and preachers had kept her awake. Before dawn, Kebede's wife fixed her a hot bath, a mutton wot breakfast, and a pot of coffee, which helped immensely. She felt energized for the rough trip ahead.

"This is all of it?" she asked Jainaba.

"We have ten trucks."

"The pack animals won't be able to keep up."

"They will be along in good time." He greeted the next driver who smiled through his open door window. "Be careful of the dynamite on your truck. And you there," he said to those perched atop the crates, "no smoking." A couple men jumped from the truck and sprinted quickly to another truck, scrambling like squirrels to the top of the load.

"I thought smoking was against their religion," Gayle said as they proceeded down the line of trucks.

"Some of these men are Muslims," Jainaba replied. "They do not smoke or drink. But most are Orthodox Christians, which is the major religion in Ethiopia."

"They all like to chew their *khat*."

"It is the substitute for beer for eighty percent of these men."

The last truck came into view, the one with the bulldozer trailered behind it. Gayle felt a chill. Maki, wearing his goatskin robe, sat cross-legged on the operator's seat now shaded by a tarpaulin canopy. Smears of pig's blood looked like the black strokes of a paintbrush. On the ground, Maki's brothers sat on their haunches, cheeks bulging with *khat*, grinning as she approached.

"Maki," she called up. "I expect you and your brothers to act civilized. No more animal sacrifices on the university's time. Is that clear?"

"We are ready, bwana."

"And there'll be no more talk about curses, Maki. I don't want you frightening the other men."

He said nothing, just stared down at her.

"Come, Miss Gayle." Jainaba took hold of her arm and turned her toward the waiting Land Rover. "We best be going."

"He'd better not cause any more trouble."

"I will drive."

"Forget it." She climbed in behind the wheel and buckled her seatbelt.

Jainaba stood outside the passenger door, hands on his hips. "Eee. I don't like women drivers."

"The way I see it, you have a choice, Jainaba. You can forget about me being a woman or you can ride on the bulldozer with Maki and his brothers."

Without further hesitation, Jainaba jumped in. "You drive a hard bargain. What made you this way?"

She started the engine. "What way?"

"Hard as a man."

"Necessity, Jainaba, necessity." She engaged first gear as the trucks began to pull out. Behind them, animal tenders began coaxing their charges into motion. "I'm an old farm girl, remember?" Spinning tires, she lurched away from Atombo Mercantile, and shifting through the gears, she quickly overtook the lead truck.

"Eee. It is more than that." Jainaba fidgeted with his seatbelt. He had little room for his spidery legs. His knees were pressed against the glove box door.

"What about you, Jainaba? Why don't you dress like your countrymen and chew *khat*?"

"I don't like it."

"Yesterday, you drank a beer."

He chuckled. "I am a Westernized Amharan, a Christian. I do not wear *shammas* and *fugus* because I choose not to, by my own beliefs."

She looked in her rearview mirror, a quick check on the convoy behind her. "What do you believe?"

"Why should it matter to you?"

"There are many religions, either someone has to be wrong or everyone is wrong."

"What do you believe, Miss Gayle?"

The Rover bounded out of Bahar Dar, where the blacktop met the molar rattling road south toward Choke

Mountain. The road wasn't much different from the gravel road between Highway 9 and her farm back in Kansas. And for a moment, she saw fields of tall corn stalks on either side of the road whizzing by, the Ford pickup fishtailing into the farmhouse driveway, her father cursing, words she'd never heard him utter before. She remembered her tears that day, the rip in her Sunday dress, and the blood. She was only fifteen years old.

"I'll kill the son of a bitch," her father said with a growl in his throat.

Frightened beyond belief, she couldn't talk. Her windpipe clutched spastically. She couldn't stop bawling. And her private place hurt, it ached and it burned. She wanted so badly to sink into a tub of hot water and wash away what the preacher had done to her down there.

It was chaos at the farmhouse. Cow dung scented the air, and flies buzzed around everything. The screen door banged, and her mother ran out to meet the pickup as it skidded to a stop.

"My poor baby." Her face was etched with horror, and tears streamed from worry-sick eyes. Younger brothers Michael and Sam, one taller than the other, stood stone-like on the porch, hands thrust into their pockets, their long faces white with fear.

Mother pulled open the truck door. Her eyes went wide at the sight of the bloodstained dress. She covered her mouth with her hand. "What did he do to you?"

Gayle couldn't speak. She couldn't find words to explain what had happened. Her young mind couldn't process the violence. All she could do was bawl and inhale with sharp jolts.

"This is your fault," her mother shouted at her father.

"It was a church picnic." He jumped from the truck. "She wanted to go, and I saw no harm in it."

"I never liked the way he looked at those girls."

"He's the preacher, for God's sake. Can't we trust

anyone with our children?" He ran around the pickup, a shoulder strap of his blue jean coveralls dangling down to his elbow, and headed for the house, boots clomping. Never before had she seen him this angry, crazy like a rooster defending his hens. He stomped up the steps, threw open the door and bounded inside.

A sudden realization bolted through her. Maybe she wasn't the only girl in church to have fallen for the preacher's lies.

"How long has this been going on?" her mother cried.

Feeling dirty and ashamed, she didn't want to talk about it. The preacher had said it was the way God loved her, the way God touched her, through him. On countless occasions over the years he'd found ways to be alone with her: after Sunday school cleaning the chalkboard, before services as she prepared the candles, and sometimes in the rectory kitchen after a Sunday evening potluck dinner. Fondling her, he said God had ordained him to do it. She'd been chosen to receive His affections. God had blessed her, and as long as she never told anyone, she would someday sit with Him on the throne in heaven. How could she have known it was wrong, it was a lie, and the lie got worse and worse each time the preacher's hands went farther and stayed longer, until today at the picnic when he dragged her into the bushes and did this horrible thing to her.

Seconds later, her father returned with the shotgun in his hands, the one he always kept over the mantel. "I may not be home for supper." He leaped back into the truck.

"No, Daddy, don't," she cried out as her mother tried to pull her from the truck. With white knuckles, she clung to the steering wheel. "The police will arrest him."

"They aren't going to do a damn thing."

"I'll tell them what he did, Daddy. Just don't go."

"No daughter of mine is going to utter a word of this to no strangers, police or not. It's devil's talk, yah hear." He pried her fingers from the steering wheel. "I'll handle this my way."

Her mother helped her from the truck seat. "It's too embarrassing any other way, Gayle honey. Everyone will talk."

The engine cranked and started with a roar.

"Thou shalt not kill, Daddy."

"Get her cleaned up," he yelled to her mother and tore off toward town in a mad rush.

Her mother guided her toward the house. "We must get you into the bath at once."

Stomach cramping and stooped over with sorrow, Gayle wanted nothing more than a hot bath.

"Don't worry, Gayle darling...Gayle...Miss Gayle...Miss Gayle Weatherbee."

Jainaba tapped her shoulder. "Miss Gayle, you have not answered my question. What do you believe?"

Gayle blinked and drew in a quick breath of reality, the Land Rover, the convoy, the dusty African road to Choke Mountain. "I was fifteen when they killed my father."

"Eee?"

"The police shot him down like a mad dog."

A big hole in the road jarred the Land Rover down to its rivets. Jainaba stiffened. "But why, Miss Gayle, why?"

"It's a long story."

"It is a long drive."

Looking at Jainaba, she hesitated to tell him any of this...the shame she'd brought upon her mother...the naïve way in which she'd become involved with a so-called *man of God*...the way the townsfolk looked at her afterwards, talked behind her back, as if it were all her fault. For the longest time she wished she hadn't called her father from the gas station phone. She should've kept quiet like the preacher had said. He'd warned her that something horrible would happen if she told anyone. And as it turned out, he was right. If she'd kept her mouth shut, her father would still be alive, and she'd probably be somewhere bouncing babies on her knees instead of digging in the African dirt for answers. Nobody else understood why she was here, so why should Jainaba?

He settled back in his seat. "I wish you would talk about it. It will make you feel better."

She could think of only one thing that would make her feel better, the truth about why man was such a violent creature. At first, she thought it was because of the brutal nature of things, the food chain, the eat-and-be-eaten way of the animal world. Kill or be killed, survival of the fittest, every living thing had to struggle to survive, but this line of thought didn't take into account the fact that only man killed for sport; only man killed for profit; only man killed for revenge, money, and power. Something was missing, something that changed mankind from hunter-gatherers into sadistic, bloodthirsty, raping, killing... Her anger flared, and gripping the steering wheel tightly, she felt compelled to let Jainaba know why. "I was raped by a preacher."

"Eee!"

"My father went to the church to kill him, but instead, changed his mind and called the police. He told them he'd made a citizen's arrest and wanted to turn a rapist over to them. The police thought my father had taken the preacher hostage. They surrounded the church, and when my father opened the door, a sharpshooter killed him."

Jainaba's eyes were wide open. "And why has that brought you to Africa, Miss Gayle Weatherbee?"

The Rover banged and clanked down an extremely rough stretch of road. Behind her, the convoy kept up the frantic pace. "On the sixth day, God created man and saw that it was good. Is it fact or fiction, Jainaba?"

He shrugged. "Evolution or creation, who is to say?"

"If it's true, then something went wrong with the part about man being good."

"Some say the devil makes a man bad."

"Isn't that just typical," she spat. "Man blames his bad behavior on something else, in this case, the devil. It's never mans' fault. Think about it, Jainaba, if God is so powerful, why does he allow the devil to get away with it?"

"Choice? Yes. It is said God gives us a choice."

"Come on! Did your father ever give you a choice? Did he say to you, 'you can be good today or you can be bad today, your choice?'"

"No, Miss Gayle, he insisted I be good or it was the business end of the stick for me."

"Then if God is our 'father,' wouldn't he have insisted we be good, or made us that way in the beginning?"

"I think it was his intention, but for some reason, it is not so."

"My point exactly. Something happened that made man a violent creature, and none of it had anything to do with God. None of it had anything to do with nature."

"And that is why you are here, Miss Gayle. And the preacher is why you are so hard. Is that what it is?"

"You understand perfectly." She spotted the cutoff to Choke Mountain ahead. "Somewhere out here lies the answer, the truth, Jainaba, and I intend to find it."

"And what happened to the preacher?"

A knot tightened in her stomach. "He got away with raping me."

Jainaba frowned. "How could this be so?"

She pulled the Land Rover to the side of the road, brakes squeaking to a stop, her mouth dry as Choke Mountain dust. For a moment, as the convoy clanked and squealed to a halt behind her, she thought about answering Jainaba's question. She knew it was a combination of the community's reaction to her father's actions and a police cover-up. They couldn't arrest the preacher after they'd killed her father. That would have been the same thing as admitting they were wrong. They'd have been chastised by the press and liable to the family. So she wasn't surprised when they bought into the preacher's explanation. Her father had been possessed by the devil. Why else would a normally sane man barricade himself inside a church and maniacally shout accusations of rape with a shotgun to the preacher's back?

Suicide by cop. The investigation was closed.

She'd tried to make them understand, but she didn't stand a chance. After all, the preacher was head of the church, a pillar in the community. She was just a distraught teenager, mourning the loss of her father and looking to blame someone for his actions that led to his death. It was her word against the preacher's, and worse, she couldn't prove she'd been raped. All the evidence had been washed away in that tearful bath. Public pressure to silence her accusations became intense: death threats, civil suits, and loan foreclosures against the farm. Her brothers were beat up at school and shunned by their friends. Eventually, her mother was committed to a mental institution, and her brothers were sent to foster homes. Their family had been totally destroyed.

In the end, Gayle realized she had only herself to count on. She shut out men; she shut out God; she vowed to destroy the very foundation that made the preacher so powerful. She would take away his God, take away his shield, and someday expose him for the criminal he really was, a brutal rapist. Until then, she would walk tall and talk tough. As far as answering Jainaba's question, she said, "I don't know how he got away with it."

"Eee. Miss Gayle. From the look in your eyes, I see it is not over yet."

In her rearview mirror, she saw Maki and his brothers approach through the swirling dust. "No, Jainaba, it's just beginning."

Chapter Nine

Janis touched Lisa's hand as the 757 descended on final approach to San Francisco. She seemed lost in thought. Out the window, he saw the Golden Gate Bridge. Boats of all sizes cut white wakes through choppy gray waters. The angular spire of the Transstar Building knifed skyward from a clutter of distant skyscrapers. He'd come to the City by the Bay to ask Lo Chin for his help. Janis hoped he wouldn't have to beg. Tracy's life hung on Lo's cooperation.

"We met down there," Lisa said breathily.

Janis looked at her blue eyes and sleek blond hair. A true California girl, she was. He could've fallen in love with her, but he'd come to his senses real quick. "I remember."

"At the Balli Club. You were meeting my dad."

A life-changing event, Janis thought. Turned his simple life at CU Boulder upside down. "Your dad's obsession with the 13th Power started all this. And now we have to do it over again." He made a fist. "Worse, I have to drag my friends into it. Lo Chin is going to have a fit."

She sighed. "Let's ride the trolley."

"There's no trolley to Marin County."

"No, silly. Just for fun."

"We don't have time for fun."

"I get so little time with you anymore."

He didn't want to talk about it. Their time together had been short for a reason. She was too young for him. She was Ray's daughter. Besides, her battle with Abandoned Child Syndrome was more than he could deal with, her mood swings, her temper tantrums. Life was better this way...for both of them, but still, it was good to see her. "Thanks for coming with me."

"I want to surprise Lo."

"I just hope he'll listen to you." Janis knew Lo had been more of a father to Lisa than Ray ever was. Her mother spent most of her time drunk, drugged up, and incarcerated, and Lisa grew up without her dad in her life, always shuffled off to one private school or another.

The jet banked right, and the landing gear dropped with a clunk. Lisa clutched the gold crucifix on her necklace, whispered something, her eyes closed.

"We'll be all right," Janis said, wondering about her newfound religious fervor. "I've never seen you like this."

"Like what?"

"You're hanging onto that cross as if it were a lifeline."

She smiled. "I've seen it all, Janis, the 13th Power, the beauty of our galaxy. We're so small in comparison, but it's not all for nothing." Her blue eyes glistened. "There's a reason for us being here."

"A grand scheme, you think?"

"I've suffered a lot, Janis, but God got me through it."

Janis grumped. "Your father and I got you through it."

The jet banked left, and as it dropped toward the airport, Lisa tugged on her seatbelt. "Don't you believe in God, Janis?"

"I'm a mathematician. I believe in numbers. They follow the rules and never lie."

"So you think this was all an accident, the earth, the universe...us?"

Janis felt uneasy about the subject. He believed there was a God because his mother said so. However, he believed nature was the true creator: physics, mathematics, action and reaction, the primordial soup from which life arose. Evolution made perfect sense to him. It appealed to his analytical mind.

Tires hit the runway, and reverse thrusters roared. Janis braced himself against the inertia of the decelerating jet. "Adam and Eve just don't cut it for me, Lisa."

"So you think we evolved from apes? That's nonsense."

"There's something missing, I know."

"Faith, Janis. That's what's missing."

"I need proof."

She squinted. "You saw my dad's recording."

"So?"

"How much more proof do you need?"

"The aliens prove nothing. They evolved the same as us."

"But God put 100,000 light years between us and them for a reason, Janis, to keep us apart. That's why my dad didn't tell anyone."

"Let me worry about the aliens. You just hang on to your necklace."

"And what are you going to hang on to, Janis?"

"You're making my brain hurt."

The jet taxied to the gate, and moments later, the gangway rolled up to the door. Lisa didn't say anything, just sat there with her arms crossed and a pout on her face. Janis stood, relieved the conversation and this flight was over. He retrieved their carry-ons from the overhead bin. "Are you coming?"

***

The San Francisco airport terminal buzzed with activity. Espresso wafted from a café on the mezzanine, and in a monotone female voice, the intercom announced, *"Final boarding call: United flight 285 to Denver."*

Wishing it was *his* flight home, Janis scanned the crowd for Lo Chin. He was supposed to meet them...

Lisa hooked his right arm. "I don't see him." She looked around. "It's not like Lo to leave you hanging."

Janis recalled their phone conversation. "Lo wasn't exactly thrilled when I called."

"Did you tell him what was going on?"

"Just that I need his help to save Tracy. I left out the details."

"He won't have anything to do with the 13th Power, you know."

"He'll do it for Tracy."

Lo wasn't anywhere to be found. He didn't answer Janis's page. A million people milled about, but the one person Janis needed the most wasn't there. Lo Chin must have decided not to help him.

More and more, as he made his way outside to ground transportation, he began to fear that Tracy was doomed. Sure, he could work out the equations and calculate the formulas, but without Lo Chin's expertise in programming the supercomputers, nothing would work. The 13th Power would not be attained, NASA's shuttles wouldn't fly, and Tracy would be executed as a traitor. He couldn't bear the thought of Tracy paying the ultimate price for this fiasco. "Damn it, Lo! Where are you?"

"Taxi," Lisa called out.

***

The cab ride across the Golden Gate Bridge to Marin County ended at the iron gate to Lo Chin's mansion, a sprawling estate with an ocean view. Janis recalled the last time he was here, when California seemed like heaven. A million years ago.

The driver pulled luggage from the trunk, took Janis's money and sped off. Turning to the tall wrought iron gate, he scanned the high brick walls on either side. "How are we going to get in?"

"I used to live here, remember?" Lisa punched numbers into the gate control panel. "I hope this code still works."

"Buzz him on the intercom first."

"And ruin the surprise?"

The gate creaked and started to open.

"After you," she said.

Janis grabbed their suitcases and led the way up the circular drive toward the front door. Lisa's sandals slapped the concrete behind him. A salty ocean breeze stirred the pine tree branches overhead. Sparrows chirped and flittered about. He saw Lo's old pickup truck and his blue Corvette parked in front of the porch.

"He's home," Lisa exclaimed, darted around Janis, and bounded up the stairs to the front door. It opened with an eerie squeal, revealing a tall man with curly hair, dressed in a black suit.

"You people are trespassing," he growled.

"We came to see Lo Chin," she said. "Are you his new butler?"

"Do I look like a fuckin' butler, lady?"

"Then who are you?"

"Lisa, let me handle this." Janis set down the luggage, fully convinced this guy was the butler, a bit rude, but Lo Chin probably told him to get rid of them. "We've got to talk to him."

"He's not here."

"His car is here," Lisa said. "Who are you?"

The suit stepped through the doorway, pulled a gun from under his suit coat. "Put your hands up."

A jolt of shock hammered Janis's chest. The man was no butler. "Now listen here—"

"Do it now." The man held the gun out, straight-armed.

Slowly, Janis complied, suddenly fearful of Lo's fate. This thug could have kept Lo from meeting them at the airport. Or killed him.

"Lo Chin is our friend," Lisa said, hands raised.

"Get the hell out of here before I call the cops."

"We're not leaving until we see Lo Chin," Janis said. "So go ahead and call the cops."

Two more suited men rushed out the doorway, waving their guns. "Enough of this nonsense," the biggest one said. Janis recognized him as the suit on the jet to NASA, the whittler, the one who'd gut-punched him in the SuperMIGGS. Peterson was his name. "I told you to get rid of them," he shouted at his accomplice, "not pull a gun on them."

Janis's stomach sank. They were in big trouble now.

The third suit was squatty and overweight. "Get 'em inside before somebody sees us."

"What are you doing here, Peterson?" Janis asked him, stalling.

Lisa gave him a dirty look. "You know these people?"

"They're from NASA."

Her expression changed from anger to wide-eyed fear. "Oh shit."

"Get moving," Peterson said.

With a gun barrel pressed to his ribcage, Janis stumbled up the steps and followed Lisa into the house. Thoughts of his last scrape with the CIA raced through his mind. He didn't know what agency these thugs worked for, but he was sure they were no less ruthless.

"What have you done with Lo Chin?" Lisa asked.

"Shut up!"

"He'd better be all right," Janis threw in, just in case they thought he might be able to do something about it.

"If not, what are you going to do?" Peterson growled.

Yes, they were screwed. Janis decided to shut up. As the suits shoved him through the front room, Lisa cast a confident glance at him, like she was thinking about making trouble for the bad guys. He wished they didn't

Terry Wright

have guns.

At the end of the hallway, he came to a brightly lit room with mirrored walls and mats on the floor. Incense scented the air. Lo Chin's dojo. He sat in a chair in the center of a large mat, his bony arms and legs bound with ropes. His silver hair was braided in back, he wasn't wearing his glasses, and he wore a white t-shirt and green boxer shorts. A thin stream of blood oozed from an angry gash in his forehead, giving Janis cause for alarm. Lo looked frail and defenseless, but he was a Karate Master. Janis figured the suits must've taken Lo by surprise, probably snuck in during the night and bullied him from his bed at gunpoint. That was the only way his unenviable situation could have come about.

The suits shoved Janis and Lisa into the room. Lo's eyes widened. "Miss Lisa... Dr. Janis. Sorry I did not meet you at the airport. I got tied up."

"Lo," Lisa cried out. She ran to him, dropped to her knees, and hugged his legs. "What have they done to you?"

Peterson turned to Janis. "I didn't expect to see you here, Dr. Mackey."

"Must be my lucky day." Janis's stomach still hurt from their last encounter.

Lisa whimpered and doted over Lo. "You're hurt."

Janis tried to divide his attention between Lisa's antics and the suits, whose attentions were now sternly on him. "What do you guys want?"

"General Brigham invited Lo Chin to NASA," Peterson said. "He declined, so we're here to change his mind. Personally, I don't see what good he is."

"He's a Chinese American and an expert computer programmer," Janis explained. "And what's more, he's my friend, so show him a little respect."

Peterson balled a fist. "And who's going to make me? You? A mathematician? A professor? President of the debate team, I suppose. You don't scare me."

Janis saw Lisa slip her hands around Lo's ankles and start untying the rope. He had to think fast. "I was a Golden Gloves boxer in my prime." He put up his fists. "Want to go a round, see who the tough guy really is."

"Great!" Peterson grinned and waved his gun at Janis. "Right here, right now. I'm so going to love fucking you up."

The squatty suit grinned.

"You talk tough with a gun in your hand." Janis hoped to keep the suits' attention on him and away from Lisa. "But I don't understand your attitude." He shuffled back and forth and threw a couple air punches. "We're all on the same side, right? General Brigham, NASA—"

"Hey!" The tall suit had spotted Lisa unwrapping the rope from around Lo's legs. As he raised his gun, the other two suits spun around in surprise.

Janis didn't have time to think. The *fight or flight* instinct gripped him, but *flight* was out of the question. He threw himself into Peterson's back, knocking him into the tall suit.

His gun went off. A wall mirror shattered.

Lisa dropped to the floor, and with a leg sweep, knocked the feet out from under the squatty suit. He hit the mat hard, dislodging the gun from his grip and sending it across the mat. Before he could scramble after it, Lisa landed a leg drop to the back of his head. Lights out.

Lo sprang to his feet, and though he was bent over with his arms still tied behind the chair, he made a spinning turn toward Peterson who was now pointing his gun at Lisa. The chair legs struck his arm, knocking the gun aside, and as Lo came around, he delivered a kick to Peterson's ribs. Air huffed from his lungs, and he staggered backward, gasping, his arms hugging his ribcage, but his hand still clutched the gun.

Janis had only a split second to react. He jumped in and delivered a right punch to Peterson's face. His knees buckled, and he dropped to the mat for a ten-count.

By this time, the tall suit had drawn a bead on Janis, but Lisa rolled across the mat and bulled her body into the back of the bad guy's legs. He fell backward. His gun banged, but agile as a gymnast, he flipped back up on his knees and now aimed at Lisa. However, he failed to notice Lo, who with lightning speed delivered a spinning back kick to the side of the tall suit's head, sending him to the mat with a groan. Lo fell over and landed on his back, still tied to the chair, bare feet kicking.

The tall suit sprang to his feet again, but Lisa greeted him with a scissors kick followed by an elbow to his temple. "Good night."

Janis dove for the gun the squatty suit had dropped, but Peterson's polished shoe stepped on it first. Janis wished he'd hit him harder.

"That's enough!" Peterson's eyes were narrow slits of rage as he aimed his gun at Lisa.

She took a step back and put up her hands.

Janis felt the agony of defeat.

"We're all going back to NASA," Peterson announced.

"I will *not* go," Lo shouted, still lying on his back in the chair.

"My orders are to bring you in or kill you, you stubborn old man."

"You go ahead, shoot me. I don't care."

"Stop talking like that," Janis said. "I need your help. They've got Tracy."

Lo frowned.

The tall suit sat up, rubbed the side of his head. "Shoot him, boss."

"Very well." Peterson turned his gun on Lo.

"Wait," Janis shouted. They were bluffing. If Lo died, Brigham's plan would fail. He was sure of it. "Think about what you're doing. Brigham needs Lo to return to the 13th

Power. How are you going to explain that you'd erased his only chance to succeed?"

Peterson aimed at Lo, right between his eyes. "I'll take my chances."

Lo just glared back at him.

"For Christ's sake, Lo, tell him you'll cooperate."

"I'll not help the general. No one can make me."

"Then do it for me, will you?"

"Not even for you, Dr. Janis."

"Then do it for Tracy."

Lo shook his head. "This thing they are asking us to do, Janis, it is bigger than Tracy and you and I. There is no honor in this alien invasion."

Janis understood that. "Tracy and I want to go home," he told Lo. "Go back to our simple life. We can't do it without you."

"It's better to die than help them disgrace humanity." He glared at Peterson. "Go ahead. I ready now. Shoot me."

"Peterson's not going to shoot anybody," Janis insisted.

Peterson lowered his gun. "Janis is right. I can't kill you, but I can't drag you through an airport, tied up and gagged either. You have to go willingly." He turned the gun on Lisa. "Change your mind, old man, or I'll blow her away."

Lisa put her hands on her heart. "Lo?"

Janis looked into Peterson's eyes for any sign of a bluff but saw only cold determination.

Peterson barred his teeth. "I'll do it, I swear."

Lo's eyes got big around. "She has nothing to do with this."

"Then Brigham won't mind if I kill her."

"She's an innocent girl."

Janis's throat tightened, barely got out the words, "You can't kill her in cold blood."

"Watch me."

Lisa's life was in Lo's hands. Was their bond strong enough, the years they'd spent together, his mentoring her in martial arts, and her companionship, or would he let her die for his convictions?

"So what's it going to be?" Peterson pressed. "A quiet trip to Florida or a dead blonde?"

"Shoot the bitch," the tall suit said.

"No!" Lo's expression drooped in defeat. "I will go."

Janis's knees wobbled under him, weak with relief.

"And no karate stuff," Peterson said.

"Just don't hurt her."

Peterson holstered his gun and looked at Lisa. "You're a tough young lady."

"I can hold my own."

Rubbing his swollen cheek, Peterson turned to Janis. "Nice punch."

"Who do you guys work for?"

"If I tell you—"

"You'll have to kill me, I know." Janis saw that cliché coming from a mile away.

Peterson grinned and turned to his partners. "Untie him and get yourselves cleaned up."

When Lo was free of the chair, Lisa took his arm. "I'll help you pack." They left the room. The goons followed them out.

Janis told Peterson, "You didn't have to come here. We had it handled."

"Brigham didn't think so, and frankly, Lo Chin is one stubborn old man." Peterson pulled a jackknife and an unfinished wooden figurine from his coat pocket. "You'd have gone back to NASA without him." He put the blade to the wood with an even, gentle stroke. "Unless of course you had threatened to kill someone he loves, but I don't think that's your style, Janis."

"Don't expect me to thank you."

"I expect you guys to send Brigham and his men to

the green planet."

"And if we fail?"

He held up the figurine he'd been carving, a bigheaded alien with almond eyes and twiggy limbs. "You'll never get Tracy back."

Chapter Ten

*Q*uestnar sped through the outer solar system. Luthes had set the thrusters to maximum outflow, which at this speed made the hull glow a dazzling blue. Ionized electrons left in the ship's wake formed an iridescent tail. He kept a trained eye on the NAV screen and a firm hand on the helmswheel. His shift was nearly over, and he eagerly awaited the relief helmsman's arrival. Four months had lapsed since departing *Latearian*. The Ice Planet was now clearly visible on the scope screen.

"ComCap on deck," came a call from the Operations officer on watch. Kerillan's entrance was always announced with fanfare, as set by Fleet Base protocol, which the crew adhered to even this far from home.

"Carry on," Kerillan said in his baritone voice. He paced across the polished amber floor, made his way between the bone white Ops and NAV consoles, nodding to the flight crewmen at their stations as he passed, and approached Luthes at *Questnar's* helm. "Another electronic letter from *Latearian*, Trantenant Rez." Kerillan offered him the folded paper. "Read it on your break."

Luthes took the message from Kerillan's long fingers. "That is three letters in forty days, sir. Verrilla is not doing well."

"She has made her own misery. *Latearian* is no place for them. As I understand it, she refuses to return to Beltzee."

"It is important that she waits for me, sir."

"Rather impetuous I must say."

"I miss her...and Sashi."

Kerillan set a hand on Luthes' shoulder. "I once had a fine woman. We missed each other as you and Verrilla do now, but the strain of Fleet Service became too much for her, and back then, there were no teleport passes for family. She soon gave up on me and married a Kedrikan banker."

"Sorry, sir."

"You are lucky, trantenant. You have a fine woman, a fine child. This is why I do not request their passes be revoked. As long as she is willing to tough it out, she is welcome to stay aboard *Latearian* until we return."

Luthes thought he should ask the ComCap to reverse his decision. Deep down, Luthes wished his family would leave *Latearian*. The bizarre possibility of a Tarreeda invasion, even if he didn't agree with Regarius's conclusions, was unnerving. If the Tarreeda had returned to reclaim their place on Beltzee, the battles in orbit would be furiously fought. He didn't want his family to be caught in the crossfire. They'd be safer at home than on the Fleet's out-base. He tucked the folded message into his pocket. "Thank you, sir."

Kerillan patted Luthes' shoulder, and without further comment made his way across the flight deck to his observation chair. Already, the second shift crew was filtering in. Luthes began preparations to relinquish his post. There would be several shift changes before entering orbit around the Ice Planet, and being the senior helmsman on *Questnar*, he had already claimed station duty for that event, in case there was a showdown.

***

The riddium power core hummed deep inside *Latearian*. Cloaked in the shadow of Beltzee, it was now on the night side of its orbit, and activity aboard the remote outpost was minimal. The last fleet supply ships had left, the crews were fed, and the kitchen cleaned. Transient quarters had quieted: the cube throwing, hollering, and cheering subsided. The lights dimmed. Verrilla tucked Sashi into her berth. "Sleep well."

"Will we get a message from Daddy tomorrow?" Sashi asked, her eyes wide-awake.

"Perhaps. He is very busy, and it takes a long time for communications to arrive." A chill tingled the fine hairs on the back of her neck. The thought of Luthes being that far away, so far that messages took several days to traverse the distance, made her feel small and insignificant compared to the vastness of space and the hugeness of her husband's mission. When he was on orbital patrol, it didn't seem as if he were so far away. Some nights, from their home in the great city of Benzatee, she could see the fleet pass overhead, their hulls reflecting sunlight like orbiting stars. *Questnar* was the biggest speck of light moving with the fleet. Whenever she saw it, she felt as if Luthes wasn't far away.

"Why are the Tarreeda bad, Mom?"

Dread jolted Verrilla. Her daughter was too young to understand the Tarreeda's vicious nature. There was no way to answer her question honestly. She didn't want to implant visions of boogiemen in her daughter's mind, images that would invade her dreams with horrors of long ago. "Your father knows more about them than I. Ask him when he returns."

Sashi whimpered. "He is never coming back."

"Of course he is." Verrilla chalked up her daughter's negative attitude to her youth and moved to the door. "Goodnight."

"Don't turn off the light."

This wasn't like Sashi. She'd never been afraid of the dark before. Concern burrowed in her chest like a Wickisheeti mole. She returned to the berth and sat with her daughter. "What is wrong, dear?"

Sashi sat up and hugged Verrilla's neck. "The

Tarreeda are coming."

"You don't know that for sure."

"Everyone is talking about it. I'm frightened."

"Oh dear," Verrilla whispered, hugging her daughter. It was all anyone talked about on *Latearian* these days. There was nothing she could do to protect her daughter from the gossip. "Get some sleep, dear."

"I want to go home."

"We will be okay," Verrilla said, mostly trying to convince herself.

***

Alarms sounded throughout the flight deck. "Repulsor stations!" Kerillan ordered from his observation chair.

Luthes brought *Questnar* within range of orbital insertion. Below her keel and rotating like a giant frost ball, the Ice Planet looked to be a frozen wasteland, its surface scarred with craters and giant pillars of ice crystals rising up like spiny mountains. As of yet, no communication links had been detected, no life forms on the barren surface, nothing moving through the thin atmosphere below. He checked his fore and aft screens, studying every mark, every speck, every glitch, any one of which could be an attacking Tarreeda Cruiser. The lives of every Beltzan onboard *Questnar* depended on his quick reflexes to evade incoming cannon fire.

"Scanners on full span."

Operations officers huddled together, pouring over data and shaking their heads. Even the interceptor strobe had detected nothing in orbit, nothing within its entire range. Finally, they came to a consensus. "It is a trap, sir. They have discovered our approach and withdrew their forces to the surface. Underground, perhaps. Draw us in close, surround us..." His voice fell away as if he couldn't say the words that would describe their fate.

Luthes didn't know what to make of that gloom and doom scenario. It went against everything he knew about the Tarreeda. They loved to fight. Death and destruction were in their blood. They'd never miss the opportunity to engage the enemy, especially a lone Orbital Patrol Ship far from reinforcements. There was only one explanation, and he didn't hesitate relaying it to the ComCap. "There is nobody here, sir."

Kerillan stiffened. "Ridiculous, Trantenant Rez. Go for orbital insertion."

Operations officers started yammering. "That is highly unwise, sir," one said, then another put in, "We should fall back and observe for a while."

Luthes hesitated working *Questnar's* controls. He knew he was right. The Tarreeda probably froze to death on this planet a thousand generations ago. However, with all the dissension going around the flight deck, doubts began to creep into his mind. What if he was wrong? What if Operations was right? What if it *was* a trap? They'd all be killed before a warning could be transmitted back to Fleet Base on Beltzee.

Operations persisted, and navigation took up with them. "Navigator to helm. Evade."

Kerillan held up his hand. "You have your orders, Trantenant Rez. Go for orbital insertion."

At that, Luthes put his hands on the throttles. The procedure was complicated, but he knew it well: reduce power to the thrusters, angle the bow and apex at forty five, and when *Questnar's* speed matched the planet's gravitational escape velocity, set the orbital ratio at one-to-one and cut the thrusters off completely. They wouldn't be needed to maintain orbit. However, should a Tarreeda Cruiser attack, precious seconds would be wasted re-firing the thrusters so he could execute evasive maneuvers. *Questnar* would be at great risk. Everyone could die. His fingers started trembling.

Operations officers continued arguing their point to the ComCap. The flight deck erupted in chaos. Then a raspy voice came over his shoulder. "You look troubled, Luthes."

He turned to see Specialist Regarius, who had entered only moments ago, wearing the maroon uniform of a crewman, his hair unkempt as usual. "I must obey the ComCap's orders," Luthes told him. "But what if it means the end of *Questnar*?"

"Believe in your convictions," Regarius said, "as you did at the briefing aboard *Latearian*."

"But there is much at stake." Luthes blocked out the loud arguments around him. "Even the experts do not agree."

"We have come a long way." Regarius patted Luthes' shoulder. "Let us find the truth."

"Yes. The truth." It was the only way to prove that he was right and Regarius was wrong. With renewed determination, Luthes bit his lower lip and began orbital insertion. The thrusters wound down to a low-pitched whine, and the bow lifted gracefully. Moments later, he finalized *Questnar's* approach configuration and awaited the NAV's data output to cue thruster cut off. Only now did he notice the silence on the flight deck. It was as if everyone's fate rested on his skill as a helmsman. These demands had never been placed on him before, and his forehead bore the sweat of this grave responsibility.

NAV beeped. He held his breath, whispered, "To Cada," and shut down the thrusters.

"Orbital insertion confirmed," navigation reported.

"Well done, Rez," Kerillan said. "I want four scanners scouring the surface for any sign of the Tarreeda's base camp, any sign of life at all. Leave two scanners and the interceptor probe sweeping the zones above *Questnar*. Repulsor stations stay ready." He settled back in his observation chair; his long fingers drummed the armrests.

This did nothing to quell Luthes' trepidation. One orbit, then two went by without incident. Specialist Regarius remained at his side, studying the scanner screens and taking notes on the back of the old flight plan, the one the transports used to relocate the Tarreeda to the Ice Planet so long ago. He seemed especially interested in the ozone levels of the ionosphere, probably still searching for an answer to those mysterious oscillations on the old flight path and the cessation of signals. Right now, Luthes wasn't concerned about the events of a thousand generations ago. His nerves were poised to react to any motion on the icy surface below *Questnar's* keel.

Orbits went by, one after another, without *Questnar* falling prey to any Tarreeda traps. In fact, there had been no sign of them anywhere. Luthes alternated his longitude and latitude courses, sweeping the planet in wide search zones.

Nothing stirred above or below.

Operations officers started in again. "They have dug in down there somewhere," one said.

Another contended, "There should be traces of carbon dioxide in the atmosphere, but there is no indication that any living thing has ever exhaled a breath here."

"And there is no residual exhaust from any power plants or transportation vehicles," another officer announced.

Kerillan leaned forward in his observation chair. "Specialist Regarius, what do you make of this?"

Regarius referred to his notes. "I am going to side with young Luthes here, sir. There are no Tarreeda on the Ice Planet."

Kerillan frowned. "It was on your testimony that we have come here."

"Luthes is right," an agitated Operations officer put in. "They must all be dead."

"On the contrary," Regarius replied. "The Tarreeda

are alive and thriving somewhere, I assure you, just not here on the Ice Planet. The cruiser's appearance proves that much. I have a theory that something went wrong back then. They never made it here. They went someplace else." Regarius pointed to the mysterious oscillation in the flight path on the old flight plan in his hand.

Kerillan scowled. "Then where did that cruiser come from?"

"Look down there," Regarius said, pointing to the scope screen. "Look at the desolation. They would not have survived here. The Ice Planet was a death sentence, but somehow they survived, and you can bet they have not forgotten, nor forgiven."

"I believe they are all dead," Luthes said, trusting his initial convictions. "We did not see a Tarreeda cruiser. It was someone else, from somewhere else."

Kerillan started to object when Regarius cut in. "There is no one else, young Rez. We are alone in the universe. The teachings of Cada have affirmed this to us. Besides, there is no way to travel the great voids between the stars, let alone the galaxies. Logistics prevent such journeys."

Luthes stood firm. "But someone has found a way."

"No, young Luthes, the Tarreeda are around here somewhere." Regarius indicated the planet orbital tracks bisecting the flight plan. "Somewhere close by."

"Do you think we can find them?" Kerillan asked Operations.

"There are thirteen planets in this system," an Operations officer interjected. "And hundreds of moons, all unexplored. The Tarreeda might be hiding on any one of them."

Another officer jumped in, "It would take years to search them all."

With that, Operations chatter subsided. It seemed as though everyone had finally agreed on something.

"Regardless," Regarius said. "We must search them."

Luthes turned to Kerillan, hoping he wouldn't order a complete search of the solar system. If he did, Luthes would never see his family again. "It's a waste of time, sir. There are no Tarreeda."

Kerillan didn't give the order but remained silent, his brows furrowed. "It doesn't make any sense," he muttered. "To come all this way for nothing."

"Unless it was a diversion," Operations stated flatly.

Kerillan's eyes shot open wide. "Of course," he shouted. "The Tarreeda have managed to draw *Questnar* away from the fleet. We have been duped. Beltzee is in grave danger."

Operations chatter broke out again. What fools they were. Luthes couldn't believe how fear had turned to hysteria. Even after all this, no one would listen to him.

There were no Tarreeda.

"We must return to Beltzee at once." Kerillan buckled his chair belt. "Trantenant Rez, get us underway, posthaste."

Chapter Eleven

In the NASA Aerospace control room, Kennedy Space Center, Janis Mackey looked over his team of scientists and engineers sitting at their computer terminals; three rows of white consoles stretched the length of the room. Lo Chin sat nearest to him, typing on a keyboard. Not much had gone right during the past six months, and not much was going right today, especially now that Brigham was here. Staring into the SuperMIGGS window, he chewed on the stub of a cigar. His mere presence put everyone on edge.

Lo pointed to his monitor. "See. It locks up again."

Janis's head ached. His formulas kept freezing the PLR program. No PLRs, no 13th Power, no green planet. No Tracy.

Brigham bellowed, "What's the problem this time?"

Janis wiped sweat from his brow. "I wonder why I ever wanted to be a mathematician."

Brigham faced the control room. "I thought you brainards were smarter than this."

Lo glared at him. "Be smartest to walk away."

"I want this contraption operational!" Brigham indicated the SuperMIGGS window. "No more delays. No more excuses."

"There's something you have to understand, General." Janis sat in his swivel chair and locked eyes with him. "The universe is mostly empty space. You don't want to get stuck out there with no way back. Let us do our jobs and quit bitching."

"You understand this, smartass." Brigham yanked the

cigar from his mouth and pointed the saliva-sopped end at Janis. "My men are ready. The shuttles are ready. I need this equipment working."

"And I need Tracy's help."

"Ah, yes, Tracy, the little traitor."

Janis wanted to bash in the general's skull. "She's not a traitor, and you know it."

Brigham grinned. "We shall see, yes, we shall see."

"She's a laser physicist, for Christ's sake, the only one who can program the PLRs."

He examined his cigar. "I'm proceeding with the indictment against your wife."

"What?" Janis couldn't have heard him right.

"In thirty days, Tracy will be brought before the Federal Magistrate in Washington, DC. I've been told she's going to plead guilty and throw herself on the mercy of the court."

"She can't do that." Janis wished he could talk to her, keep her from caving in to these government bullies. But since her arrest she'd been held at the United States Marine Corp Base in Quantico, Virginia, completely cut off from the outside world.

"Her lawyer thinks a guilty plea will save her from the death penalty," Brigham said. "However, the Justice Department is going to reject it. There *will* be a trial." He glared at Janis. "We'll get a conviction. Tracy will be executed by firing squad."

Janis's stomach hurt. "You said you weren't going to press an indictment unless I refused to cooperate." He balled a fist. "I'm working my tail off around here, and Lo too. We're trying to appease you."

"You've been stalling, Dr. Mackey."

Janis held eye contact with Brigham. It appeared as though Tracy would die no matter what they did. Or was he bluffing? Janis thought to test his theory, turned his back to Brigham. "Come on, Lo. Let's get out of here."

Lo looked up from his typing. "It's not quitting time."

"Brigham's going to lynch Tracy no matter what. He doesn't understand that she's the only reason I'm helping him. Without her, it's no use. I'm going home." Janis grabbed his suit coat off the back of his chair. "Are you coming?"

Lo shut off his monitor. "Right away, Dr. Janis."

"Now hold on there, you guys," Brigham demanded. "You can't just walk out of here."

"Watch us."

"You've got thirty days to get this project on track."

Janis glared at Brigham. The bastard didn't get it. "Without Tracy, your shuttles are never going to fly. She's the laser expert. She knows the PLRs. But, you've got her locked up like a criminal."

"We're finished," Lo said.

"Very well." Brigham's voice dropped an octave. "Tracy is going to die."

"And you're not going to the green planet." Janis feared he'd pushed Brigham too far. Thoughts of begging him on bended knees rushed through Janis's mind, but he had to stay firm and kept walking.

"Don't make me kill her just to prove a point."

At the doors, Janis stopped, looked back. "I love her. I'm going to miss her. But you're the big loser here. You bet the farm and got hog shit, a career-ender for sure."

"Before you go running off half cocked." Brigham eased himself against the MIGGS console, crossed his ankles, and folded his arms on his big belly. "Don't think you're fooling me, bluffing with Tracy's life."

"You wish," Janis said, worried that his last-ditch effort had just been derailed.

"And if I let her help you?"

"We can do it," Lo said, nodding. "Maybe it'll take three months."

"Thirty days," Brigham shouted.

"Sixty," Janis said, pushing it.

Lo frowned. "It's not possible, Janis, not sixty."

"Forty," Brigham countered. "Or she goes before the judge in handcuffs."

That wasn't enough time. Ten days more than the thirty they already had... "Okay."

Lo tugged on Janis's shirtsleeve. "No."

"Ten days is better than nothing."

***

Three days later, Janis stood on the Shuttle Landing Facility tarmac with Lo Chin on his right and General Brigham on his left. A staff car idled behind them. The driver, a young corporal, leaned against the fender and dragged on a cigarette. A balmy Florida breeze came straight off the Atlantic Ocean and smelled of fishy brine. In the distance, a Hawker jet lined up on final approach to runway 33, the fifteen-thousand-foot shuttle landing strip used by all aircraft coming in and out of Kennedy Space Center. The jet touched down with a screech, and its reverse thrusters roared. Janis's heart started pounding. Tracy was on that plane. They would soon be reunited.

Engines whining, the jet pulled up and stopped. As if on cue, an Air Force Security Police car careened onto the tarmac, its lights flashing and siren wailing. The sudden commotion alarmed Janis, but the general stood stoic, as if this development were no surprise to him.

Lo's face turned sullen. "Something smells like rotten fish."

A worse odor came to Janis's mind as the car skidded to a stop and two armed Security Policemen emerged. They reported directly to the general, saluting. "We're here for the prisoner transfer, sir."

"Prisoner?" Janis sensed a double-cross.

The general returned the salute. "She'll be here in a

minute."

"What prisoner?" Janis asked. "You're not talking about Tracy—"

"What did you think?" Brigham spat. "I'm not going to let you two set up house here, play patty cake or whatever else it is you do. She's still under arrest, released from Federal custody under my recognizance."

"But you said—"

"I said she could help you."

Janis clenched his jaw, muttered, "We're getting screwed again."

"You better hope I don't alter the deal any further."

The jet's cabin door opened, and steps dropped to the pavement. A man appeared in the doorway, his black coat unbuttoned, the breeze tugging at his thin tie. Janis recognized him as the tall suit from Lo Chin's house. Then Peterson appeared, his black slacks littered with wood shavings. Janis wondered why they were involved with a Justice Department matter. What agency did they work for?

Tracy emerged from the plane. She wore an orange prison uniform with black numbers stenciled on the front. Her red hair was tied back in a ponytail, and her hands were shackled to a leather strap padlocked around her waist. In white tennis shoes, she could only take short steps because of the chains on her ankles. Her eyes met Janis's. She sneered.

"Tracy!" Janis rushed toward her.

The SPs started after him.

"Give them a minute," Brigham ordered his men.

Standing in front of her, Janis could barely contain his emotions. The joy of seeing her contrasted with the dismay at her awful predicament. He opened his arms to hug her, but she backed off, glowering.

"How could you?"

"God, Tracy, it's good to see you."

She gritted her teeth. "You should've left me to rot."

"What happened to *I love you, I miss you, I want you,* or *thank God I'm out of that prison cell?"*

"What made you think I'd help these clowns?" She indicated Brigham and his cronies with a tilt of her head.

"I need your help to save your life."

"I'd rather sit in that stinking cell and sleep with my toilet than have anything to do with those bastards."

"You don't understand, Tracy—"

"Perfectly," she spat. "They're going to drag me through the justice system with a noose around my neck."

"They're going to kill you."

"Worse things can happen, Janis."

The suits stepped up and grabbed Tracy's arms. "Time's up, lover boy." They handed her over to the SPs who promptly ducked her into the back seat of the security car.

Janis felt his future slipping away. He stood dumfounded, sweating under the Florida sun. As the security car sped away, he realized that Tracy would rather be prosecuted than have any part of NASA's exploitation of the long-fingered aliens. Prison had cemented her contempt for Brigham and his trumped up charges of treason. Janis should have known she'd take a stand against them.

Now what was he supposed to do?

***

The next day, the suits brought Tracy into the control room. She wore the same prison uniform as yesterday, but wrinkled as if she'd slept in it. Her arms hung limp at her sides. Janis shot out of his chair and watched her shuffle in, her leg irons clanking along the tile floor, a zombie-like look in her eyes. She seemed disconnected from herself, uninterested in the control room, the technical surroundings that once appealed to her, challenged her.

His wife was a basket case.

"Tracy?"

Like a ghost, she passed right by him, past Lo and the other technicians without as much as a nod. Her shuffling steps took her straight to the SuperMIGGS' foot-thick window. Janis followed her. She stared into the massive gravity chamber, her eyes wide open. "Oh my God." Her voice was almost a whisper. "Look what they're doing, Janis."

An ominous sight, even frightening to see sixteen Aerospace shuttles suspended from the ceiling, all brightly lit by halogen beams and shining like new Christmas toys.

"They can't do this." Tracy's chest heaved as she took in a lungful of air. "Don't let them do this, Janis." She shouted this time and started pounding on the glass with the palms of her hands. "Janis. Make them stop."

"Looks like she's not impressed," Brigham said in a booming voice.

Janis whipped around. Under the stressful circumstances, he was in no mood to deal with the general. "Look what you've done to my wife."

She pounded on the glass. "We have to stop them, Janis. Stop them. Stop them."

"She's right," Janis shouted to Brigham, wishing she'd snap out of it. "This project is not in the best interest of humanity."

Brigham approached, stuck his nose in Janis's face. "I don't give a damn about humanity. Look around you, Janis. All of you," he shouted at the team. "Look at what we've accomplished. Consider what is left to do."

Tracy stopped pounding on the glass and slowly turned to Brigham. "You'll do it without me, you son of a bitch."

"I think not." Brigham snorted. "You'll do it."

"I won't!" she screamed, her fists clenched at her sides.

"Come on, Tracy." Janis took her hand and led her to a chair in front of the laser control terminal. "It's no use arguing with him. He's got us over a barrel."

"He's got *you* over the barrel, Janis, only because he's got screws in my ass. What the both of you don't realize is I don't give a shit what happens to me."

"Don't talk like that."

Brigham stepped up. "Do you give a shit about Janis?"

"He can take care of himself."

Janis gasped. She couldn't possibly have meant it.

"We'll see about that." Brigham drew his Colt, and without warning, shot Janis in the left foot.

Pain rifled up his leg. Complete disbelief hit him first, then shock. He toppled to the floor, wailing. "The son of a bitch shot me." The bullet went clear through his shoe. He grabbed his ankle with both hands. Blood was gushing everywhere.

Brigham aimed at Janis's knee. "Do you give a shit yet, Tracy?"

Her eyes were ringed in white. "You shot him."

"I'll kill him right here. Without you, he's worthless to me. What's it going to be?"

"Tracy," Janis yelled. "Do what he wants."

"It's your call." Brigham extended his shooting arm, locked his elbow. "Shall I count to three?"

"Tracy..."

"One."

"Tracy, please."

"Two."

She just sat there, glaring at Brigham.

"For God's sake, Tracy."

"Three."

Brigham pulled the trigger. With a bang, a bullet hole blossomed in the console next to Janis's leg.

"Oh darn!" Brigham scoffed. "I missed." He aimed

again.

"All right." Tracy jumped out of her chair. "I'll do it." She dropped to her knees next to Janis, touched his shoulder. "I'm sorry. I'm so sorry."

Janis locked his jaw. The throbbing in his foot felt like a thousand jackhammers. "What took you so long to change your mind?" He rasped through clenched teeth. "Are you nuts?"

Tracy looked up at Brigham. "Get a doctor."

***

Thirty days later, Janis hobbled up to his terminal and looked at the *ERROR* flags scrolling down his monitor. The Scheduler program debugging wasn't going well. He wondered if he'd ever get the formulas right. He scanned the control room strewn with wadded up paper, dinner trays piled with dirty plates, empty pop cans and candy bar wrappers. A cot had been set up under the SuperMIGGS window where he wished he could take a nap, but nobody would get any rest until this problem was solved.

Two weeks ago, his foot stopped throbbing. The doctor had said he'd be wearing a shoe again next week. Brigham never apologized, never showed any compassion, just claimed it was a firearms accident and glared at Janis as if daring him to say otherwise.

Lo had finished the Programmer codes, and Tracy's particle beams worked perfectly. She set a cup of coffee next to his keyboard. It must have been dawn...up there in the real world. Deep underground like this, he had to visualize the sun rising over Kennedy Space Center. Life on earth went on as usual. No one knew anything about what they were doing below NASA's Aerospace hanger.

For a brief moment, he thought about his home in Boulder, how the lawn had probably overgrown with weeds by now. September's fresh clean air was cool and dry in

Colorado. He missed the mountains, he missed the snow, and what's more, he missed the life he and Tracy had left behind. He wanted to go home, but he knew that wouldn't happen today and not tomorrow either. There was too much work to do. He turned to Lo. "Run the Scheduler again."

The Scheduler was a series of programs stored in the Supers' upper memory. At predetermined intervals, the hardware configurations had to be engaged, each one culminating with the next program's startup commands. The mainframe's *Programmer*, which Janis thought worked perfectly, linked the Scheduler to the control room, the SuperMIGGS, and all sixteen PLRs that would degenerate sixteen shuttles into the 13th Power.

Lo typed on his keyboard. *SCHEDULER RERUN LOADING* appeared on his monitor. "You have it right this time?"

"We'll know soon enough. Just run the damn thing." Patience was in short supply lately.

"It's still giving you fits?" Tracy asked over his shoulder.

"I thought I was good at this." Awkwardly, Janis turned on his bandaged foot to face her. The suits had let her wear civilian clothes instead of that ugly prison uniform. Today, she wore loose fitting black slacks and a red blouse. Black loafers replaced the white tennis shoes. Brigham had promised to kill Janis if she walked out. That was enough to keep her on the job.

She patted his shoulder. "You'll get it figured out."

"We only have ten days left."

"How's the foot?"

"It gets better every day. I just wish I could say the same about us."

She winced. "My cell is comfortable...but lonely."

He knew what she meant. Every night tortured him, watching the suits take her away in handcuffs, sleeping alone, thinking about her lying in that ten-by-twelve foot cell the SPs had the nerve to call *Guest Quarters* in lockup at Cape Canaveral Air Force Station. "I miss you."

"I know." Her shoulders slumped. "Brigham's right, you know. None of this would be happening now if it wasn't for the decisions I made back then, when the President asked me to work with the CIA on Star Wars. It was the career break of a lifetime. After all, how many laser physicists fresh out of Cal Tech got a calling like that? I was young, I was eager, I was foolish."

"Quit beating yourself up," Janis said. "If Ray Crawford hadn't talked me into this, we'd have never met."

She looked at him with tearing eyes. "I can't bear to think what all this is going to come to."

Janis didn't want to think about it either. Every time he did, he got a sick feeling in the pit of his stomach. The green planet and the long-fingered aliens were in danger of being annihilated by Brigham and his space cowboys. No matter how Janis figured it, everything that was about to happen would be their fault.

"Program is ready," Lo said.

"I better get back to my terminal." Tracy turned away.

Janis watched her for a moment, sighed at her lack of affection, and then checked his monitor where a *START* button flashed incessantly. He activated Engineering's two-way frequency. "Stan, we're ready up here."

Stan Burton's voice came back with a crackle. "*All clear.*"

Pressing the intercom switch, Janis made the final announcement. "Attention all personnel. Test fire will commence in ten seconds." He started the countdown clock located above the SuperMIGGS window and looked down the console at the line of techs sitting at their terminals. "Everybody ready?"

All concurred.

The clock ticked down to zero.

Janis set his mouse cursor on *START* and clicked the

left button.

The CEI engaged. Janis used the Computer Enhanced Imaging system, running in parallel with the Programmer, to record real-time events, which the Supers could analyze and, in turn, calculate a probable outcome. Command blocks in the CEI insured the actual events did not take place, even though the Supers executed all the Scheduler programs in sequence, and the equipment came online as if this run was the real thing. Using the CEI, Janis could determine the success or failure of his formulas without actually degenerating the shuttles into the 13th Power.

Screens on the consoles began to scroll formulas and lines of code, which technicians checked against a monitoring program they called MOM. MOM would identify and log formula errors for later revision, but the Scheduler and Programmer would continue without interruption as long as a conflict in command lines didn't cause the equipment to shut down.

As planned, the Programmer executed the SuperMIGGS startup cycle. It sent coded instructions to the Scheduler, which in turn activated the MIGGS computer. Receiving these coded instructions, the SuperMIGGS began to hum as its multiple bands of massive electromagnetic rings came online. The power demanded by this enormous gravity chamber caused the control room lights to dim. Automatically, the Supers readjusted the power settings by increasing voltage flow from gigantic transformers located several miles away.

Next, sixteen ion fields energized, forming protective barriers around each of the Aerospace shuttles suspended in the SuperMIGGS. If it weren't for this deflecting force field, the gravity generated inside the chamber would crush the shuttles into molecular scrap and pulverize the atoms of every passenger onboard.

ION FLOW MAXIMUM appeared on Janis's monitor. He breathed out a sigh. "So far, so good." His bandaged foot began to itch.

Lo got up from his supercomputer station and moved from terminal to terminal, conferring with techs and suggesting minor adjustments in settings and configuration. He paused at the SuperMIGGS monitor. "Janis, check this out."

He hobbled to the MIGGS terminal. "What is it?"

"The Scheduler is working perfectly." On the screen, a digitally enhanced funnel began to swirl like a typhoon. It changed colors from green to blue.

"Twenty percent," the technician announced.

The humming sound that filled the control room began to pulse like a monstrous heartbeat.

Lo studied the monitor as if mesmerized by its swirling funnel and changing colors, a kaleidoscope of rising fury.

"Sixty percent," came the next announcement.

Janis hopped to the SuperMIGGS' foot-thick glass window. The control room walls vibrated. The hum became a rumble. Inside the SuperMIGGS, a crimson hue washed over the shuttles, each encircled by blue ion field haloes.

"Ninety percent."

In the center of this eight-story monstrosity, a black mist began to form, swirling like a hurricane in mid air, engulfing the glowing shuttles, expanding, thickening, throbbing and pulsing like some kind of wicked fog.

"One hundred."

Roaring electromagnets now sounded like onrushing diesel locomotives that shook the control room violently. The SuperMIGGS had maxed-out at a 3M Star Mass gravity field, a black hole from which nothing could escape, not even light. A red event horizon appeared on the MIGGS monitor, meaning the escape velocity was over 186,000 miles per second. By now, the black mist had swallowed everything inside the SuperMIGGS. Janis couldn't see the shuttles, the blue Ion fields, or the red glow that had dominated the interior only moments ago. It was an incredibly black sight and an unnerving sensation of earthquake proportions. His eardrums ached from the noise.

Automatically, the Programmer initiated PLR firing commands in the Scheduler, which configured them with the other running programs and relayed to Tracy's laser terminal instructions for activating the sixteen PLRs mounted inside the SuperMIGGS. The CEI reconfigured these commands and only allowed the sighting beams to energize. Tracy's monitor showed four rows and four columns of crosshair sights, and sixteen target aligners.

LASER LOCKED flashed across the image on her screen.

If the black mist had not completely filled the SuperMIGGS, Janis would have seen sixteen thin lines of red laser light boring into the optical lens receptors of the Aerospace shuttles' OBMs, On-Board MIGGSs. And if the CEI were not running, the PLRs would have fired their high-energy hydrogen particle beams into those OBMs, instantly releasing Higgs bosons and degenerating the shuttles into the 13th Power. Only the intense gravity field prevented the disintegration of the SuperMIGGS, Kennedy Space Center, and possibly the Florida peninsula. Once degenerated, the shuttles would traverse the gap between the atom and the universe, via the Higgs Field, and emerge in the 13th Power, 100,000 light years away.

Bringing them back, or regenerating them, could only be accomplished onboard each shuttle. The crew would have to activate their OBM regenerating programs manually, and hopefully the regeneration program would be locked-on to the shuttles, causing them to emerge from the 13th Power at the exact point in space from which they'd degenerated.

Of course, traveling through the universe at 125 miles per second, the sun will have moved by then, and the earth will have progressed along its orbital track around the sun, as well. The shuttles would then have to fly back to earth and enter orbit where they'd execute a reentry burn, which would culminate in a landing at Kennedy Space Center's Shuttle Landing Facility. Janis realized the scale of what they were doing was beyond anything man had ever done before. However, the usual possibilities of failure were multiplied by sixteen. A chill worked its way down Janis's spine as he watched the black mist boil inside the SuperMIGGS.

"It's going to work," Tracy called from her laser terminal.

Janis cast a glance to her monitor. *LASER FIRING CONFIRMED* flashed across the screen. The CEI had determined this by calculating the outcome using Janis's formulas and Lo's programming codes. No matter how hard Janis tried to suppress his feelings, this was truly a mathematical milestone in his career. He couldn't help but smile with pride.

On cue, the Programmer began to shut down the Scheduler, first cutting power to the massive electromagnetic rings. The roar subsided in stages, to a rumble and then to a hum, and the control room stopped vibrating. Then the ion fields de-energized.

Janis returned his attention to the SuperMIGGS window. Inside, the black mist broke into towering vortexes, each swirling down into steel floor grates as the gravity equalized. The ion halos dissipated, and the halogen ceiling lights blinked on. All the shuttles were still suspended by their hydraulic arms and appeared to be undamaged.

"We did it," Tracy exclaimed, her face aglow.

"Bravo." A booming voice thundered through the control room. General Brigham was standing on the observation platform. The suits stood by his side, their feet spread and their hands behind their backs. Brigham's smile reached his eyes. "Well done, gentlemen...and you too,

Tracy."

The technical team exchanged high-fives and cheered.

Stan Burton's voice came over the two-way. *"Great job, Janis."*

MOM started clattering out formulas and lines of code on an impact printer. Each of the items listed had created error messages. Each problem had to be reformulated and reprogrammed and retested before the shuttles could go into the 13th Power.

"We shall leave at once," Brigham announced.

"Not so fast, General," Janis said as the printer continued to rattle. "The programs aren't perfected yet."

"Dragging your feet again, Janis?"

"If even one of these formulas miscalculates," he indicated the lengthening printout, "degeneration will become disintegration. All the shuttles will be lost, not to mention you and your men, which, by the way, isn't a bad idea."

"Pray that doesn't happen, Dr. Mackey," Brigham said. "The Justice Department will begin immediate steps to prosecute Tracy if we don't make it."

"You won't make it," Janis insisted. "Until we are ready."

Brigham considered this a moment. "Then double your efforts. You have ten days." He stormed out.

Janis ground his molars. At the rate the paper was rolling out of MOM, he feared he would need ten sleepless nights, as well.

Chapter Twelve

Gray sky hung heavy over Santa Barbara, and morning fog swallowed the horizons. Over Ray's head, seabirds sawed back and forth on a stiff ocean breeze, screeching and complaining. Barefooted, he walked the edge of the breaking surf. The water was chilly and dirty, but the grainy texture of sand felt good between his toes. He'd rolled up his pant legs and left his shirt buttons undone. Now, the breeze tousled his long black hair and tugged at his shirttails. Carrying his sandals by the straps, he felt like a beachcomber, a lonely beachcomber, but a sober beachcomber.

Three weeks ago, he'd started taking these early morning walks. It gave him a chance to breathe fresh air, sort through the jumble in his brain, and try to leach the sorrow from his bones. He missed Kate something awful, but Lisa was right. Alcohol wasn't the answer. Jack Daniels and Johnny Walker had done nothing to ease the pain. It was something he was going to have to live with for the rest of his life.

"Dad." Lisa called to him from the back porch of his bungalow. "Breakfast is ready."

He waved. One more lap, down to the pier and back again. One more, that was all, and then he'd be ready to face the day. During his recovery, Lisa had been a big help, though sometimes her nagging annoyed him. *When are you going to clean up this place? You're getting fat. Get a haircut. When are you going to shave?* He rubbed his stubbly beard.

Tomorrow, maybe.

A freighter's horn bellowed from the fog out at sea. He'd been holed up here for almost two years, feeling sorry for himself, mostly. Last month, after he'd fired his drinking buddies, Jack and Johnny, he'd started thinking about those books he was going to write. Took some notes. Then he thought about the fame he'd achieved, the Nobel Prize he sought, and all the things that had been important to him before Kate came back into his life, before she was murdered. The thought of her bleeding to death in his arms, her last words *I love you, I love you, I love...*God how he wanted Jack and Johnny to come back, to help him forget. He tried to toss the craving aside, but it wouldn't let him go. A burst of energy and rage welled up inside, and he took off running, running as fast as he could through the sand and up to his bungalow.

"Dad, are you all right?" Lisa held open the screen door.

Gasping air, Ray bent over, and with both hands on his knees, willed his body to recover and his mind to let go of Jack and Johnny. "I'm sorry," he rasped. "Sometimes it sneaks up on me."

She put her hand on his shoulder. "Me too."

"Of course," Ray said. "Sometimes I forget...that you lost a mother."

"Your breakfast is getting cold."

He left his sandals on the porch and stepped inside to the aroma of bacon and coffee. Lisa had fixed his eggs sunny-side-up. How perfect for this gloomy day.

"Eat. You'll feel better." She spooned hash browns from the frying pan onto his plate. "I've got your dirty laundry in my car."

"You shouldn't..."

"It's okay, Dad. I don't mind."

Sitting at the table, he felt better all ready. "I don't know what I'd have done without you, Lisa."

"Nor I you." She sat across from him.

"You've taken good care of me."

She smiled. "You're the only man in my life."

"Speaking of which..." he picked up his fork, "when are you going to find a young man, get married, and make me a grandfather?"

"Janis is a tough act to follow," she said, peering over the brim of her coffee cup.

"But the two of you never...you know...consummated your affair."

"I was in love, Dad. The rest didn't matter."

Ray sampled the eggs and mulled that over in his mind. Lisa was twenty-seven already. For most of her young life, she was shuffled from one foreign school to another, Europe and Japan, and then Canada, where she worked her way through college driving trucks for a logging firm. She was blond, she was beautiful, she was smart. But most of all, she was stubborn. She wouldn't take any money from him. She didn't want anything to do with him. Nothing. She hated him. Back then, in her crazy mixed up mind, she'd blamed him for what had happened between her and her mother. She became moody, sometimes childish and playful, other times seductive and sensual, often angry and impossible. The doctors had diagnosed her as a victim of *Abandon Child Syndrome*. They couldn't do anything to help her. Nobody could. And now she was sitting there talking about Janis and love in the same breath again. She didn't know anything about love. She didn't even know what was good for her. "You need to find a young college boy—"

"Yeah, yeah, I've heard it all before." She set down her cup and forked her eggs. "Someone I can build a future with, and not someone who's living the future he'd planned for himself decades ago." She leaned forward. "I need somebody special, Dad, somebody secure. Unique. He needs to be gentle but strong, smart but humble. And most of all, he needs to believe in love."

"You've set your sights mighty high, young lady. There aren't many men like that."

"I won't settle for less."

"At that rate, I'll never be a grandfather."

"Why is that so important?"

Now Ray leaned forward. "Kate would have wanted to be a grandmother, if she were still alive, so find yourself a college boy."

"It's my life," Lisa said. "I'll love who I want."

"Not if I disapprove, you won't."

"There you go again." Lisa's face was turning red. "Back to your old ways. Overprotective. Calling all the shots. Telling me where I'll go to school, where I'll live, who I can and cannot love. When are you going to get it, Dad? I'm not a little girl anymore."

"You'll always be my little girl."

She scooted her chair away from the table. "Maybe I don't want the job."

"Sit down and finish your breakfast." He wasn't in the mood for another one of her temper tantrums.

"Truth is," she shouted, "you'll never approve of anyone I choose to love."

"Damn it. I only want what's best for you."

Lisa stormed out and slammed the door behind her.

Ray threw down his fork, got up from the table, and headed straight for the bottom cupboard, propelled by a gnawing rage and a familiar burning in his stomach. He flung open the door. To his horror, the cabinet was empty. Panic stricken, he started throwing open all the cupboard doors, looking for Jack and Johnny. Where did she hide them? They had to be around here somewhere.

Chapter Thirteen

Ten days had passed, ten days that tested every bit of General Brigham's patience with Janis Mackey and MOM, that nuisance of a monitoring program that kept the mission on hold for so long. The scientists had just finished their umpteenth test fire. Determined there'd be no more delays, Brigham, wearing his combat fatigues, marched into the control room. "Your time is up, Janis."

The MOM printer clattered out a message: *NO ERRORS.*

"We're ready when you are," Janis said.

Stan came in with his team of engineers in tow, all wearing gray jumpsuits and white hard hats. "The shuttles are flight worthy." He set a clipboard on Janis's console. "I've programmed their space probes with data from the transporter Ray took into the 13th Power."

Janis glared at Stan. "It better be right. I've held up my end of this rotten deal. Your engineering had better hold up your end."

Eyes narrow, Stan replied, "I know what I'm doing."

"Brigham has to survive long enough to wage war on the green planet, if not, Tracy dies."

"Quit worrying," Stan said. "I'm rooting for the aliens."

Brigham smirked. "We'll slaughter them. Hell, they couldn't even destroy one little transporter."

"They didn't want to," Janis said. "That's Ray's theory."

"The theory of a drunkard," Brigham put in. "Nobody believes him. That's the only reason I haven't sent my boys to kill him."

Janis scowled. "He'd rather die than help you."

"I recall Tracy said the same thing, but you know..." Brigham lifted an eyebrow. "Even Ray has his threshold of tolerance. You were Tracy's Achilles' heel. She was yours. I wonder what his might be. However, rest assured, should he find reason to become a problem for us, my boys will take him out. Meanwhile, he's just a lousy drunk."

"He's a brilliant physicist," Janis replied. "He broke ground in this research. Don't count him short."

"I already have." Brigham grinned, confident Ray Crawford was no threat to this project. "Now let's get these shuttles launched."

"Degenerated," Stan said.

Brigham shouted into his two-way. "Load 'em up, men."

***

An hour later, Brigham stood on the SuperMIGGS observation platform, seven stories up from the steel-grated floor. The whole place smelled of slag and cement. From here, he could oversee the Aerospace shuttle loading procedures.

He wore sunglasses to shield his eyes from the intense glare of halogen ceiling lights. Everything sounded tinny, the footfalls of his Special Forces soldiers' boots on the gangways, the clatter of their weapons and gear, and the squad leaders' voices as they supervised their embarkation. They all wore camouflaged pressure suits, body armor and gloves, helmets, and oxygen masks with transparent snouts from which black-ribbed hoses looped around to tanks in their backpacks. They may have looked like some kind of alien army fresh out of a B movie, but these men were tough, all volunteers, and all specially trained for fighting in space.

Their leader was Colonel Mike Scott, a former Navy Seal and Marine Special Forces paratrooper, highly decorated. Those who'd served under him said he was brutal and compassionless when engaging the enemy. Some called him trigger-happy, as he actually enjoyed mowing down that mob in Somalia with his 50-caliber machine gun. Colonel Scott was the right man to lead Brigham's mission.

Stan Burton joined him on the platform. "Quite a sight, huh?"

He nodded. Suspended in front of him, sixteen Aerospace shuttles hung from the ceiling. NASA emblems emblazoned their vertical stabilizers. Gangways fanned out from the loading dock on level four, and extended up or down to the shuttles' middeck hatches.

The cargo bays of eight shuttles had been converted to accommodate seating for twenty four hundred troops, three hundred per shuttle, each set up much like a wide body jet with crowded rows of seats and narrow aisles. Inside six of the shuttle cargo bays, equipment for ground assault operations was stowed: M1-A1 Abrams tanks, M-198 155MM howitzers, M-270 MLRS rocket launchers, and enough ammunition and fuel to wage a six-month campaign. One shuttle carried supplies: rations, medicine, salt tablets, liquor, cigarettes, and other expendables such as toilet paper and toothpaste. His crack troops would be well fed and well cared for. The sixteenth shuttle, Brigham's *Whiskey-Xray*, carried two orbital PLRs and seven sighting dish satellites to be deployed in orbit around the green planet. Any insurrection from the inhabitants below would be quelled with deadly force from space.

"Who did you get to fly those things?" Stan asked.

"The best pilots in the world," Brigham said. Fighter pilots, all Top Gun graduates, had been recruited and trained to fly the shuttles. Each pilot had extensive combat experience in the Gulf War, Afghanistan and Iraq and Iran. Some were Navy carrier jocks, and others were seasoned

Air Force *Ace* pilots with numerous kills to their credit. The general smiled at Stan. "Their simulator performance tests were extraordinary."

"These Aerospace shuttles are nothing like the dinosaur shuttles of the 20th century," Stan said flatly. "Unlike Columbia, Discovery, Atlantis, and Endeavor, these shuttles are not gliders, but highly maneuverable combat spacecraft. They can re-enter the atmosphere, fly seek-and-destroy missions, land and take off again."

"Undefeatable," Brigham roared.

"However," Stan pointed out, "they are unable to attain orbit on their own power."

"So I've been told, but I don't understand why."

"Pulse-light engines were designed for space travel. They can propel a shuttle over ten times the speed of light, but only in a vacuum. They can't overcome atmospheric density and gravity to attain escape velocity. They need solid rocket booster assistance for that."

"Or teleportation technology," Brigham put in.

Stan nodded. "*Whiskey-Xray* will not land on the green planet because regeneration is only possible in the vacuum of space. You need to come back for the scientists and engineers who will decipher the aliens' teleportation system, unless of course, you fail to secure the planet."

"We won't fail," Brigham barked. "I just wish the brainards could fight so we wouldn't have to waste time with a second trip."

"NASA won't put the nation's top minds at risk in battle. If your men fail to secure the planet with a surface assault, you will be able to return to earth, but your soldiers will die on the green planet."

"Of course." They had explained this to Brigham before, at every NASA briefing he'd attended. It was implanted in his brain: should something go wrong, the other shuttles were expendable, and the men, too. He was to direct operations from orbit where he'd be safe. That appealed to him like a maggot in his C rations. "I'd rather be with the surface invaders."

Stan slapped Brigham's back. "Maybe next time." With that, he left.

Moments later, Peterson joined him on the platform. "I just got word you're leaving."

"It won't be long now." Traffic on the gangways was thinning out. Brigham would have to get on board soon.

"And my request? You will see to it?"

"As long as you are clear on the Tracy situation."

"Yes, sir," Peterson said. "If you don't come back, she goes directly to Quantico for prosecution."

"There's been a change of plans," Brigham said. "If I don't come back, put a bullet in her head...along with that mathematical idiot, Janis Mackey."

Peterson didn't smile. "You'd better come back...with my alien."

***

In the control room, techs chatted among themselves, checked data sheets against programming statements, and went through startup procedures for their respective equipment. Janis tried to shut them out of his head, but before long they were discussing the muggy weather. Confidence was high. He wished he felt the same.

Lo Chin seemed perplexed as he tapped on his keyboard in earnest, and Tracy kept scrolling through the PLR firing sequences as if she expected to find some misplaced and undetected error lurking within millions of lines of code. MOM had said they were good to go, but Janis still wondered what his techs were concerned about. "Lo, anything I should know? Tracy?"

Neither answered him. He got up from his terminal and strolled to the SuperMIGGS window, thankful he didn't need crutches anymore. His left shoe fit a little tighter than the right, but the doctor had assured him the swelling would eventually go down. Now he was more concerned about the sight before him.

Brigham had just ducked into the middeck hatch on *Whiskey-Xray*. ASPs (Astronaut Support Persons) wearing white gowns shut the doors, checked for secure seals, and then headed down the gangways toward the loading dock. A few moments later, electric motors whined, and the gangways retracted. The halogen ceiling lights went out, leaving the SuperMIGGS' interior awash in a crimson glow. The red lighting would help the shuttle pilots' eyes adjust to the darkness that would soon engulf them.

***

Brigham climbed the short ladder to the flight deck. The bulky spacesuit made the ascent cumbersome, but he'd been assured that getting around would be much easier once they reached zero gravity. There were two thick windows on the ceiling. Four high-back seats faced the heavily tinted front windows and took up much of the cramped space. He squeezed past a flight engineer and communications tech sitting in the back two seats. The pilot, Major Remsfield, sat left front. "Welcome aboard, General."

It wasn't easy, but Brigham worked his bulk into the right front seat. "Kind of like getting into a VW bug." Before he strapped himself in, he removed a loaded pistol from his pant leg pocket and stashed it in the center storage compartment under the radar screen.

"What's that for?" Remsfield asked.

"Never leave home without it."

Stan's voice came over the radio. "You guys about ready?"

Brigham buckled his safety harness.

"Lock and load," Remsfield said.

***

Stan's voice came over the control room intercom. *"They're ready, Janis."*

Janis didn't respond. He stood at the SuperMIGGS window and thought about the absurdity of this mission, the completely typical human nature of it all: exploration and conquest. The Egyptians, the Romans, the Huns, the Spaniards, the Germans, even the United States and countless others throughout history had invaded lands that belonged to someone else. They'd raped and pillaged as they went. Ask the Native Americans what it was like to be conquered. This was mankind's legacy, which was now about to be spread throughout the galaxy. Janis remembered the flight to San Francisco with Lisa, and how she'd said God had put a hundred thousand light years between mankind and other worlds for a reason. Maybe this was that reason. Only now did he truly understand why Ray had kept his discovery from the rest of the world.

"Earth to Janis," Lo called out.

Janis turned. His monitor displayed the Programmer's flashing *START* command. Filled with regret for his contribution to the continued degradation of the human race, he slowly walked to his terminal, as a man would walk to the gas chamber. He took hold of the mouse. His index finger hovered over the button, twitching. He paused for a long moment.

"Janis?" Tracy said. "Are you all right?"

"Go ahead, Lo," Janis said. "You start this thing."

Lo shook his head. "It's not my job."

Janis flinched at Lo's insight. He was right, of course. It *was* Janis's job. It *was* his responsibility. He'd been the first to agree to do this for NASA, for Tracy, but right about now he envied Ray Crawford, who was probably wallowing around his bungalow, drowning himself in alcohol, oblivious to what was going on. That was a luxury

Janis couldn't afford.

"*Whiskey-Xray to control,*" came over the loud speakers. "*What's the hold up?*"

"Janis is having second thoughts," the intercom tech replied.

Brigham cleared his throat. "Don't turn chickenshit on me now, Janis." His gruff voice echoed through the control room.

Janis rushed to his terminal and clicked the intercom relay switch. "One more time, General, think about this one more time." His heart was pounding. "Once we start this thing, there's no turning back. The Supers will lock out changes and—"

Clunk.

A noise at the door stopped him. A motion. Peterson entered with two of his cronies behind him. His black-gloved hand disappeared into the slat of his suit coat, and in a flash, he revealed a silver gun. "You heard the general. Proceed."

Brigham's cackling laugh came over the speakers. "*Peterson will kill you all and activate the START button himself if he has to.*"

"You wouldn't," Janis said.

"Just push the button," Peterson replied. "Or don't you have the nerve?"

"Why you son of a bitch." Janis lunged at Peterson.

Tracy shot up from her chair and grabbed Janis's arm. "It's not worth it. After all we've been through, don't get yourself killed now."

Janis sneered at Peterson who was holding the gun out at arm's length. "Someday," Janis said.

"Not today," Peterson replied.

"Let's get this over with," Tracy whispered to Janis.

"Christ!" He looked at Lo. "We should just let him kill us and be done with it."

Lo shook his head. "Wise man once said, 'It is not

unusual for a general to meet his death in battle.'"

Janis thought about that for a moment. "You're right. Brigham could get himself killed."

"End of problem," Lo said.

With that thought in mind, Janis walked to his terminal, and hoping the long-fingered aliens could defend themselves adequately, activated the *START* button.

And then it began.

Instantly, the lights dimmed as the SuperMIGGS' electromagnetic rings energized and hummed to life. All the techs sat upright at their stations and reported their systems' startup progress to Lo's terminal. The Supers checked and crosschecked the data and relayed the information to the Programmer, which in turn activated the Scheduler. The ion shield engaged and ringed the Aerospace shuttles in luminous blue halos. The hum became a rumble, then a roar. The control room started vibrating. Tracy's monitor lit up. *PLRs ARMED* flashed on the screen, which immediately switched to the sighting beam image with four-by-four rows of sixteen crosshairs.

LASER LOCKED flashed on her screen.

Tracy confirmed her settings. "I'm ready, Janis."

"Sixty percent," the MIGGS tech reported.

Janis ran to the window. The black mist was already swirling around the glowing shuttles, growing in density and size in an unstoppable frenzy.

"Eighty percent."

Everything started shaking violently, as if a runaway freight train were barreling through the control room. Then the drone of charging PLRs added to the fury. Clutching the SuperMIGGS window frame with both hands, Janis thought it was the end of the world. A thick, swirling mist swallowed everything in the gravity chamber until it became pitch black.

"One hundred."

Automatically, the Supers sent firing commands to the

laser terminals, and particle beams shot out of sixteen PLR electron acceleration rings. The power of the sun was focused into sixteen beams that tracked their respective sighting lasers straight to their targets, the OBMs on the Aerospace shuttles suspended in the SuperMIGGS. A sound like cracking thunder rumbled from the PLRs and rattled the control room windows. Janis's breath hitched. If it weren't for the gravity field that trapped the particle beams inside the SuperMIGGS, there'd be nothing to stop them from disintegrating everything within range.

"Tracy, status report." He had to yell over all the noise as he stared into the blackness beyond the window.

"I'm checking."

Inside the SuperMIGGS, flashes of light began to emanate from the dark mist, like lightning in storm clouds on a moonless night. In the distance, or what appeared to be a long way off, a small dot of light appeared. Ballooning as it drew nearer, Janis could see it pulsing and undulating as if possessed by an evil force. Fingers of light began to wriggle from its core, lashing about like tentacles. The power of this light was unmistakable; it had exceeded the escape velocity of the SuperMIGGS, something in excess of 186,000 miles per second.

It was the Higgs boson at the 13th Power.

"We're losing it," the MIGGS tech shouted.

The gravity field was weakening inside the SuperMIGGS. The lightning-like flashes around the Higgs boson increased in intensity. Should the gravity collapse all together, the Higgs boson would be released and the 13th Power would be unleashed on an unknowing world.

"More power," Janis said, his voice raspy.

Grabbing the accelerator handle on the SuperMIGGS control console, the tech shoved it full forward, increasing the power to the electromagnets. The ceiling lights brightened as the entire control room took the surge.

Suddenly, the Higgs boson broke apart into a million-billion specks of light, like stars on a dark night, all of which began to clump together, rotate, and then flatten out to form a giant galaxy of whirling stars, bulging brightly at its core. *The Milky Way.* Smaller galaxies spun in the distance. It was the most beautiful thing Janis had ever seen. In all its splendor, this tiny speck in the universe had appeared inside the SuperMIGGS, as if it were a prisoner to technology, if only temporarily.

As quickly as it formed, it dissipated to black.

The tech pulled back on the accelerator, returning the room lights to normal. Gradually, the roaring subsided as the Scheduler deactivated the SuperMIGGS. Vent fans whirred on, and the air began to smell like burnt metal. Inside the MIGGS, the swirling mist broke into tall vortexes and twisted down the floor grates as the gravity equalized. Janis blinked. All that remained inside the MIGGS were the mechanical arms that dangled from the ceiling.

The shuttles were gone.

Turning back to the control room, Janis shouted at Peterson. "Are you satisfied now?"

But Peterson was gone too.

***

Brigham's Aerospace shuttle, *Whiskey-Xray*, started shaking. He saw only blackness out the windshield. The other shuttles, though only a few feet away, were blanketed by a swirling black mist. The sights and sensations were so foreign to him, that he felt trepidation overtake his sense of reality.

Titanium joints creaked under the strain of the SuperMIGGS gravity field, which bore down heavier and heavier.

He felt pressure on his chest, and his eyeballs began to ache. The *G-Force* gauge climbed past *2*. Though he expected to hear the roaring MIGGS, everything outside was silent as death. He glanced at Major Remsfield who was wide-eyed as a boy on a rollercoaster ride.

The G-Force gauge read: *3+*. The ION Shield meter was *green.*

"Any moment now," Remsfield reported. He'd been through all this before in the simulators.

Holding his breath, Brigham clutched the armrests of his chair, waiting for something to release him from the pressure. His heart hammered as his eyes searched the black mist outside for any sign of an end to this torture. Seconds passed like hours.

Then far away in the darkness beyond the windshield, a pulsing light appeared. It was faint at first, approaching from perhaps a million miles away, or maybe just a few feet. The nearer it came, the more brilliant it shined. Beams of light arced from its core, reaching out, twisting and bending and racing forward at incredible speed.

"The Higgs boson," Remsfield said, cool as a summer salad.

Brigham gulped.

Shaking like mad, the shuttle groaned. The hull pressure gauge needles were bouncing in the red.

"We're going to be crushed."

The G-Force gauge read: *4.*

"It's nothing in here like it is out there." Remsfield pointed to the window.

Brigham could hardly breathe. The intense glow of the onrushing Higgs boson lit up the flight deck like the beam of a locomotive bearing down on a stalled car. Squinting, he didn't want to shut his eyes. He didn't want to miss a thing.

Something popped.

He flinched, expecting the shuttle's walls to cave in on him at any moment, but to his immediate surprise, the intense pressure on his body was suddenly gone.

In an instant, the Higgs boson exploded into a billion sparkles that started spinning around the shuttle, slowly at first, then faster and faster until lines of light streaked the darkness and formed a tunnel, brilliantly lit, bending and twisting, swirling down and up and around.

Brigham clenched his jaw in an effort to thwart the upchucking sensation of vertigo. Tense moments eroded into a sudden realization that the feeling of speed was just an illusion. There were no centrifugal forces pressing against him, no lurching and jerking about in his seat. He looked at the light-speed indicator. It read *Zero*. They were sitting still while everything around them streaked by at breakneck speed.

"Look at that," Remsfield said, pointing out the windshield.

Brigham could see the other shuttles again. Remsfield's hands were not on the controls, and in spite of that, the Aerospace shuttles were flying in a tight formation, wingtip-to-wingtip, rolling together, first to the right and then to the left, as if they were one.

There were forces at work here, forces greater than anything Brigham had ever imagined. For the first time in his life, he felt afraid.

Streaking through the luminous, rollercoaster-like tunnel, the squadron of shuttles rolled over in unison, faster and faster. The spinning particle-charged tunnel walls changed colors like a kaleidoscope, yellows and reds, greens and blues, and a mix of all the others. Brigham's balance flipped off kilter, his sense of direction and orientation now dizzily perplexed. Vertigo-induced nausea again clutched at his guts.

They were spinning, rolling, and spinning again.

Abruptly, the tunnel ended, and the shuttles began a freefall down into a funnel, its shape defined by sparkling lights, maybe galaxies, perhaps billions of stars.

Down. Down. Down.

Terry Wright

The squadron plunged into what appeared to be an empty well of black space, and a hollow feeling took hold of Brigham's stomach, a kind of floating sensation that made his whole body tingle.

The G-Force gauge read *zero* now, but the light-speed indicator displayed: *0 point 9*

He tightened his abdominal muscles as if that would hold his insides together. A communications headset floated in the air. The shuttle seemed to be upside down, or right side up, no, he gave up trying to find his place in time and space. His sinuses began to clog up. Stan Burton had said that spatial attitude didn't exist in outer space. Weightlessness. There was no up, no down, no level flight. There was nothing to do but hang on.

Plummeting into the narrowest part of the funnel, the shuttles raced toward an anomaly. It looked like a giant pinwheel made of luminous dust, its curving lines radiating from a center point in space and slowly rotating. Brigham did a double take at the sight before him; he wondered if his eyes were deceiving him. He could see nothing beyond the pinwheel, not a hint of light or a single star, as if the pinwheel wasn't transparent, a cosmic wall of matter or the bottom of a black hole. His heartbeat took a leap. "What's that?"

The space probe came alive, wailing an alarm.

"They never showed this in the simulator," Remsfield said. "We're going to crash."

"Stop this thing," Brigham ordered, startled by the panic in his voice.

"I can't."

"Then go back. We're going to be killed."

Remsfield took hold of his controls and pulled back on the yoke. Nothing happened.

Brigham couldn't believe it. "I thought you could fly this thing."

"I'm trying, General."

The cosmic wall was getting closer.

"Put it in reverse."

Remsfield activated the reverse reflectors and shoved the throttles forward. A shrill whine came from the engines. Streaking toward the ominous wall in the middle of space, the shuttle shuddered and shook.

The light-speed indicator read: *0 point 9.*

"We're not slowing down."

Brigham flipped the radio switch. "Janis, you there?"

Only static came back.

"Damn!" He switched to the squadron frequency. "All wings, report."

"*Alpha-Bravo,*" came a panicked pilot's voice. "*We have no control.*"

Charlie-Delta came through next. "*Our pulse-light engines are at full reverse.*"

"*Echo-Foxtrot, we have no emergency procedures for this, sir.*"

The wall now loomed before the shuttle squadron like a giant black barrier suspended in a luminescent web, dead on, an end to everything.

Light-speed: *0 Point 9.*

"*What do we do?*" came *Golf-Hotel's* frantic call.

"Get hold of yourselves, men," Brigham said to them all, understanding their dire predicament. "We're working on the problem now."

"*Hurry,*" *India-Juliet* replied.

Remsfield rechecked the throttles. They were all the way to full. Reverse reflectors: *MAXIMUM.* He tried to pull back on the yoke again. Still nothing. This space-bound aberration was intent on pulling the Aerospace shuttles down to their doom. Everything was about to end in a microburst of fire. "I'm sorry, sir."

"Janis Mackey, you son of a bitch!" Brigham wished he could regenerate back to the control room and strangle the mathematician. His only solace was knowing Peterson was going to shoot Tracy in the head, and Janis would die after seeing his wife take her last breath.

Suddenly, Remsfield's mouth fell open in awe. "Sir...look."

What Brigham saw in front of him took his breath away. The center of the pinwheel was opening like the iris of an eye.

"It must be the 13th Power," Remsfield said.

Brigham didn't blink. "That's it, an inter-galactic gateway." The opening was huge and growing larger by the second. Beyond the ballooning hole in the darkness, a galaxy appeared, rotating, its middle bulging and glowing with white and yellow star clusters and supernovas, and its stellar plane swirled trails of sparkling stars in its wake.

"Look at that." Brigham suddenly felt like an insignificant spec of matter. "The Milky Way."

Flying in formation, the shuttles streaked through the expanding iris and into the galaxy.

"We made it." Remsfield shut down the reverse reflectors.

"I thought I was going to have a heart attack." Brigham took back all the nasty things he'd said about Janis Mackey. He was a goddamned genius.

The flight clock on the overhead instrument panel began running: *T + 5 seconds*. The Higgs gauge vibrated in the green band meaning the regenerator had been charged, the OBM had trapped the particles needed for the return trip home.

Throttling up, Remsfield let the pulse light engines run full open.

The light-speed indicator read: *10 point 0*.

In spite of all the wonders that lay before him, Brigham didn't waste time gawking. "All wings, report."

His men were elated.

"We're on the other side of the Milky Way," he said to them.

"Do we have to go back?" one pilot returned without identifying himself.

"We have a job to do, men. Get into your designated attack formations, lock your space probes, and stay alert."

Brigham referred to his navigation screen. Stan Burton had programmed the shuttle's guidance system to track the same Higgs Field string recorded on Ray Crawford's previous flight in the transporter. He'd also factored in the rotation speed of the galaxy, which would ensure a direct path to the long-fingered aliens and their teleportation technology.

Moments later, the space probe began beeping. And there it was, magnified on the screen, the ringed green planet.

"Yes," Brigham shouted. "This is going to be one hell of a fight."

Chapter Fourteen

On *Questnar's* flight deck, Beltzee appeared on Luthes' scope screen, a mere ringed dot in the distance but ballooning rapidly. It had been a frustrating four-month journey back from the Ice Planet. He'd marked each day off his calendar as he and *Questnar's* crewmen went through their shift changes and sleep cycles. They feared that Kerillan's prediction of a Tarreeda attack during their absence might have been the enemy's plan all along.

Luthes didn't believe it.

Communication links, which had taken several days to traverse the great distance, were restricted to official business because the League of Beltzee was on *Extreme Alert* status. He'd received no word from Verrilla on *Latearian* in all that time, but he felt confident they were safe. The Tarreeda threat wasn't real. They'd all died on the Ice Planet a thousand generations ago.

Regarius entered the flight deck. His hair poked out over his ears, as usual, and his glasses rode low on the bridge of his nose. During the trip, he'd taken a liking to the maroon crewman uniforms and abandoned the traditional white robe of his Specialist's rank. He took his place in the jump seat behind Luthes. "Home at last, young Rez. I expect you are excited to see your family again."

"I cannot wait."

The communication link came alive with frantic voices. "Fleet Base to *Questnar*." *Squelch.*

"Kedrikans regroup!"

Click. Click. Click.

"*Latearian* is under attack."

"It is the Tarreeda...the Tarreeda...(scream)...*Boom!*"

Static.

Every nerve in Luthes' body turned to ice. This couldn't be happening.

Alarms on *Questnar's* flight deck rang out. "Repulsor Stations," came over the inner-speakers.

Luthes turned in his helmschair, wide-eyed and heart racing, he addressed the ComCap. "Sir!"

Kerillan strapped himself into his observation chair, his eyes on the scope screens and sweat beading his brow. "Take us into battle, Trantenant Rez. Maximum overdrive."

"But *Latearian*, sir."

"I know. I know. Communications officer. Try to raise her."

"Right away, sir." The officer went to work. "*Questnar* to *Latearian!*"

There was no response.

"*Questnar* to *Latearian!* Do you read?"

Operations chatter rose to fever pitch, each officer deciphering data and relaying their concerns to the others. They were in constant disagreement.

Tightening his helmschair straps, Luthes fixed his attention on his duties. He rammed the thrusters into maximum overdrive and focused on the scope screen where Beltzee's ring-plane began to appear in greater detail. "Helm to navigation, I need a vector to *Latearian*."

"Navigator to helm, steer heading nine...forty-four...three."

"Confirmed." He turned to Regarius. "Strap yourself in. It is going to be a rough ride."

"*Questnar* to *Latearian*, come in."

"Visual contact in thirty seconds," navigation reported.

That seemed an eternity to Luthes. He had trouble concentrating on his direction indicator, his mind imagining his wife and daughter trapped on the remote outpost, now under attack. A hole opened in his chest as he realized the severity of his notion that the Tarreeda had not come back. Only now did he realize how wrong he had been. His wife and daughter were about to pay the price for his mistake. He wanted to scream.

"*Questnar* to *Latearian!*"

Still no answer.

The ring-plane now loomed mightily on Luthes' scope screen, its colored bands spinning overhead at breathtaking speed. And just as navigation predicted, the sphere of *Latearian* twinkled in the distance.

But something else caught his eye, a sight that chilled him to the bone. Orbital Patrol Ships defending *Latearian* were exploding into great balls of luminous vapor. It was the most horrifying sight he'd ever seen.

Intense light beams shot out from the wingtips of several massive Tarreeda cruisers, flashing brilliantly and destroying everything in their paths. They were attacking *Latearian's* defenses, flying in diamond formations, four cruisers to a pack, hitting the fleet from all sides. The Kedrikans, flying their colors proudly, made a gallant stand, but balls of energy from their repulsor cannons, all fired in unison, were unable to repel the Tarreeda's death beams. Within moments, the Kedrikan's left flank had been thinned to only a few Orbital Patrol Ships, some already on fire and venting.

"*Latearian*, this is *Questnar*." The communications officer's voice was frantic. "Do you read? *Latearian*, do you copy?"

"Navigator to helm. Prepare to rendezvous with the fleet, nine minutes."

"Hit them from behind," Kerillan said. "Repulsors on full."

Speakers crackled. "*Questnar, Questnar, this is Latearian's Command Center.*" A young Beltzan's voice reeked with hysteria. *"Everyone in communications is dead. I just figured out how to work this communications link."*

Luthes thought his pounding chest would burst. They were all dead. What about his wife and daughter?

Kerillan worked a switch on his armrest panel. "Do you have a casualty report?"

"No, sir."

"Are you evacuating?"

"The teleport station is down. We were hit so suddenly, no one had a chance to get away."

"What about the civilians?"

"No one, sir. There are fires throughout the station. We are venting badly."

BOOM!

Static.

"Questnar to *Latearian!"*

No answer.

Dread pumped wildly through Luthes' veins. Five thousand Beltzans were trapped aboard *Latearian*, including his wife and daughter. He could see spiny geysers of vapor shooting out of *Latearian's* hull from several places. Viewports had been reduced to jagged black holes. A debris field floated around *Latearian*. Outmasts toppled. With each attack run the Tarreeda made, their death beams penetrated the outer hull, again and again. He feared the riddium power core would soon be breached. Luthes asked Cada for a miracle.

Above the ring-plane, thirty Orbital Patrol Ships appeared, teleported up from their bases on Zarakatan, Berakatee, and Retakan, their battle stripes raised high on their mastheads.

A cheer rose from *Questnar's* flight deck. Luthes felt a wisp of hope rise inside. The battle scene drew nearer on his scope screen, but not fast enough.

Without hesitation, the reinforcements joined the

battle, quickly shoring up the Kedrikans' faltering left flank. En masse, they trained their repulsor fire on a pack of Tarreeda Cruisers bearing down on them from above.

The Zarakatans opened fire first. Ten, twenty, forty balls of energy deflected the Tarreeda pack's course and sent them veering off into space. Jubilation erupted on *Questnar's* flight deck, but the clamor quickly died when another pack of Tarreeda attacked the Zarakatans from below. Death beams flashed, and in an instant, fourteen Orbital Patrol Ships exploded. Another Tarreeda pack swooped down on the Kedrikans, and then another pack hit the Berakatees, both attack runs leaving gaseous balls of vapor in their wakes.

"More speed," Kerillan ordered.

Luthes could do nothing else. The thrusters were running at maximum overdrive. *Questnar* was not yet close enough to engage the Tarreeda, though he could see their cruisers more clearly now. They were unlike any ships he'd ever seen, fat bellied and blunt nosed. Symbols adorned their vertical stabilizers: *N-A-S-A*, but there were no black crosses anywhere that he could see. Who were these vicious attackers?

The pack swung around and let loose a barrage of death beams against the Retakans. Their ships exploded in a fiery display.

"There is no way to stop them," Operations reported. "Evade."

"No!" Kerillan shouted. "Trantenant Rez, prepare to engage the enemy. Do not evade. We are *Latearian's* only hope."

Clenching his jaw, Luthes zeroed in on a pack of Tarreeda that had just strafed *Latearian*. They were flying toward *Questnar* now, and he set his course to meet them head-on.

"Navigator to Operations. Range, four-five-zero decks."

They were still too far away for the repulsor cannons. "Hold fire for two-two-zero decks," Kerillan said.

Brilliant fireballs pocked the space around *Latearian* as one after another, Orbital Patrol Ships were destroyed. Luthes could only imagine the horrors aboard those ships, the blast of heat, the ripping and tearing of hulls and bulkheads, ceilings and floors, the concussion as space sucked out the air, exploding lungs and boiling body fluids. He started blaming himself for *Questnar's* tardiness, wishing he'd pushed the Orbital Patrol Ship harder on their return voyage from the Ice Planet. Wishing that he had believed...

"Range, three-two-three decks."

The Tarreeda pack in his sights suddenly looped belly-up, and then dove toward the Kedrikan's right flank. Beams of intense light flashed from the cruisers' wings. Orbital Patrol Ships disintegrated.

Luthes felt sick. His palms were sweating. With every nerve now on fire, he steered *Questnar* into battle.

"Range, two-seven-zero-decks."

Luthes' mouth went dry. Fear swelled inside him along with an unfamiliar feeling. Rage. The sensation frightened him as much as the impending battle ahead.

The Tarreeda pack in his sights circled around, broke through the newly blown hole in the Kedrikan's right flank, and headed straight for *Latearian*. Light beams flashed with intensity, penetrating the hull. Jagged rifts of fire crisscrossed *Latearian's* exterior, which expanded with a final breath, and then exploded in a billowing ball of intense light.

Luthes' scope screen flashed bright white, the magnitude of the explosion overwhelming *Questnar's* external sensors, searing the delicate electronics and blinding him to what was happening outside. He tried the backups. They failed.

Then the concussion hit *Questnar* with a mighty

punch. The largest Orbital Patrol Ship in the fleet rolled over and over in the undulating fabric of warped space, no more significant than a leaf in the wind. Luthes clutched the helmswheel, felt the safety harness cut into his shoulder, and saw crewmen who were once standing boldly at their stations tumble around the flight deck. Most were killed outright. Consoles spewed sparks and ripped from their floor anchors, crushing technicians and Operations Officers. He ducked his head as ceiling panels flew through the air like hurled knives. Electrical equipment burst into flames.

Tumbling dizzily, he felt *Questnar's* hull sustain a hammering blow. Bulkheads groaned. Fasteners popped. Unable to see outside, he feared he'd collided with something, or perhaps an aftershock from *Latearian*...then his eardrums reacted violently to a major change in air pressure. The flight deck's blast doors closed automatically. A horrendous crashing sound came next and the screams of crewmen aft of the flight deck. He inhaled the stink of molten aluminite and realized *Questnar* had just been hit with a Tarreeda death beam.

To Cada.

Attitude stabilizing jets arrested *Questnar's* chaotic tumble. On Luthes' control panel, warning lights flashed. The thrusters had been knocked out of commission. Flight controls failed to respond to the helmswheel. As he struggled to assess the damage, he saw that the docking bay doors had been activated. Diagnostics indicated a short circuit. Backups and shutdown switches had no effect on the doors. Then an alarm rang out, warning him that the space shield had not been deployed. If vacuum were to leach into the fuel cells, the reaction would be instantaneous and catastrophic. Questnar would vaporize.

"Sir!" He turned to report the problem to Kerillan, but through the smoky haze on the flight deck, Luthes saw the ComCap slumped in his chair. Blood flowed from an angry gash in his neck.

Fighting panic, Luthes returned his attention to the opening doors and again worked the switches several times. No response. He found it unsettling to have survived this long only to be vaporized in the end, a victim of the deadly Tarreeda.

Just then, another alarm sounded. The central power system was failing. He could think of only one thing to do. It wouldn't fix anything, but it would buy his floundering ship a little time. Hoping there was enough power left, he activated the space shield. His ears popped from a welcome increase in pressure.

Only now did he look behind him to check on Regarius. His glasses had been knocked off his face, and his flight suit was covered with dust. But he was conscious, his eyes scanning the wrecked flight deck, his face white with shock. "Young Rez," he said hoarsely. "Seems I was right. It was the Tarreeda."

"Seems like it, but where are their crosses?"

Regarius coughed. "Can you save the ship?"

"Maybe Fleet Base will send help." It was his only hope.

Regarius set a hand on his forehead. "They are all gone, you know. The fleet was near *Latearian* when it exploded. We were far away and fared very poorly."

A deep sorrow engulfed Luthes. The specialist was right. Not only had he lost Verrilla and Sashi, but the fleet had been destroyed, as well, all those lives lost to the bloodthirsty Tarreeda, or whoever the aliens were. And he would be next, and Regarius, and the crew who'd survived only to finally succumb to a violent end. *Questnar* languished in space without power and control. Hull pressure gauges were dropping. Acrid smoke churned through the only breathable air they had left. Hope of rescue flickered out, as did all the lights on the flight deck.

In total darkness, Luthes awaited his death.

***

Aboard *Whiskey-Xray*, Brigham watched the gigantic alien craft list to port. It was bigger than anything he'd been up against so far, but he wasn't concerned. His Aerospace shuttle attack force had annihilated everything with surgical precision. When the space station went up, all holdouts defending it were instantly vaporized.

"Shall I blast that bad boy again," Major Remsfield said, his thumb hovering over the firing trigger for his wing-mounted PLRs. The giant ship listed in his sights.

Brigham was about to give the okay when he noticed the floundering ship's bow doors opening. "Hold your fire. I wonder what they're up to."

"They might be launching fighters." Remsfield put his thumb on the trigger. "We've got to destroy it now."

"At ease, Major," Brigham ordered.

"But it's the last one."

Brigham didn't argue the point. He sat forward in his seat and studied the enemy ship floating wounded in space. It was as long as an aircraft carrier and maybe ten stories tall, flat on the bottom and wide across the beam, like a teardrop. He couldn't see anything that looked like windows, but the strange doors opening on the bow intrigued him. It might be a way in. There might be a survivor or two...for Peterson. "Move in," he told Remsfield.

"Sir, it could be a trap. Those cannons pack a wallop."

"They rattled our molars a few times," Brigham acknowledged. "But that's all." He regarded the ship once more. "I don't think these aliens have any lethal weapons."

"I don't care to find out," Remsfield replied. "Let me just blast them and be done with it."

Brigham didn't reply, but picked up the radio mike. "All wings stand down."

"What are you doing?" Remsfield asked in a tone of

disbelief.

"The surface assault can wait. I want to get a look inside this thing."

"But what if they send up reinforcements?"

"They hit us with their best shot, Major. What are you worried about? Move this shuttle closer to those doors."

"But..."

"That's an order." Brigham keyed the radio again. *"Golf-Hotel."*

"Yes, sir."

"Colonel Scott, come along side me and follow us down. If we can board this thing, deploy your troops, search and destroy any aggressors. I need information about the planet's ground-based defenses."

"Right away, sir."

Side by side, the Aerospace shuttles glided toward the wrecked spaceship. Brigham inspected the black hole where a particle beam had penetrated the hull. Vapor vented from the molten wound.

"You think anything is alive in there?" Remsfield asked.

The huge ship loomed in the shuttle's windshield.

"I don't see any running lights," Brigham noted. "They have no power. It's probably freezing in there." He went back to his radio mike. *"Golf-Hotel*, I want your men in full pressure suits. Got that?"

"Roger."

As the shuttles approached the dark and canted docking bay, which appeared to be large enough to accommodate four shuttles, Brigham felt a rush of fear. He held his breath, not because he feared for his men's safety, but because the view out the windshield became suddenly blurred. Space turned to liquid, as if they were passing through an energy field. He hoped it wasn't lethal. The anomaly only lasted a few seconds, and he exhaled with relief as they flew into the alien spacecraft.

Remsfield shut off the pulse-light engines, and with precision bursts from the hypergolic steering jets, he set the shuttle down on the crooked floor. *Golf-Hotel* did the same. Artificial gravity held the shuttles in place.

Brigham, feeling the sensation of weight return to his body, switched on the shuttle's exterior lighting, which revealed a huge chamber that resembled an aircraft hangar. The place was in shambles. Bodies and debris were strewn everywhere. Then he spotted dark figures scurry into the shadows. "Careful, men," he said into his mike. "Aliens."

***

On the darkened flight deck, Luthes felt *Questnar* pitch forward slightly. He was attuned to subtle shifts in spatial attitude. It came from being a seasoned helmsman. "They have landed in the docking bay," he told Regarius.

"How?"

"The docking bay doors shorted open. I energized the space shield before the power went out. It's the only thing that saved us from the breached hull."

"H-how long will it last?" Regarius's voice stumbled.

Luthes coughed, the noxious air burning his lungs. "Probably longer than we will."

Emergency lamps flashed on, eerily illuminating the smoky flight deck. Luthes saw Regarius's sooty face. "The power cells won't last long."

Looking around the wrecked flight deck, Luthes cringed at the sight of smashed equipment and broken bodies that littered the floor. Blood was smeared and splattered everywhere.

"I'd rather sit in the dark," Regarius said.

Luthes glanced at ComCap Kerillan sitting limp in his chair. "Is he...?"

"He is dead," Regarius confirmed.

The magnitude of loss hit Luthes in the stomach. His

beautiful wife, Verrilla, his beautiful daughter, Sashi, he couldn't imagine their last moments of terror aboard *Latearian*. And all those Beltzans..."They are all dead."

"They died believing in you, young Rez. They died with honor and dignity, as did all these fine officers on *Questnar*, and all those who defended the League of Beltzee. At least they have been spared living under the Tarreeda's tyranny. They will give the survivors a whole new perspective on misery."

Luthes hacked. He knew there was every possibility the attackers were the Tarreeda, but one important fact remained. There were no crosses on their cruisers. It was the only thing that had kept him from being totally convinced. Even now, at the end, he doubted Regarius.

Creaking sounds came from the corridor beyond the flight deck's closed doors.

Luthes' heart rate jumped. "Who is out there?"

"Someone is alive in here," came a voice through his collar-mounted translator.

Regarius's eyes opened wide. "The Tarreeda."

Luthes licked dry lips. "My translator recognized the words. He is probably a Kedrikan crewman."

"Not necessarily," Regarius said. "Our translators are programmed with the old languages, too, including the Tarreeda's."

"But they might not be the Tarreeda," Luthes replied. "I still think they all died on the Ice Planet."

Metal clanked on metal as hammers and pry bars worked against the buckled blast door.

"We shall soon see our killers," Regarius said, his face ghostly white.

Finally, the door jogged open and smoke swirled in. "It is Luthes," someone announced and dashed in.

Luthes recognized the Kedrikan crewman serving temporary duty on *Questnar*. That accounted for the translator's activation at the sound of his voice. Satisfied,

Luthes unbuckled his helmschair straps. "How many of us are left?"

"There are twenty with me," the Kedrikan said. "But there may be others. Some of the passageways are blocked with debris."

Survivors started crowding onto the flight deck, their smudged faces filled with terror. Luthes was glad to see them.

"You gave us quite a fright," Regarius said and got up from his chair. "What are you going to do now?"

"The Tarreeda have landed in the docking bay," the Kedrikan said. "We are looking for somewhere to hide."

"We cannot hide," Regarius said, his eyes downcast. "We will be taken prisoner. Made into slaves to toil for the Tarreeda."

"I would rather die," a Beltzan mechanic proclaimed. He had lost all his crewmates in the aft maintenance galley when the death beam hit *Questnar*. Harsh lines in his face revealed the anger of that loss. In an act totally unlike any Beltzan, he picked up a broken chair leg. "We must fight them to the death."

Suddenly, a *Pop...Pop* sound came from somewhere down the corridor. A crewman screamed.

Again: *Pop...Pop*.

Fear stabbed Luthes' brain. He'd never heard that sound before. Suddenly, two other crewmen stumbled in through the smoke. One held a bleeding shoulder. "The Tarreeda have tubes that shoot fire," he said before he fell. Luthes rushed to his side, saw blood gushing from another hole in his back.

This was something Luthes had never seen before. He looked at the Beltzan mechanic with the broken chair leg cocked over his shoulder. "We cannot fight against tubes that shoot fire."

"We must defend ourselves."

Luthes could not imagine striking anyone, Tarreeda or

otherwise, for any reason.

Running footsteps echoed from down the corridor. "No!"

Pop...Pop.

"Humph!" A body hit the floor.

"Close the door!" Luthes shouted.

As the Kedrikan tried to slide the door closed, a black boot suddenly stomped on the threshold, instantly stopping the door's progress. A muffled voice activated Luthes' translator. "There's a slew of them in here, men." Several gloved hands with short fingers forced the door open again.

Panic stricken, Luthes took two steps back, and nearly tripping over a dead Operations officer, he gasped at the sight before him. Aliens in puffy suits the color of dirt and grass appeared in the smoky doorway. Their heads were covered, their faces masked behind transparent shields from which black, corrugated tubes protruded, one on each side, coiling around behind their backs. He tried to make out their facial features or hair color, anything that would tell him they were indeed the Tarreeda, but he saw nothing familiar. Whoever the invaders were, they looked huge and undefeatable as they poured through the doorway, pointing fire tubes menacingly around the flight deck. Crewmen panicked, some scrambling for the far corner, others breaking for the aft door.

Then the unthinkable happened. Screaming, the Beltzan mechanic lunged toward the invaders with the chair leg raised above his head.

Pop...Pop.

In the mad rush that followed, Luthes was shoved into the corner and pinned down by the throng of crewmen trying to escape the lethal barrage. Fire tubes popped. Bodies fell into piles. Blood rained down on the living and the dead. Advancing at will, the invaders stood on bodies and fired down on crewmen cowering and pleading for their lives. Luthes knew it would be only seconds before he was killed.

"Cease fire, men." The translator relayed a booming voice, muffled under a mask, yet one that commanded respect. Instantly, the fire tubes went silent. "Are you out of your minds? We need information, not corpses." As his subordinates stood off to the side, their leader plodded through the gruesome carnage on the flight deck. "Are there any aliens left alive?"

Aliens? Luthes had trouble understanding this and wondered when he'd become an alien.

"Colonel Scott," the leader shouted. "What happened here?"

One of the invaders stepped up to him. "General Brigham," he said with a salute. "We were told to search and destroy any aggressors, sir."

"You massacred them."

"We were attacked first." The officer pointed to the dead Beltzan mechanic still holding the broken chair leg. "We're all a little jumpy, sir."

"Looks more like trigger-happy to me."

"We had no idea what they were going to hit us with. It was self defense."

"At ease, Colonel. We're not in Somalia." Brigham looked around. "What a mess."

Luthes didn't move as the invader called Brigham started poking through the bodies strewn about. Dread pumped through Luthes' veins, for he knew the penalties he would pay for being captured. If these were the Tarreeda, they'd hang him on a cross until he was dead. It would be a horrible way to die, and he feared it more than the fire tubes. As he thought to make a dash for it, he looked up over the pile of corpses, and at that moment, his eyes met Brigham's. Luthes froze.

"Here's one," Brigham said. "Take him to be interrogated."

In total defeat, Luthes stood.

Regarius followed his lead.

At least they weren't alone.

"There's another one," Colonel Scott said.

"Take him, too."

"But he's an old man," Scott said. "He'll only slow us down. I'll shoot him right here."

Wide-eyed, Regarius thrust his palm out and shook his head.

"Look at that," Brigham said. "I think he understands us."

Luthes said to Regarius, "He will need a translator so we can talk to him."

"So you believe me now, young Rez?"

"General, they're talking to each other, might be planning something."

"The translators are proof enough," Luthes replied. "You were right. The invaders are the Tarreeda. I was wrong."

"Then you must know it will do no good to talk to them."

"Shut up," Brigham ordered.

"We have to try." Luthes felt another drop in pressure. His eardrums began to ache. "We don't have time. The space shield is deteriorating."

"We should stay here and die."

"Where there is life, there is hope," Luthes said.

The Colonel made a jabbing motion with his fire tube. "They're still talking gibberish, sir, probably plotting some trick."

Luthes glanced at Brigham who seemed content to listen to their Beltzan conversation and made no move to silence them. "We need to give him a translator."

"I do not have a spare."

"Kerillan will not need his. You must get it and give it to the one they call Brigham."

The two Tarreeda seemed perplexed, or perhaps

curious about the conversation, though their expressions were hidden behind their face shields.

"What could we possibly say to change our position with him?"

"We have to warn him that *Questnar* is going to explode. Perhaps he will be appreciative."

"I doubt it."

"It is our only hope. Now hurry."

Regarius held his hands up. "Why do I have to do it?"

"You are closest to Kerillan. Do it now."

"To Cada." Emerging from the corner with his hands high in the air, palms well exposed to the Tarreeda, Regarius climbed over the pile of bodies.

Colonel Scott rushed forward with his fire tube pointed at Regarius's chest. "Hold it."

"At ease, Colonel," Brigham said. "The old guy can't hurt anybody. Let's see what he's going to do."

Luthes held his breath.

Everyone on the flight deck watched Regarius move to Kerillan's chair and unclip the translator from his collar. Trembling, Regarius then approached Brigham with the device offered in his open hand.

Brigham stepped back but eyed the gadget with a curious tilt of his head.

Suddenly, the pressure dropped again as *Questnar's* atmosphere continued to bleed off into space. Luthes knew they had only a precious few minutes left.

Regarius pointed to the translator on his collar then pointed to Brigham's collar.

Brigham just stared at him.

Acrid air hurt Luthes' lungs. The Tarreeda had the benefit of masks and could not possibly know how dangerous the conditions were becoming. He inhaled painfully, knowing time was running out fast. "Will you hurry up?"

Regarius shoved his open hand toward Brigham.

Cautiously, Brigham took the offered translator in his gloved hand, fumbled it and dropped it. Regarius shook his head, bent over, and retrieved it from the floor. His face was turning blue as he reached out to Brigham's collar.

Brigham stiffened.

Regarius clipped the translator into place. "We must get out of here at once."

"By God, I understand him," Brigham exclaimed. "How does this thing work?"

"It sends translated impulses through your clothes and into your body," Regarius said. "The audio receptors in your brain interpret the signals. It sounds as if you are *hearing* us speak your language."

"That's incredible."

The pressure dropped again, and then one-by-one, emergency lamps started popping.

"The space shield is failing," Luthes said. "*Questnar* is going to explode."

"We've got to get back to the shuttles," Brigham said to Scott. "Assemble your men."

"What about them?" Scott indicated Regarius and Luthes with the point of his fire tube.

"I am Specialist Regarius," he said to Brigham. "This is Luthes Rez, helmsman of *Questnar*. We prefer to stay here and die with our crewmen."

"Are you nuts?" Luthes said. "I thought we already decided..."

"Trust me."

"What are they jabbering about?" Scott asked.

"They're coming with us," Brigham said as another emergency lamp popped and spit glass. He looked around the grisly flight deck floor, to his right and his left. "See if you can find any more of these gismos." He pointed to the translator on his collar. "And roundup the survivors."

Quickly, the Tarreeda invaders went to work sorting through the dead and wounded, plucking translators from their clothes until the last emergency lamp finally exploded and plunged the flight deck into darkness. Tarreeda flashlights came on and waggled about. "How are we going to find our way back to the shuttles?" Scott shouted.

Nearly freezing and filled with terror, Luthes decided to take matters into his own hands. "Follow me." He stumbled over his dead comrades as he headed for the door.

"Move out," Brigham ordered his men.

Questnar creaked and groaned.

Chapter Fifteen

In the SuperMIGGS control room at NASA, Janis sat at his terminal and watched his regeneration monitor track the Aerospace shuttle squadron, which appeared as Xs on a computer-generated galaxy, 100,000 light years from earth. At first there were sixteen shuttles. Now there were fourteen left, as two shuttles had disappeared suddenly. Either they were destroyed in battle, or they had entered the planet's atmosphere and were no longer operating in the vacuum of space.

Peterson stopped his incessant whittling and examined the monitor. "Are they all right?"

"It's hard to say." Janis swiveled his chair. "They made it. That's all I care about."

"Now we wait," Peterson said. "Everybody break for lunch."

Lo and Tracy got up and left with the other techs. There wasn't anything else they could do around here, and it had been a long morning. Janis wasn't hungry and took the opportunity to talk to Peterson. "It's time you let us go home."

"Not until they come back," Peterson said, his eyes quizzically fixed on Janis's monitor.

"We're done here."

"How do I know you brainards haven't pulled a fast one? You can make these things do anything you want." He indicated the machines around him with a wave of his jackknife. "I'd never know the difference."

"This isn't a video game," Janis said. "It's real. Brigham is in the 13th Power, as agreed, so let me take

Tracy home."

Leaning back against the console, Peterson began to whittle on his figurine again. "She's my prisoner until Brigham says otherwise."

"You know he's trumped up the charges."

"It's not for me to decide." A wood chip drifted to the floor. "That's what a judge and jury is for."

Frustration clawed at Janis's throat. He regarded Peterson's whittling obsession, which seemed a strange pastime for a government thug. His specialty was figurines of alien creatures, this one nicely detailed but grotesquely devoid of humanoid form. Peterson was a big man with thick arms, broad shoulders, and brawny hands, yet he manipulated the wood and knife with the skill of a surgeon. And the scar on Peterson's cheek intrigued Janis. Whoever cut him must've put up one hell of a fight. "What happened to your face?"

Peterson ran a fingertip along the scar. "It's just a scratch."

"Must've hurt like hell. Was it a knife?"

He stared blankly at the wooden alien in his hand, as if his mind had slipped back to another place and time. The muscles of his angular jaw twitched.

"A bayonet?" Janis guessed. "Hand to hand combat? You were a Marine, right?"

Peterson said nothing.

"A paratrooper?"

Mute.

"Don't tell me you cut yourself shaving."

"It was a plane crash," Peterson snapped. "A plane crash, all right?" His eyes bored into Janis. "I flew a Cessna into a tree. A branch punched through the windscreen. My wife was killed instantly. Are you happy now?"

Janis felt a jolt of *gotcha*. He'd opened an old wound and didn't know how to respond to Peterson's outburst. The man had lost his wife, and the scar on his face was obviously a constant reminder of the crash, probably every time he shaved. "It was an accident, right?"

"I'm going to lunch." He put the whittling project in his pocket and turned to leave.

Janis couldn't let him off the hook that easy. "Pilot error?"

He kept walking.

"You screwed up." Janis had found Peterson's sore spot. "You killed your wife, and you're pissed off at the whole world."

Turning abruptly, Peterson jabbed a stiff finger at Janis. "Shut up."

"You don't have a wife anymore...but I do." Janis stood and stormed toward him. "That really gets your goat, doesn't it? Admit it. You're out to kill Tracy, same as you killed your wife."

"It was an accident." Peterson threw his shoulders back. "I've flown everything from kit planes to Tomcats and every helicopter the Marines could throw at me. I know how to fly."

"So it wasn't your fault?"

"It was a rental." Peterson spoke with fury in his eyes. "A Sunday afternoon pleasure flight. The elevator control cable broke. Shit happens, so don't expect me to care about your problems, Janis."

"What *do* you care about, Peterson, besides carving little aliens?"

"Go ahead, piss me off. I'll—"

"You'll what? You can't even scratch your balls without Brigham's okay."

"Why you..." Peterson pulled out his gun and shoved the barrel under Janis's chin. "I ought to..."

Janis didn't back off. He had to get Peterson to give a shit about what happens to Tracy. "Go ahead," he growled through clenched teeth. "But you'll still have that scar on your face. It'll never go away, no matter what you do, so don't add Tracy's lynching to your list of accidents."

Peterson showed teeth through bloodless thin lips, his eyes slits of rage under deeply furrowed brows. For one second, Janis thought he may have pushed him too far and truly expected to see a blinding flash of light and eternal darkness, but instead, Peterson shoved him back into the chair. "It's not going to work, Janis. You're stuck here." He put the gun away. "But I'll say, you've got a lot of nerve for a mathematician."

"I'm fighting for my wife."

"You could get yourself killed."

"Not a chance. Brigham needs me too much. Your tough-guy act isn't convincing. And you whittle little aliens like your life depends on it."

"Calms my nerves between murders." The corners of his mouth lifted slightly and gave away his joke.

Janis wasn't amused. "What is your interest in this project?" He swept his hand around the control room.

"Just doing my job," Peterson said flatly.

"You're not military. Who do you work for?" Maybe Peterson would reveal some kind of motivation for being involved. "CIA?"

"It's none of your business, Mackey. Let it go."

"The Justice Department? Secret Service? You have the power to save Tracy from Brigham's inquisition, I'm sure of it."

"I can't save her," he said. "No more than I could save my wife."

"Then let us go home."

"Brigham would only hunt you down." Peterson removed a wooden figurine from his pocket, set it upright on the console like a toy soldier, and turned for the door. "You're better off doing your job until it's over." He walked out.

Janis let him go then curiously picked up the wooden figure. It was an intricately whittled alien, human in appearance and frighteningly familiar. It had a carved helmet and face shield...and extremely long fingers, an exact replica of the aliens from Ray Crawford's recording. Janis turned it over in his hands, felt the smooth wood grain, the fine ridges of detail. His heart seized with a frightening revelation.

Peterson was out to get himself a real alien.

Fighting panic, Janis reached for the phone.

Chapter Sixteen

L isa arrived at her father's bungalow early. She hadn't heard a word from him since she'd stormed out the other day. He wouldn't answer his phone. Worried, she'd thrown on a pair of blue shorts and a yellow-laced tank top and drove the short distance from her townhouse in Santa Barbara to tell him she was sorry.

"Dad?" She opened the front door and peeked inside. "Dad?"

The curtains were closed; the place looked dark and abandoned.

"Dad? I'm sorry." When she stepped into the front room, the nauseating stench of vomit hit her. "Dad?" She shouldn't have argued with him. She shouldn't have lost her temper. Sure, he was overprotective to the point of obsession. She knew it, and yet she'd pushed his buttons anyway. Sometimes she found it hard, if not impossible, to control her emotions. Her hot-headedness had gotten the best of her again, and this time it had driven her father back into the bottle. A few more steps through the bungalow confirmed her fears. She found him butt-naked, lying on the floor, face down and still as death.

"Oh my God."

Flies buzzed around him. In his left hand, he clutched an empty bottle of Jack Daniels. She bent down but hesitated to touch him. His skin was pale. "Don't be dead, damnit." Leaning over him, she got down close to his face, which was pressed to the floor and listened for any sound of breathing. She heard snoring. "Christ, Dad, you scared the shit out of me."

The phone rang.

"Wake up." She shook him hard, but there was no response. The phone kept ringing, and she wondered who could be calling at this inopportune time. "Dad?" She shook him again. Quickly, one thing became clear. He wasn't going to answer the phone. She moved to the cluttered end table and picked up the receiver. "Yes?"

"Lisa?"

Her heart jumped just hearing his voice. "This isn't a good time, Janis."

"Let me talk to your dad."

Again, she looked at her father lying naked on the floor. "He can't come to the phone."

"I've got to talk to him."

"He's passed out cold."

"I thought he quit drinking."

"It's a long story." She didn't want to tell him that she had anything to do with his relapse, their argument and all. "Call back tomorrow."

"I need to talk to him now."

"There's no way. He's comatose."

"Throw a bucket of cold water on him," Janis said. "The colder the better."

"Oh dear." She thought about how much that would piss him off. "It's best to leave him alone when he's drunk."

"Cold water, Lisa, and make it fast."

"He's going to have a fit."

"Do it now."

She put down the phone and went to the kitchen. A part of her dreaded dousing him, yet another part of her relished the thought. She couldn't find a bucket, but she knew Ray kept a cold jug of drinking water in the refrigerator. Retrieving it, she returned to the front room, and standing over the flaccid remains of her once-proud father, she couldn't help but grin. "Here goes."

It didn't take much cold water to get a reaction from him. He came off the floor like an enraged bull, cursing, staggering on alcohol-weak legs. "What the hell?" When his eyes found her, his mouth flew open in total surprise, and as if some instinct left over from the Garden of Eden hit him like a board, he stooped and cupped his hands over his crotch. His face flushed, and he couldn't walk backward fast enough, tripped over an empty Jack Daniels bottle, and stumbled to the bedroom door. Once out of sight, he let out a scream.

Proud of herself, she retrieved the phone. "Just like that, Janis? My God, I thought he was going to die of embarrassment."

"Tell him I'm on the phone."

Lisa shouted, "Dad. Janis wants to talk to you."

"He's got nothing to say that I want to hear," Ray hollered from the bedroom, his words slurring. "And the same goes for you." She heard him rifling through drawers, looking for something to wear. "What are you doing here?"

"I came to apologize."

"Where are my clothes?"

"I washed them for you, remember? What happened to the shorts you were wearing?"

"I had an accident. What have you done with my clothes?"

"They're in a basket in the back seat of my car, all clean and neatly folded."

He came out with a towel wrapped around his waist. "I suppose you want me to thank you for that."

"Don't knock yourself out, Dad."

"My head is killing me. Where's my Johnny Walker?"

She pointed to an empty bottle on the floor. "That one?"

"Damn! Get my clothes. I have to go to the liquor store."

"Talk to Janis first." She held out the receiver.

"My clothes, I mean it."

Lisa shrugged. "If you don't talk to Janis, you don't get your clothes, and if you go to the liquor store looking like that, I'm sure you'll be arrested." She smiled at the dumbfounded look on his face.

Growling, he grabbed the phone. "What is it, Janis, got your balls caught in a particle accelerator?"

"You're real cheery this morning."

"Screw you."

"Dad, be nice."

"It's done," Janis said. "Brigham has returned to the 13th Power. We just degenerated sixteen Aerospace shuttles."

Ray's face turned white. "Jesus."

"I know what they're up to, Ray, They're going to bring back an alien."

Ray didn't say anything.

"Did you hear me, Ray?"

Lisa took the phone. "He heard you. I think he's going to be sick."

"He needs to snap out of this."

Sighing, Lisa looked at her father, who had slumped onto the couch. He looked and smelled like an old boozer, his unsightly condition bringing tears to her eyes. "He was doing so well, Janis."

"Are you two fighting again?"

"Sometimes he makes me so mad."

"What happened?"

"It's the same old thing. He's overprotective."

"So you did have another fight." There was a hint of disgust in his voice.

"You don't understand. He wants me to find some college boy and fall in love."

"Sounds like good advice to me."

She shifted the phone to her other ear and turned her back to her father. "I haven't gotten over you, Janis.

Please—"

"We've been through this before, Lisa, a hundred times."

"I need more than some party boy, Janis. I need security." She looked at her father sitting dazed on the couch and remembered the loneliness she'd endured in those European prep schools, all because of him, because he and her mother couldn't get along. "Security, Janis. God knows I didn't get that from my parents. I need a man who has a grip on his life, like you, not one who thinks of surfing and beer and polishing his car on Saturday."

Janis didn't respond. She figured he was so hung up on Tracy that he'd forgotten the way he had felt about her. Back then, she was his California Girl. He was her Colorado Cowboy. Now they were nothing. He got a crummy notion that she was too young for him, that their lifestyles were too different. California and Colorado were poles apart. Just thinking about it broke her heart all over again. "I have no use for a college boy."

"If you want my advice—"

"I want you, Janis." She felt like hanging up on him. "Keep your advice."

"You can't have me, Lisa, so stop it. I love Tracy. Find somebody else."

"It doesn't matter. Dad won't approve—"

"Forget about what your dad wants. Move away if you have to."

"I'm not abandoning my father. He's the only family I have left. I just want him to let me live my life my way."

"You, of all people, should know that you don't always get what you want."

"Touché!"

"Now let me talk to Ray."

She looked at her father slouched on the couch, his hair unkempt, his bloodshot eyes staring across the room. "He's a lost cause."

"I need him here."

"Wild horses couldn't drag him to NASA."

"Doesn't he care what's going on down here?"

"No, Janis. There's nothing you can say to make him change his mind."

"Maybe if you sober him up...maybe he'll see I need his help."

"He doesn't care, I tell you."

"Then we're all in trouble, Lisa. Don't let him turn his back on us."

"I hear Tracy calling you, Janis." She hung up and screamed at her father. "You guys are driving me crazy."

Chapter Seventeen

Back from lunch break, Tracy walked into the control room just in time to see Janis slam down the phone. He sat upright in his chair and clenched his fists like a junkie trying to stave off a fit. Cautiously, she approached him, hoping he wouldn't smell cigarette smoke on her breath. "What was that all about?"

"Ray Crawford. He's back on the booze."

"He can't help us, Janis. We're on our own." Trying not to get too close to him, she leaned against the console where the regenerator monitor showed the location of Brigham's Aerospace shuttles. "What do you suppose they're doing out there?"

Janis didn't answer, just looked her up and down, a lost look in his eyes.

"What is it?"

"Do you still love me?" His voice was soft.

Her breath hitched. Speechless, she looked at him sitting in his chair, his face turned up to her, his reading glasses low on the bridge of his nose. He looked rather smart that way. She missed him during those lonely nights in that jail cell, yearned for his warm embrace, his smile, and his witty sense of humor. Their life together in Boulder came to mind, too. All those good memories couldn't outweigh the one bad thing that was tearing her up inside. She turned toward her terminal.

"I asked you a question, Tracy," Janis said sternly this time. "Do you still love me?"

She winced and kept walking.

"Tracy?" His voice was a little louder.

A flash of embarrassment knifed through her. He'd press this, she was sure of it. She stopped, then quickly turned and paced back to his station. "Janis, this is not the time or place to discuss it."

"Well, do you?" he asked louder still.

"Keep your voice down. Everyone will hear you." The control room was already teeming with techs coming back from their lunch breaks.

His eyes drilled into her. "Something is wrong between us. I know it, and you know it."

"Stop it." A hot flush crept up her cheeks. People were looking their direction. "Please."

"I sit here day after day. You sit over there," he indicated her laser terminal, "and we never touch, we never talk, we just go about our duties as if there is nothing between us. If I advance, you retreat. Hell, you don't even look at me anymore. What's the matter? Are you afraid I might smell cigarettes on your breath?"

"I quit smoking." The lie made her feel guilty. She didn't like lying to Janis, but cigarettes were at stake.

"You know I don't like it." He glared at her.

She hoped he was finished.

"Look," he said in a softer voice. "I know this has been tough on you, but that's no excuse. You're not the same person, Tracy. I want you back, the way you were before..."

"You should've thought about that before you roped me into this project. I was just fine where I was."

"In jail?"

"It was better than helping Brigham and his cronies destroy peace in the galaxy."

"I couldn't let him keep us apart."

"When are you going to understand, Janis? There are some things that are bigger than us, bigger than our love."

Janis sat back in his chair, mouth agape. "That's the scientist in you talking, Tracy. There's nothing bigger than our love. Nothing."

"Now you sound like Lisa."

"What's she got to do with this?"

Tracy raised an eyebrow. "She still loves you, doesn't she?"

"Lisa's never had any luck with love."

"That's not what I asked. Does she still love you, Janis?"

He sat there for a moment, thinking, then his eyes brightened, and he smiled. "Tracy, I'll be damned. You're jealous of Lisa."

"That's not it." She whipped around, her back to him now, and folded her arms across her chest. Janis had read her like a book, and worse, he was right. She didn't like being stuck in a jail cell while he was in California trouncing around with Lisa.

Sure, she trusted Janis, all right, but she didn't trust Lisa. No woman would. Worse, Tracy knew it wasn't Janis's problem. It was hers, her own insecurities at work. She'd never been this way, until now, powerless as she was to direct the course of events in her life. Brigham and jail and treason and aliens, everything had piled up on her. The stress, the nicotine fits, she had to let her frustrations out or explode, so in her mind, she'd made a big deal of Lisa, when the real problem was right here at NASA and what they had done. At that, she took a breath and turned to Janis who was leaning back in his chair, gloating. Everybody in the control room was watching them.

"Well?" he said. "You're jealous. Right?"

"A little," she replied, feeling better about being truthful with him.

He leaned forward. "I'm in love with you."

"I know, Janis, but Lisa isn't the problem. She was the scapegoat, and I'm sorry."

"Then what is the problem?"

"It's you."

"Huh?"

"You caved in to Brigham, and now look. He's killing aliens by the thousands."

"He was going to kill us if we didn't cooperate."

"He was bluffing," Tracy shot back.

"You don't know that."

"So what if he did kill us? How could our lives be so important compared to what he's going to do to the human race, not to mention the aliens?"

Janis shook his head. "I'm not ready to lose you, Tracy, not for the human race, not for the aliens, not for Brigham..."

"What greater cause is there to die for than saving the universe? Instead, you made me an accomplice, and you're trying to get Ray Crawford involved as well, and on top of that, you sit there and wonder if I still love you. What are you thinking?"

Janis slumped in his chair, a look of shock in his eyes. "I was just trying to keep us alive."

"In the meantime, Brigham is wreaking havoc on the green planet. It's your fault."

"It's Ray Crawford's fault. He's the one who started this."

"And it got him a life sentence in a bottle."

Janis leaned forward. "I don't like this any more than you do, Tracy, but we do what we have to do. We deal with it. We wait. We hope for the best in spite of the fact that it's going to get worse."

"Worse? What do you mean worse?"

Janis turned to his console, picked up a wooden toy, and handed it to her. It was a beautiful carving, a figurine of a long-fingered alien, and when she realized she'd seen this alien before on the space probe recording, she felt a jolt of dread. "Where did you get this?"

"Peterson carved it."

"That means he's seen Ray's recording."

"Exactly."

"But Brigham said it was Top Secret. Peterson is just a bully. How did he get access?"

"Because he's not who we think he is."

"Are you suggesting he's...he's Brigham's superior?"

Janis nodded. "And I don't think Brigham even knows it."

"But why?"

"It's obvious to me. He's going to bring back an alien."

"No shit?" Things were going to get worse, all right, but her mind kept tripping on any reason why Brigham would want an alien. "Why would he do that?"

"For Peterson." Janis pointed to the figurine.

"I don't understand." She gave it back to Janis.

He eyed the carving. "He's obsessed with aliens."

"So?"

"Peterson is aware of the nature of war. He was a Marine, a helicopter pilot, an educated officer, probably studied military history, or perhaps he works for someone who has this knowledge. He knows that prisoners of war will be inevitable. I think he told Brigham to make damn sure that happens."

"What can we do about it?"

"Like you said, save the universe." Janis held out his hand to her. "One alien at a time. Are you with me?"

She reached for his hand. "I love you, Janis."

He stood and pulled her close. "That's all I need to know."

Inhaling the scent of his cologne, she embraced him and kissed him hungrily.

The control room erupted in applause.

A door banged. Peterson bounded in. "Get back to work."

Chapter Eighteen

Heat escaping into the vacuum of space turned the air inside *Questnar* cold as the Ice Planet. Luthes shivered and rubbed his arms as he led the survivors and their Tarreeda captors toward the docking bay. The canted floor made running difficult. Worse, breathable atmosphere was leaking out through the damaged space shield at an alarming rate. *Questnar's* hull creaked and moaned. A total collapse was only moments away.

As he entered the docking bay, another fear knifed through his guts. Two Tarreeda Cruisers came into view. They were parked side-by-side and silhouetted against the star field outside the open bay doors. Their front windscreens glowed like menacing eyes. The sight tingled his nape hairs. He never thought he'd ever see a Tarreeda cruiser up close much less depend on one for his survival. Flashlight beams sliced through the dark docking bay and shown the way toward the cruisers.

Brigham was running on Luthes' right, breathing heavily behind his mask. Old Regarius was keeping up the pace, and behind them, wounded crewmates limped and stumbled along, aided by their Tarreeda captors. Dead bodies and scattered debris made the way an obstacle course.

"They're coming," someone said from under one of the cruiser's wings. Floodlights on the cruisers illuminated the disheveled docking bay and smoky air. Support girders had fallen from the deck flooring above. Bodies dangled from sagged wiring. When *Questnar* cartwheeled through

Terry Wright

space after *Latearian* exploded, everything that wasn't tied down had been violently tumbled around. The devastation saddened Luthes, his mighty patrol ship in shambles.

Brigham led him to a ladder that came down from an open hatchway on the side of the Tarreeda Cruiser. "Up. Up." Brigham said. "Hurry."

That was easier said than done. Luthes had never negotiated anything like this before. His long fingers made gripping the ladder rails difficult, but as he tried different techniques, he finally managed the dozen or so foot planks to the top where he was roughly grabbed by waiting Tarreeda and yanked aboard.

The air was much warmer, thicker, and easier to breathe, and Luthes gulped it in greedily. Only now did he get a good look around him, at the faces that were staring at him, a curiosity now. He stared back, even as he was directed away from the doorway. These creatures looked nothing like he'd read about, no dark skin, and no hairy faces. They looked as normal as any other Beltzan, except for their short fingers. The sight was so strange that Luthes felt compelled to stare in amazement.

Regarius came through the hatch next, followed by a bleeding crewman who wailed in pain.

"Medic," someone shouted.

That brought forward two Tarreeda, both wearing red armbands, each adorned with a white cross. Squatting on the floor with his back against a bulkhead, Luthes couldn't catch his next breath. The Tarreeda still adorned themselves with crosses. Though they were white and not black, and symmetrical, unlike the Tarreeda crosses he'd seen pictures of, the similarities were profound, yet not exactly right. He turned to Regarius who was now scrunched up beside him, rubbing his arms vigorously with his hands. "I'm still not sure these are the Tarreeda."

"They are," Regarius replied. "What more proof do you need?"

A Tarreeda with short yellow hair and a handsome face brought them blankets. As he bent over, a golden cross, a Tarreeda cross, swung down from a thin chain around his neck. "Cover your hands," he said with a sour look on his face.

Luthes cringed. He remembered reading how the Tarreeda wore crosses on chains around their necks, remembered the Tarreeda's disdain for the Beltzans' long fingers, how they were persecuted because of them. For the first time in his life, he felt ashamed, felt different, felt threatened for having long fingers. He quickly hid his hands under the blanket then slowly turned to Regarius who had done the same thing. "You are right," Luthes said. "These are the Tarreeda."

Brigham came through the hatch. "Close it up, boys."

As the hatch shut, the air pressure changed with a dramatic thud. A whining sound came from the cruiser's stern, and Luthes felt the ship lurch backward. Suddenly, he felt sick to his stomach. The blanket started to float off him, and he started to rise. Tarreeda drifted through the cabin as if they could fly. With terror gripping his insides, Luthes grabbed for handrails on the walls. It was obvious to him that the cruiser was not equipped with artificial gravity, and he was not accustomed to the sensation of weightlessness.

"Breathe deeply," Regarius said. He was holding onto a wall rail, his body parallel to the floor. "You will be all right." Then turning to Brigham he asked, "Where are you taking us?"

The Tarreeda leader peeled off his mask, revealing a heavy face and cold eyes. "To earth."

Luthes thought earth was the Tarreeda's name for one of the fourteen planets in their solar system. "Earth?"

Regarius said, "The Tarreeda's home planet."

Brigham asked, "What's a Tarreeda?"

"You," Regarius replied. "You are the Tarreeda. We banished your ancestors to the Ice Planet a thousand generations ago."

Brigham laughed. "We are humans from the planet earth, on the other side of the galaxy. Tarreeda. Humph."

"I could not be wrong about this," Regarius insisted.

"I knew it," Luthes said, his brain feeling a bit joggled. "I was right. They are not the Tarreeda."

Brigham called up to the flight deck. "Remsfield, deploy the Star Wars system. I want those PLRs in orbit right away."

"We're on it, sir."

"PLRs?" Luthes asked. "What are they?"

"Proton Laser Resonators. Satellite based particle beams."

"The death rays?" He'd seen them destroy *Latearian* and the fleet.

"Call it what you like. Any resistance from the planet's surface will be met with deadly force from space."

"But you do not understand. We are a peaceful people. There are no weapons down there."

Brigham grinned. "Then our invasion will be easy."

"I do not think so," Regarius said. "Fleet Base Commander Sangrean will not give up easily. They will hit you with every repulsor cannon they have."

"Then they'll die." Brigham plucked a communications device from the wall and pressed a switch with a gloved thumb. "All commanders, begin your surface assault." He replaced the device and turned to Luthes. "Back there in your ship," he said in a softer tone. "Well...I just want to thank you for helping us get out of there."

Luthes nodded but felt no comfort. Brigham's survival meant death and destruction on Beltzee.

"One thing I am curious about," Regarius said to Brigham. "Why do you humans attack us like this? We have done nothing to you."

"We want your teleportation technology," Brigham replied matter-of-factly.

"I wonder then," Regarius pressed. "Had you ever considered just asking us for it?"

"We aren't taking any chances on the strength of your defenses. Divide and conquer. It's called military strategy where we come from."

Regarius furrowed his brows. "We will never show you how it functions."

Brigham puffed out his chest with confidence. "We'll secure the planet and bring in our own scientists and technicians to reverse-engineer it."

"I fear that will not be possible," Regarius said. "It is too complicated."

Luthes agreed. The humans have wasted their time.

Brigham scowled. "You have other things to worry about. Once we get you back to earth, you'll be incarcerated and interrogated." He turned to the humans floating nearby. "Take these alien prisoners down to C deck and strap them in." He ducked through a hatch leading forward.

Regarius shouted to Brigham's back. "All this death has been for nothing."

As the humans approached to take them away, Luthes felt a great sorrow course through his veins. Verrilla and Sashi were dead. The inhabitants of Beltzee were about to be divided and conquered, and he and Regarius were to be taken to this planet called earth where violence was their way. Luthes wished he were dead.

***

Commander Sangrean stood between rows of consoles in Fleet Base Command on Beltzee. As Operations officers frantically attended to their duties, he tore off his dark glasses to better see the information displayed on the wall screens. Chatter was at a fever pitch, each officer relaying damage reports and casualty figures. The Tarreeda had returned in full force, and as it had been in the past, the death toll was rising fast.

In all his years, he'd never imagined this much destruction. The magnitude overwhelmed him. *Latearian* was gone. All aboard were lost. The fleet had been destroyed, and the Tarreeda had ambushed *Questnar* before they could get off a single repulsor round. Grief would have overcome him had it not been for the immediacy of the disaster, the shock that numbed his senses. And far more important than his own concerns were the needs of his personnel. They were counting on him in this time of crisis. Decisions had to be made...and made quickly.

Ground Operations officers loudly voiced their fears of a Tarreeda surface assault. "Repulsor batteries are on full alert," one said.

Another replied, "They are useless against the Tarreeda's death beams."

Another added, "Station perimeters must be fortified."

Someone else shouted, "We must evacuate the cities."

And so it went, on and on, mayhem, panic, and fear. The loss of the fleet had everyone stressed to the limit. Sangrean was powerless to ebb the tide of impending doom for his home world.

"The Judicials are online," a young Com officer said.

"Patch it into my office." Sangrean rushed to his desk. The door closed automatically behind him.

A hollow voice filled the room. "We trust you have matters under control, Commander."

Sangrean had no words to explain how dire their situation had become. "We are executing our planet defense initiatives."

"If you fail, you will be held accountable."

"I beg your pardon," Sangrean replied with respect. "I fear this responsibility will fall back on the Judicials. Your predecessors have brought this peril upon us."

"Our security was left to you and your fleet."

"If our ancestors had been allowed to blow the dam at Zarakatan and flood the valley where the Tarreeda were holed up, we would not have needed a fleet. Now they have returned, and our act of mercy has been set upon us like a plague. Worse, we have no lethal weapons with which to fend them off."

"Weapons are horrible things."

"We are doomed, and that is more horrible."

"Then it is Cada's will."

A Ground Operations officer banged on the door. "Commander, you must come see this right away."

"To Cada!" Sangrean said to his superior and broke the voice connection. He heard screaming outside.

"Hurry."

Following the officer, he joined a throng of personnel heading for the front doors. Everyone had abandoned their stations, and Sangrean knew they wouldn't have done that without good reason.

The flow of Beltzans burst outside and into a sunlit day. Panicked faces turned skyward, cupped hands shielding their eyes from the glare of both suns. Sangrean followed their gazes. Fireballs were dropping through the stratosphere, high up in the emerald sky, like comets with fiery tails. A chill shot through his insides. At first, there were four of these strange anomalies, then there were six, and now eight streaks of flame cut across the sky, moving from right to left at horrendous speed. Onlookers shrieked in horror. Some took off running, and others, like Sangrean, stood fast and watched the spectacle unfold. He knew exactly what was happening. Tarreeda Cruisers were entering the atmosphere.

The end was coming.

Taking his eyes from the enemy descending on his planet, he looked across the meadowlands of grain and berry bush to the horizon where sunshine glistened off the majestic spires of Benzatee, a city of economics and engineering, beautifully blue and crisscrossed with violet flightways. Feeling despair for the doomed inhabitants, he turned to his left where a long, wide band of granitite stretched into the distance. Rising from the plain, a battery of towering white repulsor cannons pointed skyward. Fifty of them stood like huge sentinels, all awaiting their call to repel the invading Tarreeda.

Beyond the repulsor cannons, the clear green waters of the Rissetan Sea sparkled. Sailing ships bobbed like corkswood in a dazzling display of multicolored masts, some harvesting the abundant fish runs, others transporting citizens and goods between the great and peaceful nations of Kedrikee, Retakan, Berakatee, and historic Zarakatan.

In the distance, the forest island of Odotzee stretched out to the horizon, a mecca of wealth in lumber and ore. The breeze blowing across the water was clear and pure and smelled of pine and wildflowers.

In his heart, Sangrean felt a great anger rise up, a feeling he had never experienced before. He knew he had to make a stand and meet the aggressors with as much malice as he could muster. He vowed to defend his home world against the Tarreeda until his dying breath.

Again he turned his attention to the sky where the plummeting fireballs faded one-by-one. Sunshine glinted off the invaders' spacecrafts as they made S turns on the way down.

BOOM! BOOM! Sonic blasts slammed to the ground. *BOOM! BOOM!* Again and again, the Tarreeda Cruisers broke the sound barrier.

A Com officer ran up to Sangrean, breathing heavily. "Kedrikee and Berakatee are reporting the same thing, Commander. It is a full-fledged Tarreeda attack."

Sangrean bared his teeth. "Mobilize all forces."

WHAMP! WHAMP! WHAMP!

Fleet Base repulsor cannons unleashed a barrage of white energy balls with a deafening roar. On the horizon,

Benzatee's defense repulsors shot a flurry of light balls skyward in a brilliant display. Death beams flashed from diving Tarreeda Cruisers. Parts of the city exploded and caught fire.

Sangrean sprinted back toward Operations and the battle to save his planet. Before he reached the door, a young yellow-haired Beltzan woman approached him at a full run with a small girl in tow. "Commander Sangrean," she called out. "Commander, wait. Have you news of my husband?"

"We have many casualties," he shouted over the repulsor cannons firing in the background.

WHAMP WHAMP WHAMP.

"Contact personnel. They should soon have a count."

"His name is Rez, Luthes Rez, from *Questnar*."

A Tarreeda Cruiser screamed overhead. Death beams flashed, and a nearby repulsor cannon exploded. Everyone hit the ground and covered their heads, everyone except Sangrean. With debris hurling through the air all around him, he resumed his dash toward Operations.

He didn't have time to tell the woman that *Questnar* had been destroyed.

Chapter Nineteen

I n orbit around the green planet, General Brigham watched through the shuttle's observation port as the last Star Wars satellite whirled from the cargo bay. A network of sighting dishes had already been deployed, insuring maximum coverage of the battle zones below. Operated by remote control from the Aerospace shuttles already engaging the aliens, the PLRs could dispatch the enemy from space with surgical precision.

Major Remsfield banked the shuttle to starboard and announced into the radio, "All commanders, orbital munitions activated."

Only a moment passed before the PLRs began firing particle beams at sighting dish satellites, which in turn reflected the beams to targets on the planet's surface. All hell was breaking loose down there, and Brigham longed to be a part of it.

However, his mission objectives were clear. He was now prepared to regenerate back to the earth to retrieve the scientists who would decipher the teleportation technology, and of course, he would turn over the captive aliens to Peterson. It was going to be one hell of a freak show.

"Ready when you are, General," Remsfield said, his hand on the regeneration control lever.

"You sure this thing is going to work?"

"Janis and Tracy have been right so far."

"Then let's go home, Major."

Remsfield engaged the regenerator, and the shuttle began to vibrate. A low-pitched rumble emanated from the onboard MIGGS and reverberated up from C deck, through middeck, and into the flight deck. Clutching the armrests of his chair, Brigham watched the green planet rotate outside the windshield. In the distance, two suns glowed against a background of embedded stars.

Then everything shrunk and disappeared as if the Aerospace shuttle had been slammed into reverse and accelerated at unbelievable speed. There was no sensation of motion inside the shuttle, no inertia, no dizzying centrifugal force as space narrowed into a swirling tunnel of starlight in which the shuttle dipped and yawed and rolled over and over.

"Yee haw!" Remsfield shouted, his gloved hands clutching the controls but having no affect on the shuttle's course.

They went down, down, down and around, around, and around. Seven seconds later, it ended. Brigham swallowed hard and darted his eyes about the flight deck. He expected to see instruments smoking and computer panels spewing sparks, but to his relief, everything was in order.

The crew cheered.

About five million miles away, earth drifted in the black soup of space. Sunlight illuminated half the planet, as well as half the moon. Brigham blinked in awe. From here, the earth looked small and fragile, and he briefly caught a hitch in his breath. He looked up as far as he could, and then down, and right and left. Other than the sun, there was nothing else close by, as if the little blue dot were alone in the universe.

"Whiskey-Xray, this is Houston. Do you read?"

"Roger, Houston," Remsfield replied.

"At 30 degrees north, contact approach on one-two-two-point-six."

"How about that?" Remsfield said. "One-two-two-point-six." He repeated his clearance, throttled up the pulse light engines, and steered the shuttle toward earth. "We should be down within an hour."

Brigham grumped. He was in a hurry to get back to the battle with his men on the green planet. Their primary objective was to take control of the aliens' teleportation facilities. It was the only way the shuttles could return to orbit where they could then be regenerated back to earth. And if the alien Regarius was correct about his Fleet Base not cooperating, Brigham knew he had to get his scientists there as soon as possible. He hoped they would be able to figure out how the alien's equipment worked. Otherwise, without launch pads or solid rocket boosters, no huge infrastructure to support a shuttle launch, they'd be stuck on the green planet forever. As he watched the earth balloon in the windshield, he felt suddenly homesick. The thought of living out his years on a strange planet so far from home made his stomach hurt.

Flying upside down, the shuttle entered orbit over India. Gazing out the windows, he watched the earth turn, bluer than any blue he'd ever seen. Asia peeked out from under bands of white clouds that stretched to the horizon, the edge of the atmosphere changing colors from the deep blue of the ocean to the blackest black velvet of space.

"Approach," Remsfield radioed. *"Whiskey-Xray* reporting 30 degrees north."

"Maintain heading one-five-zero miles. Begin your descent to Kennedy Space Center in two minutes."

"Roger, *Whiskey-Xray.*" Remsfield pulled back on the throttles. "Put your helmets on," he ordered over the intercom.

Brigham took another minute to watch the earth go by and marvel at what he saw. The mission had overshadowed everything that had happened on this foray into the 13th power, every magnificent sight he'd seen. Right now, he took in the sights before getting back to business.

"One minute to reentry."

At first he felt pity for all the helpless inhabitants of

the green planet, the pathetic aliens who couldn't defend themselves. Then he felt pity for the people on earth below, the wars they'd endured, the starvation and suffering, the terrorism, the crippled children. He could go on and on, and would have if one staggering reality hadn't come to mind. If not for misery, there could be no bliss. The strong ruled the weak. It was survival of the fittest. This was his world, and he was among the fittest. He rather enjoyed his superior position in the scheme of things.

"Thirty seconds."

He put his helmet on and settled back in his chair to await the ride down.

Somewhere above the Pacific, flying upside-down and backwards, the shuttle's pulse light engines fired. *Whiskey-Xray* shuddered, rolled on its belly, and began the fiery plunge back toward the surface. At 17,300 miles per hour, the shuttle hit the atmosphere, and the smooth ride became suddenly bumpy and violent. The view out the window turned from black to yellow, then orange, a sight that gave Brigham cause for alarm. Like a meteor, the shuttle was ripping electrons from the rarefied gasses in the upper atmosphere, which formed a plasma field around the hull so intense, it could be seen from the ground. Brigham felt suddenly isolated in this would-be fiery tomb. The shuttle creaked and moaned, but slowly he felt the pull of gravity come back, the weight of his body evident again.

Outside the windows, the fiery orange soon dissipated and darkness took its place, a darkness studded by twinkling stars above and clusters of city lights far below. They were somewhere over Texas in the dead of night, still traveling at over 12,000 miles per hour. Aerodynamic forces working on the shuttle were so tremendous that, if anything went wrong, the airframe could be ripped apart. The shuttle would literally disintegrate, and death would be instantaneous. It was an insane risk to take, one that the alien's teleportation technology would eliminate entirely.

"Whiskey-Xray with you, Houston," Remsfield radioed.

"Roger, Whiskey-Xray. Clear for your approach to Kennedy Space Center."

Gliding silently over Louisiana, the shuttle dropped out of the sky and made a series of radical S turns to bleed off airspeed. The pulse light engines were not needed for landing. Over Florida, green runway lights appeared in the distance, and the shuttle dove toward the ground steeply.

Whiskey-Xray buffeted and boomed as it decelerated through the sound barrier.

"Clear to land. Runway Three-Three," came over the radio.

Moments later, the shuttle coasted to a ghostly touchdown. The main gear contacted the concrete with a thud, and the drag chutes deployed. Then the nose gear hit with a solid bang.

The crew cheered.

Relieved, Brigham drew in a long breath.

"Houston. Wheels stopped."

"Welcome home, Whiskey-Xray."

***

Down on C deck, cheering humans sent a chill down Luthes' spine. Tied to his chair next to Regarius, he was sure they had landed somewhere, though he couldn't believe they had traveled across the galaxy to this place called earth in mere seconds. There was a great deal of commotion around the ship, and through a viewport, he could see humans milling about an area illuminated by bright lights. Strange-looking vehicles converged on the scene.

C deck was awash in a crimson glow. Along one wall and strapped into bunks, the wounded crewmen from *Questnar* moaned. Earlier, humans with crosses on their arms had attended to their injuries. Less-seriously injured men were strapped into seats behind him. Some had white bandages wrapped around their heads. One had his arm in a sling. He counted eleven men. Regarius looked scared to death. "We are going to be okay," Luthes said. "These humans are not the Tarreeda. They are probably not near as bad."

"Bad is still bad," Regarius said.

"By all rights, we should be dead already, like Verrilla and Sashi." Luthes fought back stinging tears as he remembered their smiles, their laughter, their warm arms embracing him, a happier time the humans had destroyed. "I do not know what I will do without my wife and daughter."

"A tragic loss," Regarius said and hung his head. "And ComCap Kerillan."

"He died in the Fleet's service, a brave defender of the League of Beltzee."

"To Cada," Regarius prayed. "It was His will. They are all with Him now."

That sounded comforting, but it left Luthes with a big empty spot in his heart. "Do you think we will ever see Beltzee again?"

"No."

The door opened. "Be careful, men. We've got some aliens in here." General Brigham came in first, followed by a man with a fire tube. "You're not going to give us any trouble, are you?"

Luthes shook his head. The others said nothing. They were untied, and at first Luthes felt relieved until some kind of metal clamps were put around his wrists. "These are not necessary," he said. "We will not fight you."

"Quit your babbling," the human with the fire tube said. He didn't have a translator on his collar.

"You're being transported to an isolated place for testing," Brigham said.

Regarius was subjected to the same hardware. "What kind of testing?"

"Microbiological for starters. We don't know what kind of bacteria you might be carrying. You could make us all sick."

"And what is to keep us from becoming sick because of your bacteria?"

"You will be properly immunized. Now move it. We have to get off this bird."

Roughly, they escorted Luthes out of the ship and down a ramp. Bright lights hurt his eyes. Strange little creatures spiraled in the lights. Around him, he could see nothing of this place called earth. His lungs took in air that was heavy with moisture, but there was something in the air that didn't feel right in his throat. He could smell the taint. He could taste it on the breeze. He didn't like it.

A clutch of humans approached. They were dressed in baggy white uniforms, white boots and gloves and transparent masks with breathing tubes. They gathered around him, threw a cape over his shoulders and put a mask on his face that made his breathing sound hollow. It stunk of some kind of disinfectant but relieved the irritation in his throat.

The white-suited humans ushered him into a box-like vehicle and made him sit on a bench seat against the wall. The doors shut, and with one human sitting on each side of him, the vehicle lurched into motion. Out the back window, Luthes caught a glimpse of Regarius boarding an identical vehicle in similar fashion. He wondered if he'd ever see the Specialist again.

As they sped off into the darkness, the humans said nothing to him or to each other. They just stared at his long fingers. He tucked them under the cape.

So far, the humans seemed genuinely interested in his health. The Tarreeda would have hung him on a cross by now. And he felt sure the humans were as curious about him as he was about them. Maybe they would send him home when they finished their tests, he hoped.

Then again, there was nothing left for him at home. His wife and daughter were dead, and his career was destroyed along with *Questnar* and the fleet. And after the human invaders finished their surface assault with those death beams, he feared there'd be nothing left on Beltzee but smoke and ash.

Sitting between his captors and hiding his fingers, he came to the somber realization that he'd have to face the reality of his situation. He was a prisoner on a foreign planet. He'd have to make the best of it. They were sure to feed him, clothe him, and see to his every need. How bad could that be?

Regarius's words came crashing back. *Bad is still bad.*

Chapter Twenty

In the employee quarters at NASA Aerospace, inside a room no bigger than a berth on a cruise ship, a ringing phone rousted Janis from his sleep. "Hello?"

"Brigham is back," Peterson said.

"Already?"

"He wants you in the control room."

"What for?"

"I'll send a car for you in thirty minutes."

"What about Tracy?"

"She'll be there."

"Christ." Janis hung up and looked at the clock on the nightstand. *4:30am.* He'd only slept three hours. The shuttles hadn't been gone very long, less than twenty-four hours. He yawned. Why did Brigham want him at this ungodly hour? Then a realization struck him. Brigham was back. The mission was successful. He was going to let them go home.

That was it. Of course.

Hardly able to contain his excitement, Janis showered and dressed in brown slacks and a white shirt. As he fixed his tie, whistling, a knock came at the door. He checked his watch. Only twelve minutes had passed since Peterson's phone call. The car shouldn't have arrived yet.

"Who is it?"

"Lo."

"Lo...?" Janis opened the door.

Lo stood in the hallway, barefooted and wearing his teddy bear pajamas.

"What are you doing here?"

"I got a call from a friend at flight operations." Lo pushed his way into Janis's room.

"I already know Brigham's back."

"But that's not all."

Janis wasn't interested in any new complications. He sat on his bed and pulled on his shoes. "All I care is that he's back safely. That was the deal. Then Tracy and I can go home. You too."

"No, no, Janis. My friend tell me there is something more. Hush, hush, top secret."

"What else is new?" Janis stood. "Everything around here is Top Secret. A car is on the way for me. I'm meeting Brigham and Tracy in the control room. We're going home."

"No, Janis. You can't go home."

"What are you talking about?"

"Aliens," Lo said and bowed. "My friend has seen them."

"I don't want to hear about it." He rechecked his tie in the mirror, as if that simple act would take him back in time to a point where they could start this conversation over. Of course he was going home. That was the deal. *Aliens?* How did that word enter this discussion? He was taking Tracy home. There were no aliens. It was too soon—

"Did you hear me, Janis?"

Janis retied his tie. Something about the knot wasn't quite right. He even took a moment to inspect under his chin to make sure he'd shaved the tough spots adequately.

"Brigham brought back aliens." Lo's persistence was annoying. "They're in quarantine right now. This is no bullshit."

"Jesus Christ." Denial tugged at the very core of his body. He was going to take Tracy home. But was he only lying to himself? They couldn't leave, not if they were going to save the universe one alien at a time. His worst fears had become a reality. "How many?"

"One is too many. Janis, you have to tell Ray."

"That worthless drunk. What can he do?"

"If you leave, you cannot do more."

It occurred to him that he may not have a choice in the matter. "Brigham's got what he wants. He has no more use for us. I've got a feeling he'll put us on a plane out of here whether we like it or not."

A rap on the door. The driver.

Janis grabbed his suit coat. "Fuck."

***

Janis strolled into the control room, calm and confident, though he was pissed off enough to spit nails. Brigham and Tracy were waiting at the SuperMIGGS console. Peterson looked up from a computer keyboard. Ceiling lights glowed brightly, and the aroma of coffee filled the air. The SuperMIGGS window was dark, and blinking incessantly, a red light on the regenerator terminal indicated no Aerospace shuttles were capable of regeneration. Fifteen had landed on the green planet and one had returned...with aliens.

"Great job." Brigham rolled a freshly lit cigar between his thumb and forefinger. "I was just telling Tracy how proud I am of you two. Not a hitch. Not a glitch. You brainards came through for me, for all of us."

"We're going home, Janis." Tracy wore her favorite gray pantsuit, the one she liked to travel in.

"Stan Burton and his team of engineers can handle the mission from here." Brigham looped a beefy arm around Tracy's shoulders and shook her. "And all charges have been dropped. My legal staff will have the papers drawn up by noon. Then you're free to go. Peterson will take you to the flight-line where your plane awaits."

The words Janis dreamed of hearing now sounded bitter. He didn't want to blurt out what he knew about the aliens. The security leak might be traced back to Lo Chin. That would get him and his friend thrown in jail, for sure...or worse. Janis studied the general a moment, wondering how to draw him into revealing the information himself. "How was your trip?"

"We can go home now," Tracy said. "Who cares about his trip?"

"We put a lot of work into this project. I just want to know how it turned out."

Brigham grinned. "It turned out just fine, Dr. Mackey. The surface assault should be wrapped up shortly."

"Any resistance?"

"Nothing we couldn't handle."

"And the aliens?"

Brigham examined his cigar. "There were casualties, of course."

"Any prisoners?"

"I'll say this," Brigham said. "We saw some beautiful things. The stars, the galaxies, the green planet, the spaceships, beautiful stuff."

Janis frowned. Brigham was dodging the question, and Janis wouldn't let him get away with it. "Did you have contact with the aliens?"

"You're going home. What difference does it make?"

"You killed them all, didn't you?" Janis probed for the right button to push. "You didn't take any prisoners."

"Now Janis, don't go jumping to conclusions."

Janis shoved a chair under a console. "He's nothing but a murderer, Tracy. And it's our fault. We sent him out there armed to the teeth, and he killed everything in sight."

"I told you he was going to slaughter them," Tracy added, her face scornful.

Puffing out his chest, Brigham protested. "I did not."

"Just wait 'til the press gets a hold of this. I'm going to blab it all over the country."

Peterson stepped up, his hand on the gun under his

black suit coat. "Talk like that will get you killed, Janis. What are you trying to pull?"

Brigham waved off Peterson and drew his own Colt. "I'll kill him myself."

Tracy stepped in front of Janis and grabbed his tie. "Why are you riling these guys? We can go home, so forget it."

"So much for saving the universe?"

"That's not fair, Janis. There's nothing we can do to stop these guys. What's done is done."

"And I was right about Brigham all along." Janis hoped to push the general over the edge. "He's nothing but a criminal with government backing."

"That's enough," Brigham shouted. "Peterson, get these two out of here. Make them disappear."

"They'll be alligator fodder by dawn, boss." Peterson grabbed Janis's arm.

Janis figured it was time to pull out all the stops. "What about the prisoners?"

Brigham sneered. "I killed them all, remember?" He pointed at Peterson. "Get them out of here."

"I'm talking about the aliens you brought back with you."

"Aliens?" Tracy said.

Now Peterson grabbed Tracy's arm. "He doesn't know what he's talking about."

Janis glared at Peterson. "You know what's going on here—"

"Shut up." He yanked Janis toward the control room door.

Janis pushed him back. "And you've got something to do with it."

"What are you implying?" Brigham cocked his head. His eyes were glaring mad.

The best Janis could do now was press the issue. "I want to see the aliens you brought back."

"Who told you about the aliens?" Brigham's voice was low and menacing.

"I guessed," Janis hissed. "And I'm right, aren't I? Your type can't resist bringing back a trophy from the greatest hunt in history."

"Janis?" Tracy looked pallid, as though she might faint. "Tell me they didn't...oh my God."

"So you see," Brigham said. "I didn't kill them all."

"Why did you bring them back?" Janis shouted.

"I had my orders, too." Brigham puffed his cigar while eyeing Janis and Tracy. "But it's not your problem."

Peterson jerked Janis around, went face-to-face with him. "Who told you about the aliens?"

"A little birdie."

"Do you hate living?" Peterson asked. "You know I'll kill you—"

"Stuff it." Janis was sick of Peterson's threats. He glared at Brigham. "What happened up there?"

Leaning on a console, Brigham crossed his arms. "I don't have to tell you anything."

"We're going to be alligator bait anyway, so what's the harm?" Janis was counting on Brigham's ego, his inability to resist the opportunity to brag about his exploits in space. Peterson shoved Janis toward the door and pulled Tracy along. "We deserve that much, General."

"Give them a minute," Brigham said and smiled.

Peterson jerked them to a stop. "They don't need to know anything."

"We encountered a huge alien spaceship. It was beat up pretty bad, venting gases from a particle beam hole we'd blasted through its hull. Its bow opened up, like the one we saw on Ray's recording, in fact, it might have been the same ship."

Janis recalled the recording and the spaceship with the huge bow doors. "You went in the spaceship?"

Brigham nodded. "We found some aliens who gave

me this." He pointed to a round device on his collar. "It's a translator. I actually talked to them."

"My God." Janis had heard him but could not believe the words that came out of his mouth.

"They warned us their spaceship was about to explode. We were in a tight fix, and then everything went dark. The aliens led us back to our shuttle, saved our lives, you could say. So we loaded them up and got away just before their spaceship exploded."

"What about the other ships?" Tracy asked. "There must've been a hundred on that recording."

"The big one was the last holdout."

Tracy frowned. "You destroyed them all?"

"You want to hear this story or not?"

"I'm sorry. Please, go on."

"The aliens told us what we needed to know for the surface assault, and being the honorable soldier that I am, I brought them back here rather than dispatch them in space."

"How big of you, General." Janis didn't care if he sounded sarcastic. "But I think you and Peterson planned taking prisoners all along."

"Nobody cares what you think."

"I want to see them."

"What for?"

"They're going to need help getting back home."

"Are you out of your mind?" Now Brigham's voice boomed. "They're in quarantine."

"How many are there?"

"Thirteen."

"My God." Tracy put a hand on her heart.

"But two of them might not make it. They were shot up pretty bad."

"We've got to help them," Tracy said.

"They don't need your help." The tone of Brigham's voice chilled the air. "And they're not going home. Ever."

That only made Janis more determined. "Then neither am I." He looked at Tracy. "Are you with me on this?" Of course he knew she would be. He just wanted to give her the chance to say it for herself.

"Now wait a minute," Peterson jumped in. "You two have a date with a gator."

It was obvious to Janis that Peterson was putting on a show for Brigham, but Janis didn't understand why. After all, Peterson knew about the aliens. The carved figurine proved that he'd seen Ray's recording. But why was he privy to it? And what government agency did he work for? There must've been a plan in place to get the aliens here, and it was probably illegal, or at the very least it didn't have Congressional approval. If that was the case, General Brigham could spend the rest of his life behind bars. With that thought, Janis decided to play the angle. "We can help you guys get out of this mess you're in."

"What mess?"

Janis held up a finger. "One: Congress has not declared war against the green planet. Two," another finger: "The green planet had not declared war on us." Another finger: "Three: you are holding prisoners of war illegally, a war that has not been declared." And another finger: "Four: I'm just a mathematician, but that adds up to an illegal invasion, false imprisonment, and violation of the aliens' civil rights. How long do you guys want to spend in jail?"

"You're full of shit, Janis. You aren't a lawyer. What do you know?"

"I'm an American, same as you, and you know I'm right."

Brigham regarded Peterson a moment, then Tracy and again Janis. "What do you propose?"

Peterson didn't say anything. He was holding his breath.

"Tracy and I will get with Stan and prepare the

transporter...the one Ray took into the 13th Power. It'll need to be fitted with a heat shield and landing gear."

"Then what?" Brigham asked.

"When the prisoners have recovered sufficiently, we'll send them back where they belong. A one-way trip. No one will be the wiser."

"I don't like it," Peterson put in. "The aliens don't know how to fly the transporter."

"Ray could teach one of the aliens."

"That drunk?"

"I'll sober him up. What do you say? After all we've done for you, let us do something for them."

"The aliens aren't going anywhere," Brigham said.

"Why are they so important to you guys?" Tracy asked.

"That's none of your business," Peterson shot back.

Brigham said, "We could send them back when you're done with them."

Peterson glared at Brigham. "The aliens are not going back."

That pretty much laid out the pecking order between these two guys. Peterson was calling the shots. But why? Janis asked him, "Can we see the aliens?"

"No."

Brigham cleared his throat. "What's the harm?" he asked Peterson. "Without them you wouldn't have your aliens. Show a little appreciation."

"General, don't fall for their malarkey."

Brigham snuffed out the cigar on the heel of his boot. "Any funny business, you have my permission to kill them."

"I don't need your permission."

"Quit being such a hard ass. It's unbecoming."

Peterson relented and released their arms.

Tracy rushed into Janis's embrace.

He glanced at Peterson. The guy wasn't all bad. He

had an agenda, for sure, but maybe he had some self-imposed penance to pay for the death of his wife, and it just might have started with cutting him and Tracy some slack, and the aliens too, hopefully.

***

As the sun rose over Florida, Janis pulled himself out of the staff car and inhaled the salty smell in the cool and damp morning air. Tracy and Brigham got out, and Peterson shut off the engine. They all joined him in front of a corrugated steel warehouse painted blue.

"It doesn't look like much from the outside," Brigham said.

A lieutenant met them at the door. His nametag read *Swanson*. "Welcome to SIU," he said and let them in. The reception room was painted brilliant white, top to bottom.

Janis asked, "What is this place?"

"The Sterilization and Isolation Unit," Swanson said. "Part of NQF, the NASA Quarantine Facility. It was designed to quarantine anything we might bring back from Mars. Before the expansion project two years ago, moon rocks spent a lot of time here. They weren't much of a bother, but our newest guests, well, that's a different matter."

"Are they combative?" Peterson asked.

"On the contrary. It's just that they require intensive medical care."

"We're here to see them," Brigham said.

"This way."

"Go ahead," Peterson said. "I need to use the computer."

Janis, Tracy, and Brigham followed Lieutenant Swanson. They passed through a security door, traversed a white hallway, and entered a room with a glass wall. Dim lighting allowed for a better view of the well-lit area on the other side of the windows. Technicians wearing white protective clothing and hooded masks moved around an area that looked like a hospital ward. People lying in the beds were covered with white sheets up to their necks. Janis counted thirteen of them. A few beds were equipped with IV bottles, and heart monitors stood nearby, beeping.

"Where are the aliens?" Janis asked.

Swanson pointed to the window. "You're looking at them."

"But they look just like us."

"Wait until you see their hands. They're spooky."

"Long fingers," Brigham said, wiggling his fingers.

"Are they sick?"

"Hyponatremia," Swanson explained. "Depleted sodium levels in their blood. Potassium levels are sky high. The doctors are giving them saline injections and salt tablets."

Tracy asked him, "Will they be all right?"

"I don't know. They're not getting any better."

Through the glass, one alien locked his gaze on Janis, then lifted his head from the pillow and tilted it slightly. Gray hair stuck out over his ears. Janis felt the alien's stare, and though it gave him an unsettling chill, he couldn't bring himself to break eye contact. The only thing he could think to do was give the alien a slight nod. The alien returned the gesture, put his head back down, and closed his eyes. Janis's heart raced. "How long do they have to stay in there?" he asked Swanson.

"Until we're certain they aren't carrying an alien virus that could wipe out the population. A few days, maybe a couple of weeks."

"And if they have a virus, what then?"

"All of them and everything in that room will be incinerated."

Janis glared at the general. "Jesus Christ, Brigham."

"Don't look at me," he said, frowning. "I don't make

the rules."

Tracy groaned. "How are we going to help them?"

"Don't worry about it," Brigham replied. "From the looks of them, my guess is they won't last a week."

Janis shuddered. A week didn't give him much time. "I've got to go back to California."

"What for?"

"Ray Crawford might know how we can help them."

Tracy said, "He's a lost cause, Janis."

"I've got to try. You stay here and watch over them." He indicated the aliens. "I'll be back in two days."

"Peterson's going with you," Brigham said.

"I don't need a babysitter."

"And I don't have the time or patience to argue with you. I've got to get back to the green planet. Stan and his men are installing a passenger module for the scientists into the shuttle's cargo bay as we speak. In the meantime, I'm going to get some rest. He executed a military about-face and walked out.

Janis turned to Tracy and flinched when he saw that an alien had walked up to the window behind her. He wore a white hospital gown and looked sickly pale. His hair was cut short, and he had a dimple in his chin, round nose, and brown eyes.

Tracy must've sensed Janis's surprise. She whipped around, staggered backward, and almost tripped. He steadied her by the elbow and stared in awe at the alien's long fingers. Spidery and fluid-like in motion, they were beckoning him to come near the glass. "What does he want?" Janis asked under his breath.

"You'll need one of these." Swanson clipped a device to Janis's shirt collar. "It's a translator. Go ahead. Say hello."

"You've got to be kidding."

"No, it's all right."

Janis stepped to the window and right away noticed

the alien had a similar translator attached to his hospital gown.

"My name is Luthes Rez," the alien said, his voice muffled behind the glass.

Janis understood the alien perfectly. "I'm Dr. Mackey, and this is my wife Tracy."

Luthes glanced at her, nodded, and returned his attention to Janis. "I was the helmsman aboard *Questnar*, the mightiest Orbital Patrol Ship in the fleet."

Janis touched the translator on his collar, amazed at the technology the aliens possessed.

"What did he say?" Tracy asked.

"Something about a patrol ship, helmsman," Janis told her and then said to Luthes Rez, "I'm a mathematician here at NASA. Welcome to earth." Boy did that sound corny.

"I am not happy to be here," Luthes replied. "Your human counterparts have destroyed my ship. They have killed my wife and daughter, and they have made me a prisoner on this planet where the air bites my throat. I certainly hope your day was much better than mine."

Janis didn't know what to say. The tragedy befallen this alien was greater than anything he could have imagined. He felt heavy-hearted and gravely responsible.

"What did he say?" Tracy asked.

"You don't want to know." Janis didn't have the heart to tell her.

"I want to go home," Luthes said.

"The green planet, is that your home?"

"Beltzee, yes. We are sick in this place called earth. We must go home before we die here."

"The doctors are trying to help you."

"Let us go home." Luthes put his hands up, his palms flat on the glass. "Please let us go home." Tears trickled down the alien's face.

Janis stepped back, his heart wrenching at the pitiful sight before him. He could hardly breathe. For all the things they'd accomplished, all the science, and all the discoveries, none were worth this alien's suffering.

"Let us go home," Luthes cried out.

Masked technicians rushed to the window and subdued Luthes, dragged him back to his bed and strapped him down.

Removing the translator from his collar, Janis looked at Tracy. "You were right. We shouldn't have helped Brigham do this, even if it meant losing our lives. I'm sorry I didn't listen to you."

"What are we going to do?"

He handed Lieutenant Swanson the translator. "We'll be back."

***

The next morning in California, rain came down in straight lines, a gloomy drizzle that matched Janis's mood. A frigid ocean breeze tugged on his suit coat as he stood on Ray's front porch and banged on his door. Peterson waited in the rented Ford parked across the street, whittling another alien figure.

"Come on, Ray. Open up."

"Go away," he shouted from inside.

"I'll break down the door, I swear."

"I don't want anything to do with you sons of bitches, now go away."

A car door slammed. Janis turned, startled, and then saw Lisa running toward the porch, a basket of laundry wrapped in her arms. She wore a white tank top, blue short shorts, and white sandals. Long blond hair trailed behind her.

"What are you doing here?" she said breathlessly as she ducked onto the porch.

"I need Ray's help."

"Good luck." She keyed the lock. "Come in if you can

stand the smell of him." She pushed open the door.

"Get the hell out of here." Ray was sitting at the kitchen table in his underwear, hunched over a bowl of cereal. His hair went every which way. A bottle of Jack Daniels sat within easy reach. "Can't a man eat in peace?"

Janis stormed through the front room, grabbed a chair, and sat at the table with Ray. "Got an extra bowl?"

Lisa took a bowl from the cupboard and found Janis a spoon. He grabbed the box of Raisin Bran off the table. "I haven't had this since I was a kid." Ray just glared at him through booze-red eyes while Janis poured cereal into the bowl. "Remember when we were in college?"

Ray said nothing.

"Professor VanBlought got us thinking about the possibilities of the 13th Power, set a challenge before us, and let us go at it." Janis poured milk on the cereal. "You were really something back then, you know. With fire in your eyes, you went about conducting experiments that you believed in, to the point of obsession, if I remember correctly."

Ray just stared at him.

"And the Board of Trustees, now those guys really got your negative electrons flowing. When they cut funding for the project, I thought you were going to blow a gasket."

"I did blow a gasket," Ray said, his face tightening. "The bastards wouldn't listen."

"You were so mad, you lit out of there like the place was on fire."

"I had no use for them, like I've got no use for you or those NASA bastards."

"Nothing was going to stop you from achieving your goal. The 13th Power, man, you lived and breathed the theories, the possibilities."

"That was a long time ago." He chucked a spoonful of Raisin Bran.

"Your dream came true, Ray, but look at what it's

done to you."

"Never mind how I look." He reached for the bottle of Jack.

Janis stopped him with a firm hand on his arm. "The aliens are here, Ray. I've seen them. I've talked to one of them."

Ray dropped his spoon.

"The long-fingered aliens," Janis pressed. "Remember, from the green planet?"

"They're here, Dad. Our aliens."

Ray looked at Lisa blankly.

"That green planet has a name," Janis said. "It's called Beltzee. And the alien has a name too. It's Luthes Rez. He said he was the helmsman of that spaceship you encountered when you were in the transporter. The pilot, Ray."

"He could have killed us, Dad, but he didn't."

"My God," Ray said.

"Luthes told me that his ship was destroyed, and his wife and daughter were killed. And you know what else he said to me, Ray? He said he hoped I had a better day than he did. Now you tell me, why do you think he said that?"

Ray just sat there with a faraway look in his eyes.

"He wants to go home, Ray. There are twelve others with him, most wounded in varying degrees of severity." Janis leaned forward. "And they're sick. Our air hurts their throats. They want to go home. They want to live. Then there's you, Ray Crawford. Look at you. You're a disgrace."

Scowling, Ray yanked his arm free of Janis's grasp. "You don't understand."

"You're pathetic," Janis said. "And what's your excuse? You lost your wife. Well, Luthes Rez lost his wife too, and his daughter. He's got nothing, Ray, except his dignity, which is more than I can say for you. Here you sit wallowing in self-pity, drinking yourself into a stupor every day, and treating the rest of us like garbage." Janis wanted to reach across the table and knock some sense into him. "You still have your daughter. You still have your health, which is more than I can say for Luthes Rez."

Brows flexed, Ray looked at Janis. "They're sick?"

"The doctors say there's not enough salt in their blood. Saline injections and salt tablets aren't helping them get better."

Ray's eyes opened wide. "Damn." He knocked over his cereal bowl, spilling Raisin Bran everywhere. "They're poisoning them."

"What?"

Ray looked mad as hell and somewhat sober. "Sodium chloride, Janis. It's foreign to them."

"How do you know that?"

"I remember the space probe's surface analysis indicated fresh water on the green planet."

"Beltzee," Janis corrected him.

"No salt."

"Salt. It's no wonder the aliens are sick," Janis said. "The ocean air..."

"Not to mention the food." Ray grabbed the box of Raisin Bran and read the nutrition label. "Look. Three hundred fifty milligrams sodium." He tapped the box. "It's alien rat poison."

"The doctors are pumping them full of the stuff." Janis looked at his uneaten bowl of cereal. "They need a no-salt diet."

"Salt is a staple of life on earth, so common that we never give it any thought. Every living thing depends on salt in one form or another, for cell osmosis, digestion and metabolism, and nerve and muscle functions."

"But not on Beltzee. Their entire body chemistry must be different from ours."

"You have to get them out of Florida," Ray said. "Someplace like Colorado. Boulder is at high altitude and a long way from the ocean."

That was a good idea...and doable. "I'll work out something with the university. I can pull some strings with the board, make some arrangements—"

"No you won't!" Peterson's voice boomed from the kitchen door. "The aliens aren't going anywhere."

"I thought you were waiting in the car."

Ray frowned. "Bring some muscle with you this time, Janis?"

"He's my babysitter."

Peterson sneered. "It's my job to see that he doesn't talk to the press. Now I find him plotting to take the aliens to Colorado. I warned you, no funny stuff."

"They're going to die," Janis said.

"What do you mean?"

"Florida is killing them," Ray said. "It's the salt. We need to move them."

"You can't have direct contact with the aliens." Peterson said it with authority.

Janis knew that exposing the aliens to the outside world could result in a plague of biblical proportions. "Of course. We have to be sure it's safe first."

"I'm not talking about safety," Peterson said. "It's against the law."

"What?"

"Title 14, Section 1211 of the Code of Federal Regulations, the Extra-Terrestrial Exposure Law. On July 16, 1969, Congress made it illegal for anyone to make contact with aliens."

"You're shittin' us," Ray said.

Janis blinked. How would Peterson know that such a law existed? "Who are you working for?"

"The aliens," he said.

"Then they need your help."

"Brigham won't allow them to leave Florida."

Janis frowned. "Don't you mean you won't allow it?"

Terry Wright

"You're not making any sense, Dr. Mackey."

"I think you're in charge of this operation." Janis slammed his hand on the table.

Ray jumped.

"You don't know anything about me."

"I know your wife is dead."

Peterson scowled. "Leave her out of this."

Ray said to Peterson, "My wife is dead, too."

"Welcome to the club," Peterson replied.

"Kate was gunned down by a drug dealer's father. What happened to your wife?"

"She died in a plane crash." Peterson clenched his fists. "I was the pilot. A cable broke. I couldn't keep the plane in the air."

"Must've been terrible," Ray said.

"I haven't flown since. Can't take the responsibility anymore."

Ray asked, "Do you visit her grave? Talk to her?"

"No."

"I visit Kate's grave," Ray said. "I miss my wife."

"Is that why you drink so much?"

"I handle it my way." Ray fiddled with his spoon.

"You're not an alcoholic," Peterson said. "You're an escape artist."

"And you turned into some kind of tough guy?"

Peterson yanked his hands from his pockets and stepped forward.

"That's enough," Janis said, having discovered a common link between the two men. "Luthes lost his wife, too. Now he's going to die if we don't help him."

"Dad, we have to do something."

Janis leaned back in his chair. "Tracy and I are going to help them get home."

"I thought Brigham arrested her for treason."

"All charges have been dropped," Janis said. "Are you going to help us, Ray?"

"Why do you need my help?"

"Stan will get the transporter ready. I need you to teach Luthes how to fly it. It'll save their lives."

"The aliens could have killed us," Lisa reminded Ray. "Return the favor."

"All right." He pushed his chair away from the table. "Make some coffee. I'll be in the shower."

"I'm going to NASA with you, Dad."

"I wouldn't have it any other way." Standing up straight, he made his way toward the bathroom with as much dignity as any man could muster when dressed only in his underwear.

Lisa gave Janis a thumbs-up sign.

He felt a ray of hope.

Peterson sat in a chair at the table. "I can't authorize you to send them back."

"Then get someone who can." Janis passed him the cereal box.

With furrowed brows and narrow eyes, Peterson stared at the Raisin Bran like a man with a lot on his mind.

Chapter Twenty-One

At Fleet Base Command on Beltzee, the entire battery of repulsor cannons lay in twisted heaps of charred ironite, forever silenced by the Tarreeda. In the distance, plumes of smoke rose from the magnificent city of Benzatee. Refugees, hungry and terrified, poured into the countryside. There were no emergency services available to provide care for them. After all, this invasion should never have happened. The fleet should have repelled the Tarreeda, but no one was prepared to go up against weapons of such destructive power.

Having witnessed the carnage on multiple viewers, Sangrean slumped over his communications terminal in total despair. The devastation was the same all around the planet. The powerful Tarreeda had overwhelmed the League of Beltzee, destroyed its meager defenses, and set most major cities on fire. Reports of roaming assassination squads soon poured in, the atrocities of murder, rape, and arson being a common denominator as the invaders advanced from one island nation to the next, pillaging as they went. Never in his worst dreams had Sangrean ever thought something this horrible could have happened on his watch.

His Operations control room lay in shambles, running on backup power. Electronics short-circuited and spewed sparks. Sharp rays of sunlight shot down from holes burned through the roof and walls. All around him, an acrid haze drifted in the air, so thick he could taste it in the back of his throat. The smell of molten ironite and burned flesh made his stomach turn over.

Surviving crewmen and Operations officers began sifting through the rubble in search of wounded comrades. "Medical," someone called out.

A wounded crewman moaned.

"Commander?" Someone tapped his shoulder. "Commander, are you all right?"

Sangrean looked up, relieved to see his wide-eyed communications officer staring at him. As Sangrean sat upright, a sharp pain knifed through his left shoulder. "I must have caught a flying chair or something." Rubbing the ache, he got to his feet. "Get me a casualty report as soon as you can."

"Yes, sir."

"And..." He paused suddenly remembering the yellow haired woman and her child asking about Luthes Rez, just as the attack began. They were lying on the ground out front when he last saw them.

"Sir?"

"Never mind." Sangrean headed for the front doors, kicking debris aside as he made his way down the darkened hallway. He had to step aside as a rescue crew barreled toward Operations, toting stretchers, fire extinguishers, and ladders. The outside doors hung bent and crooked on their hinges. A part of him wanted to stay inside Fleet Base headquarters, but he needed to know if Luthes' wife and daughter had survived the attack. Clenching his jaw, he pushed the broken doors aside and stepped into sooty daylight. Smoke from fires burning throughout the compound blackened the sky. Bodies were strewn everywhere, some still smoldering. A lot of them were easily recognizable, duty crewmen and Operations technicians who had made a run for it. He could tell by the color of their scorched uniforms. Other victims' remains were in horrific condition, dismembered and charred to the bones. They had been nothing more than target practice for the attacking Tarreeda.

As he approached the area where he'd last seen Luthes' wife and daughter, his heart suddenly clutched. Two bodies, one larger than the other, were slumped together on the granitite, smoke curling from their charred remains. Sangrean felt deathly ill.

"They are coming back," the communications officer shouted from the doorway.

A Tarreeda Cruiser screeched overhead, banked to port, and descended to the granitite where the repulsor cannons once stood. Tires barked and threw smoke. A drag shoot deployed. Seconds later, another cruiser dropped from the sky and landed, then another, and another.

Sangrean looked once again at the remains of Luthes' family. "Cada be with you." He dipped his chin, turned, and sprinted toward the door.

"What are we going to do?" the officer yelled.

"Surrender," Sangrean said. "I want all my officers out here at once. Parade formation. And no stun-wands."

"Yes, sir."

Turning to the Tarreeda Cruisers, which were taxiing toward him in single file, Sangrean wiped dust from his uniform sleeves, stood up straight, thrust his chin forward and hoped he had the strength to keep from falling to his knees at the Tarreeda's' feet. He knew that life on Beltzee had been altered forever. He blamed himself for that. As Fleet Base Commander, he had failed to thwart the enemy invasion. Whatever the punishment for that might be, he hoped he had the courage to face it with dignity.

***

Inside the SuperMIGGS, Brigham stood on the boarding ramp to *Whiskey-Xray* and took one last look around. Stan Burton and his team had installed a crew module into the shuttle bay in record time. One hundred fifty of the world's top scientists, mechanical engineers, and electronics experts were already onboard. It would be their job to decipher the alien's teleportation system and ensure the Aerospace shuttles' ability to return to earth. Something fluttered deep in the pit of his stomach as he worried that he would never again set foot on this planet. Regarius had told him that the teleportation system was too complicated to decipher. Failure would mean he could never leave Beltzee. Vowing not to fail, Brigham tapped his boot on the hatch's threshold and stepped inside the shuttle.

"Houston Departure," Major Remsfield said into the radio.

Brigham strapped himself into his seat. Two mission specialists secured the entry hatch.

"*Whiskey-Xray* is ready to go on your mark."

"*You're clear for degeneration, Whiskey-Xray. Have a nice flight.*"

The SuperMIGGS ceiling lights went out, and a crimson glow filled the steel chamber.

Brigham held his breath.

***

Sangrean heard the footfalls of his top officers as they assembled behind him. "Remember, Beltzans, whatever happens, you have served the League of Beltzee with honor. If Cada wills it, may you die with honor."

"Yes, sir," they replied in unison.

Sangrean thought to turn and face his officers, but he didn't want to see the fear in their eyes. Dread pumped through him as the massive cruisers approached, their engines whining, their huge wheels rolling toward them. They didn't attempt to steer around the bodies lying in their paths. They just ran over them, leaving gruesome stains on the granitite tarmac.

Within moments, the cruisers lined up wingtip-to-wingtip and coasted to a stop in front of the wrecked building that once was the vibrant hub of Fleet Base Command. Hatches came open. Ladders dropped to the ground.

Sangrean swallowed hard. He was about to see a Tarreeda for the first time, a prospect that sent a chill down his spine. They would erect their crosses somewhere nearby, and after a lengthy and painful interrogation, they'd hang him and his officers up to die a slow and torturous death.

First down the ladders came swarms of Tarreeda dressed in forest-colored uniforms. They hit the ground and fanned out, forming a line in front of Sangrean and his officers. The invaders wore helmets and carried strange weapons in their short-fingered hands. Sangrean's heart beat faster at the sight before him, the overwhelming number of Tarreeda now gathered around, their dark eyes glaring.

The next Tarreeda down the ladder appeared to be an officer, because he commanded the respect of several invaders who raised straightened fingers to their eyebrows and drew them away with a quick jerk.

"Colonel Scott, they are offering no resistance," a Tarreeda reported.

Sangrean's knees felt suddenly weak. His translator had translated the Tarreeda's words. Then he noticed the Colonel had a translator clipped to his collar and wondered how he'd come by it. But more important, Sangrean could communicate with him. "Colonel Scott," he said. "I am Sangrean, Commander of Fleet Base Operations for the League of Beltzee. I beseech you to spare my crewmen and officers."

Stepping up to Sangrean, the Tarreeda Colonel glared at him eye-to-eye. "Nobody gave you permission to speak, soldier."

Never before had he seen such a hateful look as the

Tarreeda Colonel gave him. "But it is my duty—""

"Silence." Then turning to his line of Tarreeda, the Colonel barked out, "First Squad, clear the building. Second Squad supply cover fire if they run into resistance."

"Yes, sir." The squads formed, and they ran toward the building.

Sangrean was concerned about the weapons they carried in with them. He spoke up. "My men are inside collecting the dead and wounded. They will not fight you, Colonel."

Scott whipped around, a scowl on his face. "What are you, stupid?" His boots stomped the ground, and a fierce growl came from his throat as he approached. "I warned you not to speak."

"But force is not necessary."

"Baker."

"Yes, sir," a Tarreeda answered from the ranks.

"We need to teach this alien a lesson. Do the honors."

"Who, sir?"

Scott frowned. "Your choice."

"Yes, sir."

The Tarreeda named Baker came forward, his weapon held out and pointed at the communications officer whose face suddenly drained of color. "That one."

Two Tarreeda comrades stepped forward and yanked the officer out of line behind Sangrean, brought him to the front of the formation, and shoved him to his knees.

"Let this be a lesson to all of you," Colonel Scott shouted.

Baker put the end of his weapon to the officer's head.

Before Sangrean could figure out what was happening, a sudden explosion eruptcd from the weapon, knocking the officer over on his side. Blood gushed from a hole in his head. Having never seen anything like this before, Sangrean succumbed to a wave of nausea. He fell to his hands and knees and vomited violently.

The Tarreeda laughed at him. Colonel Scott kicked him in the ribs. "You're all a bunch of girl scouts."

Pain shot through Sangrean's insides. "We are Beltzans."

"Stand up and fight, you coward."

Sangrean's officers stepped back, their eyes wide with shock.

"Get up." Scott bent over Sangrean and yanked him to his feet. "Show some backbone."

"Do with me as you will," Sangrean snarled. "I will die with honor as did my communications officer." He could only hope his gutsy stand would help fortify his remaining officers, whom he was sure would also fall victim to the Tarreeda's wrath.

Scott pulled a similar weapon from a pouch on his belt. "I'll kill you myself."

Suddenly, a speaker squawked. *"Golf-Hotel. This is General Brigham. Come in, Colonel Scott."*

With sweat beading on his forehead, the Colonel ignored the call and pointed the weapon at Sangrean's head.

"Colonel Scott. Do you read me?"

Another Tarreeda approached with a handheld communications link. "You'd better take this, sir."

The Colonel sneered at Sangrean. "Must be your lucky day." He returned his weapon to his pouch and took the call. "General Brigham, your timing is impeccable."

Sangrean took a much-needed breath.

"Send up your coordinates."

"Yes, sir."

It appeared to Sangrean that the Colonel had a superior. With any luck, this General Brigham might put an end to the Colonel's homicidal behavior.

Scott said into the link, "Navigation, send him a fix."

"Right away, sir."

At that, the Colonel returned his attention to Sangrean.

"Just wait 'til Brigham gets here. He'll hang you out to dry."

Visions of crosses came to Sangrean's mind. Any hope he'd held for a reprieve evaporated. They were all going to die, arms spread and wrists nailed to Tarreeda crosses.

First Squad came out of the building with captured crewmen in front of them. "Second Squad is making a final sweep," a Tarreeda reported to the Colonel.

"Get these aliens in line with the others."

"Here he comes," someone said, pointing to the sky.

A fireball shot across the stratosphere, arching into the pull of Beltzee's gravity. Sangrean didn't understand how a Tarreeda cruiser could withstand that kind of heat and pressure on reentry. Within moments, the fiery streak dissipated.

BOOM!

A Tarreeda Cruiser appeared, glinting sunshine from its fuselage. Wheels came down from its belly as it turned on final approach, and within seconds, touched down on the flat of granitite, its tires throwing smoke and a drag chute straining in its slipstream.

Sangrean turned to his officers and gave them a reassuring nod, though he wasn't entirely sure it would do any good. He was proud of his men. He wanted them to know that.

The cruiser rolled to a stop. A ladder came out, and a burly Tarreeda emerged. He had little stars on his collars, as well as a translator. This totally confused Sangrean. He could think of no logical reason why the Tarreeda had translators.

"What happened here?" the general asked, indicating the dead officer lying in a pool of blood on the ground.

"We had trouble with him," Scott said.

"That is not true," Sangrean jumped in. "My communications officer did nothing. Your Colonel Scott

Terry Wright

shot him because I talked out of turn."

Scott backhanded Sangrean, sending him to the ground. "Nobody asked you."

"At ease, Colonel," the general bellowed. "You want to start an intergalactic incident here?"

Scott chuckled. The Tarreeda broke out in laughter.

Sangrean failed to see the humor. He sat up and put the back of his hand to his bloody lip. "This is my Fleet Base Command, General. My officers and I understand your reason for returning to Beltzee with force. We know you are angry for what our ancestors did to you. I hope you realize that banishing your race from Beltzee was not our doing."

"What are you talking about?" General Brigham offered Sangrean a hand up. "Colonel Scott must've hit you harder than he intended."

Taking the general's hand, Sangrean pulled himself to his feet. "The Tarreeda Wars could have ended much worse for you. The Ice Planet was a better alternative than complete annihilation."

"You're the third alien who's called us the Tarreeda."

"How could that be?" Sangrean said. "I am the first alien you have spoken to...unless, but of course, a Beltzan had to have given you that translator."

"We boarded your big spaceship, *Questnar*, I believe it was called."

"But *Questnar* was destroyed."

"Not until after we got out...with the help of a couple of your men, that is."

"You have prisoners?" Sangrean asked, his heartbeat accelerating. He couldn't believe there were survivors from the fleet. "Who are they?"

"Some young fellow, Luthes Rez."

"Luthes is alive?" Sangrean couldn't have heard better news.

"And a specialist who goes by the name of Regarius.

~226~

Spunky old coot, I'll say."

Sangrean turned to his officers. "Luthes and Regarius survived."

"To Cada," his officers cheered.

Suddenly, the image of Luthes' wife and daughter burned to death on the ground came crashing into his mind. "Oh dear."

"There are eleven other survivors," the general said. "My medical people are attending to them now, back on earth."

"Where?"

"I hate to disappoint you, Commander, but we are not these Tarreeda you've been talking about. We are humans from a planet on the other side of the galaxy."

"That is not possible," Sangrean said. "There is no other intelligent life in the universe. Cada is very specific about that."

"Cada?"

"Our God."

"Your God is wrong."

"Then why are you here, if not to reclaim your place on Beltzee?"

"We came to get your teleportation technology."

"Just like that." Sangrean snapped his fingers. "You want us to give it to you?"

"Or we're going to take it from you."

Unfamiliar anger ballooned in Sangrean's belly. "You invade our planet, destroy *Latearian*, destroy the fleet, burn our cities, and kill our citizens for something we would have gladly shared with you in peace? Forget it, General Brigham. You will not dishonor us in this way. We will not give you what you seek to take by force. You have wasted your time."

"Regarius told me you'd be uncooperative. However, we're prepared to deal with you."

Just then, Second Squad stormed out of the building.

"We found them hiding in a storage closet," a human said. They threw their new prisoners to the ground, a woman with yellow hair and a girl child.

Sangrean couldn't believe it. Luthes' wife and daughter were alive.

Chapter Twenty-Two

B lasting and grading, Maki, his brothers, and a crew of fifty men widened the winding road up the hillside to Dr. Spears' dig on Choke Mountain. It had taken the better part of two weeks, time Milton spent marking his site with stakes and yellow ribbon. Another thirty men worked with brushes and spades in the excavation area. They wheelbarrowed the extracted dirt to a sifting area where another crew left no stone unturned. Jainaba and Gayle Weatherbee spent most of their time with these men to be sure anything of value was not overlooked or secretly pocketed.

"Trucks are coming," a lookout announced.

Battered and dusty, a duce-and-a-half and a flatbed semi barreled into camp and parked in an area Maki's bulldozer had previously graded flat.

Milton heard all the commotion from his communications tent. He threw back the insect fly. To his delight, on the flatbed sat the folded hydraulic boom of a backhoe he'd ordered from Addis Ababa. His superiors had said he was foolish to use such a heavy piece of equipment on an archeological dig. After all, the machine was more suited for clawing out trenches. However, he had already figured a way to minimize the risk to anything valuable. In the other truck, he expected to find a GSP, Ground Sonar Propagator, capable of producing sound waves that would penetrate deep into the ground. He planned to use the machine to map buried images and then dig around them, thus speeding up progress. With a burst of excitement, he set his hat on and dashed from the tent.

Jainaba ran up to supervise the unloading. "Eee, it is a big shovel, Dr. Spears."

"Yes it is," Milton replied as the backhoe's diesel engine rattled to life. Black smoke spewed from the exhaust stack. The operator nimbly worked levers in the cab and raised both the front bucket and the aft excavating shovel into the air. His skill was apparent as the knobby-tired machine climbed down from the flatbed like a clumsy scorpion.

Maki's bulldozer clanked to a stop on the upslope grade. He and his brothers stood on the track, watching the newcomer's arrival. Their faces turned scornful.

***

Meanwhile, in the anthropology office at Addis Ababa University, Emmett Collins sat at his desk and opened a package he'd just received by armed courier from the radiocarbon dating lab. He was concerned about the condition of Dr. Spears' artifact. Knowing a part of it had to be destroyed in the carbon dating process, he quickly unwrapped the piece. Examining it closely, he saw the area where a shaving of metal had been removed from the exposed edge. He also noted that some of the cement-like clay had been scraped off. His left cheek twitched. He'd expected to see more damage and wondered if the lab had tested it thoroughly, as he had instructed.

The report that came with the package drew his attention next. As he started reading it, he began to think that Dr. Spears was trying to orchestrate a hoax on the university. Analysis of the artifact concluded that there wasn't enough carbon to test: *less than 0.04%*. This indicated that the piece was NOT produced in an ancient charcoal furnace but sometime after the industrial revolution of the 19th century when steel was produced in regenerative furnaces, which among other advantages reduced the carbon content of the steel.

Too much carbon made steel brittle.

For example, the report said, cast iron contained four to six percent carbon, making it impossible to stamp or forge, but when molten, it poured easily into molds for machine casings and engine blocks. Less carbon made steel softer, more resilient, and easily forged into tools and weapons. He knew that household scissors contained 1.4% carbon, which made the steel malleable when heated, yet strong when cooled, but not brittle.

The report indicated the steel in Dr. Spears' artifact could not have been produced 20,000 years ago. The technology didn't exist, and that meant only one thing: Dr. Spears was trying to pull a fast one. He'd planted this artifact on Choke Mountain, probably so he could make it look as if he'd found something grander than Don Johnson's *Lucy*.

Milton hadn't gotten over missing that discovery, but there was one thing Milton didn't know. The problem he'd been sent to address at the Department of Antiquities that day was just a diversion to get him off the Rift Valley dig site. Emmett had set the whole thing up so Don Johnson wouldn't have to share the glory of finding *Lucy*, an honor his investors had paid Emmett well to secure. Now Milton might have uncovered the plot and may have been out for revenge. "Well, Dr. Spears," Emmett said to himself. "You won't get away with it."

Convinced of a get-even scam, he read on. The report began explaining how an Accelerator Mass Spectrometer was used to separate the stable C-12 and C-13 carbon atoms from a sample, leaving the unstable C-14 atoms to be accelerated and counted in a detector. He wondered what this information had to do with the artifact but continued reading the report. It went on to explain how Carbon-14 atoms were formed in the atmosphere when cosmic rays struck nitrogen atoms and changed them to Carbon-14 atoms, which were distributed in the biosphere by the movement of weather patterns. Plant leaves absorbed these unstable atoms, which then became part of the plant and its pollen. When the plant died, the absorption process stopped, and the C-14 atoms began to decay at a rate of one half-life every 5700 years. The report assured Emmett that organic material up to 50,000 years old could be radiocarbon dated.

Then he came to the part in the report where the lab tested the clay that coated the artifact. Embedded in this coating, they'd found spores, pollen, and many elemental traces of flora. As Choke Mountain was once a tropical jungle, this information did not surprise him, but the carbon dating results did.

The organic material preserved in the clay was 20,000 years old. That meant the object coated by the clay would have to be at least that old. The revelation took Emmett's breath away.

Because archeologists often dated artifacts by the age of the environment in which they were found, he now believed Dr. Spears' artifact was in fact 20,000 years old. What he didn't understand was how the artifact could have been manufactured that long ago and who had the advanced technology to make it.

Examining the piece again and feeling the rough clay coating, Emmett's heart began to pound as he realized the answer rested with the artifact itself.

That got him out of his chair. He rushed to the lab. Bounding through the door, he scanned the room, which was sparsely equipped. Florescent light fixtures hung above wooden workbenches along the walls. Several microscopes sat on the benches amidst an array of tools. An old freeze-drier sat in the corner, and there were several chemical storage cabinets linked to a fume extraction system.

The space was divided into several workstations, one of which was a wet area used for cleaning artifacts. There, a Nigerian student sat at the sink, diligently working on an old medallion. Emmett recruited him to clean Dr. Spears' piece.

Within moments, it was soaking in a tray of soapy water to loosen the clay and make easier work for a stencil brush. Conserving an iron artifact of this age had never been done before, so Emmett needed to proceed cautiously, applying the least harmful of cleaning techniques first, and then moving on to harsher chemical processes later, if needed.

As the assistant went about his chore, brushing and rinsing, he commented, "It's pristine."

Left cheek twitching, Emmett leaned over the student's shoulder. "What do you mean?"

"There's no crud on it."

This was the college student's term for Copper Carbonate, Copper Sulfate, or Sulfide, the greenish-blue and black encrustations which infested metal objects that had been buried in the ground for centuries. Because metal artifacts were made of refined ores that had been heated, purified, and alloyed with other metals, most commonly copper, they became very unstable. In a process known as patination, a metal artifact, when exposed to the natural elements in the ground, combined with them and returned to its more-stable state. So over a period of hundreds, or even thousands of years, a buried artifact would develop a layer of these related minerals on the surface of the metal: hence, the crud.

However, this artifact did not have any crud on it, and this abnormal condition led Emmett Collins to only one conclusion: the metal and alloys in this artifact did not occur naturally in the ground. The implication greeted him with a cold rush of fear. It was alien.

He grabbed the piece away from his assistant and dismissed him. Alone now, he used a stencil brush and a brass pick to remove the remaining clay. The tedious process took over an hour, and when he finished, he placed the 20,000-year-old artifact on a clean white towel and stared back at it in total confusion. He had seen this symbol before: a pyramid surrounded by sunrays, and in the center, an eye. Though it looked similar to a human eye, the pupil wasn't round. This eye wasn't of this world. It was an alien's eye.

The hair on his neck prickled.

Standing again, he paced, amazement rising with his thoughts. Anyone who ever knew Emmett Collins would say he was a little fish in a big pond, and every time he made a big splash, a bigger fish got the credit. But this time would be different, he swore. After all, he was the conservator and head of the antiquities committee. He was responsible for conserving, mending, and cataloging everything that came into the lab, including everything that was found at the Choke Mountain dig. This put him in an enviable position, as provenience cards were easily altered and often misplaced.

With this thought in mind, he approached a chemical storage cabinet and began rummaging through its contents. He found undiluted hydrochloric acid, the most destructive chemical he could use on an artifact. Chuckling at his own ingenuity, he switched the provenience card for Dr. Spears' artifact with the medallion the Nigerian student had been working on earlier. He then unceremoniously dropped the medallion into the acid. By morning it would be unrecognizable.

After pocketing the artifact he believed to be alien, he picked up the phone and called for the helicopter. He wasn't going to rush to Choke Mountain to inform Dr. Milton Spears of his amazing find. No, this was one discovery that he intended to claim for his very own, not because it was the greatest archeological find in history, but because there was undoubtedly more valuable artifacts still waiting to be unearthed on Choke Mountain. However, to force Dr. Spears from his dig site, Emmett needed to falsify a report to the Ethiopian Department of Antiquities, and he was headed there now.

***

Dr. Spears prepared for the first shot of the GSP, the ground sonar propagator. It had taken two hours to set up sensor links to the computer in the communications tent and plant green flags along the fall line. His measurements of the landslide area had convinced him that an ancient settlement could lie anywhere along that line, probably at a depth of fifty feet. Now, as he sat in front of the monitor, he was itching to get started.

Gayle looked over his shoulder at a blank computer screen. "I don't think this is going to work."

"Of course it will."

"But the sonar has to penetrate too much ground, a good five stories down anyway."

Milton had the same concern, so he'd been careful to select the correct model propagator for the task. "This GSP is designed to work down to sixty feet," he told her. "I expect to see the signal diminish with depth, so if nothing is revealed in the top half of the echo image, we can be sure it's safe to dig down to that depth. After that, we'll take another series of shots before digging deeper."

"Shoot and dig, shoot and dig. Very clever."

"That remains to be seen." Outside the tent flap, Jainaba and two of his strongest men wheeled the GSP up the slope, east of the camp. This propagator was a Rayleigh wave-based forward-echoing blaster that worked in ranges above three hundred hertz. It looked like an appliance dolly cradling a large vertical cylinder. And it was as heavy as a refrigerator.

When Jainaba reached the first green flag, Milton called him on the two-way. "I'm ready."

Breathing hard, Jainaba responded, "Give us...one moment."

Milton waited while Jainaba inserted a powder-filled shell into the firing mechanism atop the cylinder. The computer screen scrolled the message, *AWAITING SENSOR DATA.*

"Okay, be ready." Jainaba and his workers donned ear protection. Men working in the dig set down their tools and covered their ears.

The GSP fired with a thundering crack. Expanding gasses in the cylinder drove the ram downward where it struck the *foot* with tremendous velocity. The impact made the dust jump as it directed a fierce sound wave into the ground. Sensors placed in the soil picked up the returning echoes, and a digital image of the subterranean rock appeared on the computer screen, a chaotic jumble of black and gray spots. It reminded Milton of television static. But at a depth of thirty feet, the image turned bone white. He wondered if the echo had been lost, or absorbed, or the GSP had somehow malfunctioned.

"What is it?" Gayle whispered.

He looked at her over his shoulder. "I don't know."

"Maybe you should try again."

The laser printer rolled out a copy of the image, and quickly studying it, Milton saw nothing of significance. "We'll stick with our original plan." He got on the two-way. "Jainaba, go to the next flag."

Jainaba and his helpers moved the GSP to the next green flag, and the process was repeated until they had covered the entire fall line, an operation that brought them to the end of daylight.

With a sandwich in his hand, Milton worked by the light of a single forty-watt bulb that hung from the center tent beam. He poured over the printouts arranged on the table in order of their position on the fall line. Most of the images were bone white after thirty feet down. However, those at each end of the array displayed varying shades of gray down to sixty feet, through an area where he had hoped to see echoes of dwellings, hearths, pottery, tools, or even human skeletons. This told him the propagator was capable of resounding to the depth it was designed for, but the blank portions of the center printouts frustrated him.

He knew that sand or an open area, such as a cave, could have accounted for the lost echoes, but a cave could not have been located above the original slope of Choke Mountain, and sand would have eroded down-slope long ago. An air pocket under the landslide was a possibility, of course, however the weight of fifty feet of broken rock would have collapsed any air pocket after 20,000 years, especially one of this size, which looked blimpish in shape, bigger than the Hindenburg.

Mentally exhausted over the dilemma and lacking any better explanation, he concluded that a glitch in the equipment or software had created the bone-white blank spots. He gulped down the rest of his sandwich and killed the generator.

Tomorrow he would find out for sure.

***

The next morning, Milton didn't bother to shave. He threw on his clothes and headed down-slope to Maki's encampment where, next to the bulldozer tracks, a cook fire smoldered under a tin pot of bubbling lentil mash. Squatted on their haunches around the fire, Maki and his brothers paid no attention to Milton's approach, as they were preoccupied with dunking scraps of *injera* into the mash and devouring the drippy goop. It was an ugly affair. "Good morning, Maki."

Maki didn't look up from his meal, nor did his brothers.

"It's hot in the sun and I wish to finish my business

with you quickly. I need your bulldozer to cut away twenty feet of the fall line that I've marked with green flags."

"We are not finished with the boulders," Maki managed through a mouthful of food.

"You've been pushing grass and rocks around for two weeks. It's time to dig."

At that, Maki looked up, his albino eyes glaring. "Use your fancy new machine. We are busy."

Milton detected resentment, or perhaps even jealousy from Maki's tone. After all, the new backhoe was beautiful compared to his rattletrap bulldozer, all dented and smeared with dried pig's blood. "If you want your check, you will dig."

Maki stood, his goatskin robe shedding dust. "We will dig when we are ready." His brothers looked up and showed toothy grins.

This Milton took as a gesture of solidarity. He was well aware of the curse on Choke Mountain, and he respected the Oromo farmer's reluctance to cut a deep gash in the ground, but they had made a deal. "That earth must be moved by nightfall. I suggest you get started right away."

The glare in Maki's eyes sharpened. He drew his Massai knife in what Milton hoped was just a symbolic act of defiance. However, when the brothers stood, he knew he'd been gravely mistaken. Jainaba had warned him that Maki was dangerous, and it appeared as though Milton was about to find out just how dangerous when a roaring rush of wind suddenly engulfed them in dust.

A helicopter had risen from beyond the east escarpment. The sound of its engines, once blocked by the mountain, now battered the air with fury. Flying over the dig site in circles, it scattered dirt and animals and Africans in all directions. Tornadic winds buffeted the tents, straining the tie-downs, some to the point of complete failure. Around and around the helicopter flew until the entire camp was in chaos.

During the confusion, Maki and his brothers dispersed.

Milton ran to the dig in a panic. Workers struggled against the tempest to cover the bare ground with plastic sheets in order to keep their work from being blown away. Jainaba and Gayle were with them, ducking the onslaught fearlessly and shouting orders over the hammering helicopter hovering above. "Cover this up. Cover it quickly."

As Milton jumped in to lend a hand, the helicopter finally retreated to the landing area. He didn't have time to express his growing anger as he assessed the damage, the blown-over stakes and missing markers, the trampled soil samples, and the spilled water jars and scattered tools.

"Just who does that guy think he is?" Gayle shouted from her knees.

"Eee, I think he is crazy," Jainaba put in.

Milton brushed dirt from his hands and climbed out of the dig with murder on his mind. There was no call for that kind of recklessness. Someone was going to pay for this.

As he ran toward the idling helicopter, he saw the pilot pointing upslope toward the communications tent as if the person responsible for this outrage had gone up there. Confused, Milton sprinted to the tent, and when he burst in, he discovered the white-suited culprit.

Emmett Collins closed the refrigerator door and popped a beer, his left cheek twitching. "You're going to need this," he said, offering it to Milton.

"What's the matter with you?" Milton shouted. "You've set us back a month with that stunt."

"That's all right." Emmett held up the beer can in salute, and downed a swallow. "You're finished here, anyway." From his top pocket he removed a yellow paper, his gray eyes cold and hard as iron. "Read it and weep."

Milton took the paper. It was from the Ethiopian

Department of Antiquities, an order to cease all operations on Choke Mountain. Unable to grasp the reason for such an order, he read it again and still came away breathless. "Why?"

Emmett grinned, and from his pocket he removed a horribly deformed artifact and flipped it to Milton. "Tried to pull a fast one, huh?"

"What?" Milton examined the piece carefully. He could tell from its red discoloration that it had been soaked in hydrochloric acid, but he couldn't recall having seen it before. "What is this?"

"That's the piece of junk you claimed to have found on this site." Emmett helped himself to another swig of beer. "It's a worthless plant, a fake, and because it's my duty as conservator of this dig, I reported the fraud to the authorities immediately."

Astounded, Milton couldn't say a word in his own defense.

Emmett went on. "The Department of Antiquities has ordered a complete investigation. They put me in charge." He scowled. "Oh yes, Dr. Spears, we are going to get to the bottom of this. You have twenty-four hours to vacate. I expect you to be gone when I return." He downed the last of the beer and crushed the can with one hand.

Still, Milton stood speechless. Emmett retreated to the helicopter, which soon rose in a rush and was gone. Eviction notice in one hand and a worthless medallion in the other, Milton collapsed into a chair. What truck had just hit him?

Shortly, Gayle and Jainaba rushed in. "What was that all about?" Gayle asked.

He noticed her knees had been scraped during the fracas. "You should put something on that," Milton said with defeat in his voice.

Jainaba stepped forward. "You look like you have seen a ghost, Dr. Spears. Has someone died?"

"What's wrong?" Gayle prodded.

He showed them the order. "We have twenty-four hours."

After reading the eviction notice, Gayle handed it to Jainaba. "Why?"

Now Milton showed them the worthless artifact. "This."

"I've never seen it before," Gayle said.

"It's the piece I found."

"It looks like bronze to me," Jainaba commented.

"That's because it's been soaked in hydrochloric acid." Anger stabbed Milton's chest. "Emmett ruined it."

"But still..." Gayle plucked the magnetic screwdriver from Milton's pocket. "It's steel." She touched the screwdriver tip to the artifact, but there was no attraction. Again and again she tried, but nothing happened. "I mean...it should still be magnetic. This *is* bronze."

Rage set fire to Milton's chest. He shot up from his chair. "Emmett switched it."

"Eee, why would he do that?"

"The real artifact must be worth a fortune," Gayle suggested.

Pacing furiously, Milton realized Emmett had betrayed him once again, as he had done on the Rift Valley dig, but Milton doubted that the artifact was worth enough money to motivate Emmett to mutiny. There had to be something in this dig site that he wanted, something much more valuable, something buried much deeper. Emmett was one to look for glory, and whatever he had found here would soar him above kings.

Milton bared his teeth. The only way to stop Emmett was to unlock the mystery of Choke Mountain himself, and he had only twenty-four hours to do it.

Chapter Twenty-Three

Halfway around the world, Luthes Rez, Specialist Regarius, and the eleven surviving crewmen of *Questnar* were dying. At NASA's Sterilization and Isolation Unit, doctors worked frantically trying to restore sodium chloride levels in the aliens' blood, but each salt tablet made Luthes sicker, and he prayed to Cada that this hour would be his last.

The ceiling lights were always on, and there was always activity in the room. Humans in white coats went from bed to bed, checking and medicating the captive Beltzans. He wished they'd just leave them alone to die. His veins pulsed with high blood pressure, his ears rang, and his sweat smelled acidic. Curled up under a white sheet, he tried to ignore the pain in his kidneys. He constantly felt the urge to urinate but couldn't, and he was thirsty, but the humans wouldn't let him drink. Conditions on earth were unbearable.

He didn't know if it was day or night outside. The only window in the room looked out to a hallway where he'd seen humans gather to observe them. He'd felt violated by their stares of astonishment, as if he were on display like an animal in a cage, an oddity because he was different. He wasn't sure how long ago it was, but one of those humans had talked to him. His name was Dr. Mackey. Luthes knew from the look on the human's face that he was deeply concerned and hoped he would find a way to help them.

Trembling, he looked at Regarius lying in the next bed. He hadn't said anything for several hours, and when he wasn't sleeping, he stared at the ceiling.

Luthes was about to close his eyes again when voices from the other side of the window activated his translator. He heard a man shouting, "You're poisoning them." When he turned to the window, he couldn't believe what he saw. Familiar faces, faces he'd never forget. He'd seen them on *Questnar's* scope screen in the windshield of the Tarreeda cruiser, a man with black hair, and a woman with yellow hair. Intrigued, he forced his weak body up on one elbow and stared at them.

The man was shouting at a group of humans wearing white coats who had gathered around him. They were talking loudly, and his translator picked up only a few words: "give them water," and "get them out..."

Then he saw Dr. Mackey. The yellow-haired woman who looked like Verrilla was standing next to him, her mouth agape and her blue eyes staring at Luthes. He stared back, at first with amazement and then with sorrow as the death of his wife came back to him. His arm gave out, and he dropped his head back down to the pillow.

The next thing he knew, a bustle of activity exploded into the room. Humans grabbed his arms and forced him to sit up. Another human offered him a bottle of water, which he drank from greedily. Other crewmen around him, those who could sit up, were being given water too.

"Leave me alone," Regarius protested, obviously annoyed with the vigorous attention he was receiving.

"You need to drink this water," a human insisted.

"What is happening, Luthes?" a crewmate cried out.

"Let me explain," came a voice from the open door.

Luthes turned as the man with black hair entered, the only human to have come into this room without protective clothing. He wore blue slacks, a jacket with a translator clipped to his collar, and a bush of hair under his nose. Luthes couldn't take his eyes off him.

"We now understand why you're sick," he said as he

walked down the row of beds. "Please help us make you well by drinking a lot of water. This will cause you to urinate more frequently. We'll also give you masks to breathe oxygen from."

"What is wrong with us?" Regarius asked. His face was drained of color, and still looking at the water, he did not drink.

"We call it hypernatremia, a condition brought on by an overdose of sodium chloride in your bodies."

"I do not understand," Regarius replied.

"You're going to have to trust me."

"Why should we? Humans have done nothing but harm us."

Luthes couldn't contain himself any longer. "I have seen you before," he said to the black-haired man. "And since then, life has become terrifying."

The man approached with a curious look on his face. "Were you in that huge spaceship?"

"I saw you on my scope screen, and the yellow haired woman with Dr. Mackey. You were looking out the viewport of your cruiser."

"My God," the man said and sat next to him. "I want you to know that this is my fault. I take full responsibility."

Luthes felt dizzy being this close to the first human he'd ever seen. "You must be very smart to have found your way to our planet."

"I was foolish."

"My name is Luthes Rez."

The human extended his hand. "Ray Crawford. I wish we didn't have to meet like this."

Luthes recognized the gesture the human put forward, the clasping of hands, but he hesitated to give his hand in return. "I was helmsman of *Questnar* before the humans destroyed it. I was a husband and father until they killed my family."

A look of shock came over Ray Crawford's face. "I'm

sorry...but tell me, why didn't you destroy the space transporter and kill my family?"

"We are not like you or that General Brigham."

"We're not all like him."

"You expect me to believe that?"

Ray shook his head. "I don't expect you to forgive me either, or to forgive the human race, but please understand, we are here to help you." Ray didn't retract his offered hand.

The entire room was silent as Luthes looked at Ray's hand and then at his sincere eyes. "What do you propose?"

"We're going to send you home," Ray said. "But it will take time to prepare. Until then, you have to trust me. We need to get you out of here, but the journey won't be easy."

"And if we refuse?"

"You'll die here," Ray replied.

Luthes saw no problem with that, after all, he didn't have to get much sicker to die. He looked at Regarius, and then at the expectant faces of his crewmates. He could see they wanted to go home, and they looked to him for direction. With that, he accepted Ray's offered hand, and as strange as it felt to touch his short fingers, he found a measure of comfort in the connection. "What must we do?"

"The water we are giving you is distilled of minerals," Ray explained. "The air in the masks is pure. You'll eat fruits and vegetables, which are high in potassium chloride. This will restore the chemical balance in your bodies, and you'll start feeling better soon. Then we are going to leave."

"For Beltzee?"

"To a city far from the salty air that has made you sick until we're ready to send you home. In the meantime, you and your people are our guests. You'll be treated with respect and given every comfort affordable."

"How is it that you have the power to do this for us?"

"I don't." Ray stood and addressed them all. "Like I said, the journey won't be easy. There are humans who will try to stop us. It'll be dangerous. Are you willing to take the risk?"

Again, Luthes looked at his crewmates and at Regarius. He nodded then drank down his bottle of water. The other Beltzans followed his lead. They were going home.

***

The next day, in the SuperMIGGS control room at NASA, Janis stood in front of the thick window and stared into an empty gravity chamber. "Now let me get this straight," he said to Ray who was standing at the console behind him. "We need to send thirteen aliens home in a transporter with three seats?"

Stan Burton sat at the chief engineer's station. "I can equip the space transporter with a heat shield and landing gear, no problem. And I can use the galley and the onboard MIGGS instrument compartment to make room for three more passengers, but thirteen? That's impossible."

Ray leaned on a console and crossed his arms. "Then someone will have to stay behind."

"That's not acceptable, Ray, and you know it. We need a shuttle." Janis turned around and faced Stan. "Can we convert Discovery?"

"I thought you wanted to keep this hushed up."

"He's right," Ray said. "A project of that scale would require everyone's participation at NASA."

"If Brigham gets the Beltzan's teleportation system working—"

"That's not likely," Stan broke in. "I should have been on the scientific team."

"You're needed here," Janis replied.

Ray asked, "Is everything ready in Boulder, Janis?"

"Dean Billings will get back to me this afternoon."

Peterson dashed in. "It's all set." He pulled off his sunglasses. "A Special Ops C-130 transport will arrive in the morning. We've got to be ready to go by 7:00."

"How did you pull that off?" Janis asked.

"I have my connections."

"Why doesn't that surprise me?"

"A simple thank you would be nice."

Janis knew he'd have to ignore his concerns over Peterson's involvement, for the aliens' sake. He turned from the MIGGS window. "Sure, thanks."

"How are our aliens doing?"

"They're much better," Ray said.

Peterson strode to Ray sitting at his console. "So it was the salt?"

"The way I understand it," Ray began, "the Beltzans' body chemistry is similar to our own except for one thing: sodium chloride."

"Salt."

"There are different kinds of salts," Ray said. "Sodium chloride doesn't occur naturally on their planet, but potassium chloride does. Both salts are needed for our bodies to function properly, but Beltzans rely on only the potassium chloride, and they have no tolerance for sodium chloride. Around here, salt is everywhere: in the air, the food, and the tap water. They're alive now because Janis didn't give up on me."

"Yeah, he can be a persistent pain in the ass."

"I'm glad to be back on my feet."

It had taken something this big to make him care about anything again.

Peterson kept things businesslike. "Will the Beltzans be ready to move?"

Janis said, "Lisa and Tracy are handling logistics for the trip to Boulder. Clothes are coming from the Base Exchange at Cape Canaveral Air Force Station. Two wounded Beltzans are still not able to get around on their own."

"We'll manage," Peterson said and took from his pocket another whittling project, a long-fingered alien with a handsome face. It was the likeness of Luthes Rez.

The aliens were extremely important to Peterson, Janis could see, but he didn't know what Peterson's connections were and still didn't trust him.

***

Lisa tore into another box of clothes that Lieutenant Swanson had set on the floor in SIU. "Is this all?"

"There's more coming."

"I hope there'll be enough." She sorted slacks and shorts and shirts by size, and laid out shoes in pairs. Underwear and socks had come in another box earlier, and those items had already been distributed to the Beltzans. They treasured the clothes as if they were Christmas gifts.

The first thing she'd realized while working with the Beltzans was their kind and gentle nature. Even under the worst of conditions, they didn't complain...well, except Regarius. He could get cranky, but she didn't blame him. He was the oldest captive. Luthes Rez was the most handsome, and she'd picked out a set of clothes that would fit him nicely. They hadn't spoken, of course, because she didn't have a translator. There were only a few spares, which the doctors needed. Bearing gifts, she approached Luthes' bed.

He sat upright when she neared, his eyes fixed on hers, which caused a jolt of electricity to speed up her heart. "These are for you." She held out the stack of folded slacks and shirts, one hand underneath, one hand on top. His oxygen mask slipped up his cheeks as he smiled. Taking the clothes from her, his hands touched her fingers and he paused, setting off fires in her bloodstream.

"Dedure cadree," he said, his voice distorted behind the mask.

Though his words meant nothing to her, she wasn't going to let that interfere with their conversation. "Your hands are warm," she said, knowing that meant he was feeling better.

His cheeks reddened. *"Taulde."*

Regarius, in the next bed, chuckled. *"Chidru gamar tog de."*

Luthes laughed.

"That's not fair," she said. "You guys can understand me, but I can't understand you."

With that, Regarius removed the translator from his hospital gown and offered it to her with a smile. Exhilarated by the prospect of talking with Luthes, she nervously clipped the translator to the white lace on her blouse. "What did you say?"

Luthes laughed again. "You are kind and I thanked you."

"Then what did Regarius think was so funny?"

"It was nothing."

"Tell her," Regarius said. "What do you have to lose?"

Shyly, Luthes repeated Regarius's words. "The beautiful woman likes you."

Lisa had hoped she wasn't being that obvious, then again, why not? She dipped to Regarius and then said to Luthes, "May I sit with you?"

He patted the mattress. "Most certainly."

"This is so weird," she said, sitting with one leg tucked underneath her. "I mean...I'm actually talking to an alien."

"As am I," Luthes replied. "But there is something I wish to tell you."

"Yes?" She wondered what great galactic revelation he was about to reveal to her.

"The fact that we can speak to each other on these devices does not mean that we will ever understand each other, for where I come from, the violence of your people is beyond our comprehension. You have caused us great suffering and loss."

Lisa nodded. "Maybe something good will come of this."

"I have lost everything," Luthes said sternly. "My wife, my daughter, my fleet, my home, and yet you take this as a means to betterment. Our understanding of each other is a long way apart."

Jumping to her feet, she shouted, "I'm just trying to be nice to you."

"By shouting?"

"You don't know anything about us."

Luthes frowned. "Oh, yes, we have experienced tyranny much like this in our past. Your ways are not unlike the Tarreeda."

"Who?"

"Our enemy once terrorized our world, hunted and enslaved us, slaughtered us for spectacle and sport, and why...?" He showed her his hands. "Because we were different."

"Humans are not like that." She suddenly realized she'd spoken before thinking.

"Perhaps not entirely," Luthes said, and the color faded from his lips. "The Tarreeda would have hanged us on their crosses by now."

A crushing weight landed on her chest as she envisioned Jesus on the cross. "We would never do that to you," she insisted anyway. "And we won't let the Tarreeda do that to you either, if they come here."

"They were banished to the Ice Planet," Luthes said. "And they have since perished."

Regarius made a noise and shook his head, which gave her cause to believe that the old man disagreed with

Luthes. Then she thought about her necklace tucked inside her blouse, the gold crucifix that meant so much to her, her savior on the cross, dying for her sins. If Luthes saw this, he would think of the Tarreeda, and their understanding of each other would be ripped even further apart. So she said nothing, returned the translator to Regarius, and feeling numb inside, went back to unpacking the boxes.

***

The next morning, a Special Ops C-130 Hercules transporter arrived at the Shuttle Landing Facility right on time. Lieutenant Swanson brought the Beltzans in a sealed, oxygen-enriched passenger van. They were dressed as tourists, complete with baggy pants, colorful shirts, sunglasses and all. Under no circumstances were they to reveal their hands to anyone.

The cargo ramp whined to the ground, and the loadmaster waved Swanson aboard. He drove the van up the ramp and into the belly of the aircraft. Once inside, the Beltzans donned their oxygen masks before the doors were opened to the salty air. Lisa and Tracy helped them disembark and get settled into web seats along the fuselage wall.

Janis met Ray on the tarmac as the mighty turboprop engines idled loudly. "Where's Peterson?"

"I thought he would be here by now," Ray shouted over all the noise. "Did the Beltzans get their immunizations?"

"Last night," Janis yelled. "And their decontamination showers this morning."

"This is risky," Ray said as they headed toward the cargo ramp, ducking the propeller backwash. "If they get sick—"

"They're fine," Janis replied. "The medical team will accompany them to Boulder." A short run up the ramp and they were inside the aircraft where the air was alive with vibrations. "And the University of Colorado is going to take over from there. It's all set."

On the loadmaster's signal, Lieutenant Swanson backed the van down the ramp and sped off. Janis stood at the back of the aircraft and scanned the flight line for any sign of Peterson. He was nowhere in sight.

Concerned, Janis retreated into the shadowy cargo bay and found Tracy helping the long-fingered Beltzans fidget with their safety harness buckles. They were definitely designed for hands with short fingers. The wounded Beltzans were transferred to gurneys and strapped to the front bulkhead.

Ray shouted, "There's Peterson!"

Janis whipped around, saw a jeep careen onto the tarmac, tires smoking.

"He's in one hell of a hurry."

Then Janis saw the reason why. Air Force squad cars were in hot pursuit of the jeep, sirens wailing and overheads flashing. "We've got to get out of here." He dashed for the cockpit, shouting, "Tracy, buckle up."

The cockpit was located above the cargo bay, and Janis took the doglegged stairway two steps at a time. "We gotta go!" he shouted to the pilots, who jolted up from their checklists.

"What are you talking about?" the captain asked.

"Look!" Janis pointed to the approaching cars.

The pilots looked at each other, and the copilot said, "Jesus Christ." Immediately, he got on the intercom to the loadmaster. "Leave the ramp down. We've got to move."

"What about Peterson?" Janis asked.

"He's on his own." The pilot shoved the throttles forward, and four turboprop engines roared to high RPM. The C-130 Hercules began to roll.

Janis clung to the stair railing and looked back to the open cargo door, wishing Peterson was already onboard and none of this was happening.

As the huge transport picked up speed, the dragging ramp threw up a shower of sparks from the concrete. Lisa and Tracy clung to their safety harnesses, joggling about like toy dolls, and caught in the rush of wind, their hair whipped toward the open cargo door.

Then from the left, Peterson's jeep raced up behind the accelerating plane and lurched wildly up the ramp. He slammed on the brakes and skidded to a stop inside the cargo bay.

A half dozen blue security cars careened in behind the plane, fishtailing and throwing smoke. In the next instant, Peterson jumped from the jeep and pushed it backward out the cargo bay. It banged down the ramp and violently upended itself on the runway in a spectacular display of flying debris as it cartwheeled and crashed into the onrushing pursuers. Squad cars skidded and veered and slammed into one another while pieces of the jeep rained down in a storm of metal hail.

Peterson jammed his hand on a lever. Hydraulics whined, and the cargo ramp began to rise up.

Barreling down the runway, the C-130 shuddered and shook, but the captain talked calmly to the tower. "Roger. Aquarius is ready for immediate departure."

"Clear for takeoff, Aquarius," the tower replied.

Janis thought it was odd that the tower gave them permission to takeoff under these conditions. "Why are they letting you go?" he asked the captain.

"Agent Peterson can answer that better than I."

"Agent Peterson?" Janis felt as if he'd been hit with a board. As the Hercules roared down the runway, questions battered his mind. *Agent? From where? Who? Why?*

Seconds later, the giant transport clawed its way into the Florida sky. The cargo ramp closed with a bang, quelling the tempest and noise. Crimson lights now illuminated the hold and the passengers' terrified faces.

Terry Wright

"What the hell was that all about?" Ray shrieked at Peterson. Before Janis could get down the stairs, Ray had already grabbed Peterson by the lapels of his black suit coat. "You son of a bitch."

"Ray! Ray. Stop it, Ray." Janis threw his body between the two men, but the steep angle of the aircraft's ascent caused him to bowl them over.

Even sprawled on the floor, Ray still managed to slug Peterson in the jaw. "Now the whole world knows about this."

"Get a hold of yourself, Ray." Janis knew Peterson had a gun, but during the ensuing brawl, he didn't draw it, and Janis wondered why.

The loadmaster staggered across the rocking cargo bay toward the heap of combatants on the floor, and with burly hands, he helped Janis separate Ray and Peterson. "That's enough."

Peterson sat up and wiped blood from his lower lip with the back of his hand. "I can explain."

"It better be good," Ray spat and wrenched his arms free of Janis's grasp.

"Lighten up, Ray," Janis shouted. Then he looked at the Beltzans strapped in their web seats, their eyes wide in disbelief of the ruckus they'd just witnessed. Luthes and Regarius disapprovingly shook their heads, and Janis felt a flush of embarrassment. The aircraft leveled off, and after a quick glance at Tracy and Lisa, he gave Peterson a hand to his feet. "Why was the Air Force chasing you?"

"They want the aliens."

"You told them?"

"The problem with you guys," he pointed to Janis and Ray, "you're amateurs. This thing is way over your head."

"And I suppose you're the expert," Ray said, still seething.

Peterson inspected the blood on the back of his hand. "I'm from the National Security Agency."

~254~

Droning, the C-130 bucked, and everyone lurched.

"Do any of you remember *Project Aquarius?*"

"That's been defunct since 1969." Ray hung on to a cargo strap suspended from the ceiling. "Since the Air Force released *Project Blue Book.* They'd found no credible evidence of any aliens, so the government got out of the UFO business."

The plane banked left.

"That's what they'd have you believe," Peterson replied. "But *Project Aquarius* has been operating in secret ever since, under a National Security Agency directive using CIA confidential funds. It's been our job to prepare for any possible future contact with aliens and collect intelligence on them: scientific, medical, and technological information."

"What for?" Janis asked. "The Air Force decided it was a waste of taxpayers' money."

"Ray's discovery set off a firestorm at the National Security Agency, and our heightened activity attracted the attention of Air Force brass."

"What do they care?" Ray asked.

"Don't forget, they're the ones who said that aliens didn't exist."

"And now they've got a black eye over Blue Book," Janis said.

"So they want the aliens eliminated," Peterson replied. "Once and for all."

Janis had to sit down. He found a web seat, and Peterson sat next to him. "Don't you see? These aliens have been dropped into our laps, and it's our job to protect them."

"From the United States Air Force?" Ray shouted. "We'll all be killed."

"We were going to keep the aliens locked up at SIU," Peterson went on, "until you and Janis figured out why their health was in danger. Over the years, we've prepared for just this sort of thing...aliens among us. Roswell was a wakeup call. Back then, there was no plan in place, no way to care for the aliens, to transport them, to study them. Everything was makeshift and haphazard."

"Now wait a minute," Janis cut in. "Roswell was a weather balloon."

"You think?"

"Are you saying that *EBE* the alien, the autopsy, and a flying saucer really happened?"

"And then some," Peterson assured him.

Ray asked, "Why didn't the Air Force investigate Roswell during Project Blue Book?"

"They did, but we fed them misinformation, same as the media."

"So they weren't privy to the facts."

"But because of our efforts, there is now an underground railway in place to transport, safeguard, and study aliens. *Project Aquarius* is the only thing that makes it possible for us to move the Beltzans to Boulder."

"You m-mean," Janis stumbled, "the pilots, this plane, the clearance for takeoff and even SIU allowing us to remove the aliens from quarantine, that's all part of it?"

He nodded. "Air Traffic Control and the University of Colorado are in the loop too. Aquarius is High Priority. If we hadn't continued with our work..." he pointed to the pallid survivors of *Questnar*. "These Beltzans would be dead already."

Janis scowled. "What about your kill-everybody attitude?"

"I had to be sure Brigham trusted me—"

"So you could get your aliens," Janis finished for him.

Peterson grinned.

Now Janis understood how Peterson knew about Title 14 of the Code of Federal Regulations, the Extra-Terrestrial Exposure Law. On one hand, the government had denied the existence of aliens, and on the other hand, they'd passed a law forbidding anyone to have contact with them. That was so typical of the government. Janis surveyed the Beltzans still clutching oxygen masks to their faces. He gave Tracy a wan smile. "At least we're all safe."

"*Agent Peterson.*" The captain's frantic voice came over the intercom. "*You'd better get up here.*"

***

Peterson bounded up the steps to the flight deck. "What is it?"

"Look." The copilot pointed out the starboard window where an F-15 Strike Eagle had flown within yards of the C-130's right wing. "Strategic Air Command."

The jet pilot was gesturing down with a pointed finger.

"He wants us to follow him, and look, he's not alone." The radar display showed a jet tailing them two miles back. Just then, the RWR, Radar Warning Receiver, beeped. A radar lock had been detected. "It's a radar-guided Sparrow missile."

"How do you know that?"

"This Special Ops C-130 is equipped with identifier electronics and state of the art countermeasures." The copilot indicated the blips on the radar screen. "Trust me, these guys mean business."

"What do you want us to do?" the captain asked Peterson.

"Stay on course." He squeezed into the flight engineer's seat, strapped himself in then donned a headset. "Give me air to air," he told the copilot. When the frequency display activated, Peterson pressed the transmit switch. "Aquarius to Air Force escort, do you copy?"

"*We have orders to take you down or shoot you down,*" the fighter pilot replied. "*Your choice, Aquarius. Over.*"

"Be advised," Peterson said. "You are interfering with a National Security Agency Priority-One designated flight."

"Follow me," came back.

The captain announced, "We're coming to our next waypoint. What do you want me to do?"

Now Peterson had to test the fighter pilot's resolve to shoot down a C-130 Hercules. "Make your turn, captain."

When the transport made a steep bank to the left, the F-15 veered off in the opposite direction. Within moments, its radar blip was flying alongside the trailing jet, and seconds later, the RWR chirped, indicating a missile had been launched.

Peterson felt a chill.

"Seven seconds to impact," the copilot said.

The captain moved the *Arm-Safe* switch on the Dispenser Control Panel, and a red *ARM* light glowed. The DCP indicated it had a full load of chaff cartridges and infrared countermeasure flares. He moved the selector switch to *C* for the chaff cartridges and pressed the fire button. Mounted in the tail section, a dispenser ejected fifteen cartridges packed with aluminum foil strips, which exploded into an array of radar-confusing blossoms. Immediately, the captain pushed the yoke down and put the transport into a sloping dive to port. The missile sliced through the chaff, and continued blindly on course until it exploded a mile downrange.

"Heads up," the copilot reported as the RWR chirped another launch warning. "It's a heat-seeking Sidewinder."

As the C-130 continued its plummet, the captain pulled back on the throttles to reduce engine exhaust heat, moved the DCP selector switch to *F* and pressed the fire button, launching a dozen M206 infrared countermeasure flares. Glowing balls of superheated magnesium shot out behind the transport, and at the last instant, the captain pulled back on the yoke. Groaning, the C-130 climbed out of the missile's flight path and veered to starboard. The Sidewinder honed in on the hot magnesium shield and exploded.

The RWR chirped again as the captain pushed the throttles to full power. Four turboprop engines roared. "Status!"

"Another Sparrow."

Again, chaff bloomed behind the transport, and again the captain put it into a dive.

Peterson's stomach was in his mouth. "How do I get a land line?" he managed to ask the copilot.

"Use the panel keypad to dial."

The bewildered Sparrow spiraled off into the distance.

Peterson knew his private emergency call numbers by memory, but punched them clumsily due to the rough ride. Missing the nine, he had to start over, but as the captain banked the transport hard to starboard, pulled it out of the dive, and climbed, Peterson missed the seven. Everything shook and rattled. "Can't you hold this thing steady?"

Another chirp, another Sparrow, another dive.

Dialing again, he finally heard the National Security Council hotline ringing in his headset, then a click. "What is it, Peterson?"

He could barely hear the man's voice over the roaring turboprop engines. "Mr. Secretary, we're under attack, two F-15s out of SAC. Tell the President to get the Air Force off our backs."

Chirp! Chirp! Chirp!

"Sidewinder!"

Another volley of flares spewed into the sky, and the Sidewinder took the bait, but the DCP now displayed warning lights indicating the dispenser was out of flares. After rotating the selector switch to C, the captain began flying a zigzag course, banking left and right almost ninety degrees each way, leaving an uneven trail of exhaust heat in the transport's wake. Peterson thought he was going to puke but maintained his vigil on the phone as the NSC attempted to get Presidential intervention to SAC headquarters and override the pilots' orders.

The RWR chirped.

"Sidewinder. We're out of flares."

The captain leveled the wings and pushed the left rudder pedal to the floor. This cocked the nose left so he could better see the missile's approach.

"Five seconds to impact."

The missile would home in on the engines, and it didn't need to strike them to detonate, but only get close to the heat source. As the phone line remained silent in his ear, Peterson feared he had only seconds to live.

"Where is it?" the copilot asked, looking back and forth in frantic confusion.

"Port."

The missile was coming on fast, but Peterson could see it veering wildly as it passed through the uneven trail of engine exhaust and tried to make radical course corrections. By the time it neared the transport, it was considerably off course but still near enough to knock them out of the sky.

"Now," the copilot shouted and pulled back on the throttles.

Pushing the yoke down and right, the captain sent the transport into a nosedive, straight down. The Sidewinder's sensitive infrared electronics immediately determined it was as close to the target as it was going to get and detonated. Ballooning, the fireball momentarily engulfed the diving transport, and the concussion belted it with a shuddering blow. The aircraft shook violently. Though they'd eluded the Sidewinder's lethal strike, another problem developed quickly. The airspeed indicator needle was buried in the red, meaning the airframe could not withstand full or abrupt maneuvering control inputs or the wings would be ripped from the fuselage. On top of that, extreme left rudder had caused the aircraft to go into a dead-man's spin.

Centrifugal force plastered Peterson to the engineer's console, and his head was dizzily disoriented when a voice came on the line. "The President has been notified, Peterson. What's your position?"

"We're going down."

"Help me with this," the captain shouted. He and his copilot strong-armed the controls, easing the C-130 out of the spin, but outside the windshield all Peterson could see was the ground getting closer, a plowed field, a road, a pond, and cows running in every direction.

"Pull her back easy." Straining, the pilots gently muscled the giant Hercules back to level flight, but they were immediately confronted by two towering grain elevators not fifty feet apart.

"Hang on."

The captain turned the yoke hard right and, with the help of full left rudder, flew the plane between the elevators, wings damn near vertical. Sparks spewed from a wingtip as it nicked one of the towers.

Twisting the wings level again, he executed full throttle. The massive propellers grabbed air as the captain fired the booster jets, and the C-130 lumbered back into the sky.

"Jesus." Peterson thought his whole life should have flashed before his eyes. Gulping air, he heard the Secretary's voice in the phone. "Is anybody there? Peterson?"

Flying two hundred feet above the treetops and somewhere over Georgia, the RWR chirped again.

"Sparrow."

"We're never going to shake these guys," Peterson shouted.

The captain deployed the last of his chaff, and because there wasn't enough altitude to evade, he stayed on course until the Sparrow hit the blooming aluminum cloud. Then he executed a hard right turn under full power. The Sparrow screamed past them and hit the hillside in a billowing display of fire and smoke.

"Peterson!" the NSC Secretary called out.

"Get these bastards off our tail."

"The President has given SAC the order to disengage."

"They're not listening," Peterson shouted.

"Give them a few minutes to pass the order down to the pilots."

"We don't have a few minutes."

As the C-130 flew low, and the RWR remained silent, the copilot said, "They've thrown three Sidewinders and four Sparrows at us."

"They should have one more Sidewinder between them," the pilot speculated and glanced at a muddled radar screen. "I wonder where they are."

"There's too much ground interference down here," the copilot said, looking out the windows. "Let's go up."

A wooded and hilly landscape appeared up ahead. "I've got a better idea." The captain dropped down to the treetops and hugged the sharp bends of a river valley. Startled horses reared up in their pastures, and local folks gawked up in awe of the monstrous aircraft roaring by so closely overhead. Banking and rocking, the captain negotiated the course as if he were flying a Piper Cub.

Within seconds, Peterson lost his connection to the NSC. Three minutes passed, and still there was no sign of the F-15s. Thinking the jets had been called off, he breathed a sigh of relief. "Take her up, captain."

The transport bulled its way out of the valley. At two thousand feet, the RWR beeped, and the radar screen revealed two jets bearing down on them from five miles away.

"Radar locked," the copilot reported. "Another damn Sidewinder."

"We're out of flares," Peterson reminded them.

The captain shook his head. "This just isn't going to be our day."

"Four miles," the copilot said. "They're coming up fast, Mach point nine."

"Why haven't they fired?"

"Three miles..."

"Still no launch!"

"Two miles..."

Suddenly, the RWR indicated it had lost the radar lock.

The copilot said, "They've disengaged."

"What are they up to?" the captain asked.

Peterson suggested, "They've given up on the missiles, so they're going to shoot us down with their machineguns."

The captain shook his head. "We can't outmaneuver them."

"One mile..."

"You've got to try."

"Brace yourselves." The captain started working the yoke, waving the wings up and down, moving his aircraft erratically in an attempt to make it harder to hit with machinegun fire. The rattling ride became nauseating, but within seconds, the F-15s were flying alongside the transport. They were so close that Peterson thought he could smell the pilots' aftershave, but at least they weren't shooting. Confident the President had overridden their orders to terminate the flight, Peterson waved at them.

Nodding, the pilots gave him a two-fingered salute and peeled away.

Peterson slumped in his seat, and under the protection of *Project Aquarius*, the C-130 transport roared on toward Boulder, Colorado.

Chapter Twenty-Four

It couldn't have been a more miserable morning on Choke Mountain. Rain drizzled from a slate-gray sky, and the hillside was alive with trickles of muddy water streaming downhill and jogging every-which-way, crisscrossing, and merging, growing in volume and velocity and finally forming torrents that cascaded down into the Blue Nile Valley. Milton feared a mudslide might ruin his dig site.

Rain pattered on the communications tent as he sat in front of his blank computer screen awaiting the next series of ground sonar shots. Yesterday they'd moved ten feet of earth and planted sensors in the newly formed floor of the dig. He'd found the artifact in section 42, and he thought perhaps more items might be buried in the same area. Having no time to dig carefully, thanks to Emmett Collins' eviction notice, Milton had thrown every resource into a final and desperate attempt to uncover Choke Mountain's secret.

It was well past sunset before the last sensor was positioned in section 42, along with green flags that marked the grid for each shot. Last night, sleep had escaped him, and this morning the storm blew in.

Now, the dig site was a mud pit. After considerable effort, Jainaba and his sopping men had moved the propagator into position for the first shot. Maki and his brothers were watching the show, perched on their parked bulldozer, silent as vultures.

The propagator went off with a boom.

Milton's monitor came alive but revealed nothing.

"Next," he said into the two-way, and through the tent flaps, he watched the men drag the muddy propagator to the next green flag. Dressed in a yellow poncho, Gayle Weatherbee joined them, her bare legs streaked with mud and her hair hanging straight down. As she lent them a hand wrestling the heavy machine, she slipped and fell into the slop. Dancing raindrops in the mud puddles around her reminded Milton of scenes from Fantasia. He felt as besieged as Mickey Mouse.

Booming again and again, the propagator sonically explored each flagged area, but every returning echo revealed nothing but gray shades of rock and clay, and that unexplained bone-white area. An hour passed in total frustration, and then two hours. Milton felt a black despair come over him.

Jainaba had been working outward from the center of section 42, and he finally came to the deepest part of the dig, on the uphill side, by a ten-foot wall of earth from which muddy water cascaded into the dig site and onto the men. Undeterred, they took the shot.

Scrolling, the monitor revealed the echoes, and in the midst of all the muck, a couple of solid black images appeared. Milton stared in amazement. One spot was symmetrical, not square, not rectangular, but possibly cubical, and the other was more long and straight. A rush of curiosity hit his brain, and he shot a glance out the tent flaps. Jainaba and his men were already moving to the next flag. "Wait!"

Gayle looked up to the tent, squinting against the rain. Jainaba's voice came over the two-way. *"Eee, we need a break."*

"Shoot it again," Milton replied. He had to be sure it wasn't a fluke. As the printer rolled out the image and Milton waited to take the paper, he realized his hands were shaking.

The propagator boomed again, and again the echoes

revealed the same images. Whatever they were, they were ten feet down and twenty degrees right. He started the 3D image processor, which displayed the sensor grid they'd laid out, and rotating upward, it showed the buried images' positions in relation to the grid. After the printer rolled out the results, he threw on his hat and sprinted from the tent, the paper in his hand quickly becoming soaked with rain.

Slogging through the mud, he shouted. "It's here," and paced off the distance from the green flag. He turned, faced the propagator, and looking at the printout, took two steps forward. "This is where we dig, ten feet down. Get the backhoe up here. I'll do the rest by hand."

"You can't be serious," Gayle shouted.

Rain dripped from the brim of his hat as he trudged toward her. "We're running out of time to do it any other way."

"What's down there?" she shouted.

"The truth."

Before long, the backhoe was in position. The stabilizer legs came down; their pads sank into the mud. Wearing only a shamma over his head, the African operator sat in a metal seat at the back of the rig, and working levers, he extended the hydraulic arm out and angled the bucket to bite into the earth. The diesel engine growled under the strain as the bucket drew toward the backhoe and gouged out a mammoth helping of mud and dirt. Swiveling to the left, the bucket disgorged its contents, and then went back for another helping.

Now Maki and his brothers stood on their bulldozer, rain pouring on them as they chanted: "Kaang, Kaang, Kaang!" With each bite of earth taken, their chanting became louder.

"Kaang, Kaang, Kaang!"

Some of the locals joined in, while others cowered. The whole affair began to unravel Milton's already-frayed nerves as he stood ankle-deep in mud.

And the rain kept coming down. It was a cold rain, wet and miserable. Standing between Gayle and Jainaba, he watched the trench become longer and deeper with each stroke of the backhoe.

As the diesel belched smoke and roared, Maki and his brothers became more and more frenzied:

"Kaang, Kaang, Kaang!"

And the locals became more and more agitated.

Milton saw terror rising in their eyes as they stood around watching the machine do its work. Occasionally, the bucket's teeth would grate on a big rock, and the operator would have to work to free it, causing the backhoe to lurch and jump on its braces. The growing pile of removed dirt was already eroding away in rivulets of muddy rain-wash.

At one point during the digging operation, Milton assessed their progress. He took the grid printout from Gayle and called out to the operator. "*K'um!* Stop."

Maki and his brothers fell silent when the bucket stopped digging. Relieved that the chanting had ended, Milton jumped into the trench, tape-measure in hand. Granules of clay rained down on him, and because he feared the possibility of a cave in, he worked quickly to measure the depth and width of the trench and compare his findings with the three dimensional grid. His calculations told him they had to dig down another two feet. The buried objects were safely one foot away from the trench wall. Satisfied, he knelt in the rain-spotted clay, and after gathering up a handful of dirt, he crumbled it with his fingers. From this he knew the clay hadn't seen moisture in a long time, hopefully in 20,000 years, which gave him reason to believe that the objects he sought were well preserved. Being this close to something that old drew a shiver up his spine. He climbed out of the trench, and the backhoe went to work again.

Maki and his brothers took up their chanting: "Kaang, Kaang, Kaang!"

The next time he jumped into the trench, Milton took a shovel with him. As Gayle and Jainaba peered down over the edge, he started digging into the trench wall, vigorously at first, then more carefully as he cleared away the first foot of clay. When he heard a *chink*, his heart rate sped up. Grid printout in hand again, he determined that it was the long and straight object which he had encountered. The cube-shaped object was about three inches farther in and eleven inches to the left. He looked up to the rain-streaked opening above him. "Pass down a garden spade and a flashlight."

"Let me bring them down to you," Gayle said.

"You're staying up there," he shouted. "All of you. It's too dangerous down here."

"Why do you risk your life for this?" Jainaba shouted down.

"Just drop me the spade and flashlight."

He caught the flashlight, and the spade hit the dirt beside him. Now he went to work freeing the long, straight object. After fifteen minutes, he had it in his hand, but covered with clay, he had no idea what it was. He set it aside, and on his knees he continued digging, expanding the hole in the trench wall until the flashlight illuminated the edge of the cube-shaped object.

The patter of rain seemed suddenly far away, as did the idling diesel engine and the beating of his heart.

He worked mechanically, chipping and clawing at the clay until, after an hour, the object finally came free. Holding the box-like artifact in his hands, he now understood how Don Johnson felt when he'd unearthed *Lucy*. In spite of the fact that Milton was soaked to the bone, coated with mud, and every joint in his body ached, he felt charged with energy. It was the highest high he'd ever known.

Using the palm of his hand, he rubbed crumbling clay from his artifact. It wasn't heavy, and he saw a seam and something that looked like a sliding latch. He wanted to

open the box right now, but instead, he took out his magnetic screwdriver and touched it to the cover. It stuck, exactly what he expected, but still his excitement was hard to contain.

Leaving the flashlight, spade, and shovel where they fell, he grabbed the long, straight object and drunkenly clambered out of the trench.

The sight of him emerging from the ground with the artifacts in his hands set off Maki's brothers again. They jumped up and down on the bulldozer, chanting: "Kaang, Kaang, Kaang!" Maki wasn't anywhere to be seen, but right now Milton didn't have time to worry about the crazy Oromo farmer.

Milton summoned Jainaba. "Put the men to filling the hole. Then pack up the equipment. I want nothing left behind that can be of use to Emmett." He headed for the communications tent with Gayle running behind him.

Inside, he set the artifacts on the table and shed his sopping hat and coat. Gayle took off her poncho. Her hair was stuck to the side of her face, but her eyes were wide and full of wonder. Gathered around the table as rain pattered on the tent roof, neither of them could take their eyes off what he had found.

The box intrigued Milton most, so he picked up the long straight object first. As he cleaned off the clay deposits, he noticed that there had been no patination of the metal. Once he'd sufficiently cleaned it to identify it, he could see that it had a wide end and a narrow end, and it was folded into a ninety-degree angle along the length of it.

"It looks like a broken table leg," Gayle said.

Milton had thought the same thing. After all, the landslide would have smashed everything in its path. He didn't say anything to Gayle, but moved on to the box. His throat went dry. From the refrigerator, he got a bottle of water and took the time to take a long drink, which helped to suppress his inflamed curiosity. He didn't want to get careless. He didn't want to break anything.

"Are you going to open it?" Gayle asked.

"Get me the tool kit."

She rushed out of the tent, and by the time he'd moved the folding chair from in front of the computer monitor to the table and sat down, she was back with the tools. He took out a ruler first. The rain was coming down harder, as he expected it would in the afternoon, but in spite of the harsh conditions, he was determined to stick to procedures. On a yellow pad, he painstakingly recorded the object's measurements: nine inches high (assuming he had identified the top correctly), twelve inches wide, and ten inches deep. The seam that separated the lid of the box from the body was four inches from the top. Its surfaces were void of any symbols or decorations, but the texture reminded him of brushed aluminum.

Gayle set a digital scale on the table.

He weighed the box: six pounds, two ounces. That completed, he pressed his thumb on the sliding latch, but it wouldn't budge. Or perhaps he wasn't operating it correctly. From the tool kit, he took out a stencil brush and a brass pick and went to work cleaning the area around the latch.

"Shouldn't we be doing this back at the university lab?" Gayle asked.

"This thing isn't going anywhere near the university."

"Or Emmett Collins?"

"Exactly."

Click.

To Milton's astonishment, the latch suddenly snapped open. He figured he must have inadvertently touched some sort of release mechanism with the brass pick.

"Open it," Gayle said in a voice of boundless enthusiasm.

Milton set his tools next to the box. He took in the sound of the rain on the tent, and noticed the wind rise, the tent flaps now shuddering with intensity. A huge foreboding came over him, and for the next moment, he felt as if he were about to open Pandora's Box.

Gayle said over his shoulder, "Hurry."

Dismissing his anxieties, he placed both hands on the lid, one on each side, thumbs to the front, and lifted. With a hiss, 20,000-year-old air escaped as the lid came off.

Gayle gasped. A pleasing scent wafted through the tent. Milton had never experienced this aroma before. It made him feel lightheaded.

Gayle put her hand on her forehead. "Oh my." She keeled over. A chair toppled, and a computer monitor crashed to the floor with her.

Fearing the aroma was some kind of poisonous gas, Milton held his breath, dropped to the floor, and crawled to Gayle's side. Fighting disorientation, he got to his knees and dragged her toward the tent door, all the while trying to comprehend what had just happened. Gayle had been standing behind him, looking over his shoulder. She'd inhaled the gas with a gasp as it rose from the box. Her smaller frame and body weight had made it easy for her to be overpowered.

Outside, he gasped fresh air and noticed his dizziness subside with each lungful. The wind drove the rain with biting force, and gray clouds overhead rolled with a ferocity he'd not seen around here before. It was as if all of nature had become suddenly enraged.

He placed a finger on Gayle's neck. She was alive. "Thank God."

A few moments later, her eyes blinked and came open. "Dr. Spears?"

"Are you all right?"

"Why am I lying in the rain?" She sounded drunk.

"Christ." Milton pulled her to a sitting position. "Breathe deeply. Do you remember what happened?"

A look of serenity washed over her face. "No."

"You've got to stand up." He helped her to her feet.

"I feel dizzy."

"Breathe, breathe."

"It's raining." She giggled like a little girl.

Milton looked into the tent at the open box on the table. He hadn't gotten a chance to look inside it. Everything had happened so fast, and he had no explanation for any of it. The wind was sure to dissipate the gas, he guessed, but thought it best to stand in the storm a little longer.

"Dr. Spears, I'm cold."

"Keep breathing."

She leaned into him. "Gee, you're cute."

Now he knew she was bombed. He decided she should lie down, so he helped her negotiate the few steps to her tent, unsnapped the fly, and led her to the cot, into which she promptly plopped. "Good night, Dr. Spears."

As he covered her with a blanket, he felt the shotgun she always slept with. "I'll check on you in a while."

She was snoring.

In a rush, he headed back to the communications tent, but before stepping inside, he held his breath. With rain still dripping from his hat brim, he sidestepped the smashed computer monitor and approached the open box. What he saw inside was beyond anything he could have ever imagined.

An eye stared back at him from inside the box, a 20,000-year-old eye of providence, a human-looking eye inside a triangle surrounded by sunrays. It was embedded in the cover of a book, and when he carefully opened the cover, he could see it was a book with thin silver pages and the black writing of a language he'd never seen before, and Milton had seen them all during his career. And he was sure this book was important. It had been sealed in this box and, to all appearances, protected with a poisonous gas. Whoever had written it was more highly advanced than the humanoids that roamed this planet 20,000 years ago. There was no doubt in his mind; this artifact was alien. He'd found it in the "cradle of mankind", and its existence could destroy every theory of man's origins. Worse, Emmett must have figured it out, as well. He was going to steal the dig site on Choke Mountain, and there was nothing Milton could do to stop him. There was only one way to safeguard this discovery. He would have to take it to the University of Colorado...himself.

Just then, Maki leaped into the tent, startling Milton to no end. "Get out of here."

"When I am through," he said in a sandpaper voice. Rain dripped from his scraggly black hair and amplified the stink of his goatskin robe. His albino eyes glared with ferocity at the alien box on the table. "You have awoken the curse of Choke Mountain," he said, approaching too close for Milton's comfort. "I beseech you to bury this thing you have found and leave the past where it belongs."

Swallowing panic, Milton stepped back until a table behind him stopped him. "What do you know about this?"

"You have come to Kaang's doorstep."

Milton knew the story well and respected the locals' beliefs, but their god was not going to get in the way of the truth. "This is bigger than Kaang."

"It is wrong that you take this thing from him. Put it back before it is too late."

"I appreciate your concern. You're a wise man, but you have no say in the matter. The artifact is going to the USA."

Now Maki's hand hovered over the hilt of his Masai knife. "It is going back in the ground, even if I must take it by force."

Milton wasn't about to give up this artifact without a fight, not like he'd caved in to Emmett Collins. Not this time. "You should have brought your brothers," he growled.

"I do not need them." In a blur, Maki drew the knife.

Milton darted to the table and grabbed the brass pick. It was a puny weapon compared to Maki's knife, but Milton brandished it menacingly. The gesture brought a cackle from Maki's throat, and he lunged forward but stumbled over the computer monitor on the floor that Gayle had dragged down with her when she passed out. His goatskin robe complicated matters to the point he had to forego his attack just to keep his balance.

Milton took advantage of the moment and sidestepped around Maki, who quickly regained his stance and pivoted sharply, lunging again. Milton grabbed Maki's wrist, and in the cramped confines of the tent, the ensuing struggled sent chairs toppling and office equipment crashing to the floor. Milton dropped the brass pick in favor of grappling Maki with both hands.

Maki fought like a wild animal, reeling and thrashing, his Masai knife often grazing Milton's face and finally knocking off his hat. The commotion brought Jainaba and his men running, as well as Maki's brothers. They met as enemies on a battlefield and began beating on each other in the mud outside the tent. It was all-out bedlam before a shotgun blast rang out. Everyone froze, including Maki.

"What's the matter with you people?" Gayle held the shotgun up in the air. "This is what I was talking about, Jainaba. Look at you." They were all covered with mud and dripping rain, and their eyes were fierce and their fists were clenched. "God didn't mean for man to be like this."

Milton glared into Maki's albino eyes. They were nose-to-nose, locked in their combative embrace. "She's right, Maki, drop the knife."

"No."

Gayle entered the tent with the shotgun level at her hip. "Drop it, Maki."

Groaning, he gave up the knife. "Kaang will have his curse."

Milton tossed the knife on the table. "If you're so worried about it, then you should know that Kaang's real enemy is Emmett Collins. He's coming back tomorrow with diggers of his own."

"Why would he do this?"

"He's looking for..." Milton hesitated, thinking Maki wouldn't grasp the meaning of aliens, so he decided to stay with what Maki feared most. "He's looking for the door to Kaang's underworld."

Maki's albino eyes got big around. "He will find the word that will destroy all men."

"Not if I can help it," Milton assured him. "But there's something I must do first. I'd like for you to stay here while I'm gone."

"Where are you going?" Gayle asked.

"Boulder, Colorado. You and the others can wait for me in Bahar Dar." To Maki he explained, "This artifact," he pointed to the box, "is only a clue to what's buried here. I need to study it in the lab at the University of Colorado. I must learn what it is, what it means."

Maki clutched the amulet hanging from his neck. "It is better that you don't."

"That's why I need your help."

"I have already tried to help you."

"Keep an eye on Emmett for me." Milton knew that Maki and his brothers would cause Emmett a lot of trouble, and that would hinder his progress while Milton was in Colorado. "Will you stay?"

Looking at his soaked and muddy brothers standing outside the tent, Maki nodded. "We will need another pig."

Chapter Twenty-Five

At the University of Colorado, there was once a dormitory building called Aquarius Hall. It was built in 1973, four years after *Project Blue Book* ended all government involvement in UFO investigations. Twelve years later, the building was expanded into what became known as the Center for Astrophysics and Space Astronomy. The construction project suffered huge cost overruns due to the difficulties encountered in maintaining the integrity of the original building hidden within the new design. Only a few people knew about the existence of Aquarius Hall, until today, when thirteen Beltzans became its first residents.

Luthes was breathing much better now, though he often found himself holding his breath at the beauty of this place called earth. The blue sky dazzled him most. There were mountains and meadows and trees and red rock on Beltzee, of course, but the sky was a dull blue-green, and he thought he'd never see anything different. From the look on Regarius's face, Luthes thought he too must have been equally amazed.

Quarters were comfortable and adequate. He had his own room, as he had on *Questnar*, but his bed was spacious, and the windows were large and bright. Fancy designs adorned the walls. A table with a vase of flowers sat in the corner, and there was a box on a counter that reminded him of his scope screen.

Regarius knocked on the door and stepped in. He wore pants the humans called blue jeans and a short-sleeved shirt with symbols on the front: *C-U-B-U-F-F-S*, whatever that meant. His white shoes squeaked on the smooth floor as he walked, and his gray hair was going every which way, as usual. "Just think," he said. "We could be dead by now."

Looking out the window, Luthes was about to reply when a horrifying sight met his gaze. A building on the corner had a cross on the roof, a black Tarreeda cross. The sight stabbed his chest with fear.

Regarius moved to Luthes' side and made a wheezing sound. "There is still something very unsettling about this place."

"It is just a coincidence," Luthes replied. "The Tarreeda did not survive on the Ice Planet."

"I am not convinced."

"There is no other explanation."

Regarius sat on the bed. "The matter of the oscillations in the Tarreeda's' flight path has not been resolved."

"The problem with you specialists is you cannot take anything at face value. You have to pry into every nook and cranny, looking for something that does not exist. The facts are clear. We are on earth, guests of the humans who will send us home soon."

"Why do I think it is not that simple?"

"You always say that."

Another knock on the door, but it didn't open. Luthes turned from the window. "Yes?"

"Luthes?" Lisa's voice activated his translator.

He'd been stern with her before, when they were sick and housed in the place they called SIU, and he didn't expect she'd ever visit him again. Her unexpected arrival sent him rushing for the door. "Come in, please." The first thing he noticed when she entered was the translator clipped to a shoulder strap of her pink top. She wore matching shorts and white sandals, and her yellow hair glowed like the fire of Beltzee's twin suns. The second thing he noticed, she was carrying a tray.

"I thought you might be ready for some real food." The plate on the tray was heaped with food he'd never seen before, and a glass of white liquid.

"It is not fruit and fish?"

"It's steak."

His translator sent him an image of a sharp wooden stick, but his eyes told him that was incorrect. "I do not understand."

"Steak." She set the tray on the table. "T-bone, you know, beef, meat."

Meat he understood, and a sudden terror engulfed him. Wide-eyed and speechless, he stared at the plate, the hunk of meat and bone, and he couldn't imagine the brutality inflicted upon the unfortunate donor animal.

"You're not hungry?" Lisa asked.

He stepped back. "I would rather starve to death than eat what you have brought me."

"What?"

"Only the Tarreeda eat meat." His stomach turned upside down just saying it.

Regarius said, "Another unsettling development, Luthes?"

He thought he was going to be sick. More and more, Regarius appeared to be correct in his hypothesis that these humans were in fact the Tarreeda. "Take it away."

"Okay," Lisa said. "I'll get you something else, but first, I want to show you how things work around here." She flipped a switch on the wall. "Lights." She went to the box on the counter. "TV." When she pushed a button, the screen came alive with pictures and sound, running animals with humans on their backs, fire tubes puffing smoke and an awful yelping sound. "Cowboys and Indians," she said, then picked up a small device and pointed it at the TV. "Remote," she said. Working buttons on the remote, the scene on the TV changed to a human singing. "One hundred ten satellite channels. I'm sure you'll find something of interest."

Everything about these humans interested Luthes, and he was sure this fascinating machine could help him to understand them better, though the eating of meat would be impossible to accept.

Lisa put the remote in Regarius's open hand. He started switching channels, one after the other, and Luthes became confused. His brain tried to focus on something, but an instant later, another image bombarded him, then another. Lisa must've become equally frustrated because she grabbed the remote from Regarius. "We call that channel surfing. It's very annoying." She turned off the TV.

Luthes wanted it on, but before he could protest, Regarius beat him to it. "More."

"There's one in your room."

With that, Regarius left in a hurry.

Lisa sat on the bed. "I'm sorry about last time." She offered him a place to sit on the bed with her. "You're right about us humans. We have our problems, and sometimes we're not very nice to each other, but that's not all of us all of the time. We're not all bad."

She would be hard pressed to convince him of that, and then pointed to the window. "Why do you put black crosses on your buildings?"

"Huh?"

"Look outside."

"Oh, the church. It's a symbol of our religion." She reached inside her shirt and took out a necklace that struck terror into Luthes' soul. "Like this one."

It was a small Tarreeda cross with a nearly naked human hanging on it, his arms spread, and there were spikes in his hands and feet.

"It's very important to us."

Luthes panicked. He couldn't help himself. His feet started moving, and he leaped off the bed, but his knees wouldn't hold him. He fell to the floor and scooted into the corner under the table, knocking over the flower vase. His heartbeat was at maximum overdrive.

"Luthes. What's the matter?" She closed her eyes and clutched the tortured human in her fist. "I'm sorry."

"Why did you show me that?"

"It isn't what you think."

"I am not stupid. I know what it is."

"Let me explain. You won't be afraid." She held her hand out to him, the morbid object of torture and death tucked inside her blouse. A compassionate glint sparkled in her eyes. "Please?"

But he couldn't imagine her saying anything that would make him understand the atrocity she wore around her neck. The earth was a beautiful place, he'd seen, but the humans who lived here were as ugly as the Tarreeda. They did things to each other, as the Tarreeda had done to the Beltzans, and he feared it would be just a matter of time before he too was hung on a cross.

"This happened a long time ago," she said. "Please, come out from under there and listen to the story."

"I do not trust you."

"Humans don't do this anymore." She righted the flower vase. "Let me explain."

"But you did it in the past, like the Tarreeda."

"We're not like the Tarreeda."

He wondered if she realized how lame that sounded.

"You want to know what happened, don't you?"

Of course he did. He wanted to know everything. His curiosity was just as intense for these humans as it had been for the Tarreeda. And he had to admit his interest in Lisa was mounting as well. He thought it must've taken a lot of courage for her to reveal the necklace to him, and now he wondered if that was because she was interested in understanding him also. If so, the least he could do was meet her halfway. With that thought, he crawled out from under the table.

"That's better," she said. "Sit with me, and I'll tell you the story of this man on the cross. Then you can watch TV all you want."

***

Dr. Milton Spears arrived at the University of Colorado after a grueling eighteen-hour trip from Ethiopia. The cab ride from DIA to Boulder took over an hour, as traffic on the Boulder Turnpike moved along at a crawl. He'd forgotten what city congestion was like, and he was appalled at the urban sprawl Denver had suffered. It was only a *cow town* last time he was here. However, he understood that recent earthquakes in California had sent the populace running to more stable ground in Nevada and Colorado.

Donning his bushman hat and still dressed for an African safari, he paid the cab driver and then bounded up the steps to Administration. He carried with him two items: a small suitcase and a heavily wrapped package that contained the box he'd found.

"I'm looking for Dean Billings," he told the receptionist.

"Are you guys going fishing?" she asked.

He tipped his hat. "I always dress like this."

Moments later, the balding Dean Billings appeared, dressed in suit coat and tie. "Dr. Spears. Please, come this way."

They went through a swinging door, and as they walked down the hall together, Milton said, "I'd like to get to the lab as soon as possible."

"What do you have there?" Billings asked, eying the package.

"It's from the dig on Choke Mountain."

Billings cleared his throat. "You should have followed

the prescribed channels, you know, through Addis Abba University, I mean...this is highly unusual."

"I'll explain later." Milton didn't want to get his adrenaline flowing over his problems with Emmett Collins.

"What are you up to?"

"Wait until you see this, then you'll understand."

"But first, wouldn't you prefer to freshen up a bit. We have a nice room for you at Aden Hall."

"There'll be plenty of time for that later."

***

In the lab, groups of students were gathered around tables, working on various projects. Dr. Spears donned a lab apron and unwrapped his alien artifact. Because Billings oversaw all departments at CU, he was privy to what he was about to see. After all, it was his university's money that had funded the Choke Mountain dig.

Before long, the box rested on the examination counter in plain view.

Dean Billings pressed in closer. "What is it?"

"Watch this." Using a brass pick, Milton activated the latch and opened the box, leery that a fresh dose of gas might greet him. However, there was none, just the strange eye of providence staring up at him.

"My God," Billings said. "Where'd it come from?"

"It's not from around here," Milton explained. "By that I mean it's not from this planet."

"Alien?"

"That's right." He reached into the box and gently lifted the book cover. "This is unlike any language I have ever seen."

Leaning in, Billings asked, "What does it say?"

"I don't know. I have to translate it somehow."

Billings stepped back, his eyes open wide. "I wonder..." Taking Milton's arm, he led him to a vacant wash sink far removed from the students. "There's something you should know," he whispered. "You're not going to believe it."

Milton sensed excitement in Billings' grip. "What?"

"Project Aquarius has been activated."

It meant nothing to Milton. "What's that?"

"The National Security Agency has a super secret project to harbor and protect aliens."

"So?"

"They have thirteen aliens...here at the university, right now."

He couldn't have heard the dean correctly. "Thirteen what?"

"Aliens."

That's what he thought Billings had said, but the notion was beyond belief. Milton laughed, drawing the attention of several students.

Dean Billings tugged on Milton's shirtsleeve. "I'm not joking."

"Let me get back to work."

"Listen to me." Billings wouldn't release Milton's shirt. "I know how this must sound, but perhaps these aliens can help you translate your book." He pointed to the box on the table.

The idea struck Milton with a rush of excitement, but even as he wanted to believe Billings, his distrust of university politics gave him cause to remain cautious. For all he knew, Billings had concocted the unbelievable alien story in order to horn in on the discovery, as Emmett Collins had done. "No thanks. I'll figure it out myself."

Billings let go of Milton's shirt. "Very well," he whispered. "Have it your way, but when you're totally stumped and tired of wasting time, come see me. You will be enlightened." He turned and left the lab.

Milton was happy to see him go. Standing in front of his alien book, he grumped, "Aliens? Here? No way." That was as impossible to believe as this alien book he'd dug out of Choke Mountain. But he had found it. It was alien. So it wasn't impossible. He wondered if that meant aliens at the University of Colorado were possible too. Now he didn't know what to think.

He looked at the book. A cold rush of fear spread through him as he stared at the cover and into the eye of providence.

Chapter Twenty-Six

An ugly gloom hung over Fleet Base Command on Beltzee. In the days following the invasion, Sangrean's men were made to toil as slaves for the victorious humans. They had taken over crew quarters, forcing the defeated Beltzans to pitch makeshift tents on the south lawn. They were forced to live as refugees in a camp of squalor, the air fouled from the stench of sewage sumps and smoky cook fires.

The upside of all this misery came in the repairs to Fleet Base Command. Materials had been shipped in from Odotzee, and under armed guard, shifts worked day and night to mend the broken buildings and pile up the repulsor cannon debris on the granitite plain. Word came to the camp of similar operations being undertaken in the city of Benzatee and several other centers that had been sacked during the invasion. The humans had a curious way of destroying everything, and then rebuilding what they had destroyed.

Sangrean didn't take part in any of these activities. He sat on a cot in a locked room the humans called detention. There were no windows, and the air was stale from lack of ventilation. The fact that he hadn't taken a shower in several days hindered his comfort as well.

Clanking keys drew his attention to the door, which opened with a squeak. He was surprised to see Verrilla entering with his ration of bread and water.

"It is not much." She set the tray on the small table.

The human guard closed the door.

Sangrean wiped sweat from his forehead. Brigham

had sentenced him to bread and water and told him he wouldn't see the light of day as long as he refused to cooperate with their mission to steal the Beltzan's teleportation technology.

"Bread and water. It is better than nothing." He noticed she was wearing the same dress he'd seen her in before, but now it was torn. "Why have the humans let you visit me?"

She looked at him with sullen eyes. "I have been made a slave in the kitchens. It is like it was before, a curse to be a Beltzan woman in the hands of the Tarreeda."

Alarmed, Sangrean stood. "But these are humans from the planet earth, not the Tarreeda. What are you telling me?"

"If actions are their measure, I see no difference."

"What have they done to you?"

She hung her head as if shamed. "I wish I had not left *Latearian*."

"Do not talk like that," Sangrean approached her. "You would have been killed."

Falling into his arms, she said weakly, "With Luthes dead I do not have the strength to go on."

"But I must tell you—"

"Sashi is made to work in the kitchen, too, but unlike before on *Latearian*, the humans are brutal taskmasters. She has been whipped as I have, and we have not slept but a few hours each day."

He sat her on the cot and kneeled in front of her. "Do you know of anyone who has been hung on a cross?"

She shook her head.

"Then these humans are not as brutal as the Tarreeda."

Shakily, she stood, unbuttoned her dress, and let it fall to the floor, revealing a once smooth body crosshatched with red whipping welts, front and back. Some had leaked blood. "Humans are brutal nonetheless." Bending, she pulled up her dress and refastened the buttons. "And they take their favors violently."

Bile roiled in Sangrean's stomach as another rage came over him, that same sensation he had as the humans began their vicious attack. It was a strange feeling, but with it came a rush of energy and determination. In his mind, acts of retribution appeared in the form of dismembered humans. Inner satisfaction followed the gruesome images. Though violence was not a normal Beltzan reaction, perhaps it could be a learned response that, if applied properly, would help save his people and his planet.

"Are you all right?" she asked, her hand on his arm.

Sangrean felt a twinge of hope. "You must be strong, Verrilla, for Sashi...and for Luthes."

She looked at him with startled eyes. "Luthes?"

"Yes. He is alive."

"But *Questnar* was destroyed."

"As impossible as it may seem, Luthes was captured and taken to the humans' planet."

"Oh Cada. We have to get him back."

***

Sitting at a desk in the newly repaired command center, Brigham lit a cigar. All around him, radar and communications equipment beeped and crackled. His men busied themselves with their duties. Everything had gone as planned, making the smoke from his cigar taste sweeter than honey.

He thought about Sangrean and felt confident that a diet of bread and water would bring him to his senses, but so far he'd steadfastly refused to cooperate, and following his lead, his officers were just as obstinate. Brigham needed to know who on this planet had expertise in the teleportation system, who the operators were, the designers and the engineers. However, no amount of torture had made them reveal that information.

Up to this point, Brigham had found himself besieged with logistical problems for his soldiers, as well as the team of scientists he'd brought in. By commandeering the existing facilities, many of these problems were settled in short order, and after deciding to make Fleet Base his command post, he began to initiate repairs to the facility. Prisoners were mobilized into work gangs. Progress was swift. Security had been established. M1-A1 Abrams tanks patrolled the perimeter. He was sure any counterattack would be dealt with efficiently; however, he thought it strange that local resistance was nonexistent.

Colonel Scott came in. "Sir, the men have finally cut through the doors."

Brigham rose to his feet and snuffed out the cigar on his boot heel. The scientists had found what they believed to be the teleportation machine, but the aliens had sealed the doors during the invasion. And these were no ordinary vault doors. They were the size and thickness of the nuclear blast doors at NORAD inside Cheyenne Mountain, Colorado. Complicating matters, the doors were made of unfamiliar composites that resisted the heat of cutting torches. Proposals to use a shuttle's particle beam to blast open the doors were quickly dismissed, as the equipment inside could have been irreparably destroyed. So day and night, the torches assaulted the barrier. The delay was unfortunate, but now they'd made it over the first hurdle...getting inside. And they'd done it without Sangrean's help.

The short walk to teleportation brought Brigham to his mission objective, and at first his mind couldn't fathom the enormity of the task before him. Inside the teleportation machine, he saw gadgetry that struck him with awe.

The most striking device stood in the center of a huge chamber, a transparent ball of a glass-like material that towered ten stories high. Inside it, a reflective sphere hung in the center with no visible means of support. It rotated illustriously like a mirrored disco ball over a dance floor on prom night. Shards of reflected light from this ball streaked across a domed ceiling, which was covered with mirror tiles that dispersed those shards of light in a million directions, down to the reflective floor, across to the mirrored walls, and back to the ceiling. The combined result of this reflected light produced a soft glow that seemed to hang in the air like a luminous fog.

The scientists filtered in. A group of them gazed at the vast spectacle with open-mouthed wonder. They milled about in silence, each one contemplating the mystery before them. Brigham noticed that a few of them found a short stairway, which led to a door about five feet off the floor. The door opened automatically, and the men went inside. Curiosity drew Brigham to follow them.

Inside the room, he suffered another mental setback as the scientists around him gazed dumbfounded at the equipment they had found. It was obviously the control room. One entire wall clearly revealed the inside of the chamber, and he realized right away that he was standing behind a two-way mirror. The most puzzling thing about this room was the total lack of switches, dials, levers, and knobs of any kind. There were consoles, of course, but their surfaces were covered with millions of colored tiles, some large as a foot, some small as an inch. The mosaic was beautiful but perplexing.

One scientist approached a console and touched one of the smaller tiles. A voice echoed through the room, startling everyone. Brigham's translator relayed the message. *"Incorrect input. Please try again."* Other scientists began touching tiles and got similar responses. Then they huddled together, shaking their heads.

It was obvious to Brigham that whoever operated this device had to know the exact sequence in which to touch the tiles to get the machine to work. Not only would Brigham's scientists and engineers have to figure out the hardware, but also the secret to operate it. A cold chill of defeat crept through him, a stark realization. Without Sangrean's help, he was going to die on this stinking planet.

Chapter Twenty-Seven

Several days passed as Milton toiled in the lab at the University of Colorado, working long hours in an attempt to translate the language in the alien book.

Some of the symbols looked vaguely familiar, possibly a cross between ancient Sumerian pictograms, Akkadian cuneiform, and Egyptian hieroglyphics, but not similar enough to make any sense. He couldn't determine if it was written left to right or right to left, and because the symbols were also aligned in columns, he thought it could possibly read top to bottom or vise versa.

He took photographs of the pages, and after scanning them into the computer, he superimposed a database of ancient languages onto the alien writing. Working backwards, it seemed as though he was witnessing human language regress back before the time of Mesopotamia. The more he studied it, the more it became evident that the alien text hadn't been derived from any known language but was probably the root from which all language grew. With that stunning hypothesis plaguing his mind, he picked up the phone and dialed Dean Billings. It was time to have a talk with his aliens.

***

Two hours later, Milton arrived at the C.A.S.A. building, and after taking a special elevator, he met Dean Billings at the bottom floor. Billings led him down a hallway to a room with a bookcase. A loose book revealed a switch. Billings touched it, causing the bookcase to rotate, revealing a secret passage. The security system was so clichéd that Milton understood why it was effective. No one looking to penetrate Aquarius's security would ever think that access to the hall would be that simple. However, a tight grid of sensors in the passageway announced their presence to black-suited National Security Agents on watch. One man with a scar on his face greeted them. "Welcome to Aquarius Hall. I'm Agent Peterson."

"Dr. Milton Spears." He shook the man's brawny hand.

"Dean Billings has told me of your alien book," Peterson explained. "Aquarius is at your full disposal."

"I'm hoping your aliens can help me decipher the language."

"Wouldn't that be something?" Peterson replied. "You'll need this translator." He clipped a device to Milton's collar. Billings didn't get one.

"Aren't you going in?" Milton asked him.

"Not tonight," he said. "Good luck."

"Thanks."

"The old man's name is Regarius," Peterson said as they strolled down a bright hallway. "He's a specialist, a scientist with expertise in genetics."

"I need an expert in alien language," Milton replied.

"You only get what we've got."

Until now, Milton hadn't considered what these aliens might look like, his problems with the book more pressing. "Why did you refer to the alien as an old man?" he asked Peterson, thinking his concept of an alien's appearance would never draw such a parallel. "Do they look like us?"

"Except for their long fingers," Peterson replied. "And they don't have any hair on their faces."

"Interesting," Milton said, though he thought that was an understatement. Being an expert in evolution, he knew that even minute changes in environment and circumstance produced vastly diverse organisms, and he could only assume that the differences between two planets would be so huge that the inhabitants of each would more likely be immensely different rather than even slightly similar.

He considered human DNA, which was ninety five percent identical to a chimpanzee's, yet the five percent difference was enormous, encompassing grasping feet, quadruped locomotion, and full body hair as being the most significant phenotypical dissimilarities in the two species.

And human DNA was also seventy five percent similar to a nematode worm, which in no way would lead Milton, or anyone for that matter, to infer that round worms were three-quarters human. However, he would assume that aliens who possessed the same physical characteristics as humans must also have the same DNA as humans, and that would be impossible considering the galactic distances between their individual evolutions.

They came to a door and stopped.

Peterson knocked. "Regarius?"

Inside, a TV was blazing guns.

He knocked again. "You have a visitor."

The door opened. A blast of sound greeted them. Milton held his breath as his eyes fell on the alien in the doorway. He looked like Albert Einstein less the bushy mustache.

"Come in, come in." He motioned with a long-fingered hand that immediately fascinated Milton. "Have some popcorn."

"Unsalted microwave popcorn," Peterson said. "Alien gold. They love the stuff."

Stepping into the blaring room, Milton didn't know how to act in the alien's presence. Should he bow? Should he offer a handshake? The dilemma quickly faded as Regarius rushed back to watch the TV. "They are killing each other."

It was *The Alamo*. As a ladder-full of Mexicans toppled over backwards, Regarius hugged the popcorn bowl and looked as if he were about to pass out from fright.

"He's been watching way too much TV," Peterson explained. "I keep telling him it's not real, but he doesn't believe me." Peterson turned off the set. "I want you to meet Dr. Milton Spears."

Regarius stared at the blank screen, his face drooping with disappointment.

"He has a favor to ask of you."

Sighing, Regarius stood. Popcorn bowl cradled in one arm and his free hand extended, he said, "What can I do for you?"

Milton felt a sudden urge to step back, but instead, he grasped the alien's long-fingered hand and shook it. He'd never forget the sensation. "Would you look at something for me?"

***

Luthes had spent the last five days greedily taking in everything on TV. Some of it was beautiful, and he especially enjoyed the nature programs and the wide variety of life on this planet called earth. Lisa would sit with him for hours, explaining things as they appeared, and sometimes Regarius would come into the room with popcorn, and they'd watch a movie together. The TV presentations were often interrupted with short takes on human products. Lisa called them commercials. He found them entertaining as well as informative.

However, most of what he saw on TV was horrifying and violent, especially the History Channel, which replayed wars of the past, recounting the horrible death and destruction humans had inflicted upon one another. He saw the mushroom cloud of an atomic bomb, ruined cities, and skeletal human corpses piled up like firewood. And from what he'd heard on the *NEWS* channels, humans had learned nothing from their past mistakes: reports of war and terrorism, murder and assault, robbery and corporate fraud. The death of children at the hands of their parents upset him deeply. Through all this, he came to believe that humans were every bit as violent as the Tarreeda.

Tonight, he and Lisa cuddled together on the bed and watched a terrifying movie called *Jurassic Park*. As they clung to each other for comfort, Luthes found himself paying more attention to Lisa's warmth than to his fear of the monsters. She'd been with him nearly every waking hour, and he enjoyed her fussing over him, touching him, and the way she often looked at him with her soft blue eyes. He wanted to tell her how he felt, but thinking of Verrilla, he quickly returned to the raptors' murderous rampage.

As the movie progressed, he began to understand human's scientific resourcefulness and their inherent struggle for survival. It wasn't like that on Beltzee, at least not after the Tarreeda were banished to the Ice Planet.

During the spine tingling part when the raptors were stalking the kids in the kitchen, Regarius came in. He was with two humans, one Luthes had not seen before. "We must go with them," Regarius said.

"I am watching this."

"It is important."

The unfamiliar human removed his hat. "My name is Dr. Milton Spears."

Regarius said, "He needs our help."

"Why me?"

"We are in this together," Regarius replied. "Come on."

Then the mathematician, Janis Mackey, came in with his wife Tracy. "What's the hold up?"

The room was getting crowded. "All right," Luthes said. "Where are we going?"

"The anthropology lab. Ray Crawford will meet us there."

Moaning, Lisa turned off the TV. "I'm going with you."

"I don't think so," Peterson said.

She looked into Luthes' eyes and took hold of his long fingers. "We're in this together, right?"

He liked the sound of that. "Of course."

"Wait one second," Janis blurted out. "What's going on here, Lisa?" Frowning, his accusing eyes darted back and forth between her and Luthes.

"He trusts me." Lisa rubbed his arm.

"I've seen that look in your eyes before," Janis said. "You're in love."

"I am not."

"Your father will have a fit."

"Leave my father out of this." Lisa's voice was loud.

Luthes didn't like it. "Please," he said softly. "It is nothing."

"Nothing?" Lisa shot him a sharp glare. "Fine." She stormed out.

***

The lab was a few blocks from Aquarius Hall, and they rode over in a vehicle called a minivan. The street lights fascinated Luthes.

On the way, Milton talked about the dig on Choke Mountain and what he had found under an ancient landslide. "When we opened the box, a gas came out and almost killed us."

The Tarreeda had developed a poisonous gas to exterminate Beltzans they'd rounded up from the cities. It produced a euphoric effect before turning lethal. Fresh air was the only antidote, but only if it were administered quickly.

"Inside the box," Milton said, "there is a book with thin silver pages and black inscriptions. I'm hoping you might know what it says."

"Why would we know of a book found on your earth?" Luthes asked.

"Because it's older than our history," Dr. Spears said. "And made of materials unknown to us."

Luthes leaned back in his seat. He didn't understand why this should matter to him.

"The writing in the book isn't familiar, either," Milton added as the van stopped.

Luthes looked at Regarius, puzzled.

"I told him we would see it," Regarius said.

The doors opened. Luthes got out and inhaled aromatic air. "What is it that I smell?"

"Pine," Milton said.

"It is delightful," Regarius put in.

A night breeze rustled the trees as they negotiated a lighted sidewalk that led them to a building's door. Inside, it was bright and hollow sounding as they walked down a hallway. "Why does the air smell different in here?" Luthes asked.

"That's floor wax," Peterson replied.

Luthes didn't know what he meant, this floor wax, but he liked the aroma anyway.

Ahead, Ray Crawford was standing at an open door. His hands came out of his pockets when he saw them approach. "What took you so long?"

"Nothing," Peterson said, but Luthes knew Lisa's outburst had detained them. They had to wait while Dr. Mackey and Tracy searched for her, but she was gone. They'd decided to stay behind to continue their search. Now Peterson stood outside as the others went into the lab.

"Right here." Milton rushed to an artifact safe, one of several positioned throughout the lab, and opened the locked door. From inside, he removed a silver box.

"Ritainium," Regarius said, his eyes wide with surprise.

"What?" Milton set the box on the counter.

"I have seen this metal before."

"Then perhaps you'll recognize this." Milton opened the box.

The room fell silent. Regarius stepped back, his hand patting his chest as if he couldn't catch a breath. Luthes moved forward warily, his gaze on the open box. A knot formed in his stomach at what he saw. "The eye of Cada," he said in a whisper. "The ever-watchful Cada."

Ray leaned forward and looked into the box. "We call it the eye of providence. Look." He pulled a piece of paper from his pocket. "A one dollar bill," he said and turned it over. "On the back, see, the eye of providence. It's also on the United States Seal, and the Masons call it the Masonic Eye. It's nothing new."

Milton added, "It's been around a long time, in one form or another, even without the triangle. It's appeared on obelisks in Egypt, pottery in Mesopotamia, and on the walls of temples in Turkey 8,000 years ago. However, the one on this book is over 20,000 years old."

Ray shot Milton a disbelieving look, brows arched. "How's that possible?"

Regarius said to Luthes, "Seems we have another unsettling development."

"What do you make of it?" Milton asked him.

"Beltzans did not use this symbol for Cada."

"What's Cada?"

"The one god of the universe." Regarius held out his hand, palm turned up. "Our Cada symbol is an open palm." He pointed to the eye on the book cover. "This one belongs to the Tarreeda."

"That means they have been here." Luthes couldn't believe his own words.

Milton frowned. "Who are the Tarreeda?"

Luthes explained about Beltzee's enemy. When he came to the part about banishing them to the Ice Planet

20,000 years ago, Regarius jumped in.

"The Tarreeda never made it to the Ice Planet, but somehow they traveled across the galaxy, to earth."

"Maybe this will tell us what happened." Milton took the book from the box and handed it to Regarius.

With long fingers, he opened the book carefully.

Luthes looked over Regarius' shoulder and recognized the Tarreeda inscriptions immediately.

Regarius studied it for a moment, flipped through a few pages, and then he looked up in amazement. "This is a ComCap's report...from one of the transport ships, BA1133, *Docknor*."

"Like a captain's log," Milton said.

"There were seven ships." Luthes recalled what happened after the battle of Zarakatan. "Each carried fifteen hundred Tarreeda. They were given food and water, but no weapons."

Ray asked, "What does the book say?"

Turning pages, Regarius studied the writing. "There are daily entries." He pointed a long finger. "Here, it says the Ice Planet is in view." He turned the page. "Now they are about to go into orbit." Another page...and he looked up. "They crash-landed."

Milton leaned forward. "Where?"

"The ComCap wrote: *It was most frightening. We were flying left wing in formation for orbital insertion when a strange ball of light engulfed our ship. Suddenly without control of navigation and steering functions, we were thrust into a tunnel of spinning stars streaking through space with brilliance. In a dizzying spiral, the transport tumbled into a space well where the bottom blocked out all light. Just as we were about to crash, the wall came open and we regained our controls, but not a moment too soon, as we were suddenly plummeting through a blue atmosphere. There was a lot of screaming onboard from the women and children. The helmsman kept the nose up and set us down violently in a forest. He and some others were killed, and we buried them on the side of this mountain. There has been no contact with the other transports, and I do not know where we are, but the ground is unstable here, rumbling constantly, and all the survivors have now gone down to the valley below. I see a river and many lands to conquer.*" Regarius looked up from the book. "It is the last entry."

"He must've sealed the box and set it on a table before the landslide hit," Milton said. "We found a table leg."

Luthes noticed Ray's white face and asked him, "Do you know how this could have happened?"

Ray wrung his hands. "It could be..." He paused and inhaled nervously. "The Tarreeda ComCap described a phenomenon I have seen before, the tunnel of swirling stars. We call it Higgs degeneration. The Tarreeda must've been caught in a Higgs Field storm that transported them into the 13th Power and across the galaxy to earth."

"How do you know about this Higgs field?" Luthes asked.

"That's how we were able to travel to your planet, through the same spinning tunnel, the same space well."

"Tell me," Regarius said to Milton. "What humans lived on this planet 20,000 years ago?"

"Homo sapiens, and there were the Neanderthal, who coincidently disappeared about that same time."

"But they roamed Europe and Asia," Ray said. "Homo sapiens came out of Africa."

"True," Milton put in. "From Ethiopia, and some theories suggest that Homo sapiens exterminated the Neanderthal."

"The Tarreeda killed them," Luthes said.

"Why would they have done that?" Ray asked.

Regarius answered, "The Tarreeda possessed a defective gene, one that predisposed them to violence. Killing animals and each other was what they did best."

"They most likely spread across your planet in a violent wave," Luthes added. "Destroying everything in their path, raping and pillaging as they went. Great civilizations rose in their wake, and there was war all over the land."

"That's about the way it happened," Milton replied. "But not for another twelve thousand years. Until then, Paleolithic man wandered in small tribes. They followed animal migration routes and stayed in seasonal camps for short periods. There wasn't much raping and pillaging for the Tarreeda to do back then."

"What about the salt problem?" Ray asked. "Wouldn't it have killed them in a short time?"

Milton said, "Choke Mountain and the Ethiopian highlands are much like Colorado. By the time future generations migrated down to the sea, they could have genetically adapted to the salt, after all, it would be another 12,000 years before Homo sapiens settled in Mesopotamia." Then a wide-eyed look of terror came over Milton's face, as if he'd just had a horrible thought.

"What is it?" Ray asked.

"My God," Milton said. "They crossbred with Homo sapiens."

"The Tarreeda interfered with the natural evolution on your planet," Regarius agreed, "and passed on their defective genes to your ancestors."

"But there was only a one-in-four chance of that," Milton suggested. "There were so few Tarreeda and so many Homo sapiens, the odds of that gene surviving would have been slim."

"It is obvious in my mind that it did survive," Regarius concluded.

Ray said, "I don't believe it."

"Look around you. You have crosses on your buildings, the Eye of Cada on your money, and you have weapons of death. Watch your TV. Look at your history. I see the Tarreeda in everything here. You possess their defective gene."

"Not me," Ray insisted.

Milton challenged him. "Haven't you ever wanted to slug the guy who butted in line at the grocery store, or cursed someone who cut you off in traffic? Don't we have to teach our children to be nice to the other kids?"

"Yes, but..."

"Of course we do. I think Regarius is right. We all have the defective gene, though I surmise some of us are better at controlling it than others."

Just then, Lisa stormed into the lab with Janis and Tracy following close behind. Janis was saying, "Take it easy, Lisa," but it was too late. She stomped up to Luthes and put her face up to his. "You think we're *nothing*?" she shouted, her eyes ice blue. "Is that the thanks I get for showing you the ropes around here, being nice to you? Nothing?"

Luthes felt a surge of panic, and unable to speak, he backed into a counter. Lisa turned to her father jabbing an index finger at him. "Luthes is the kindest most wonderful and sensitive man I've ever met—"

"Now listen here, young lady—"

"And I don't care if you approve of him or not."

"What are you saying?"

"I'm in love with him." She was shouting, which made Luthes cringe.

"He's an alien."

"I don't care if he's Frankenstein."

"He's going home to the green planet," Ray shouted back. "Back to Beltzee, so find yourself a nice college boy."

"You can't tell me who to love."

Luthes didn't know what to think. All this yelling was making him crazy. He wanted to tell Lisa everything would be all right. He wanted her to calm down, but right now something much graver troubled him. "Lisa, you are acting like a Tarreeda."

She swiveled around. "I'm a human who loves you."

"Love? It is too soon since we have met. Your love is superficial, self-serving."

"What do you know about love?"

"It is the most important thing on Beltzee. We care about each other. We respect each other. Beltzans love deeply, wholly, completely. There is no time wasted on shouting and fighting."

"Then you don't care enough for each other to fight."

"Violence is not necessary."

"It's necessary here on earth." She poked a finger at him. "To understand my love, you have to stop prejudging me as one of your enemies, your Tarreeda. Give me a chance. Give each of us a chance. Judge us as individuals if you must judge us at all."

Cowering, he said, "At this moment, I am not very impressed with the way you love me."

"Because you're being an idiot."

"Lisa, please," Janis said. "You're scaring him to death. Tracy? Talk to her, will you?"

Tracy shrugged. "There's nothing I can do. She's in love."

"Damn right I am." Lisa grabbed Luthes by the shirt, pulled him to her, and kissed him hard. "Take that back to the green planet with you."

"Beltzee," he managed, shocked at the taste of her tongue on his lips.

She turned and stomped out.

"Wait, Lisa..." Janis and Tracy ran after her.

Confusion was a whirlwind in Luthes' brain.

"Even in love, humans are violent," Regarius noted.

"I rest my case, Ray," Milton said. "You have the gene and passed it on to your daughter."

Ray's shoulders slumped.

"Well, young Rez," Regarius said and leaned on the counter. "I was right after all. The defective Tarreeda gene has survived."

A lot of things were going through Luthes' mind. He knew the Tarreeda were cold and merciless killers, but from the TV shows and movies, and from those who had been helping them, he'd seen many sides to human nature, so he thought he should listen to Lisa. When he looked at Regarius, he saw an *I-told-you-so* smile, but refused to accept defeat. "Lisa is right. We should not judge all humans on history alone."

"From what I have seen," Regarius said. "Not much has changed in 20,000 years."

"Humans are not exactly like the Tarreeda."

"Perhaps not, however, there is still the matter of this book. I trust it will not bring out the best in these humans." Regarius turned to Milton. "What would happen if it became known that humans are descendants of aliens?"

Milton shuddered. "Chaos."

"Worse." Ray moved to Regarius and put a hand on his shoulder. "When I first discovered your planet, I feared our world was not ready to know that you existed. The truth would cause pandemonium, so I destroyed the evidence, or so I thought. Now it's worse than I imagined. What we've discovered here must never leave this room. If it does, creationists and evolutionists will be at each other's throats, and their verbal battles will escalate into all out war. Everything mankind has ever believed about his origins, his god, and his place in the universe will be destroyed."

Milton's face drained of color. "There's an African myth of a curse buried on Choke Mountain. It warns that if man should open the door to the underworld, Kaang will destroy his beliefs with the utterance of a single word."

"Tarreeda," Luthes said. "That's the word, *Tarreeda*."

Regarius held up the book. "It does not appear here."

"Then it must be written somewhere else."

"If a landslide buried this book," Regarius said. "Then perhaps the Tarreeda transport ship is buried there also."

At that, Milton rushed to the safe and retrieved a series of printouts, which he quickly arranged on the counter. Everyone gathered around. "These are the echoes I recorded from the ground sonar shots on Choke Mountain." He pointed to the bone white areas. "I didn't know what to make of these until now. It must be the hollow hull of a huge spaceship."

"Quite nicely buried," Regarius said.

"As it should remain," Luthes added. "It is probably charged with the same poisonous gas as the ritainium box."

"Only in greater quantity and under higher pressure," Regarius concurred. "Should it be released, the consequences would be deadly for everyone nearby."

Milton's worried expression changed to one of gaping horror. "Emmett is going to dig it up. We've got to stop him."

Chapter Twenty-Eight

T he next morning, Peterson made all the arrangements. Through Project Aquarius's extensive network, flight reservations to Ethiopia had been confirmed for himself, Dr. Milton Spears, Ray Crawford, Luthes Rez, and Specialist Regarius. When Ray informed Lisa that she wasn't going, she threw another one of her famous hissy-fits.

"Like hell I'm not going." She dragged her suitcase out of the closet.

"You're too emotionally involved."

"Like hell. You're just determined to keep Luthes and me apart." She slammed the suitcase on the bed. "Well, it's not going to work. I go where Luthes goes."

"He thinks you're a lunatic."

She put her hands on her hips. "Is that what he said?"

"I saw the look in his eyes. You can't treat him like that."

"He'll get over it." She yanked open a dresser drawer and grabbed an armful of bras and panties. "I'm not letting him get away, not like Janis, not this time." She tossed the underwear into the suitcase and turned toward the closet. "If I have to buy my own ticket, I will."

"I need you to stay here with the other Beltzans."

She wasn't the aliens' babysitter, damn it. "Janis and Tracy can handle it."

"They're going back to NASA to help Stan prepare the transporter. There's a lot of work to be done before they can send the Beltzans home."

At the open closet door, Lisa paused, a finger tapping

her chin. "What do they wear in Ethiopia?"

Ray stepped in front of her. "Forget it."

She glared at him. He was never going to change: always overprotective, always demanding, and always afraid he'll lose her again. It was his way of overcompensating for making her grow up without him. Sending her away all the time, different schools. Different countries. He'd alienated his only child. Well, not now. Not this time. This was going to be the end of it. "Get out of my way."

"Don't do this to yourself, Lisa." His voice was softer, like a father's. "He's only going to leave you."

"No."

"He's going to break your heart."

"I know what I'm doing."

"Enlighten me," Ray said.

It wouldn't do any good to explain it to him. His mind was set. He didn't want her to have anything to do with an alien. But she knew Luthes had nothing to go home to. His wife and daughter were dead. *Questnar* was gone. His home was probably smoldering in the aftermath of Brigham's invasion. Luthes would be better off here on earth, with her, and she was going to make him see it that way. After all, there was room for only six Beltzans on the transporter, and Luthes was the kind of person who would give up his seat for someone else. All she had to do was make him want to stay. "You'll never understand."

"Lisa—"

Peterson came in. "We're loading the van. Are you ready, Ray?"

"I'm going too, but he won't let me pack." Lisa pointed at her father.

Ray huffed. "There's no room for you."

"As a matter of fact, there is." Peterson examined the half-packed suitcase on the bed. "Regarius decided to stay."

Anger and determination became a rush of

excitement. "Then I'm going in his place." She pushed past her father and started grabbing pants, shorts, and blouses. "What's the weather like in Ethiopia?"

"I thought Milton needed Regarius at the dig site."

"Luthes is the Tarreeda expert." Peterson replied.

Lisa piled shorts and halter-tops into her suitcase.

Peterson backed out of her way. "Regarius is going to study the human genome."

"Why?"

"He wants to find that defective Tarreeda gene."

"But we need him in Ethiopia," Ray insisted.

"Shoes?" She stooped to her closet floor and sorted through sandals, flats, and heels.

"He has the full support of *Project Aquarius*. In the meantime, we're going to dig up a spaceship."

Lisa shoved one pair of each kind of shoe into the suitcase, already piled above the rim and overflowing.

"And what about this Emmett Collins character Milton told us about? He sounds pretty shifty."

"You let me worry about him."

"If the media gets wind of this..." Ray ticked his tongue. "We're all in deep shit."

"If we came from the green planet, I need proof, Ray. And people need to know the truth."

Lisa folded the suitcase, but it was too full to close.

"You know the old saying *the truth will set you free*?"

"What about it?"

"This time it's *not* true. The truth will ruin everything we've ever believed."

"I know, with a single word humanity is doomed. We'll get over it." Peterson frowned at Lisa. "The van is waiting, girl."

She jumped on the suitcase lid, and with considerable effort managed to secure the clasps. Stuff was sticking out the seams. "I'm ready."

Pointing to the dresser, Ray said, "You forgot your

makeup case," and walked out with Peterson.

Lisa screamed in frustration. "You better wait for me."

***

In 1887, Emperor Menelik founded the capitol of Ethiopia. Today, Addis Abba was a thriving metropolis of four million people nestled in the foothills of Mount Entoto, 8,000 feet above sea level. Modern buildings and traditional African architecture coexisted in this meeting place of past and present cultures. This morning, a fierce and dusty wind blew through the city as an Ethiopian Airlines 747 touched down on the rubber-scarred runway at Bole, six miles from downtown. Milton's stomach grumbled for breakfast.

The newly constructed terminal boiled with activity. Milton led Agent Peterson, Ray, Luthes, and Lisa through baggage claim. In a small café, they enjoyed black coffee and sweet cake before heading outside where hawkers and panhandlers, young and old, besieged them, offering up everything from worthless vases to wild women and the best hashish in Africa. Milton knew the routine, and though he sympathized with their impoverished plight, he shooed them away. As a departing jet roared overhead, Jainaba drove up in a dusty gray van that squealed to a stop at the curb. Gayle Weatherbee jumped out. "Dr. Spears."

Surprised, he gave her a quick hug then greeted Jainaba. "Thanks for coming. I know it was a long drive."

"Eee, you are back very soon."

"I only hope we're not too late. Did you bring the gear we talked about?"

"Of course, and the dynamite."

"Good. We've got a grueling ten-hour drive to Choke Mountain. Help us load this stuff."

Jainaba climbed to the roof luggage rack, and Milton

handed up the ritainium box that he'd painstakingly wrapped for its journey back to Africa. Though Dean Billings had asked him to leave the box at the university, he had other plans for his alien artifact.

"I'm glad you're back, Dr. Spears." Gayle gave him a quick hug.

"I didn't expect to see you here."

"You're not happy that I came?"

"I asked Jainaba to meet us. Not you." Milton handed a suitcase up to him. "We'll drop you off at the university."

"Oh no you won't." Her brown eyes glared at him. "I'm going with you."

"It's going to be too dangerous for a woman."

"Don't give me that." She shrugged at Lisa who was handing her suitcase to Jainaba. "What about her?"

"I was against her coming too, but I was outvoted. You, on the other hand, are not subject to the same democratic process. As long as you are my student, you are my responsibility, and you'll do as I say."

"That's not fair, Dr. Spears."

"You're right, but you'll thank me for it later."

"Fine. I'll go back to the university, if that's what you want."

Milton felt relieved that she'd come to her senses.

"And I'll tell everybody what's going on," she added like a knife blade in the chest.

"You don't know anything," Milton shot back, trying to hold his temper.

"I know enough," Gayle pressed. "I know you found something alien. I know Emmett Collins knows. I know he's digging on Choke Mountain right now. He's trying to steal your discovery. Again. I'll tell everybody."

"Now *you* are being unfair."

"I'm as much a part of this project as you...and a million times more than her." She thumbed Lisa's direction.

Milton's determination faltered like a stalled motor. He couldn't risk her talking to the media, a woman scorned and all, and he had to stop Emmett from finding the spaceship. The bastard would take the credit even if it meant the total collapse of civilization as they knew it. And time was running out. "I just don't want you getting hurt."

"I've been hurt before."

"What's that supposed to mean?"

Gayle didn't answer him. She just stood there, the glare in her eyes replaced with pleading.

Lisa bounded up. "Hi. I'm Lisa Crawford."

"Gayle Weatherbee." They shook hands. "What are you doing here?"

The two couldn't have been more different: *slick and sexy meets rough and tumble.*

"I'm with my dad, over there." She pointed to the man talking with Jainaba, "and my boyfriend." She presented Luthes.

"Luthes Rez, miss." He offered his hand.

Shock flooded her face but she deftly accepted his long-fingered handshake. Then she shot Milton a what-the-fuck look.

"It's a long story," he said and introduced her to Agent Peterson. "He's from the NSA."

Gayle didn't say a word, just stared at Milton.

"All right. You can come along." This wasn't the first time Gayle had gotten her way, and it probably wouldn't be the last. He hoped he wouldn't regret it. "Let's go, people."

After everyone was aboard the van, Jainaba catapulted into the driver's seat. With gears grinding and engine belching smoke, the van lurched from the curb like a drunken beast, vibrating and clanking. A few nerve-wracking minutes later, it lumbered down Ring Road toward the expressway to Addis Ababa.

Ray and Peterson sat up front with Jainaba, Milton and Gayle shared the second seat, and Luthes and Lisa sat together in the back. Behind them, boxes and bags of gear were piled to the ceiling. Gayle had twisted in her seat and glued her gaze on Luthes.

"Turn around," Milton told her. "It's not polite to stare."

"I don't understand," she whispered. "His hands, his fingers, who is he?"

"Not now," he replied.

"He has something to do with that book, doesn't he?"

"The fewer people who know about him, the better."

It took an hour to negotiate the sprawling suburbs of Addis Ababa in traffic so congested that Jainaba rarely shifted out of first gear. Every imaginable mode of transport cluttered the way: trucks overloaded and tilting, weaving taxi vans, and poky donkey carts. Endless lines of ghostly figures walked along the road as if time had no meaning. Jainaba worked the steering wheel, and one hand constantly punched the horn until they got out of the city.

The road to Bahar Dar was lined with wide swaths of refuse on both sides. Giant potholes wreaked havoc on the van's old suspension and Milton's overstressed nerves. In this country setting of green fields and forests, the dust cleared, and the pedestrian traffic dwindled to nothing. Jainaba took advantage of the clear going. The van picked up speed. Cows and goats grazed in the gutters, and to the north, the rocky summit of Choke Mountain rose from the highland plateau. The sight caused Milton's nerves to quiver.

"What is it?" Gayle asked.

He didn't answer her. He glanced back at Luthes and Lisa. They were sleeping with their heads together. It had been a long journey from Colorado, and he too felt the need for sleep, but there would be no time for that luxury.

Jainaba drove faster.

"We have to stop Emmett," Milton whispered to Gayle.

"I know, but how?"

"Jainaba and I have a plan. I just wish you weren't involved."

"I wouldn't have it any other way. That artifact you found, the book, Lisa's boyfriend, come on, Milton, I wouldn't miss this for the world."

"What's in it for you, Gayle?"

She looked away. "I don't want to talk about it."

A long silence passed between them as the rickety van sped along the crest of a two thousand foot ravine, swerving violently and sending their gear crashing to the floor. Milton feared the luggage on the roof rack would topple off. The book was up there. "Slow down, Jainaba."

"Eee, it is the brakes. They don't work."

The van creaked and shuddered as if it were going to disintegrate under the strain of speed and inertia in every twist and turn of the treacherous road.

"What the hell, Jainaba?"

Gayle screamed. "Stop this death trap."

Milton turned around. Luthes and Lisa were thrashing side to side like rag dolls with big round eyes. Only their seatbelts prevented them from going airborne.

Tires skidded through a curve. Loose rocks plummeted over the edge and down into the deep ravine.

Milton grabbed Jainaba's seatback, leaned forward, and saw him gritting his teeth as he wrestled the steering wheel and pumped the brake pedal like mad. The emergency brake handle was pulled up, and Jainaba had already shut off the engine, but gravity wouldn't release its fatal grip on the crippled van.

Ray and Peterson appeared frozen in their seats. Milton's jaw muscles locked in terror. The Ethiopian highlands whizzed by the windows in a blur. He felt as if he were in an airplane that was spiraling toward the ground, his final seconds of life ticking away on an African road that wound down toward the Blue Nile Valley.

Rocks and potholes tore at the van's suspension like the teeth of a hungry lion, each chomp an eardrum-shattering bang. The muffler broke off, hit the road, and flung itself over the edge and down into the rocky abyss. Tire smoke and dust choked the air. Jainaba looked white as any white man.

Suddenly, a slow-moving truck appeared, overloaded with tilting bales of hay as it rounded a curve up ahead.

"Look out," Milton shouted.

The truck driver must've panicked when he saw the van careening toward him with smoke and dust in its wake. He jerked the steering wheel hard right and plowed into a tree. Hay bales flew across the road, and the van plowed into them at full speed, a bone jarring blow that actually slowed their plummet until a fender crunched into the rocky embankment and stopped the van with a jolt.

"Oh!" Gayle said, her brown eyes ringed in white.

Hay floated down around them like golden rain.

***

In Dejen, on the other side of the Blue Nile Gorge, Milton watched a mechanic crawl out from under the van. "It is as I suspected. There is a cut in the brake line."

Milton had been sitting in the dirt with everyone else, recovering from frazzled nerves, and this news startled him. He got up and slapped dust from the seat of his pants. Perhaps Emmett had a hand in this near disaster. "You think it was deliberate?"

"It is hard to tell, but I will fix it with a splice and have you on your way soon."

Jainaba stood next to Milton. "Eee, I had the van serviced in Bahar Dar for the trip to Bole. It was fine then." He scratched his head. "A rock or the rough road did damage to the brakes."

Patting Jainaba's shoulder, Milton hoped he was right.

"We owe you our lives. Thanks."

"You are welcome."

While Jainaba went to help the mechanic work on the brakes, Milton sat with Gayle. "Are you all right?"

"We were almost killed."

"Maybe now you'll answer my question. What's in all this for you?"

She looked at him, her eyes still dazed from her near-death experience. "You're right," she said finally. "I was fifteen years old..." Gayle told him about her father, the preacher, and her quest to find the truth about the origin of man and how he'd become such a violent creature on this otherwise beautiful earth.

"The world is a violent place," Milton said. "The ground shakes, volcanoes erupt, hurricanes and tornadoes and lightning kill thousands every year. There are bacteria and viruses, predators and prey. Good men and bad men. Women too. It's the natural way of things. Why can't you accept that?"

"In the Bible it says that on the sixth day God made man and said it was good. Look at us. Look at what we've done to the world. Look at how we treat each other. How could God have been so wrong about that?"

Milton didn't know the answer, and he wasn't going to try to appease her. As things were now, he had his suspicions. There was Luthes, sitting in the shade of a tree. There was an alien book and a defective gene and a secret buried on Choke Mountain. Did any of these things have anything to do with mankind's inherent propensity for violence? Or was man just a reflection of his environment, a reflection of life on earth?

He stood. "Let me tell you what I know." Pulling her to her feet, he put his arm around her shoulders and coaxed her to walk with him down the path to the river. "The alien book is the beginning..." he said, and by the time he got to the part about Regarius's theory of the defective gene, they'd reached the riverbank. "Each mating between the Tarreeda and Homo sapiens would have had a one-in-four chance of passing the gene on to the next generation."

"Then how can we all have it?" Gayle asked. "Only one in every four humans would be violent."

"And therein lies the problem with his theory."

"Did you tell him that it only answered for a quarter of the human race?"

Milton picked up a rock. "I'm going to let him figure it out for himself." He threw the rock into the river. "Meanwhile, we're going to bring Choke Mountain down around Emmett's ears."

***

It was well after dark by the time Milton and his bunch reached Choke Mountain. Jainaba parked the van off the road in a thicket of trees. Upslope, the hillside was invisible against a pitch-black sky, but a dome of light illuminated the dig site. The growl of generators and rattle of diesel engines tainted the night air. Already, the temperature had dropped to forty degrees, and Lisa was the first to complain.

"I thought it was hot in Ethiopia." She cuddled into Luthes.

Milton sighed. These city people weren't cut out for this kind of work.

It took Jainaba a few minutes to unload the gear, and then he distributed flashlights, jackets, and backpacks. He handed out apples and *injera* to everyone, and they sat with Milton on a rock, eyes cast uphill, eating their meal and drinking water from plastic bottles.

Jainaba sat next to Milton. "Eee, they are very busy up there."

The sting of wishful revenge stabbed Milton. "I figure we'll hike up the east flank. It's not more than a mile. Take the high ground above the dig."

"Emmett will not be happy to see you."

"Feeling's mutual, I assure you." Milton stashed his water bottle in his backpack, along with the ritainium box that contained the alien book. "However, we're not going to let him see us until we get a good assessment of the situation."

"Eee, are there guards with guns, do you think?"

"You can bet on it." Milton recalled Emmett's personal Berretta in his briefcase.

Peterson strode over. "If everybody's ready, follow me."

Milton leaped from the rock and grabbed Peterson's arm. "I'll lead the way."

Peterson shot him a how-dare-you glare. "I'm in charge of this operation."

"You're out of your environment here, Agent. I know this mountain, damn near every boulder."

"He is right," Jainaba said. "There are many cliffs and snakes."

"Snakes?" Peterson swallowed hard.

"I can get us up there safely." Milton released Peterson's arm. "Okay?"

"Snakes?"

"And scorpions," Jainaba added.

Milton slung the pack over his shoulder, and flashlight in hand, he motioned to the others. "Let's go."

"Scorpions?"

Chapter Twenty-Nine

D uring the long days of incarceration, Sangrean hardened his resolve to thwart Brigham's plot to steal their teleportation technology. Messengers relayed information to him through Verrilla, detailing the invaders' progress, or lack thereof, which assured him the human scientists and engineers were failing miserably. Patience was his plan. They would soon give up.

Verrilla arrived with the evening meal.

The guard let her into the room, and then collapsed to the floor, vomiting.

Puzzled, Sangrean bent over the human. His face was pallid, lips blue. By the time Verrilla set the food tray on the small table, the guard had passed out.

"Oh, dear," she said, backing away. "He is not well."

Sangrean felt the human's clammy forehead, hot with fever, but he was still alive. "Get some help."

"But look, the door is open and unguarded," she said. "You should escape."

The thought had crossed his mind but... "I am needed here."

"Luthes would escape if he could."

"To get home to you, I think you are right."

She blushed.

Sangrean stood. "Besides, Brigham would only find me, maybe shoot another one of my officers as punishment. It is better that I am here. Now go for help."

She left. The guard moaned. It wasn't long before a human with a white cross on his armband entered. After a quick examination of the patient's eyes, he said, "lethargic."

"Is that bad?" Sangrean asked, unfamiliar with the word.

Then Brigham came in. "Another one?"

"Yes, sir," the medic said. "We're going through salt tablets like toilet paper."

"Get him out of here."

They loaded him on a stretcher, pressed past Verrilla holding the door, and raced away. Brigham walked to Sangrean's food tray on the table and lifted the cover. "Bread and water, just as I ordered. Are you enjoying your meager fare?"

"It is better than nothing." Sangrean sat in a chair at the small table, and for effect, tucked a napkin into the front of his shirt. "Care to join me?"

Brigham swelled up like a balloon, and with one mighty swipe of his hand, he knocked the tray on the floor, sending the bread and water flying across the room.

Sangrean flinched, unsure how to react to such a violent display. "You wish that I eat off the floor?"

"I wish you would help me with the teleportation system."

A moment went by in silence as Commander Sangrean regarded General Brigham and came to the conclusion the human leader was near the end of his Tarreeda noose. Sangrean removed his makeshift bib. "We have a saying on our world, that honey draws the beautiful gibberdy and vinegar attracts only the ugly barragwa."

"Are you saying you'd cooperate if I fed you better?"

"I will not cooperate for any reason, but you have got the message."

Enraged, Brigham stormed out.

Verrilla stooped to pick up the spilled meal. "He does not get the prize for congeniality today, Commander."

"Humility will do him good."

***

Outside, under the double blast of Beltzee's twin suns, Brigham stomped across the compound toward Fleet Base Headquarters. He noticed a group of soldiers standing in the shade under a shuttle wing. These were guards he'd posted to patrol the area around the shuttles. His first instinct was to severely reprimand them for leaving their posts, but when he approached them, he saw they all looked sickly. One of them was lying on the ground, moaning. Vomit dripped from his face. Several men were popping salt tablets like M&Ms.

"We've called the medics, sir," a sergeant reported immediately upon Brigham's arrival. "But they're overloaded with emergencies."

"They told us to stay with him here in the shade," a private said. His face was pale and his uniform sweat-soaked. "I don't feel good either, sir. My salt tablets are gone."

Just then, the roaring engine of an M1-A1 Abrams tank patrolling the perimeter not fifty yards away caught Brigham's attention. Everyone turned at once to face the commotion. Tank crewmen leaped from the turret as the tank crashed through a fence and into a stand of trees, finally slamming to a stop against a boulder. The tracks flung dirt until the engine lugged down and stalled.

"What was that all about?" Brigham shouted into his two-way.

"The driver passed out at the controls, sir."

"Christ." Brigham had a full-scale epidemic on his hands.

A truck loaded with occupied stretchers raced up. Medics scooped up the downed guard, tossed him on the truck with the rest of the sick men, and sped off toward the tank crash.

The private keeled over. Brigham knelt at his side.

Another man collapsed. Granted, Brigham thought it was hot, maybe a hundred degrees, and it was humid, probably ninety percent, but it wasn't any worse than summer in Florida. He didn't understand why his men were dropping like flies. In fact, there were no flies...or mosquitoes though the ocean was only a half-mile away. He could see it clearly, but it didn't smell like an ocean, and there was no briny taste in the air.

The private moaned, and when Brigham looked down at him again, he noticed his own shirt had become sweat-soaked. He was losing water at an alarming rate. Standing, he felt a wave of dizziness and dug in his pocket for his bottle of salt tablets.

The sergeant handed him a canteen. "You'd better get out of the sun, sir."

For the first time since they'd landed on Beltzee, Brigham felt the hot bite of fear. He tapped two tablets into his hand and gave the bottle to the sergeant. "In case anyone else runs out."

"Thank you, sir."

The truck returned for the downed men, and Brigham caught a ride across the compound to Fleet Base Headquarters. Inside, it was cool, but voices were frantic. A committee of scientists and engineers had gathered around his office door. They were in heated disagreement over something that he was sure to get the brunt of at any moment.

Colonel Scott met him first, a communiqué in his hand. "General, we are getting reports from our units in Retaken and Berakatee. The men are getting sick there as well. They want to know what's happening. Are we falling ill to an alien virus?"

"Tell them to double-up on the salt tablets."

"Their supplies are exhausted, sir."

That wasn't good news. "Send them some of ours."

He shook his head. "We have only enough for five

days."

That was worse news. "Tell them we are working on the problem."

"Yes, sir."

Brigham turned his attention to the ruckus before him. "Gentlemen, what is your problem?"

They all spoke at once, an unintelligible blast of jabber.

A raised hand shut them up. "One at a time, for Christsake."

"I will tell you," an old scientist said, stepping from the crowd and speaking with a Russian accent. "It is Heir Bindlen. He is sick, and his notes we cannot decipher."

"We don't need the notes," another scientist said. "We'll start over."

"You're making a mess of everything," an engineer complained. "General, please tell them to stop taking things apart without prior approval. The drafts have to be made first."

"Reverse engineering must proceed only after science and physics of operation are understood," the Russian argued back.

As they verbally lit into each other again, it became obvious to Brigham that there was no consensus among the experts as to how they were going to approach the task at hand. "People! People. Do you have any idea what you're doing?"

Silenced, they looked at him dumbly.

"We have only five days left to figure out this technology, beam us up Scottie, and get back to earth. Is it doable?"

They shook their heads. They too were pale and perspiring, the outcome of which was sure to land them in the infirmary along with half of his men. Time was running out. If he didn't solve this medical dilemma, they were all going to die on this godforsaken planet. Two-way radio in hand, he said, "Colonel Scott, get me a ride to the infirmary."

***

Ten minutes later, Brigham walked among the dead and dying. He passed row after row of cots that had been assembled in a Beltzan warehouse. When he left earth, he'd taken with him two physicians and seventy medics. One doctor had already died, and the other looked as if he were going to pass out at any moment.

"General," the doctor said, setting aside a vomit bucket. "What do you make of your great invasion now?"

"We're not whipped yet."

The doctor sat on a cot next to a sweltering patient. "Could have fooled me." Sweat ran from every pore of the doctor's body as he applied a wet towel to his patient's forehead.

"What's your status?" Brigham asked.

"Half of my medics are dead, the other half are sick. Riflemen from Third Platoon are filling in where they can."

Brigham looked around the huge room, sweat beading on his own forehead. "Is anyone getting better?"

"Everyone is suffering from Acute Hyponatremia," the doctor replied.

"In English."

"It's a lack of sodium chloride in our bodies, but worse, a massive overdose of Potassium chloride."

"It's not a bug?"

"We could kill a bug," the doctor said. "Against this, we have no defense. You see...our bodies are always seeking a balance between the two salts, about nine parts potassium to four parts sodium. On this planet...in the humid air...in the water, there is more potassium chloride than on earth and no sodium chloride. The balance is tipped to a lethal point. Brain cells swell, resulting in lethargy, seizure, vomiting, and death."

"All that because of a lack of table salt?"

"Exactly."

It couldn't be that simple. "And there's no salt anywhere on this planet?"

"Sodium chloride, none. Correct."

"But these men have been taking salt tablets."

"Yes. The recommended dosage, which is sufficient on earth but highly inadequate on this planet due to the excessive potassium chloride."

"How many tablets should they be taking?"

"Four times the recommended dosage."

Instant rage boiled inside Brigham. "Why wasn't I informed of this? I could have instructed the men."

Shaking his head, the doctor stood, leaving the wet rag on his patient's forehead. "We would have used up all our supplies three days ago. Every one of us would be in this room by now." Slow as the Grim Reaper, he moved to the next cot, the next patient, and the next to die.

Brigham was not about to let something as simple as salt defeat him. He'd return to earth to get more. However, in order to do that, he'd have to attain orbit, and that meant his scientists would have to figure out how the teleportation system worked.

Sweat trickled down his forehead. Precious salt was bleeding from his body. It would only be a matter of time before he too fell ill like the others. He reached for the bottle of salt tablets in his pocket, and then realized he'd given them to the sergeant outside. Panic set in. He wiped the sweat from his brow with the palm of his hand and licked it off. It was Sangrean who had reduced him to licking his own sweat, but Sangrean was the only one who could save them.

***

That evening, in the room the humans called detention, Sangrean was content to sit by himself. It was quiet, mostly, except sometimes the guard outside the door would cough. He was the third replacement today, as one after another, the humans were succumbing to an ailment of some kind. The thought of Brigham fighting on two fronts gave Sangrean reason to smile. He would be content to sit and wait him out.

Verrilla came to the door. "Commander Sangrean, look." She twirled into the room. "A new dress."

"A pretty one at that." He noted the pink bell and white lace. "Is there a special occasion I should know about?"

"I wish Luthes were here to see it."

Sangrean rose and bowed to the lady. "Dance?" They did a two-step shuffle, clumsy at first, and there was no music. "So tell me about this new dress of yours, how did you come by it?" He led her toward a corner, sashayed back to the center of the room, and gave her a twirl. Her hair swung around like a golden fan.

"The human General Brigham had it sent to me by special courier, and there was a bath drawn for us in B quarters."

"And Sashi, did she get a new dress?"

"With flowers and sunrays."

Sangrean pictured Brigham's frustration. Perhaps he was tiring of the ugly barragwas. "How did Sashi like her new dress?"

Verrilla spun around and came back into Sangrean's dance frame. "She was happy until she thought of her father and how he would not see her in the dress. Then she cried and asked when he was coming home. I do not think she understands how far away he is."

"An impossible distance, it seems." He gave her a dip, saw a tear swell in her eye.

"I miss him."

Terry Wright

"I know."

"Will I ever see him again?"

"Cada willing," he told her and sat on the bed, somewhat winded from their little dance.

She came to him and sat, her dainty frame barely depressing the hard mattress. "We should rescue him."

"But there is no fleet."

"The humans came here. We could go there."

"We do not know how they did it."

She played with a button on her dress. "But we have something they want."

"Are you suggesting a trade, the teleportation technology for Luthes?"

"Yes, please. They will—"

He cut her off. "You know I cannot do that."

The guard outside the door fell over with a thump.

"But it is for Luthes, helmsman of *Questnar*, the grandest Orbital Patrol Ship in the League of Beltzee, and there is Regarius, too, and the others, we could get them all back."

Sangrean stood. "You must understand, Verrilla." He wanted to be kind with words that were going to sound cruel by their nature. "To give Brigham what he seeks, for any reason, would dishonor everything that the fleet has ever stood for, everything every Beltzan has died for. It would be defeat in the worst sense of the word, to have lost the battle and the war. No Beltzan's life is worth that degradation. I am sorry, but that includes Luthes, also."

"You would let him die?"

"Not if I could help it."

She smiled. "You promise?"

"I will do what I can, but I will not give Brigham what he wants."

Her smile faded. "Then I will never see Luthes again." She buried her face in her hands.

A wonderful aroma wafted into the room. Sangrean

~326~

recognized it immediately: white fish, cavou roots, and yampamam gravy, his favorite.

"Don't be so sure," he told her with warmth rising inside his chest. "I do believe General Brigham is looking for beautiful gibberdies. We may be able to save Luthes yet."

Verrilla looked up, teary-eyed. "You think so?"

Directly, a pallid human entered the room with a linen clad table and two padded chairs. He went about setting down plates and utensils and poured peach-cherry delight into crystal glasses. The steaming dinner presented, he directed Sangrean and Verrilla to the chairs.

"Well, now..." Sangrean lifted his glass in salute to the human. "This is swell."

It was the best meal Sangrean had enjoyed in a long time, and when he was finished, he patted his lips with a fine napkin. Verrilla giggled. The peach-cherry delight was beginning to blush her cheeks.

Brigham stepped into the room. His entrance seemed to have been timed perfectly with the meal's conclusion. Colonel Scott appeared next and leaned on the doorpost.

"I trust you are pleased," Brigham said.

Sangrean nodded. "Your favors are graciously accepted, but I told you I would never cooperate. However, now that you are here, please join me in a glass of delight."

Brigham turned to the pallid human and nodded. He produced another nice chair as if that too were preplanned. Now sitting across from Sangrean, Brigham said to Verrilla, "Please excuse us now. I must talk with the Commander in private."

Verrilla rose.

Sangrean touched her wrist. "Please, be seated." He glared at Brigham defiantly. "You have made her my confidante. She shall remain in my service."

"Very well," Brigham replied. "I've no time to play cat and mouse with you."

"What is this cat and mouse, a game?"

"My men are dying, Commander."

"It must be Cada's will."

Frowning, Brigham pressed on. "I'm here to appeal to your true spirit as a leader of Beltzee, an honorable man, to save lives and end this conflict."

"How do you suggest I do this?"

"Give us the technology, and I promise we will leave this planet immediately."

"You know I cannot do that," Sangrean said and sipped his drink. "It would dishonor us all."

"Yes, of course, and I understand fully, so I'm prepared to make you a counter-offer."

Sangrean tweaked an eyebrow, his curiosity ablaze.

"Allow me to teleport one ship into orbit, with one pilot so that he can go back to earth and return with the salt we need to stay alive."

"Not good enough," Sangrean said. "But I have a better idea." He set down his glass and leaned forward. "I will agree to teleport your entire fleet into orbit so you may all go home now."

Brigham grimaced. "You want me to go back empty handed?"

"Or die here."

"I would be dishonored on my planet."

"It is your choice."

"What about Luthes?" Verrilla put in. "And the other prisoners? We want them back."

"That's impossible," Brigham said. "We have no more shuttles on earth."

Verrilla touched Sangrean's arm. "Then send one ship as Brigham has proposed, for the salt, however, he can bring Luthes and the others back also."

Brigham snorted. "They would take up too much room on the shuttle. We need all available space for the salt."

Shaking his head, Sangrean said, "Verrilla, your plan doesn't address the main problem, which is getting these violent humans off our planet. They leave without the technology they came to steal, or they die. It is the same in the end. They will eventually be gone."

Verrilla stood. "A thousand generations ago, we did not let all the Tarreeda die at the battle of Zarakatan. Why would we let these humans die here when there is a way to save them?"

"I do not want to save them," Sangrean replied. "They destroyed my fleet. I want them to suffer for that." A hot sensation started boiling up inside his chest. It made him feel powerful. "They will either give up on the technology and live, or they will stay here and die."

Colonel Scott leaned over and whispered into Brigham's ear, as a counselor would at a meeting of the Judicials. Brigham's eyebrows lifted in agreement. "I've decided to accept the young lady's suggestion. If you will agree to teleport one shuttle and one pilot into orbit, we will return with the prisoners and the salt."

"It is not satisfactory," Sangrean said. "Unless you all leave, I will not agree."

Brigham grinned. "Then you alone have condemned your own people to remain prisoners on our planet."

"It is you who took them there, thus their fate is your doing."

"He is right." Verrilla sat down, her hand again touching his arm. "You see, Brigham has given you the opportunity to save Luthes and the others without giving up the technology. You cannot deny him, or their deaths will be on you."

"Brigham is very smart," Sangrean said to Verrilla. "But the humans will still be on our planet, and they will continue their quest for the teleportation system until they prevail."

Again, Colonel Scott leaned to Brigham's ear.

"Yes." Brigham cleared his throat. "We will agree to leave your planet if we have not succeeded by the time the shipment of salt has expired."

"Unconditionally," Colonel Scott added. "All or nothing."

Sangrean sat back in his chair and regarded Brigham with caution. It seemed as if he was genuinely interested in saving the lives of his men, but to go through all this effort and then unconditionally retreat without the technology seemed highly unlikely. And by now, his scientists should know that the task was monumentally beyond their capabilities. They could not possibly succeed. Sangrean's instincts told him that there was more to this offer unseen, possibly one of those cat and mouse games. "You'll all go, or no one goes," Sangrean said.

Verrilla shot out of her chair. "How could you?"

"You are a hard man," Brigham said.

"I do not trust you."

Suddenly, the pallid human guard dropped to the ground, vomiting and convulsing.

"Then trust this," Brigham said. "When I last saw Luthes, he was sick too, like my men are now."

"Oh no," Verrilla cried.

"Your potassium is killing us here, while on our planet, sodium is killing Luthes and the other prisoners. As you can see," he pointed to the human writing on the floor, "it's not a pretty sight."

"You can't let them die like that," Verrilla shouted.

Sangrean turned his eyes away from the sick human. The thought of Luthes in that condition being preventable, Sangrean couldn't bear the responsibility for not saving him when the opportunity was presented.

"All right." He pointed one long finger into the air. "One shuttle, one pilot who will bring Luthes back with the other Beltzan prisoners and as much salt as your shuttle will hold."

Brigham agreed.

As Verrilla squealed with joy and hugged Sangrean's neck, he noticed a sly grin form on Colonel Scott's face.

The cat and mouse had begun.

Terry Wright

Chapter Thirty

In the hallway to the teleportation chamber at Fleet Base Command, Brigham and Sangrean arrived to make preparations for sending *Whiskey-Xray* back to earth.

"Get Major Remsfield in here," Brigham ordered the sergeant on watch and stepped to the huge door they had cut open earlier.

"This will need repair," Sangrean said.

"I'll put a crew on it right away."

They stepped into the chamber. The place looked like a junkyard. Brigham's jaw clamped shut. "What have you people done?" he hissed through clenched teeth.

Sangrean looked dumfounded. "They have ruined it."

The scientists and engineers had disassembled much of the machine. There were parts scattered all over the floor, and in the control room, the panels of colored tiles had been cut open, their innards of tubes and wires and alien gadgetry exposed like intestines spilling from a gut-shot wound.

"You made a mess of it," Brigham accused the scientists.

The Russian stepped from a clutch of his cohorts. "We had to take it apart to see how it works."

"Put it back together."

An engineer said, "That's not possible at this time."

Brigham grabbed the engineer's coat lapels. "Don't give me that. Put it together now." He shoved the engineer back and was about to slug him when Sangrean intervened.

"Violence is not necessary. We will fix it." At that, he stepped up to what appeared to be a blank wall. *"Keeda beveedo narroda,"* he chanted.

The wall slid up and revealed a blinking array of colorful tiles, which Sangrean began touching in sequences with practiced precision. He turned to the astounded general. "My repair crews will be here shortly. I must prepare for their arrival, but please, dismiss these men who have done all this damage."

Brigham stepped aside. "We haven't much time."

"We will hurry." Sangrean left the chamber. The others filed out after him.

Remsfield rushed in. "You called for me, sir?"

Looking around, Brigham assured himself they were alone. He took Remsfield by the arm, and they walked out the control room to the base of the towering glass ball. "I have a special mission for you."

"Sir?"

"You're going back to earth to get more salt tablets."

Remsfield raised his eyebrows. "My God. How did you arrange that?"

"Sangrean expects you to return with the Beltzan prisoners."

"Ah," Remsfield said and then frowned. "Expects is the key word here?"

"That's right." Brigham put his hands behind his back. "You will not waste one square inch of cargo space for prisoners. The salt takes priority."

"But when I come back without them..."

"You let me worry about Sangrean." Brigham rose up on the balls of his feet. "He's going to have bigger problems."

"What are you talking about?"

"Colonel Scott and I have it all worked out. When you return with the salt, we are going to give Sangrean an ultimatum. Either he gives us the teleportation technology or we'll use the Star Wars system to eliminate his cities, one at a time, until he agrees or his entire planet is wiped clean of life."

Remsfield took a step back, open-mouthed. "You'll kill everyone?"

"Strategy, Major. I don't think Sangrean will let it come to that, though I'm sure millions will die before he cooperates."

"But, sir. Innocent civilians?"

"Every last man, woman, and child if need be."

Major Remsfield snapped to attention. "Pardon my candor, sir, but it's against the military code of conduct to—"

"At ease, Major. I want off this stinking planet, and I'm not going back defeated. You hear me?"

"Don't get me wrong, sir, I'm a fighter pilot, a soldier, hell, I'm the first one to pull the trigger in a combat situation. Against that fleet of space ships up there, we had no idea what they were capable of doing to us, so I had no qualms about the use of overwhelming force, but now...now that we know these Beltzans are peaceful—"

Brigham slammed a fist into the palm of his hand. "Don't go soft on me, Major."

"They haven't even launched a counter attack, sir. They've surrendered completely. There's no way we can legally justify more hostility."

"You have your orders, Major. Return with the salt, that's all."

"What do I tell the prisoners, that their entire planet is going to be destroyed?"

"They don't need to know." Then an afterthought hit him. "On the other hand, do you remember Luthes Rez?"

"The helmsman of *Questnar*."

"I met his wife and daughter, a very nice family."

Remsfield squinted. "But he told us they were killed when *Latearian* exploded."

"They weren't on it. So when you get back, make sure Luthes knows they're still alive. It'll make his death that much more gratifying for me."

"I'm sure he'll appreciate the good news from home."

"You're dismissed, Major."

***

Eight hours passed before Beltzan technical personnel had restored the teleportation machine to partial operational status, enough to teleport one vehicle into orbit. The Aerospace shuttle, *Whiskey-Xray*, had been towed to a ground elevator pad just outside the building, in preparation for its insertion into the machine.

Confident of his upcoming victory over Sangrean, Brigham stood next to Major Remsfield under the shuttle's nose. The gigantic platform began its descent down a lighted shaft. Machinery rattled all around them. As the ensemble sunk beneath the surface, huge sliding panels closed overhead, blotting out a starry night sky. On the slow journey down, Brigham regarded the Major and his glum face. "You don't look excited about going home."

Remsfield stared forward blankly. "I didn't sleep well."

"A case of conscience, Major?"

"You wouldn't understand."

Brigham grunted. "I'd go myself if I could fly this thing." He tilted his head toward the shuttle.

The Major stiffened. "May I be frank, sir?"

"Of course."

"I want the record to show that I was against the course of action you and Colonel Scott have plotted." Remsfield turned to face Brigham. "And rest assured, if this comes to a court-martial, I will not go down with you."

"I'm the law on this planet," Brigham said. "You have nothing to fear."

"Except you, sir."

"This isn't like any war on earth," Brigham said,

thinking Remsfield a bit too frank. "We are the pioneers of intergalactic warfare. We have to make up the rules as we go. There's no Geneva Convention here, Major. And rest assured, if we don't execute this plan perfectly, Sangrean could win this war without firing a single shot."

"So you're going to use the lives of his citizens against him?"

"Brilliant, isn't it?"

"It's barbaric."

"I'm not going to lose, Major. Is that clear?"

"Perfectly, sir."

The elevator stopped at the bottom of the shaft, where it opened into a bright subterranean cavern of arcing support beams and smooth walls. With a clank, the elevator pad began moving sideways into the cavern. The air smelled of sulfur and tasted like tin. A vibration tingled the bottom of Brigham's feet.

Within a few minutes, the floor stopped, clanked, and began rising. Brigham looked up where ceiling panels moved apart, revealing the teleportation chamber's glistening interior.

The lift stopped.

Sangrean appeared. "We are ready to proceed. Quickly now."

The giant glass ball that dominated the domed chamber came alive with arcing blue sparks, which radiated from the core to the inner facing of the glass ball, plying its surface like the open palms of an electric mime. An ominous sizzling filled the air.

Brigham watched this anomaly for a moment, his stomach twitching. Perhaps this technology was, in fact, way beyond mankind's comprehension.

"I don't like this," Remsfield said. "How do I know Sangrean isn't planning to fry me in this godforsaken machine?"

"It is quite safe," Sangrean replied. "Your atoms and

those of the shuttle will be detached from each other, beamed into orbit, and reassembled in perfect order."

Remsfield's eyes bugged out. "You're going to reduce me to atomic dust?"

"The finest," Sangrean confirmed.

"And what if Humpty Dumpty isn't put back together again?"

Sangrean grinned. "I am not familiar with your Humpty Dumpty, but I assure you, it will not hurt a bit."

Remsfield turned to Brigham, grimacing. "I don't like it, sir."

Heat hit Brigham's bloodstream. He'd never considered exactly how teleportation worked, but he immediately recognized a tactical disadvantage in this. Grabbing Sangrean by the front of his shirt, he yanked him to his face. "If you pull a fast one on me, I'll kill you."

Sangrean asked, "Is *fast one* like *cat and mouse*? I am not familiar with these things."

"This better go off without a hitch."

"Yes," Sangrean replied and glanced at his technical team. "No hitch."

Remsfield squared his shoulders. "Sir, I request to be dismissed from this assignment."

"Request denied, Major." Brigham's entire face felt hot. "You have a job to do. All of us are depending on you to bring back the salt."

"And the prisoners," Sangrean put it. "Do not forget Luthes and the prisoners."

Remsfield cast him a solemn look. "Yeah, the prisoners."

"Get onboard," Brigham said, fearing the Major's forlorn reaction to the prisoner issue might tip Sangrean to their planned deception. "That's an order, soldier."

Snapping upright, Remsfield saluted. "I hope you don't regret this, sir." He turned and climbed the ladder.

Brigham watched him duck inside, all the while

thinking the Major had better not screw up. The hatch closed and within moments his face appeared in the windshield, helmet on. He saluted.

***

Remsfield went to work, configuring the shuttle for space flight. Frayed nerves short-circuited and made his fingers tremble as they flipped switches and checked dials. If the aliens had been fooling around with the equipment, he wanted to find out now and not later. It wasn't hard to picture them sitting in these seats, bouncing up and down like kids in their daddy's car, pretending to drive, or in this case fly, or whatever it was called when one's atomic structure was dismantled, moved through space and time, and reassembled.

Green lights displayed across the overhead console. The radar screen blinked on, the sweep beam plowing through ground clutter. It appeared that the aliens had not tampered with it, though the screen was blotched with fingerprints. Then he remembered the gun in the storage compartment. Had they found it while rummaging through the flight deck?

He dropped down the cover. The gun was still there. Shutting the compartment, he began to feel as if he'd become a paranoia junkie. "Stay focused," he muttered and picked up the radio mike. "Ready when you are."

***

"Ready when you are," came Remsfield's voice over the intercom.

"Come on," Sangrean said.

Brigham followed him up the short stairway to the control room. The door closed behind them, and he rushed to stand in front of the wall of two-way mirrors where he could see everything that happened inside the chamber.

Whiskey-Xray was poised for teleportation.

He put his right hand on his Colt. If this went bad, the first bullet had Sangrean's name on it. "Do it."

High voltage activity escalated in the huge glass orb. A crackling sound filled the air. Behind him, technicians pressed colored tiles in precise sequences to activate the most technologically advanced systems ever engineered.

Enormous fingers of electrical charges swept around inside the glass ball as if desperately seeking an avenue of escape. Light flashed from these bolts of energy and reflected off the mirrored ceiling, walls, and floor of the chamber, gaining in intensity with each passing second until the interior glowed so brightly that the shuttle became a ghostly image.

Colored tiles in the control room began blinking automatically, created swirling patterns on the consoles and walls and chiming musical tones with no particular tune but gaining an octave with the passing of each second. Brigham's senses were bombarded with these sensations until he thought he would scream.

Then the domed ceiling slowly parted, revealing a wondrous night sky divided by a glowing, color-streaked ring-plane. In an instant, the teleportation chamber's interior glow rose from the floor, and surrounding the translucent shuttle, seeped into the glass ball, and in a beam of intense light, shot out the open dome and into space. Brigham's heart beat wildly as he watched it ascend and dissipate. He looked again at the chamber floor.

Whiskey-Xray was gone.

***

All Major Remsfield saw from his seat in the shuttle was a glow of light out the windshield, a glow so intense he couldn't stand looking at it. When he tore his eyes away, he noticed the controls were glowing also, and as he reached up to touch the steering yoke, his hands and now his arms were aglow too, a condition that made his heart beat spastically.

In the next second, his hands began to tingle as if they'd fallen asleep, then his arms, and now his entire body took a wave of this sensation deep to his core. He felt as if he was crawling out of his skin. His back stiffened violently, and he felt a euphoric release...

Then there was nothing.

When he regained consciousness, he had no sense of time. He could have been out for only seconds, or perhaps a millennium. However, he didn't care, the sensation of euphoria was so strong he savored it. He stared out at a star-studded void. The shuttle's glowing hull began to dim, and the tingling in his hands subsided. Then he saw the green planet of Beltzee turn slowly underneath him, which brought him back to reality. He gulped air, patted his chest and his face to be sure everything was intact, and then he laughed. "That was fucking cool."

The radio crackled. *"Whiskey-Xray, do you read?"*

"Roger," he replied to General Brigham. "I'm all right." He checked his instruments. "All systems are online. Tell Sangrean I said thanks for the ride."

"You tell him when you get back."

Looking out the windshield again, Remsfield saw a Star Wars PLR satellite drift by. Its multi-ringed laser barrel pointed toward the planet's surface. A sudden chill worked its way up the back of his neck. From his short stay on Beltzee, he'd come to know that the Beltzans weren't only a peaceful people but a technologically advanced civilization that deserved a better future than General Brigham had planned for them. Complete annihilation. The only way to stop him was mutinous, a sure and swift court-martial guaranteed. And if the law on this planet was now in Brigham's hands, execution by firing squad would be swiftly doled out. At that, Remsfield resigned himself to his duty as a fighter pilot in man's first galactic war, a soldier bound to serve his commanding officer without reservation. The mission came first. He activated the regenerator. A rumbling sound came from the shuttle's OBM as the electromagnetic fields intensified.

"I'm beginning regeneration now," he reported into the radio.

"Good luck, Major. See you on the flip flop."

***

Alarms rang out in the control room at NASA Aerospace, which sent technicians scrambling to their stations. Janis shot up from his chair. "What is it?"

Lo checked his terminal for status reports. "A shuttle is regenerating," he reported.

"Brigham must've won the war." Janis ground his molars. "He's got the teleportation technology. I'll be damned. Are the other shuttles behind him?"

"Just one coming in," Lo said.

"ETA?"

"Five seconds to orbit, an hour to wheels stopped."

"Somebody get Tracy in here," Janis shouted. "Where is she?"

Lo shook his head. "Now, Dr. Janis, don't worry. She needed a break."

"You mean she needed a cigarette."

Lo stood. "I will find her."

Janis shucked his lab coat. "We're meeting that shuttle when it lands."

Tracy rushed in. "What's all the excitement?" She was sucking on a breath mint.

"A shuttle is coming back," Lo said.

Tracy popped another mint. "Who do you think it is?"

"I'm more interested in why there's only one." Janis grabbed a two-way radio. "We've got to find a ride to the flight line."

***

Thirty minutes later, a jeep pulled up at the administration door to NASA's Aerospace hanger. Janis helped Tracy into the front seat. He hopped into the back. "Shuttle Landing Facility," he told the driver, a young lieutenant with a top-secret security clearance, same as everyone at NASA Aerospace.

As the jeep tore away from the curb, Lo's voice came over the two-way. *"Janis, the shuttle is on its way down."*

"Thanks, Lo. Keep me updated."

Janis noticed it was a balmy afternoon in Florida, the sky hazy with sea mist and scattered cumulous clouds. A light breeze blew in from the ocean, bringing with it a fishy, salty smell. He clung to the roll-cage as the jeep careened onto Kennedy Parkway, thankful the conditions were satisfactory for a landing here rather than at Edwards Air Force Base in California.

The two-way clicked. *"Houston approach, this is NASA Aerospace shuttle Whiskey-Xray with you."*

"It's Brigham's shuttle," Tracy said.

"Why did he leave his troops behind?"

"Whiskey-Xray, this is Houston approach. You are clear for landing at Kennedy Space Center. Begin your S turns now."

"Roger," came *Whiskey-Xray's* reply.

Janis studied his watch. "That'll put them here in twenty-six minutes."

Tracy smiled. "I have time for a cigarette."

"Stop it," Janis spat.

***

On the tarmac at the Shuttle Landing Facility, Janis stood with Tracy in the jeep, their eyes scanning the sky.

Boom!

The sonic blast reached them before Janis spotted the shuttle. "There." He pointed to a spot in the sky much higher than he'd expected to see the shuttle, not realizing its glide path was much steeper than a passenger jet would come in. Its approach speed was over 260 miles per hour, double that of a Boeing 737. As it neared, two F-16 Hornets flanked the shuttle to escort it down, an impressive sight.

"Boys and their toys," Tracy said.

Seconds later, the shuttle glided to a perfect touchdown, and the chase jets screamed by, overflying the runway before pulling up and banking around to land.

Under the whining power of pulse-light engines, *Whiskey-Xray* taxied toward the tarmac. A dozen or more service vehicles trailed behind it like little ducklings. As it turned off the ramp, Janis saw Major Remsfield's face in the windshield. "I don't see Brigham," he told Tracy.

With her hand shading her eyes, she said nothing.

Television vans screeched up. Channel 2. Channel 9. Fox News. "Damn! Why did Base Operations let them on the flight line?"

When the shuttle stopped, technicians chocked the wheels, and the hatch opened. A truck with stair-steps pulled up to the hatch. Remsfield got out. He was wearing sunglasses and waving to the crowd that had gathered. News cameras whirred.

"Major," a reporter shoved a microphone into his face. "Could you tell us where you've been?"

Remsfield brushed past him.

"Let's go." Janis jumped from the jeep, and with Tracy on his heels, ran toward the shuttle, pushing through the crowd. "Major Remsfield."

"Hello, Dr. Mackey."

"Where are Brigham and the others?"

As they shook hands, Remsfield drew Janis close and

whispered, "We have to talk."

"I've got a jeep waiting."

More cameras and microphones appeared. The crowd surged forward, threw out a barrage of questions all at once. "When was the launch?" a woman reporter asked. A man shoved her aside. "What was your mission?"

"No comment, everyone." Remsfield turned to the shuttle maintenance crew chief. "I want a quick turn around."

Janis understood the term. "He's going back," he said to Tracy.

"I wonder why."

Remsfield said, "Get me out of this circus ring."

"This way."

They sprinted to the jeep. Tracy sat up front again. Janis sat next to Remsfield in back.

The jeep lurched into motion.

"Why only one shuttle?" Janis asked Remsfield.

"Brigham is in over his head. I've come for salt tablets, as many as the shuttle will hold."

"Salt?"

"Our men are dying on Beltzee for lack of salt."

The jeep turned onto Kennedy Parkway and headed toward the NASA Aerospace hanger, the monstrous gray building that languished eerily in the distant haze. "How many casualties?"

"We didn't lose a single man during the invasion, but before long, we started dropping like cockroaches. The planet is beautiful, Janis, but it's not fit for human life. Colonel Scott quadrupled the officers' salt tablet rations, which stripped the enlisted men of their supplies. Brigham has only three day's supply left."

Tracy twisted around in her seat, her red hair whipping across her face. "The Beltzan prisoners were dying from too much salt. We sent them to Colorado."

"So Luthes Rez isn't here?"

"No."

"Brigham told me to give him a message. His wife and daughter weren't killed in the invasion after all."

"He'll be happy to hear that," Tracy said. "Even more reason for him to be glad to go home."

Brakes squealing, the jeep stopped for a traffic light.

"What about the teleportation technology?" Janis pressed.

"It's incredible. I'm telling you, that machine took me apart and reassembled me again. There was a brilliant light and a tingling sensation, and everything glowed..."

"But does Brigham have it?"

Remsfield shook his head.

The jeep accelerated away from the stoplight.

He explained the situation on Beltzee and Brigham's plans to use the Star Wars system to bend Sangrean's will.

"Then why did Commander Sangrean agree to send you for salt?"

"Because he expects me to bring back the Beltzan prisoners."

"Now you tell us." Tracy glared at Remsfield. "That's big, that's really big, and you said nothing until now. Why not?"

"Because I'm not taking them back. Just the salt. Brigham's orders."

"So it's a double cross," Janis said, understanding Brigham's treachery and despising him even more. "Brigham gets his salt and turns Star Wars against the citizens of Beltzee."

"I have my orders."

"Screw your orders," Tracy said as the jeep turned into NASA Aerospace. "Janis, don't give him the salt."

"All our troops will die without it," Remsfield said.

Janis didn't want that on his conscience. The salt would have to be rounded up. But sending the Beltzan's back would be like tossing them into the fire. With

Brigham's ass in a sling, there could be a way to save most everyone. The key would be getting Remsfield to agree to a double-double cross.

The jeep squeaked to a stop in front of the door to Administration. Janis jumped out, waited for Remsfield and Tracy, and then as he led them toward the door, he turned on Remsfield and stopped him. "You can't be okay with Brigham's plan."

"I follow orders, like them or not, and these stink, but the general is the law up there."

"Don't let him get away with it."

Tracy stepped up. "What are you thinking, Janis?"

"The Beltzans go back on this shuttle, all of them."

Remsfield said, "Now wait a minute. I need the room for salt."

"Take enough to make everyone fit to fly."

"No way." Remsfield took a step back. "Brigham will have me shot. He's the law on Beltzee."

"Without enough salt, he won't have enough time to court-martial you."

Terror oozed from Remsfield's eyes. "He'll put a bullet in me. Bang. I'm a goner. You're asking me to go against my orders. It's suicide."

"Not necessarily." Janis opened the door and motioned him inside. Walking down the hallway to the hanger, he explained, "It's going to take at least three days to get you turned around. By that time, Brigham will be desperate."

"He's already desperate."

"So let's put him on the critical list. You, on the other hand, will be healthy enough to take over negotiations with Sangrean. Agree to leave without the technology."

"Sangrean already offered Brigham that deal."

"See," Janis said. "It's not a suicide mission after all."

They'd reached the elevator that went down to the SuperMIGGS control room. Remsfield hesitated getting on.

"There's one thing you don't understand, Janis...Tracy." He glared at them sternly. "Brigham won't lose. He'll unleash Star Wars on Beltzee. Particle beams will rain down on the cities. He won't stop until every man, woman, and child is destroyed. That's how determined he is to beat Sangrean."

"Yeah. I believe Brigham would do that." Janis stepped into the elevator. "Then it'll be up to you to take away his big guns."

Tracy followed Janis onto the elevator and turned to the wide-eyed pilot. "You coming?"

Remsfield just stood there. "In three days, there won't be a pilot healthy enough to fly. The shuttles will be useless."

"So he can't use them?" Tracy confirmed.

"Correct," Janis said, his finger hovering over the down button, waiting for Remsfield to get on. "And the tanks and rocket launchers?"

"Everyone will be too sick to fight," Remsfield said and stepped on the elevator. "The Star Wars satellites are his only hope to defeat Sangrean."

"Then you have to take them out."

"Huh?"

Janis pushed the down button. "There are only two PLRs in orbit. The sighting dish satellites multiply their efficiency."

Remsfield's brows furrowed. "I get it. When I get back, you want me to destroy Brigham's PLRs. Are you nuts? Do you know what my life expectancy will be? He'll shoot me on sight."

"Of course," Janis said. "It's risky."

"I don't see you volunteering for this."

Janis shrugged. "I can't fly."

Tracy rubbed his arm. "But he would if he could. Don't you see, Major? You're the only one who can save the Beltzans and end this war."

"Just think," Janis said. "If he doesn't have any salt,

and he doesn't have Star Wars hanging over Sangrean's head, he's going to give up."

The elevator stopped at the control room.

"Okay fine," Remsfield said as the door opened. "Let's say this works and Sangrean teleports enough shuttles into orbit so that Brigham and all the surviving soldiers can come home." They stepped out. "He'll court-martial me for disobeying orders, for destroying US government property, and worse, for treason. I'll get the death penalty."

Janis moved to his console. There was every reason to betray Brigham, but only one reason not to: Remsfield's life. "You're right," Janis said. "Go back with the salt, let Brigham carry out his plan. You'll return with the technology, after the blood of all those Beltzans stains the green planet red. But how are you going to feel knowing you could have stopped him?"

Tracy said, "You'll be an accomplice to mass murder."

"I'm a soldier. That's what we do, kill the enemy."

"They're civilians, Major. You don't massacre non-combatants. My guess is you could be tried for war crimes...right alongside Brigham."

"Come on, you guys. Either way, I'm screwed."

"Then help us," Tracy said softly. "Come back a hero, not a murderer."

Chapter Thirty-One

The climb up Choke Mountain was harder than Milton had anticipated, fraught with spiny thickets, sharp-bladed grass, and bruising rocks. An occasional scorpion scurried away from his flashlight beam. Minutes turned into hours, and it was midnight before he'd secured a position upslope from the dig. Sleep tore at his eyes, and fatigue threatened to cramp every muscle in his body. And it was cold: mountain air cold, teeth-rattling cold. While everyone else huddled together for warmth amidst a clutch of boulders, he and Peterson crawled to a rock embankment and peered over the edge with binoculars. The activity below caused waves of anxiety in Milton's stomach. There were guards, all right, a dozen soldiers in camouflaged fatigues with rifles. And big dogs padded at the soldiers' heels as they patrolled the area.

A dark helicopter sat by the trailhead, among trucks and jeeps parked helter-skelter. Maki's bulldozer was there too, unattended.

Moving left, the binoculars revealed an encampment of newly-hoisted tents, tables and chairs, and rows of portable toilets, a luxury only Emmett Collins could have arranged.

Down in the pit, legions of men worked with picks and shovels under the glare of bug-infested floodlights. Barefooted and dressed in dirty fugus and shammas, the locals chanted and sang like prisoners on a chain gang. An armed supervisor paced among them with watchful eyes. Emmett Collins was nowhere in sight.

Assessing their progress, it looked to Milton as though

they'd already dug away ten feet of earth from the mountain and extended the length of section 42 twice over. Two backhoes were digging side-by-side, and the floor of the pit had grown another ten feet deeper for their efforts. He knew from his ground sonar shots that the Tarreeda spaceship was still thirty feet into the mountain and twenty feet farther down. Realizing Emmett's mistake, Milton chuckled. "He's digging in the wrong place."

"Those soldiers are going to be a problem," Peterson noted. "Why would Ethiopia use government troops up here?"

"They're remnants of the rebellion in Eritrea," Milton speculated. "Hired guns. However, I've got a plan."

Back with the others, Peterson went to speak with Ray.

Milton stepped over to Jainaba, "You're on."

Quickly, he gathered up his backpack and a coil of rope.

Ever curious Gayle rushed up. "Where's he going?"

"Up there," he pointed, "to rig the cliff with explosives."

"Alone?"

"Yes."

"I'll go with him."

"Eee, Miss Gayle, it is safer that you stay here." He handed Milton the remote detonator. "Besides, I will not be coming back."

Milton kept his voice low. "He'll descend the north face of Choke Mountain and return to Bahar Dar on the back road. That way we can blow the east escarpment tomorrow morning. If we have to wait for him to get back here, Emmett will have another day to dig."

"He shouldn't climb alone." Gayle insisted. "Especially in the dark." She shined a flashlight in Jainaba's face. "We'll go together."

Milton didn't want Gayle to go, but then he hadn't

wanted her here in the first place. He shoved the remote detonator into his backpack. At least with Jainaba she'd be out of harm's way. Besides, it was safer to climb in pairs. "Get going," he told them. "We'll see you in Bahar Dar." As Gayle brushed past him, he stopped her with an outstretched arm. "Be careful."

She looked into his eyes. "You too."

When they were gone, Milton moved to Peterson and Ray to break the bad news to them. "We're going down to the dig site."

Peterson stiffened. "What are you up to, Milton?"

"We have to give Emmett and his people fair warning before we blow this mountain."

"Explosives?" Ray asked. "Where?"

"Up on the cliff. Emmitt will have until dawn to clear out before I bring the mountainside down on the dig site."

"You can't do that," Peterson said. "I want that spaceship."

"It's probably booby trapped, like the ritainium box that held the book."

"I'm this close to a real alien spacecraft." Peterson displayed a gap between his thumb and index finger. "I'm not going to let you take it away from me."

"Don't be a fool," Milton said. "We have to bury the dig site."

The response he got from Peterson was so unexpected it was too late to duck his punch. The night erupted in a brilliant flash of light, then nothing.

***

Lisa patted Milton's cheek. "Milton. Milton." Luthes had dragged him behind a boulder to shield their flashlights from view of the encampment down the hill. Ray went after Peterson, in the dark, and hadn't come back. "Milton." She held a wet bandana to his forehead.

Finally he stirred. "What happened?"

She helped him sit up. "Peterson slugged you and took off."

"I've got a splitting headache. Where's Luthes?"

"He's watching over the camp."

Drunkenly, Milton got to his feet and nearly toppled over. He leaned against a boulder. A nasty welt swelled over his right eye.

"We have to get you to a doctor," she said.

"I'm all right. We gotta stop Emmett." He retrieved the water bottle from his backpack. "How long was I out?"

"Less than an hour." She wasn't sure. "I think you've got a concussion."

"Jainaba should have reached the cliffs by now." He drank water, poured the rest over his head.

Milton wasn't listening to her.

"You and Luthes work your way back to the van." He tossed the bottle then removed the detonator from his backpack. "I'll take it from here."

"Oh no you don't," she said. "There's no way we're going down this mountain alone and in the dark. We're staying with you."

"Forget it. This is between Emmett and me."

Luthes ran up in a rush. "Something is wrong in the camp. Come quickly."

"Peterson," Milton said.

Rushing to the embankment with Milton and Luthes at her side, she came to the rocky ledge and peered over. Dogs were barking and a group of soldiers had their guns drawn. They were pushing a captive along, his hands tied behind his back, and his shirt torn. When he glanced upslope, Lisa saw the horror on his face. She gasped. "Dad?" A dizzying rush of fear hit her like a bus. "We've got to do something."

A man dressed in white slacks and a white sport coat emerged from a tent. He carried a gun in his right hand.

"Emmett Collins," Milton murmured.

Two armed guards joined Emmett, and they dashed toward their new captive. The head- draped diggers cowered together with uncertainty on their faces.

"Are they going to kill Ray?" Luthes asked. "Like on TV?"

"We have to assume the worst," Milton replied.

Lisa knew she had to get down there.

Ray was shoved to the ground, and the soldiers were kicking him and yelling. It was bedlam as Emmett strode up to the dusty brawl.

He laughed and pointed his gun at Ray.

Lisa stifled a scream. "They're going to kill him."

"Not if I can help it," Milton said. "You two stay here." He got to his feet and disappeared in the darkness.

Ray's painful wails rose up the side of Choke Mountain.

Fighting panic, Lisa's first instinct was to barrel down the hill and rescue her father, but two important facts held her emotional charge in check. First, there were a dozen men with guns, and second, there were the dogs, German Shepherds and Dobermans. Her karate skills couldn't defend against bullets and attack dogs, neither of which had any regard for self-preservation.

"What do we do?" Luthes asked.

"You stay here." Lisa ripped off her backpack.

Suddenly, a growl came from the darkness behind her, low and venomous. She whipped around. A dog's vicious bark tore through the air. Her flashlight beam revealed glowing retinas and gleaming canine teeth charging forward without restraint. The next moment filled her with panic and pain, her right arm suddenly wrenched in the grasp of murderous jaws and her body thrust backward as if she were hit by a truck. The flashlight went flying.

Luthes let out a horrifying scream.

She hit the ground hard, the dog on top of her,

growling and tearing flesh.

Shouting voices reached her, unfamiliar words. Two men. Their flashlight beams crisscrossed the dark and dusty scene. With every muscle flexed and acid-hot blood pumping through her veins, she clenched her jaw and kicked the dog in the groin. Yelping, the dog's hind legs buckled. She knocked the dog over and rolled the opposite direction. But the beast came back, lunged at her, snapping and snarling. She scrambled to the right. The dog jumped on her again.

The soldiers shouted. Flat on her back, she didn't know if they were ordering her to give up or the dog to stop his attack. Dust boiled from the ground, burning her lungs, and her right arm felt as if it were on fire. Fangs snapped at her face. She inhaled the dog's rancid breath. Fueled by the grip of terror, she fought the dog, pushed him, kicked him, but her arms were beginning to tire. She had all she could do just to keep the dog's jaws away from her face. But the dog wouldn't be denied. Its weight bore down on her, its drooling muzzle lunged for her throat, bit her jaw. Only her tattered right arm kept him from ripping out her windpipe.

"No!" She kneed the dog in the ribs, but nothing stopped his attack. The dark scene shrunk to tunnel vision. Sounds became garbled. Blood streaked her face, got in her eye. Everything moved in slow motion.

Then she heard Luthes scream, not a scream of terror, but one of rage. The dog's weight was suddenly gone, teeth no longer biting her arm. She heard the dog yelp, managed to look up, saw two soldiers training their flashlights on Luthes. He held the wriggling dog by its scruff and tail, hoisted over his head.

"Get back," he shouted to the soldiers.

They raised their rifles.

He hurled the dog at the soldiers. Men and flashlights scattered. A gun went off, and the dog hit the ground near a boulder, whining as if it had been shot.

Lisa struggled to her feet just in time to see Luthes bowl over one of the armed soldiers, the dusty scene eerily illuminated by the beams of dropped flashlights. By now, the other soldier had aimed his gun at Luthes. An unknown force drove her forward, slammed her foot into the soldier's temple. He hit the ground hard; his gun flipped into the dirt.

Approaching voices rose from the darkness. Reinforcements were making their way up the hillside, men probably alerted by all the commotion.

"Luthes!" With her right arm bleeding profusely, she stooped, grabbed the soldier's gun. "Come on." She picked up a flashlight and her backpack, and then led him through a gap in the boulders, the sound of heavy boots in hot pursuit.

***

Milton scrambled down the hillside, sending loose rock and dry earth cascading ahead of him, his boots barely able to maintain enough traction to keep him from falling. His flashlight revealed blurry images of boulders and thorny snags rushing by. Only his memory of the area saved him from fatal injury. He didn't care if he made noise and attracted the soldiers, as capture would be the fastest way into Emmett's camp.

It was only minutes before his approach was discovered. He surrendered to the soldiers. At gunpoint, he entered the dig site, more angry than afraid. The generator-driven floodlights hurt his eyes. Ray Crawford lay motionless on the ground, curled into a fetal position.

"Emmett! Let him go."

"He's a spy."

The soldiers kicked Ray again.

"No! He's a nuclear physicist. It was his technology that brought this alien discovery to us."

"To me," Emmett shouted. His left cheek twitched.

"You have nothing."

"Have it your way, but let him go."

"Enough," he told his soldiers, and they backed off.

Ray moaned. "Milton!"

"Can you walk?"

Straining to get to his feet, Ray asked, "Which way?"

"Turn around and walk," Milton said. "Don't look back."

That's when Emmett nodded to one of his soldiers who struck Ray on the back of his head with a gun. He dropped to the dirt in a heap.

Milton snarled at Emmett. This was only the beginning of his cruelty. "You bastard."

"Nobody is going anywhere." At the tilt of Emmett's head, the soldiers dragged Ray's limp body toward the tents, his heels leaving furrows in the dirt. Then Emmett turned a full circle, fired his Berretta into the air. "The rest of you get back to work."

The digging commenced with full fury.

He returned his attention to Milton. "What are you doing here?"

"Do you have any idea what you're looking for?"

"I have a theory. It's something alien."

"That's all?"

"It's bigger than a breadbox."

Milton was in no mood to play games. "It's a spaceship."

"Oh?" Emmett examined his Berretta.

"And we believe it's charged with a poisonous gas. If you open it, you will die, and so will all these men."

Emmett groaned. "You'll have to do better than that, Milton."

He could see that Emmett wasn't impressed. "Let me show you something else I found. It's in my backpack, if I may."

"Certainly."

He retrieved the ritainium box and held it up for Emmett to see. It was risky, he knew, showing it to the thieving bastard, but it was Milton's only hope of talking some sense into him.

"Why, Milton, you've been holding out on me."

"There's a book in here, written by the ComCap of the spaceship that landed here over 20,000 years ago."

Emmett stepped toward Milton, the Berretta still in hand. "Let me see it."

Carefully, Milton opened the box and showed the book to Emmett, the eye of Cada on the cover throwing shards of light in every direction. "We must leave these things buried here forever."

Emmett examined the book with dreamy eyes. "Amazing." He looked up. "And you're going to stand there and tell me you deciphered this?"

"I had some help." Milton didn't want to tell him any more.

"I've never seen writing like this before. Who could have helped you?"

"That's not important..."

Emmett showed perfect teeth. "Holding out on me again?" He raised the gun.

Milton hoped it wouldn't come to this. "All right. The aliens who know this language are here on earth, and one has come with me."

"Is this some kind of joke?"

"Emmett, please, this is bigger than us, bigger than our differences. What is buried here has the power to destroy the human race as we know it. Cover the dig and leave this place before it's too late."

At that, Emmett laughed. Milton hated that laugh. It reminded him of the time Don Johnson discovered *Lucy*. Emmett had laughed at Milton the same way then. And just as it was back then, there was no reasoning with him. Milton felt as though he had no choice but to use the detonator in his pocket. "Give the order to abandon camp, Emmett."

He stopped laughing. "Are you mad?"

Milton drew the detonator and extended the antenna, hoping Jainaba and Gayle were already clear. "The upper escarpment has been rigged with explosives, and when she blows, the mountain is going to come down on this dig. I'm sure you don't want to be around when it happens."

Emmett froze, his face wrenched in anger. "You wouldn't."

"I suggest you start clearing your men and equipment out of here."

Cheek twitching, he turned and looked back at the dusty pit and the men digging under the bright lights. "Very well," he said and stuffed the Berretta under his white jacket. "Very well, indeed." He walked a few steps before turning around. Hands behind his back, he looked relaxed. "Go ahead, Milton. Blow it up. Bury it forever."

Milton froze. He knew Emmett was a cold-blooded bastard, but he didn't think he'd risk the lives of all these men. "Call for the evacuation."

"Blow it up now. If what you believe is true, what are the lives of a hundred of us compared to the entire human race?" He squared his shoulders. "I am ready to die with you. Blow it up."

Milton jabbed the antenna upslope. "I'll do it, I swear. Evacuate the dig."

Emmett remained statuesque. "I'm waiting."

With his thumb on the detonator button and with all the best intentions in the world, Milton hesitated, his mind reeling with this dilemma. Should he sacrifice his life? Should he make the decision for all these men? Did he even have the right? The delay cost him his credibility.

"Ah, hah!" Emmett said. "It's as I thought. You can't do it." He grinned. "Again, Milton, you have proven that science and discovery outweighs the consequences, even if they are fabricated. You could no more destroy this site than I could. It's in your blood. That's who you are." He stepped forward and snatched the detonator from Milton's hand. "It was a bluff all along, and a lousy one at that." He pointed the antenna upslope, his finger on the detonator button.

"No don't." Milton lunged forward.

Emmett pushed the button.

Dumbstruck with fear, Milton fell to his knees. Seconds passed before he realized that there was no explosion, no rumble of a landslide bearing down the hill, nothing.

"See." Emmett tossed him the detonator. "We are quite safe from your silly threats."

"But...I...don't understand." Milton tried to figure out what had gone wrong. Something must've happened to Jainaba and Gayle. They had failed...

Emmett chuckled.

Then a familiar voice shouted out from the darkness. "Are you looking for this?" A bulging backpack arced through the air and landed on the ground with a thud and a puff of dust.

The surprised soldiers raised their weapons, but the sight that met their eyes stopped them cold. Milton couldn't believe his eyes. Agent Peterson. He was strolling into camp as if he owned the place. Two prisoners led the way, hogtied together, Gayle Weatherbee and Jainaba. The wind went out of Milton's lungs.

"Sorry, Milton," Peterson said. "I couldn't let you do it." Then he addressed Emmett. "If I had let them plant the dynamite, you'd all be dead right now, you stupid bastard."

Emmett stepped back, his face drained. "You mean...?"

"That's right. The dynamite is still in the backpack. See for yourself."

"Very impressive," Emmett said to Milton. "My, you

are full of surprises, aren't you? But I must wonder..." He turned to Peterson. "What's your interest in all this?"

"I want to see what's in this hole you're digging."

"I don't trust him," Milton said. "He's been handing us that line of bull since Colorado."

"What do you have to say to that, Mister...?"

"It's Agent, Agent Peterson," he said from behind his human shields. "If there's a spaceship in this hole, I'm taking charge of it under the international laws of quarantine in the name of the United States National Security Agency."

Emmett cleared his throat. "Forgive me for not being up-to-date in these matters, but it seems to me that the Ethiopian government might be at odds with that."

"Let them. I guarantee we have more firepower."

"And what do you want with my spaceship?"

"It's my job to investigate, preserve, and protect any and all alien objects, your spaceship included."

"Is that so?" Emmett said, his hand inching toward the Berretta under his coat. "Then perhaps we can come to some sort of terms that are equally beneficial to us both."

"I've got a better idea," Peterson growled. "Perhaps you leave the area right now."

"Perhaps not." Emmett grabbed for the gun.

"Look out!" Milton shouted.

Jainaba dropped to the ground, taking Gayle with him and leaving Peterson without cover. Gunfire erupted from the soldiers' rifles and Emmett's Berretta.

Milton dove behind a backhoe just as the bucket came around and dumped a load of dirt. By the time he got up and looked back, Peterson was gone. And so was the backpack full of dynamite.

"I'll get you, you son of a bitch," Emmett shouted into the darkness. A group of soldiers sprinted in the direction Peterson must have gone, their dogs baying in pursuit.

Gayle and Jainaba sat up, looking none the worse for

wear.

Relieved, Milton slumped onto the dirt pile. Soldiers surrounded him with guns drawn, but he was too tired to fight them.

For the next two hours, he wished he had at least tried to escape. Tied to the tracks of Maki's bulldozer, he refused to answer Emmett's questions. The soldiers beat him. Emmett interrogated him again, and the soldiers beat him some more, until finally he'd reached the end of human endurance...and told Emmett everything.

Chapter Thirty-Two

As the mountainous horizon began to glow, Luthes was relieved to see the beginning of a new day. At least now he could see his surroundings. During the night, he and Lisa had picked their way down the dark hillside, working north and away from the lighted dig site, until finally they ended up huddled together in a rocky gully. Hounds bayed in the distance.

Though darkness had been their shield during the night, it also concealed dangers that announced their presence with alarming calls: the hideous cackle of hyenas, the chatter of monkeys, and once, the throaty grumble of a leopard nearby. He'd learned the names of these animals from TV programs he'd watched, though he'd never imagined he'd be roaming among the wild beasts of earth.

Even sitting in this gully, Earth's creatures assailed him, biting and pinching. He swiped the little creatures off his arm.

"Damn ants," Lisa muttered.

His hands were bleeding, cut and scraped while scrambling over rocks and plowing through thorn bushes. As the rising sun brightened the sky, Lisa's wounds became visible: her bloody and torn shirt, her ripped jeans, and the dog lacerations to her jaw and right arm, which drew flies.

"We must keep going," he told her.

"Water." She breathed. "Just some water and a little rest." Wheezing, she batted a fly away. "Then we have to go back."

"You are serious?"

"We have to get my father."

"You're in no condition to fight those humans."

She withdrew a gun from her waistband, the gun the soldier had dropped. "Then you'll need to learn to shoot this."

Luthes cringed at the thought of shooting anyone with such a weapon. "I cannot."

"Take it."

"No."

"What are you afraid of?" She pointed the gun at a wiry tree overhanging the gully. "Point and shoot." She pulled the trigger. The gun responded with a bang and a jerk. A tree branch went flying. "Now you try."

"You shoot trees?"

"Target practice. Take it."

He reached for the gun as if it were a hot coal, daring not to get too close, but finally finding the nerve to touch it, to take it in his palm and wrap his long fingers around it.

"Trigger," she said. "Your finger goes there."

"Yes, I see."

The gun felt comfortable in his hand, though he felt uncomfortable holding it.

"Point and shoot...that boulder over there, the big one...see if you can hit it."

How could he miss? Luthes aimed and pulled the trigger. The blast and recoil startled him, but worse, a spray of rock dust shot up from a different boulder down the ravine. "I missed."

"Don't pull the trigger," she groaned. "Squeeze it."

He held his breath, concentrated on the boulder, held the gun steady, squeezed the trigger.

BANG!

The boulder cratered dead center. A warm feeling of pride came over him. "I did it. Point and shoot."

"Way to go," she said. "Don't use it...unless you have to."

Pride turned to dread. "I could never shoot anyone."

"That's what I thought," Lisa rasped, "but once I had to shoot a man to save my father's life."

"You killed someone?"

She looked to the sky. "The sun is almost up. Get the water...in my backpack."

Luthes gave her the gun, happy he wasn't holding it any longer.

She tucked it into her waistband.

He dug through the backpack for the water bottle. She drank from it greedily.

"Not too much. You are hurt badly. We must find help."

"No." She struggled to her feet. "I can make it." She stumbled and keeled over.

"Lisa?"

She was out cold, her face in the sand. He felt suddenly alone and totally lost, but he knew that if they didn't keep moving, the soldiers would soon find them, especially if they'd heard their target practice. Lisa had gotten them this far, so he would take her the rest of the way to safety...or die trying. But where would he find safety?

After taking a gulp of water, he gathered up Lisa in his arms, same as he'd held Sashi so many times, and began walking, working his way down the rocky gully one step after another. Her limp body was dead weight, and with her head lolled back and mouth open wide, she looked dead, but he pressed on until a huge pile of rocks blocked his progress. He threw Lisa over his shoulder and started climbing.

A snake slithered out a crack and startled him so badly he tripped and nearly took a tumble. Lisa flopped over followed by a clunking sound behind him. He looked back. The gun flipped and bounced down into the ravine, crashing against rocks until it was gone. It had come loose from her waistband. She was going to be very unhappy with him. He grabbed a lungful of air and plodded onward.

An hour passed. The sun beat down on his back, sapping his strength. His muscles ached, and his need for sleep numbed his senses, but he kept going for another hour, until finally he couldn't take another step. Lisa slipped from his arms, and the ground rushed up to meet him. He spit sand and tried to get up, but he fell again. The last thing he saw was black bare feet before he passed out.

Luthes expected Cada's hands to raise him from the ground, relieved of all torment and pain, but when he opened his eyes, he became instantly afraid. Black humans with white teeth and painted faces loomed above him. It took a moment for him to realize that they were children, small and thin and scantily clad. Even though they seemed harmless, he wanted to run from their frightening appearance. He made a sudden move to get up.

They gasped.

Larger hands appeared from behind the children and held him down. An old black human with painful eyes and a feathered crown came into focus. His face was hard and his demeanor businesslike. Mumbling, he waved a smoking stick over Luthes' face. The scent of it soothed him.

He realized he was lying on a thick woven blanket spread over a cushion of reeds on the floor. The ceiling was high and reminded him of a shade tree, green and leafy.

Another black human bent over him, this time a woman with large gold rings dangling from her ears and sagging bare breasts that gave him a fright. Her smile showed choppy teeth. She offered him a colorful cup from which he drank sweet liquid.

The children giggled.

Inhaling more smoke, he felt warm inside...and dizzy.

"He's awake?"

Lisa's voice activated his translator. He turned his head and saw her ghostly form stoop into the room of grass walls and colorful decorations. She was wearing a white band of cloth tied around her breasts, and another around her waist that hung down halfway to her knees. The children rushed to her, giggling with glee and reaching up with wanting hands for her Tarreeda necklace. She brushed past them and knelt on the blanket beside him. "Thank God you're all right."

"Where am I?"

"In good hands."

He noticed water dripping from her hair. "You are wet."

"I was at the spring. It was wonderful."

"And you...are you...all right?"

"You saved my life, Luthes."

"But your wounds..."

"These people have their remedies." She showed him her arm wrapped in broad leaves, and a greasy ointment had been applied to her jaw lacerations. "We are indebted to this man and his family. They raise goats."

"And they found us?"

"His children were tending the flock."

The black woman pressed him to drink more. "You need this for your strength," Luthes' translator relayed. He lifted his head and drank until the liquid was gone. Then she smiled, and the old man beside her said, "You will rest." He rose, and she and the children followed him out of the strange room.

"Your father," Luthes said as his head began to clear. "What about your father?"

"Something went wrong at the dig. There was no explosion this morning."

"That means they are still digging for the Tarreeda spaceship."

"We have to stop them."

"Yes." He sat up.

She embraced him, warm and hard. Uneasy feelings surged through his body. The sensation of her embrace caused him to remember Verrilla, the way she had held him before, the way she had looked at him with loving eyes. His heart sank as he remembered how she died, and Sashi. He wanted Lisa's embrace to end so he might lose the image of them, the heartbreak. "We will go back tomorrow."

"Can you walk?"

"I think so."

"Then we'll go right away."

"But we must rest."

Lisa hugged him tighter. "I can't believe it, Luthes. You saved me from the dog...and the soldiers."

"My intent was only to use the force required to repel the humans."

"I didn't think you had it in you...any measure of violence."

"I thought you were going to die. I could not let that happen, not like what happened to Verrilla. I couldn't save her."

Lisa looked at him with a soft blue gaze. "What was she like?"

"Kind."

"I bet she loved your teddy-bear-brown eyes."

Verrilla liked his eyes, but he didn't know about teddy bears.

"What color were her eyes?"

"Emerald green like Beltzee's sky." Tears threatened but he willed them back.

"Your sky is green?"

"Yes. And your sky is as blue as your eyes."

"We had something in common," Lisa said, smiling.

"Including yellow hair."

Lisa snuggled into him. "What's it like on your world?"

Luthes knew he could never explain it to her completely, a life without violence and fear. "There is no hate on Beltzee. There is harmony, mostly. Disagreements are not uncommon, but we do not fight because of them. We compromise. It is peaceful and prosperous for everyone...at least that is how it was before Brigham brought his death beams of murder."

"I'm sorry."

"My family is gone. My fleet."

Lisa leaned back and looked into his eyes. "Then stay here with me on earth. Start a new family."

He saw the same loving look that Verrilla always gave him, but as her words sunk in, his next breath stuck in his lungs. Her suggestion was beyond considering. "There is too much pain in your world."

"But there is love too," she said. "As I love you."

"You do not love me, Lisa. You are in love with the idea of being in love."

"I've been looking for love all my life, Luthes. My father made me grow up without him. My mother was an addict. I wouldn't wish that heartache on any kid, much less my own."

"Do you love me enough to let me go home?"

She shook her head. "I don't want you to go."

"That's superficial love, Lisa."

"I had to let Janis Mackey go. I can't lose another love again."

"Did you have a choice?"

She sighed. "No."

"Then it is not the same. To let someone go is true love."

"But you don't have to go. I don't have to lose you too. We'll live in Colorado, far away from the salt that makes you sick."

"But when it is time for me to leave, will you love me enough to let me go?"

"Luthes," she said, her tone direct. "There's only room for six Beltzans on the transporter. You won't leave one of your crewmen behind just so you can go back."

"I am a helmsman. I am needed to fly the transporter."

"My dad can teach one of your other men to fly it. Besides, you have nothing left to go back to and everything here to stay for."

Luthes gripped her shoulders firmly in both hands, the truth in her words self-evident. "Even so, your father will not allow us to be together. It is no use."

"You let me worry about my father." She drew him to her. "You have no reason to go back and every reason to stay with me and start again. I want to give you another child, a new family."

"You are serious?"

"Give our love a chance." She put her lips on his again, only this time her tongue slipped into his mouth. It was an unexpected surprise, pleasant and warm, and he took it in gently at first, then greedily. Her words of love and a future for them sounded sincere. He began to believe a new life was possible.

The kissing made his heart beat faster. His fingers traced the curves of her body. Her hand stroked the inside of his thigh. He knew he wanted to join with her, but his arousal was incomplete. Something distracted him, the strange room perhaps, or maybe the aroma of the goat man's smoking stick that lingered in the air. No. It was the disturbing necklace Lisa wore: the Tarreeda cross.

His hands slipped behind her neck, and his fingers released the clasp. She said nothing as he set the Tarreeda cross aside. Relieved, he closed his eyes and drew her soft body into him. He felt dizzy from the smoke. The room spun as his pulse escalated.

She pressed her body against his and moaned.

Wrapped in each other's arms, they fell to the blanket, wiggling and gulping air. His excitement became evident, his arousal complete, though he thought he should restrain himself from going any further. But Verrilla and Sashi were gone. The life he knew before Lisa had ended. She was right; it was time to start anew. Perhaps someday they could both come to love each other deeply, wholly, and completely. As it should be.

He let go of his past and embraced his future with passion and orgasmic release.

***

Barking dogs awoke him. Luthes opened his eyes. A small flame flickered on a stick by the door. It wasn't there earlier. Lisa was standing there, peering out around a black and white striped hideskin drape, her nude form aglow in the dancing light. Outside, goats bleated and children screamed. A gunshot rang out. His translator activated. "We know they are here."

Lisa said, "It's Emmett's hired soldiers."

Luthes shot up from the blanket, the screams troubling him. "Are the children in danger?"

She tied the white cloth over her breasts, clipped the translator in place. "What?"

"The children, are the soldiers shooting them?" He put on his pants.

The barking got louder.

"No." She tied the other white cloth around her waist and clipped the Tarreeda cross around her neck. "They're firing into the air." Her tennis shoes were on but not yet tied when she grabbed her backpack. "Hurry."

Luthes had just gotten his shoes on when two soldiers burst into the hut, guns lowered.

"Hold it right there."

Lisa crouched into a fighting stance, her fierce eyes on the soldiers. Luthes saw tension in every curve of her muscles. He feared she was outnumbered. But before she could move forward, two dogs squeezed past the soldiers' legs, snarling and straining on their leashes.

Terror darkened her eyes. She stepped back. Her

hands went up in the air in surrender.

Luthes followed her example.

***

They rode in a jeep back to the dig site, bound at the ankles and wrists during the bone-jarring ride. In spite of her unenviable position, Lisa was relieved about one thing: the goat man and his family were unharmed.

However, it was different with Luthes. She saw fear in his eyes. So quickly things had changed for them, one minute they were lovers with a future, the next, prisoners.

Activity in the dig was at a fever pitch. Droves of men sweated over shovels and picks. Digging machines rattled and squealed. A giant hole had been dug in the side of Choke Mountain, an ungodly gash in the earth.

She inhaled dust as the jeep skidded to a stop in front of a large safari tent. Roughly, soldiers yanked her from the seat and dragged her inside. Over tables and chairs, a single light bulb dangled on a rope between two supporting center poles.

"Lisa!"

"Dad!"

Sitting spread-legged on the floor, he was bruised and beaten and tied to a tent pole, his arms behind his back. Milton and Gayle were tied to the other pole in the same fashion, their heads lolling.

"What happened to your face?" Ray asked. "Your arm?"

"It's a long story."

The soldiers pushed Lisa to the dirt floor behind her father and tied her to the pole with her back to his, their arms entwined.

"Are you all right?" he asked.

"Never better."

"Where are your clothes?"

"A dog ate them."

Gayle said, "We thought you got away."

"So did we." Lisa strained against her bindings. The knots held firm.

The soldiers walked out, she assumed to get Luthes, but when they didn't return, a horrible new fear came over her. "Milton," she called out.

His head bobbed a little, his hat teetered, but he only grunted. Dim lighting revealed his badly deformed mouth and one eye swollen completely shut. He didn't look like he was in any condition to carry on a conversation. "Where's Jainaba?"

Ray said, "They're forcing him to dig with the others."

"He was supposed to blow the mountain. What the hell happened?"

"Peterson stopped us," Gayle said.

"Is he helping Emmett?"

"We don't know," Ray said. "The chickenshit NSA agent ran off when the shooting started, tail between his legs, I guess."

Lisa looked at Milton again, a beaten man. "What happened to him?"

"They tortured him," Ray explained. "Beat him until he told Emmett everything."

Lisa gasped. "He knows about Luthes?"

"Worse. He knows about the Tarreeda. He was especially interested in their method of torture and death."

"What?"

"The cross. He knows about the Tarreeda cross."

A hot rush of panic flared in Lisa's chest. The cross was Luthes' greatest fear. She started yanking on the ropes again, with more ferocity this time. No matter what, she had to get free. But the ropes only cut into her skin.

***

Two soldiers grabbed Luthes by his arms and dragged him from the jeep. Fear gripped his lungs so tightly he could hardly breathe. One soldier drew a knife. "I should cut you, you freak." Instead, he bent and cut the ropes from around Luthes' ankles, but left his hands tied behind his back. "Get moving."

They pushed him to a tent farther down the row. It was brightly lit inside, with a desk, a large bed enclosed in sheer veils, and various cases and boxes stacked about. A man sitting at the desk looked up and removed his dark glasses. "I'll be damn." He stood. "A real live fuckin' alien."

Luthes immediately saw a translator clipped to the man's white jacket. An instinctive fear came over him, being in the presence of this human. His expression was curious, his manner cold as he approached, and Luthes suddenly recognized him as the human in the white suit he'd seen the night before when Lisa's father was captured. "What do you want with me?"

"Untie him."

The soldiers untied his hands.

"Hold them out. Your hands. I want to see them."

Luthes offered up both hands for inspection. He turned them palms up and palms down and wiggled his long fingers, all the while thinking how much he despised the human that made him display himself this way. He was different, but he was determined to be proud of it. "Satisfied?"

A look of loathing came over Emmett's face. "Milton thinks you are his prize, but I'm going to find your spaceship."

"It is not mine."

"You know Agent Peterson, right?"

"Yes."

"Where is he?"

"I don't know."

Terry Wright

"He has caused us a lot of trouble."

"I wish to be with Lisa now."

"Got yourself a girlfriend, huh?" Emmett cackled. "What are you, some kind of alien Playboy?"

The soldiers laughed, but Luthes didn't get the humor. "I will not cause you any trouble."

"I've got other plans for you." Emmett moved to the tent door, which looked out to the dig site where men and equipment toiled, a constant sea of motion and noise. "Milton tells me there's a spaceship buried here, and your Agent Peterson wants it."

"If there is, it should be left alone."

"You know I can't do that. Finders keepers."

"Why is it important to you?"

Emmett walked back to his desk and lit a cigar. "Let me tell you something about our history." Acrid smoke clouded the air. "It was common practice, thousands of years ago, to execute criminals by hanging them on crosses. We would torture our prisoners, our debtors, and our rivals. The Romans perfected the practice, even nailed the son of our God to a cross. Millions of people were killed in this manner, strung up to suffer and die where everyone could see their torment. It was a very effective deterrent to dissent from the populous and instilled fear in the enemy. Simply brilliant, I must say, but I wonder...was it truly a human invention?"

"It was the Tarreeda's custom," Luthes said. "They are the ones—"

"That's what Milton told me. But according to history, it was ours, so I ask you, did we invent it or remember it?"

Luthes stiffened. "I do not understand."

Puffing smoke from the cigar, Emmett regarded the glowing ash then glanced up, a piercing glare in his eyes. "I think we remembered it," he said and smiled crookedly.

A chill went through Luthes, cold as the Ice Planet. "Why do you say that?"

~374~

Now Emmett's eyes narrowed. "Because the thought of hanging you on a cross pleases me."

"You can't mean that."

"String him up, boys."

The soldiers grabbed Luthes' arms and dragged him outside. To his horror, more soldiers approached carrying a wooden Tarreeda cross.

"No!"

They wrestled him to the ground and forcefully bound his arms and legs to the cross as Emmett stood looking down on him and smoking the cigar.

Lying on his back on the splintered wood, Luthes' heart hammered. "Why are you doing this to me?"

"You're going to help me get Peterson."

"How?"

Emmett cackled. "Alien bait."

"No!" Luthes fought his bindings as the soldiers hoisted the cross in the air. "Cada, help me!" They took him to a knoll overlooking the dig site, thrust the cross upright, and planted it in the ground. Luthes screamed in agony, as did his ancestors over 20,000 years ago. His arms and legs ached from the strain of his weight. His skin burned from the abrasive ropes. Looking down on the upturned and laughing faces of Emmett and his soldiers gathered around, Luthes no longer had any doubt in his mind. He was going to die at the hands of the Tarreeda.

He screamed. "Lisa, the Tarreeda are killing me!"

Emmett said, "That should get Peterson's attention." He turned to the soldiers. "Now bring me the girl."

***

Lisa heard Luthes screaming her name, his voice laced with terror. She couldn't imagine what torture he was enduring at the hands of Emmett Collins. If only she could free herself and rescue him, but no matter how hard she struggled, the ropes wouldn't come loose. Already, the leaf bandage on her arm had fallen off. The dog bites were bleeding again.

"Lisa," Luthes wailed.

"Luthes," she cried out to him.

"They're killing him," Ray said. He too was frantically trying to free himself.

Milton raised his head. "What's Emmett doing to my alien?"

"Lisa!"

"Try to lift the tent pole, Dad. I'll slip the ropes out from underneath it."

He strained to lift it, and even working together they couldn't budge it.

"It's cemented to the ground," Milton said.

Two soldiers burst through the tent flaps, one with a leashed and growling dog. The dog and its handler remained at the doorway while the other man went directly to Lisa. He showed her a nasty smile. "The boss wishes the pleasure of your company. Dressed as you are, I do not blame him."

Suddenly the white strips of cloth she wore seemed hugely inadequate. She felt naked, but as her hands came free of the ropes, she had only one thought. Leaping to her feet, she shoved the soldier backward, pivoted on one heel, and landed a spinning back kick to his head. He fell into a table, which broke under his weight and crashed to the floor in a splintered heap.

The dog went crazy, snarling and showing teeth. Its handler had all he could do to hold it back. "I will let him go," he warned.

Lisa crouched to defend herself, but fear and common sense prevailed. The dog was sure to win, and Luthes wasn't around to save her this time. She stood, hands raised. "Call off the dog."

Like a drunkard, the downed soldier struggled to his

feet. "I should kill you for that." He kicked a chair.

Lisa gave him a canted glare. She wasn't afraid of him, or five men just like him, but the snarling dog sent chills of terror up her spine. Looking down at her father still tied to the pole, she said, "I'll be back."

The soldiers pushed her outside.

Cold night air nipped at her bare skin, but Luthes' screams, coming from somewhere near the lighted dig site, made her stomach knot with horror. Diesel smoke tainted the air as the digging machines labored alongside the men in the pit. Two backhoes and a bulldozer crowded with locals were moving tons of earth at an alarming rate. It was a dusty and noisy operation.

"Keep moving." The soldiers pushed her along a path, until they came to a brightly lit tent. Just beyond it, on a knoll overlooking the dig, she saw the most horrible sight she'd ever seen. Silhouetted by floodlights, Luthes was lashed to a cross, writhing and screaming, his long fingers clawing the air. Soldiers stood around him, laughing and poking him with their rifles. Had they already bartered for his clothing?

Her blood ran cold. There was no limit to the cruelty man inflicted on one another, and seeing the horror of a crucifixion first hand compelled her to grasp her gold necklace and yank it off her neck, breaking the chain. It wasn't only a symbol of sacrifice, but also a reminder of man's brutality to man. She tossed it to the ground and looked up to the cross. "Luthes."

"Lisa, help me."

"I'll get you down, Luthes."

"I'm afraid."

"I love you."

The dog growled.

The soldiers jabbed her with their rifles and pushed her inside the tent. She saw a table set with fine dinnerware complete with a lighted candelabrum. A linen-covered serving cart stood beside the table, and behind it, a veiled bed, elegant as any fancy hotel.

Emmett Collins rose from behind his desk. He wore white slacks and loafers, a white shirt with the sleeves rolled up to his elbows. His strawberry-blond hair was handsomely slicked back, but his dark eyebrows and stormy gray eyes ruined any illusion of chivalry.

"Congratulations," he said, strolling toward her. "You people have managed to mess up everything for yourselves. Did you really think you were going to stop me?"

Lisa spit on him.

"I'll take that as a no." Standing in front of her, he waved his soldiers to leave them. "They will be right outside," he assured her. "So don't try to be a hero."

"Let Luthes go," she demanded.

"I like him just fine where he is." Emmett eyed her up and down with raised eyebrows. "You've had a rough time of things I'd say from the sight of you." She tried to look away, but he forced her chin into the cradle of his hand and traced the laceration on her jaw with his thumb. "What a shame."

"Let him go. He's terrified."

"I'm sure you're hungry."

She wrenched her chin from Emmett's grasp, not able to stomach his touch any longer.

"Look what I have for you." He walked to the cart and removed the white linen, revealing the silver dome of a serving plate. "Roast beef." Lifting the lid, he set loose a wonderful aroma. Whole white potatoes and corn on the cob surrounded a slab of beef the size of Texas, thickly sliced, and stabbed with a carving knife. "Plus all the trimmings. Care to join me?"

Her stomach begged her to say yes. "I'd rather be tied to a cross."

"Have it your way." Sitting at the table, he tucked a napkin into the front of his shirt. "I prefer eating a good meal before dessert." He regarded her up and down with an impious grin.

Lisa swallowed dryly. The nerve of the pompous bastard. He'd rape her for dessert. But the food looked good. She'd play along with his egotistical game. Moving to the cart, "You're quite the ladies man," she said and reached for the slice of beef closest to the carving knife.

With lightning speed, he grabbed her wrist, his eyes on the knife handle. "You'd like that, wouldn't you?"

She huffed. "I don't need a knife to whip you."

"Talk is cheap, little girl."

"Am I invited to dinner or not?"

He released her wrist.

She snatched the slice of beef and began devouring it in both hands as crudely as she could. Emmett seemed undaunted by her barbaric antics, so she picked up a potato and bit it in half.

"Would you like some champagne with that?" He indicated an uncorked bottle nestled in a pail of crushed ice. His demeanor was suave and disgusting.

"Sure." She grabbed the bottle and brought it to her lips.

Emmett shot to his feet. "Try to be civilized," he shouted, his left cheek twitching.

Hesitating to drink, she glared at him. "You should be careful who you invite to dinner...especially when it's your last meal." She guzzled from the bottle.

"Is that right?" His cheeks were mottled with rage. "I don't care if you're dead or alive when I have my dessert, so choose your words wisely."

She set the bottle back into the ice. "That dog outside is the only reason you're still alive."

He looked at her for a moment, smirked, chuckled, and then began howling with laughter. "I've got to tell you," he croaked out, "that's the funniest thing..." he bellowed and fell back in his chair, "the funniest thing I've ever heard." Now he roared, and Lisa found his jubilation contagious. She remained stern-faced, and then deliberately joined him in raucous elation, looking for any opportunity to grab the knife.

An explosion suddenly rocked the camp, and then another. Men started yelling. Rifles banged.

Emmett jumped up, stiff-armed Lisa aside, and sprinted to the tent flap.

Another explosion flashed in the sky.

She rushed to see what the commotion was all about. A sparkling stick of dynamite arced out of the darkness upslope and exploded in midair, driving workers in the dig to the dirt.

Soldiers guarding Emmett's tent and those milling around Luthes on the cross were now sprawled on the ground and crawling for cover. Yelping, the Doberman took off running. Another sizzling stick of dynamite plummeted from the sky and boomed.

"It's Peterson!" Emmett shouted. "After him!"

The soldiers took up their weapons and were gone. Lisa stepped back as Emmett turned around, fury glaring from his eyes. "Now for my dessert."

"You've forgotten one thing," she said.

"What's that?" He grabbed her arms.

"No dog."

Emmett's eyes narrowed in confusion.

She dropped backward, pulling him over the top of her and sending him flying into the dinner table. The lit candles crashed to the floor, instantly igniting the sheer draperies surrounding the bed. By the time she got to her feet, a crackling wall of fire licked at the canvas ceiling.

The unfolding disaster spurred Emmett into a rage. Bolting to his feet, he came at her full speed, teeth bared and fists balled, as if brute force alone would make him victorious. But he didn't understand that she could use his momentum to her advantage. A forearm to the chin greeted his advance, a sidestep took her out of his path, and an elbow in the ribs knocked the breath out of him. Wheezing, he wheeled around only to be greeted by the bottom of her tennis shoe, right between the eyes. He fell backward out the door of the burning tent and slammed to the ground, unconscious.

Ducking under the layer of smoke, she retrieved the carving knife, ran outside, leaped over Emmett's limp body, and rushed to the cross on the knoll. Already, the fire had attracted the attention of men in the dig site, their upturned faces illuminated in the fiery glow. She didn't see any soldiers or dogs. They were all out chasing Peterson, but she knew the fire would soon bring them back.

"Lisa," Luthes called.

"I'm here." She assessed the towering project before her. His feet were at her eyelevel, his arms high up and out of reach. "I'm going to cut the ropes."

"Hurry."

The carving knife quickly freed his legs. "You have to help me. Hold your feet stiff, toes out." She grabbed his shoe and pulled down on it. His foot gave. "Hold it tighter."

"Oh, like a step."

She tested his foot again. "Good. This might hurt." With the carving knife clenched between her teeth, she jumped up and grabbed hold of his belt.

"Ah!"

Kicking her foot up, she stood on top of his shoe. The tent fire and floodlights gave her plenty of light to see by. Ignoring the pain in her dog-bitten right arm, she pulled herself up to a standing position on top of his straining feet. Her left arm went around his neck. With the knife in her right hand, she clung there, face to face with Luthes. She wanted to kiss him.

"Hurry. You are breaking my feet."

She reached out and cut the ropes binding his left arm to the cross. This caused his body to rotate right, upending the whole tipsy affair and sending her to the ground. When she looked up, she saw him hanging by his right arm. "Lisa."

"Here." She tossed him the knife.

"Lookout," he shouted.

She was knocked to the ground from behind. A man was on her back, beating her with fists, each blow nearly bashing her into unconsciousness.

"You bitch!"

Emmett! He was crazed beyond belief.

Lying flat on her stomach, she tried to keep her face from slamming into the ground. She couldn't get any leverage to throw him off. On top of that, her injured arm responded with crippling sharp pains. His surprise attack had given him the advantage. All she could do was cry out. "Luthes."

The next thing she knew, Emmett was dragged off her, and when she turned over, her dazed brain struggled to sort fact from fantasy. Flames leaping into the night sky revealed Luthes on top of Emmett, beating his face with fists as big as sledgehammers. In the distance, she heard the nightmarish sounds of baying dogs and men yelling. Again and again, blow after blow Luthes pummeled Emmett until she finally realized that Luthes was about to kill him. "Luthes, no. Stop."

But he didn't stop. He just kept hitting Emmett. Already his eyes were glazed over. His head slammed back and forth with each blow, his arms limp at his side. He was no longer able to defend himself.

Fighting panic, she found wobbly legs, jumped on Luthes' back, and threw her arms around his neck. "You're killing him."

"He deserves to die." Luthes hit him again. "He is a Tarreeda."

"No. Luthes, please. He's a human, a bad human."

"Humans do not hang people on crosses." He slugged

him again. "Only the Tarreeda."

"Don't kill him."

Luthes stiffened, his fist held high for another blow. Slowly, he turned and looked at her, the burning tent illuminating the horror in his eyes. "Cada." Then he looked at his bloodied fists. "What have I done?"

"It's all right." She embraced him. "We have to go."

The clicking of cocking firearms suddenly surrounded them. Soldiers and growling dogs had left no route to flee.

Emmett spit blood. "Get off me, you freak."

Chapter Thirty-Three

Three wasn't a bone in Milton's body that didn't hurt, a muscle that didn't ache. Tied to the tent pole with Gayle Weatherbee, he barely had enough strength to lift his head. Even his hat seemed heavy. His left eye felt like a brick and wouldn't come open, thanks to Emmett's soldiers.

"Milton," Gayle shouted.

He didn't answer her, just passed his tongue over his swollen lips and wished for a drink of water.

"F-fire!" she screamed.

Jolted, he turned his head, and with his good eye, he saw a glow outside the tent. A shot of adrenaline hit his system, made his heart beat harder, his wounds hurt worse. Fire could spread quickly through the camp. Worse, they were in no position to escape the flames.

Then he heard the rhythmic chants of men, the clang of pails, and the sloshing and splashing of water.

"Someone get us out of here," Ray shouted, tied to the other pole.

"Help!" Gail screamed.

Four soldiers stormed in dragging Lisa and Luthes behind them.

"What's going on out there?" Ray demanded.

"Did you miss me?" Lisa replied as the soldiers tied her to the pole with Ray.

Milton saw no humor in her greeting. "There's a fire."

"Emmett's gonna need a new tent." Lisa grimaced as a soldier tightened the rope around her arms.

"Never a dull moment with you people, is there!"

Milton craned his neck so he could see them. Luthes appeared to be in shock, limp and lethargic. The soldiers tied him to the pole with Lisa and Ray. Milton asked Lisa, "Is he all right?"

"He's having an identity crisis," she said.

"What happened to him?"

Emmett stormed in, pushing past the soldiers, his white suit now soiled and bloody. "Let *me* tell you." He set the ritainium box on a table. His bruised and swollen left cheek twitched spastically. "They've just signed your death warrants."

"Sore loser," Lisa said.

Emmett scowled at her. "I'll deal with you later."

"What's wrong, Emmett?" Milton glared up at him one-eyed from under the brim of his hat. "Are you having a bad day?"

"That alien damn near killed me." He pulled out the Berretta and ejected the clip. "But things are about to improve dramatically around here." Glancing at the cartridges in the clip, he added, "Problem is, how to dispose of your bodies."

"Don't stress yourself," Milton said.

Emmett jammed the clip back into the gun. "But first..." Emmett paced to Luthes. "The alien dies." As he raised the gun to Luthes' forehead, boisterous cheering rose from the dig site.

A soldier rushed in. "They found it."

Still holding the gun on Luthes, Emmett turned his head, a smile growing on his beaten face. "Hear that, Milton? What a shame you won't live to see it."

"You owe me that much," Milton shouted.

Emmett whipped around, his gun now pointing at Milton. "You deserve nothing."

"Like *Lucy*?" he shot back. "Don Johnson stole her from me."

"You're wrong!" Emmett cackled. "I stole her from

you."

"What?"

"And his financial backers paid me well to do it."

"You lousy..."

Emmett waved the gun. "However, I made a mistake. Johnson took all the credit. He's famous. His name is in all the textbooks, and what did I get for making it all possible? Money. And that's long gone. I realized too late that I should have stolen *Lucy* for myself."

"You're just an administrator, Emmett. What would you have done with her?"

"I'd have sold her for a fortune on the black market." Emmett grinned. "This time I know better."

"What are you going to do, hock a spaceship?"

"You catch on real quick."

"What for?"

"The technology, Milton. Whoever possesses it will upset the balance of power in the world. Bidding starts at fifty billion dollars. Israel is already onboard, and the oil-rich Saudis want in on it, too, not to mention North Korea."

"The United States won't stand for that." Milton gasped. He could see it now, the consequences of Emmett's plan. "You son of a bitch, you're going to start World War III."

Emmett grinned. "And the winner will be the highest bidder." He bent over until his eyes were level with Milton's. "Better yet, I won't be playing second fiddle to the likes of you or Don Johnson anymore."

Milton could believe it. Emmett's ego was at the root of all this. The little fish with the big splash could very well drown in his own pond. For that to happen, Milton needed a change of strategy. "Brilliant," he said, still staring down the barrel of Emmett's gun.

"Genius is more like it." Emmett stood upright again, shoulders back.

"Yes," Milton lied. "You are a genius."

The workers in the dig were cheering wildly now, their revelry sounding more and more riotous. "A rich genius," Emmett added.

"Seeing as how you're going to kill us anyway," Milton pressed. "What harm could there be in letting us see what you found? After all, you have certain bragging rights."

"Then you agree it's mine?"

"Do I have any choice?"

His gun arm stiffened. "I'll just kill you now."

"You've already won, Emmett. We can't stop you."

Licking swollen lips, he nodded. "Yes, I have won, haven't I."

"Then show us your prize. Rub our faces in it. Revel in your victory."

"Very well." Emmett considered the others tied to the poles. "But they stay here." He turned to a soldier. "Free him. If he does anything stupid, kill them all."

Milton could hardly stand up straight, his ribs hurt so bad. "Thank you, Emmett," he muttered. "You have no idea how much this means to me."

"Fine then. Let's go outside and see what the celebration is all about."

Painfully, Milton followed Emmett across the west escarpment and down into the brightly lit dig, which looked more like a deep mining pit than an archeological site. The men were crowded together around the bulldozer, and now Milton realized what all the noise was about. In heated argument, the locals were discussing the meaning of what they had found. Maki stood tallest on the bulldozer, his brothers squatting around him. "It is the door, Dr. Spears," he called out. "The door to Kaang's underworld."

"Superstitious bastards," Emmett spat. "Move along."

Pushing through the crowd, they finally came to the deepest part of the pit, at the foot of a cliff-like wall, which towered six stories high and shed a constant sprinkle of dirt. There, under the brightest lights, a backhoe's scar in the earth revealed the silver hull of a Tarreeda spaceship that had not touched air for over 20,000 years.

Milton thought his knees would fail him. He moved to be near it, reached out and touched it with the palms of his hands in much the same way one would touch the Wailing Wall in Jerusalem or the Vietnam Memorial in Washington, DC. Reverently. He sensed the power and magnificence before him and felt tiny in comparison.

The surface of this spaceship felt like brushed aluminum, as did the ritainium box, but thicker, solid and unyielding. He couldn't tell how high up it went, nor how far down, but it seemed as if it went on forever. Cautiously, he put his ear to the hull and detected a sound similar to the wheezing breaths of an old man. Startled, he jumped back.

Emmett laughed. "What is it, Milton, the boogieman?"

With his good eye wide open, he looked across the pit at the locals gathered around, the soldiers with guns and dogs, and at Emmett, dirty and bloodied. "We're all going to die."

"The harbinger of doom has spoken." Emmett mocked him.

His soldiers joined him in laughter. The locals stood around, their eyes filled with horror as a team of men brought up cutting torches to assault the hull. Milton couldn't save any of them.

Maki shouted, "It is the door, Dr. Spears."

Of course, the door, the curse of Choke Mountain, the curse the locals feared. It wouldn't hurt to add a little more tension to Emmett's already stretched nerves. Milton began the chant. "Kaang, Kaang, Kaang."

"Shut up," Emmett ordered.

Milton thrust a fist into the air. "Kaang, Kaang, Kaang!"

A look of horror washed over Emmett's face. "What

are you doing?"

The locals joined in. "Kaang, Kaang, Kaang!"

"Milton!"

Maki's face lit up with a smile. His brothers rose to their feet on the bulldozer, jabbing fists in the air and chanting, "Kaang, Kaang, Kaang!"

Cutting torches spit fire. The soldiers put them to work on the exposed hull.

"Kaang, Kaang, Kaang!" The locals were going wild.

"I'm warning you, Milton."

Jainaba appeared from the throng, climbed the bulldozer to Maki's side, and joined in. "Kaang, Kaang, Kaang!"

Maki raised his arms, spreading his goatskin robe and making himself appear larger and more powerful. In Amharic, he spoke to the locals.

Molten sparks began to fly from the hull.

"Kaang, Kaang, Kaang!"

The locals cheered Maki, and at Jainaba's lead, they all began running from the pit in a frantic wave, overpowering the soldiers and trampling them to the ground. Dust rose in the floodlights like a swirling storm, and within minutes they were all gone, a human avalanche spilling down the mountainside.

Emmett's face was a red ball of fury. He looked like he was going to explode.

Milton felt the glow of satisfaction. "Now you have no one to dig for you."

Shaking with anger, Emmett growled. "I will kill you for that."

The last thing Milton saw was the butt of a soldier's rifle.

When he came to, he was again tied to the tent pole. His nose felt like it was broken. Blood had dried on his face. A hellish thirst burned in his throat. "Gayle?" he mumbled.

"Dr. Spears!" she cried out. "It's Dr. Spears. He's awake."

"Where's my hat?"

"What happened out there? It sounded like a riot."

"The little fish has an employee problem."

"The locals are gone?"

"Ran like jackrabbits. What time is it?"

"The sun is coming up."

"The spaceship? Have they gotten into it?"

"Not yet."

A wailing sound rose from the pit, like a hundred-car freight train with the emergency brakes applied. The sheer volume and pitch overpowered Milton's senses.

"What's happening?" Gayle shouted.

"They've breached the hull."

The wind came up, a tremendous howling, swirling with the force of a hurricane that lashed out at the tent and ripped it from its moorings, leaving the captives fully exposed to the elements.

Lisa screamed.

Milton winced against the bite of gale-driven dirt.

His ritainium box shot straight up into the sky and disappeared into boiling clouds. Tables and chairs flew away like litter. Soon all that remained were four terrified humans and one petrified alien tied to two poles cemented in the ground.

Keeping his good eye open, Milton saw the horizon aglow with the rising sun. It silhouetted Choke Mountain and the ungodly dig site boiling smoky gas from its belly. In the turbulent currents of wind, a gray mist whipped around them, and Milton knew it was the Tarreedas' poisonous gas. His clothes fluttered wildly in the wind. Stinging dirt pelted his face. "Hold your breath," he shouted, hoping the others had heard him over the tempest. "It's the gas."

"I can't see," Gayle shouted.

"Don't breathe the gas."

Milton already felt lightheaded. He held his breath as the gaseous storm from the pit grew in height and intensity, now towering skyward, an expanding pillar that blotted out the dawning sky's light. Billowing up like a volcanic plume, it generated enough friction to create static electricity. The sky came alive with lightning and thunder. It was the end of the world.

At the pit's edge, Emmett and his soldiers stood in breathtaking awe of the spectacle unfolding before them. "It's beautiful," Milton heard him crooning. "Beautiful." He knew they were under the euphoric effects of the Tarreeda gas. They swayed back and forth and waved their hands as if greeting a long-lost friend.

Milton's lungs began to burn, but he didn't dare take a breath of lethal air. Glancing at the others, they looked like Raggedy Anne dolls banging together, their hair and clothes whipping in the wind's fury.

And still the maelstrom expanded, rising higher and higher. Ribbons of gray gas circled them and flew off, swung around the pit and came back at them with a whoosh, then raced away. The wind roared, its sheer force buffeting the helicopter tied to the pad and rocking vehicles on their suspensions.

"What is it?" Gayle cried out.

While the gray ribbon of gas circled the pit, Milton gulped fresh air greedily in preparation for the gas's next return pass. "It's the truth you've been looking for," he told Gayle. "Emmett has opened the womb of modern mankind."

"And this was the beginning?"

"The beginning of the violence."

The gaseous ribbon of mist came back, swirled around them. Milton held his breath again. Dust raced along the ground, streaked toward the center of the pit, and then shot straight up into the boiling plume, plucking the Tarreeda cross from the knoll and sending it spinning up and up with the rising storm.

The raging wind lifted Emmett and his soldiers into the sky. It whirled them around and around at dizzying speeds. They screamed in agony, spinning in midair, arms and legs splayed until their bodies imploded and dissolved into the dust.

Lightning cracked and thunder boomed.

When the land was stripped of every loose thing, the wind abated, and the towering plume began to collapse, swirling back down into the pit like water down a drain until it was gone. Then from a calm sky, the ritainium box spiraled back toward earth, spinning down into the pit, followed by the wooden Tarreeda cross.

There was a thump, and then there was silence.

Milton exhaled and quickly gulped fresh air. "Is everyone all right?"

"Yes," Ray said. "Lisa?"

"I'm okay, Dad."

"Luthes?"

"I want to go home."

They had survived. The worst was over—

A droning sound emanated from the pit. It oscillated in frequency as if produced by a rotating machine, and it rose steadily in volume to eardrum-slamming intensity. The ground began to tremble, a little at first and then more violently as each second passed.

Shaking in terror, Milton looked up the face of Choke Mountain. The morning sun's first rays peered over the horizon and illuminated the upper escarpment in a brilliant yellow hue.

"Cada!" Luthes screamed.

It was as if God were looking down on them...but why?

The tremors became more intense. Rocks began breaking free from the cliffs above. Rumbling now, the mountain unleashed jagged boulders that tumbled down the mountainside, bouncing and crashing and smashing everything in their paths.

Gayle shrieked.

The underground rumbling got louder and louder.

"Lookout," Ray shouted.

Alarmed, Milton whipped his head around and saw Peterson approaching with his knife in hand, staggering and stumbling on the trembling ground. His clothes were ripped to shreds, and blood leaked from wounds all over his body.

"Get away from us!" Milton yelled at him.

Choke Mountain shook with fury. The high cliffs finally crumbled into a tumbling wave of rock that crashed down the mountainside. Quickly, the landslide grew in volume and speed. It bore down the mountain straight for them. Milton clenched his jaw. They were all going to die, if not by Peterson's knife, then crushed under tons of rock and debris.

Peterson reached them and fell to his knees.

Milton cringed, thinking the knife would penetrate his back. Instead, he felt a tugging on his arms. The ropes came loose. Peterson had cut him free, and then Gayle. She was already on her feet by the time Milton rose drunkenly on the shaking ground.

Seconds later, Peterson finished cutting loose the others, and they too were on their shaky feet. "Follow me."

The landslide was already halfway down the mountain, churning and rumbling with an intensity Milton could not have imagined. He knew there was no way to outrun it, but he staggered after Peterson, tripped and fell, and Gayle came back and helped him get up. Clutching each other and stumbling along, Milton glanced behind him to make sure Ray, Lisa, and Luthes were keeping up. It became quickly apparent they were all heading toward the helicopter.

Peterson got there first and released the tie-down

ropes. Milton opened the side door and ushered everyone in. By the time they were seated, Peterson was sitting at the controls, sweating. His hesitation was alarming.

"What's the matter?" Milton asked. "No key?"

"It's been a long time since I've flown."

"Get us out of here or we're all going to die."

Peterson exhaled and cranked the engine. It turned over with a slow and mournful whine, popped and wheezed. He reached for the knob to adjust the mixture, but everything was shaking so violently that he had difficulty operating the controls properly.

Upslope, the landslide was nearly on them, roaring down the hillside, just above the pit now, tossing boulders like beanbags.

Peterson tried the engine again. Finally, it sputtered to life and throttled up. The helicopter lifted from the ground just as the landslide cascaded over the dig site. A storm of rocks pummeled the fuselage, breaking a window.

Gayle screamed.

Boulders the size of Volkswagens just missed smashing into the helicopter's skids. The rumble overpowered the whine of the engine as it rose. Milton looked down and watched Choke Mountain reclaim its secret in a boiling mix of rock and dust. Maki's bulldozer tumbled with the crushing wave and was covered. The tent poles they'd been tied to snapped like toothpicks and were gone. By the time the landslide churned to a stop, a hundred feet of rubble had reburied the Tarreeda spaceship.

Milton looked up. The jagged cliffs that remained on Choke Mountain's summit reflected the rising sun's golden glow. "God stretched out his right hand," Milton said. "And the earth swallowed them."

The helicopter banked toward the valley.

Gayle hugged his neck. "You're saying God caused the landslide?"

Luthes explained. "Cada saved the Tarreeda from a

death sentence on the Ice Planet and sent them here, to earth, far from Beltzee where they could no longer do us any harm."

"Until I came back to Beltzee," Ray said. "On the same Higgs Field string that saved the Tarreeda."

Milton said, "Now God just saved us humans from the Tarreeda."

"No," Luthes replied. "He saved you from yourselves."

Gayle glared at him. "What do you mean?"

"I understand," Milton said. It was all perfectly clear to him now. "The Tarreeda didn't pass on their defective genes to us Homo sapiens."

Luthes shook his head. "No they didn't."

Milton looked out the window at the lush and rugged landscape of the Blue Nile Valley slipping beneath the helicopter. "On the sixth day, God created man and said it was good...and it *was* good...until the Tarreeda arrived. One of seven ships landed here on Choke Mountain. The survivors multiplied and migrated across the land. It took over 12,000 years, until the rise of Mesopotamia, for them to kill every human they encountered, including the Neanderthal and the Homo sapiens. And when they dominated the earth, they began killing each other." He took a breath and muscled up the courage to admit the truth. "We destroyed our enemies without compassion, learned to enslave other men, and greedily took from the world."

"We?" Gayle asked.

"Yes. We *ARE* the Tarreeda."

Everyone looked at Milton with astounded eyes.

"That's why we hurt and kill each other, and violence is the way of our world."

"Why doesn't God stop the violence? He's so all-powerful."

"He put us on earth so we'd stop killing the Beltzans,"

Milton said. "It's up to us to change ourselves, not God. And so there's the answer to your question. Your quest is over, Miss Gayle Weatherbee. You can go home now."

Ray said, "And Luthes is going home, too."

Lisa twisted in her seat and faced her father. "He's staying, Dad."

"Don't be ridiculous."

She smiled, rubbed Luthes' arm. "We've decided."

"Like hell you have."

Chapter Thirty-Four

L isa heard the news reports about the tragedy on Choke Mountain. A landslide had buried Emmett Collins along with his team of archeologists and security people. In an unprecedented act of courage, Emmett had managed to evacuate over a hundred local workers, leaving no time for his own escape. The rubble was so deep that officials deemed it impossible to recover the bodies. By an emergency act of the Ethiopian government, the area was designated hallowed ground, thus establishing a permanent resting place for those who had lost their lives. A towering cross would be erected on the site. She knew they didn't understand its true significance.

Milton and Gayle went back to the university in Addis Abba. They talked about searching for the other six Tarreeda transports that had landed or crashed somewhere on the globe. Luthes tried to talk them out of it. No such luck.

Peterson was the real hero, Lisa thought as she boarded a 747 at Bole. He'd tied himself to a boulder during the maelstrom, and once he witnessed the power of the Tarreeda spaceship, he abandoned all hope of studying it for *Project Aquarius*. In his report to The National Security Agency, he stated that the spaceship had been destroyed in an explosion that caused the landslide on Choke Mountain. His recommendation to the agency: return the aliens to Beltzee.

On the flight back to the states, she sat between Luthes and her father, who wasn't speaking to her, which was fine. He wasn't going to change her mind. Luthes was

Terry Wright

staying. She was moving to Colorado, and that was that.
For once in her life she'd found love, and she wasn't going
to let it go. Not again.

Jet engines droning, the flight was smooth over the
Atlantic. Taking Luthes' long fingers in her hand, she
caressed his bruises and cuts. "They'll heal nicely."

He looked at her thoughtfully, and then at his hands.
"Emmett proved to me that you were right. Violence is
often necessary to protect your home, family, and loved
ones. Beltzans forgot that, and we paid dearly for doing so.
We are not naturally violent, as you Tarreeda are, so we
need to learn this."

"We have to be violent to survive here."

"I fear your world." He squeezed her hand.

"We'll be fine."

Ray said, "Luthes doesn't belong here."

Lisa turned to her father, upset with his eavesdropping
but more-so with his attitude. "What you really mean is he
doesn't belong with me."

"He belongs back on Beltzee where we found him."

"We had to travel a long way to find the right man for
me, Dad. Why can't you understand that?"

"You're not thinking, Lisa. Your children are going to
have long fingers."

"There's a one-in-four chance of that, yes, but we'll
love them no matter what."

"I'm sure you will, but what about the salt? Will
future Crawfords have to live in a bubble?"

"You're the one living in a bubble, Dad."

Ray crossed his arms and fell silent.

Luthes said, "I hate to see you two arguing."

"Get used to it."

***

They landed in Atlanta to switch planes for Denver.

Lisa walked with Luthes, Agent Peterson, and her father toward their next gate when the intercom announced: *Ray Crawford, yellow courtesy phone, Ray Crawford.*

"Now what?"

They found a phone and huddled around Ray as he picked up the call. "Janis? Of course, what's up? Really? Gate B22...got it. We'll be there." He hung up, stared at the phone a moment, and then turned around. "We're going back to NASA."

Fear stabbed Lisa's heart. There was no reason to go to NASA, at least none that she could think of. Besides, Luthes could get sick from the salt again. "What about Colorado?"

"Our luggage is being transferred to a chartered Hawker at Gate B22." He looked up and down the concourse. "Which way is it?"

"Dad."

He didn't look at her. "This way."

"Colorado, Dad? Are you forgetting about Colorado?" When he turned toward her, she saw the face of a man walking to the gallows. "Dad?"

"We have to hurry."

***

The Hawker set down at the Shuttle Landing Facility at two in the afternoon. Lisa wasn't speaking to her father. During the entire flight, he'd refused to tell her what Janis had said on the phone, only answering with a lame, "You'll find out soon enough." Now, as the jet negotiated the taxiway, she feared bad news was coming fast.

A Sanitation and Isolation Unit van glided to a stop on the tarmac. Jet engines whined down. The door opened and let in a burst of sunshine. Lieutenant Swanson boarded with an oxygen bottle and mask, which he administered to Luthes before disembarking. Before Lisa had a chance to say goodbye, they'd climbed into the back of the van and sped away.

"Where are they taking him?" she demanded.

"Come on," Ray said. "Janis is waiting."

***

In the SuperMIGGS control room, techs busied themselves at their consoles, headsets in place as if something big was about to happen. Lisa rushed to Janis sitting at his terminal. Tracy stood behind him, rubbing his neck. Nearby, Lo Chin pecked away at a keyboard.

"Hello, Lisa," Tracy said. "What happened to your face?"

Lisa touched her healing dog bite wound. "It's nothing." She glared at Janis. "What's going on here?"

"We're sending the Beltzans home."

Her knees almost gave out. "But not Luthes. No. Not Luthes."

"Why not?"

"He's staying here with me."

Janis frowned. "What do you think you're doing, Lisa?"

"Now go easy on her," Tracy said.

Panic rising, Lisa rushed to the SuperMIGGS window, saw a lone shuttle suspended from the ceiling. A ramp extended from the loading dock to the open hatch. Beltzans were getting onboard. Why weren't they in Colorado? She whipped around. A terrible foreboding gripped her throat. "Where did that shuttle come from?"

"It's Brigham's," Janis said. "He sent Remsfield back for salt."

Lisa couldn't breathe. "That means you can send all the Beltzans home."

"That's the plan." The phone rang. Janis answered it. "Yes, Stan...Are you about ready?"

Lisa bit her lower lip. "Oh no." When the plan called for six Beltzans to return in the transporter, she was sure Luthes would choose to stay behind so one of his crewmates could go home in his place, but this...now things were different.

Just then, Lieutenant Swanson entered the control room with Luthes and Regarius. They were dressed in bulky white environmental suits and hoods with clear face shields.

"Luthes." Panic raced through her heart like a wild fire. She rushed to him. "What are you doing?"

"They want to brief me." His voice came out muffled from under the hood.

"Tell them you're not going. You're staying with me."

He put his arms around her, the puffy sleeves of the suit making movement awkward. "There is only room for six."

She looked at him through the hood's face shield. "They have a shuttle."

"Don't worry," he said, patting her shoulder with a gloved hand. "There is nothing left for me on Beltzee. I am staying here with you...unless they make me go...they wouldn't do that...would they?"

"They can't." She glared at Janis, who was still talking on the phone. "I won't let them." Hugging him, she inhaled the plastic odor of his suit and watched Regarius walk up to her father standing at the console.

"Earlier," the Beltzan specialist said, "you asked about the salt and why it did not kill the Tarreeda?"

"Yes," Ray replied. "In the lab at the University of Colorado."

"I have discovered two things in my genetic research at your university. The human and Tarreeda genome are identical, which means humans are the Tarreeda."

"Tell me something I don't already know."

"Identical includes genes that require sodium chloride.

Terry Wright

Beltzans do not have these genes, and as if Cada knew the Tarreeda's fate from the beginning, he gave them the gene they did not need until they arrived here."

"So they thrived on earth in spite of the salt."

"You thrived," Regarius said. "The defective gene that causes your violence is deeply imbedded in everyone here."

Ray glanced at Lisa and grimaced. "Don't remind me."

Contemplating her own defective gene, Lisa saw Peterson standing in the doorway. His feet were spread, his hands clasped behind him. "Luthes, I have a going away present for you."

"I am not going anywhere." He tucked Lisa under his arm protectively.

She savored the gesture.

With a reassuring smile, Peterson moved to Luthes and handed him a wooden figurine. "I carved it myself."

It was a human dressed in a finely engraved suit. There was a scar on his left cheek, just like Peterson's. "Something to remember me by."

"I will treasure it always." Luthes put it in his pocket. "Thank you."

"Perhaps we can meet again under better circumstances, exchange technology and ideas. That spaceship may have been more than *Project Aquarius* could handle, but even though you're leaving, I'm still in the alien business, you know."

"I will be in Colorado," Luthes said.

Peterson huffed. "I have a date with my wife."

Ray asked, "So you're finally going to visit her grave?"

"It's about time I told her I was sorry, don't you think?"

"You're not afraid to fly anymore. After all, you flew us off Choke Mountain in that helicopter."

"I didn't have much time to think about it." Peterson tapped Luthes' shoulder. "Goodbye, my alien friend."

"There are no aliens," Luthes replied. "We came from the same place. We have the same god. Will I see you in Colorado?"

"Sorry, Luthes." Peterson waved and left the control room.

Lisa didn't like the tone in Peterson's voice or the finality of his gesture. He knew something that she wasn't privy to, thanks to her overprotective father. They were up to something. She nestled deeper into the crook of Luthes' baggy arm as if only he could protect her from the hurt that was coming.

Janis got off the phone. His face looked hound-dog sad. Lisa rushed to him. "Don't make Luthes go. Please." She tugged on his lab coat, holding back tears.

"We aren't going to make him do anything he doesn't want to do," Janis said in a soft and assuring voice. "But there's something he needs to know first."

"What's that?"

Janis stepped up to Luthes, warily glanced at Regarius, who nodded, and then began to explain the situation. "There is no sodium chloride on Beltzee. Brigham and his men are dying, so he made a deal with Commander Sangrean, you know him?"

"Yes," Luthes replied. He looked at Lisa. "He is the commander of my fleet...was..."

Janis went on. "Sangrean teleported one shuttle into orbit, with one pilot. Major Remsfield was given two things to do: first, bring back as many salt tablets as the shuttle will hold, and second, he was to give you a message."

Luthes stiffened. "Me?"

"What message?" Lisa blurted out, her heart drumming in her chest.

Janis glanced at her sympathetically. "Please, this is hard enough as it is."

"Are they going to rebuild the fleet?" Lisa asked. "Is Luthes needed...?"

"What did your pilot say?" Luthes pressed.

Janis squared his shoulders, regarded Luthes a moment then said, "Normally this would be good news, however, under the present circumstances..." he glanced at Lisa, "I'll let you be the judge." He took a quick breath. "Your wife and daughter are alive."

Luthes gasped and staggered backward. "Verrilla and Sashi?"

Lisa took the news like a punch in the gut. "Oh dear."

"My wife and daughter are alive?"

"Yes," Janis affirmed. "And they want you to come home. It's your decision, of course." Janis turned to Lisa. "I'm sorry."

Luthes looked at her with wide eyes. "They are alive." His face beamed with joy.

But for Lisa, time came to a sudden stop. The room began to whirl. She was happy for Luthes, of course, but shocked nonetheless. Her breath came in sharp hitches as the reality of this news cut into her chest like a dull blade. Surely he wouldn't change his mind. He wouldn't go back. He wouldn't leave her.

Behind the hood's facemask, the surprise in his eyes drained to confusion, as if he too suddenly realized the magnitude of his dilemma. "I can go home?"

Janis nodded. "The others are boarding as we speak."

"And the salt tablets?"

"This has to end right now," Janis said. "There's only a minimal supply, enough to get the survivors on their feet. Major Remsfield will have to convince Brigham to give up and come home. If he doesn't, they'll all die."

"Your general does not seem like the kind of Tarreeda who would just give up."

Lisa couldn't stand waiting any longer. She had to know what he was going to do. "You're staying, right,

Luthes?"

He moved to her, and slowly reaching up, he removed his hood, revealing a sad face and tearing eyes. The dimple on his chin quivered. "You have been my pillar of strength, Lisa."

She threw her arms around his neck. "And you mine."

"You gave me hope for a future."

"And you gave me love."

"And because of you, I now understand the Tarreeda. My enemies have now become my friends, and I have become a better Beltzan."

"But what about us?" Her soul was melting away, draining from her chest in a river of dread.

"Verrilla and Sashi are alive. I am suddenly torn inside. What I once lost, I can now have again, but to do that I must let go of what I hold so dearly to me now. Either choice I make, I will give up something important. I do not know what to do. Just say the word, Lisa, and I will stay."

"Stay," she choked out.

Without hesitating, Luthes said to Regarius, "Tell Verrilla and Sashi that I love them, but..."

"No," Lisa blurted out. "You can't." Deep down inside, she knew that he couldn't stay. If he did, Sashi would be forced to grow up without her father, as Lisa had grown up without Ray. She couldn't bear the thought of being the reason for that little girl's loss. And though she'd promised herself to never let go of this love she'd found, for Sashi's sake, Lisa knew she had to let him go. "You must go home, Luthes." She hugged him tighter, unable to believe she'd said the words.

"But I thought we were going to be together, we were going to have a family."

"I want that more than anything," she said. "But we have to think of Sashi."

"Yes but..."

"Please don't worry about me, Luthes. Go home to

your family." Her heart fell into the pit of her stomach. "But know that I will love you until the end of time."

"As I will love you, Lisa."

In a silent control room, as they embraced each other again, she remembered Luthes telling her that Beltzans loved deeply, wholly, and completely. He'd said her love was superficial, and that he was not in love with her. Since then, they'd been through a lot together, and for him to say that he loved her now meant that he'd come to realize that her love for him was genuine, after all. She had earned his love. Now, as she savored his strong arms around her, she was losing him, yet, for the first time in her life, she wasn't thinking of herself but of Sashi and Verrilla waiting for a father and husband to return from war. It was an unselfish thing to do. That was true love.

Tracy moved to Janis and put her arm around him. "It's time."

Luthes released Lisa, and then he pulled her into his arms again and hugged her one last time before stepping back. "Goodbye, Lisa."

Holding back tears, she unclipped the translator from her blouse and placed it in the palm of his gloved hand. "I won't be needing this anymore. Goodbye, Luthes."

He closed his long fingers around it.

Janis patted Luthes' shoulder. "They are waiting."

Regarius shook Janis's hand. "Perhaps we'll meet again."

"Perhaps."

Hood back in place, Luthes turned to the door. She could barely see him and Regarius walking away through the tears welling in her eyes.

Hugging Tracy, Janis said, "Let's do this so we can go home."

She smiled at him. "Thank you."

"For what?"

"For helping me save the universe."

He smirked. "Now if I can just get you to quit smoking."

She kissed his cheek, and as she moved to her laser terminal, she smiled at Lisa. "That was a brave thing you did, letting him go like that."

"You're lucky to have someone to love."

"I know."

Lo reported, "The Programmer is activated."

"Let's send them home." Janis sat at his control terminal and swiveled his chair to face the monitors.

Lisa rushed to the SuperMIGGS window and peered teary-eyed inside. Luthes walked up the ramp to the shuttle. Regarius was in front of him. At the hatch, they turned and waved goodbye, and then disappeared inside. She waved back. He couldn't have seen her, but it made her feel better, just the same.

The ramp retracted, and the ceiling lights went out, leaving the gravity chamber awash in a crimson glow. Electromagnets started humming.

Ray moved to her side and put his arm around her shoulders. She cringed, still angry with him for the things he'd said about Luthes not belonging here. But as much as she wanted to shove him away, she couldn't. She needed him now more than ever.

"I'm sorry," he said. "I didn't realize how much you loved each other."

Leaning into him, she stared at the shuttle, her heart breaking again. "Tell me you're not happy to see him go."

"It hurts me as much as losing Kate."

"When is life going to work out for us?"

"It already has. We have each other."

Within moments, the SuperMIGGS roared, and the black mist swallowed the shuttle. In a flash it was gone.

"I'm going to miss him, Dad." She buried her face in his chest and cried.

Chapter Thirty-Five

T he command center on Beltzee should have been bustling with activity. Brigham surveyed the remnants of his operational staff, most of whom were slumped over their consoles, wheezing and sweating. All field sorties had been called off. His surviving troops had returned to Fleet Base headquarters. Man's first intergalactic war was turning to defeat, not for lack of military prowess, but for lack of salt.

"Goddamned salt," Brigham muttered, his voice ragged. Sweat had drenched his shirt, and his underwear stuck to his backside as he walked to the Star Wars console. The technician there had passed out. "Get this man to the infirmary," Brigham ordered.

Nobody moved to help him.

Colonel Scott reported in. "It's been three days, sir. Where's Remsfield...and the salt?"

Turning, Brigham noticed the Colonel looking spry as he entered the room. "You're holding up pretty well."

"My connections are running dry." He displayed a bottle of salt tablets. "These are the last ones I could get."

"The shuttle should be here soon." Brigham coughed, wondering how many enlisted men the Colonel had cheated out of their salt rations.

Scott strode to the Star Wars console and dragged the unconscious man from his chair. "We don't have much time left." He dropped the limp soldier on the floor.

"I haven't had salt for four days," Brigham put in. "I've been drinking water like a whale."

"You're gonna have to stop pussyfooting around with

Sangrean. It's time we started pulling out his fingernails and sticking pins in his eyeballs. He'll talk, I tell you."

"Not to save himself, he won't."

"Sir." The radio operator cupped his hands over his headset earphones. "I've got him. Remsfield. He's back."

That was the best news Brigham had heard all day. He almost smiled. "Put him on the speakers."

"Whiskey-Xray to command, I repeat, do you read?"

"Loud and clear, *Whiskey-Xray.* Your approach vector is thirty-by-thirty-nine at ten degrees. We see you on the scope."

"Roger that, command."

Brigham examined the radar display that fixed the approaching shuttle's telemetry in orbit along with the Star Wars satellites they'd deployed earlier. Each blip identified altitude, attitude, and status. But the shuttle's trajectory was wrong. "What's he doing?"

"Whiskey-Xray, you're off course."

"I'm fine, command."

Colonel Scott stepped up. "The son of a bitch is headed for PLR One."

Fighting panic, Brigham donned a headset. "Remsfield, you're not playing hero, are you?"

Only static came back.

Moments later, PLR One's blip went out.

"He disintegrated it," Scott shouted. "The bastard is taking away our advantage."

"I bet Janis Mackey had something to do with this. Get a fix on that shuttle."

Scott seated himself at the Star Wars console and started typing. "Activating PLR Two. We'll get the bastard before he gets us."

The status and attitude numbers for the last remaining PLR began to change as it calculated the firing angles and aligned the sighting dish satellites it required to hit the shuttle. Remsfield was going to pay for his treason,

Terry Wright

Brigham swore.

"Target locked," Scott said, his finger on the firing button.

The shuttle was heading straight for the PLR. It would be an easy shot, Brigham thought just as the consequences of his actions suddenly occurred to him. The salt. If he gave the order to fire, not only would Remsfield pay with his life, but so would he, so would all of his surviving troops, and the scientists... "Wait!" Brigham shouted.

"It's in range of his particle beams," Scott reported.

"We can't shoot and destroy the salt he's bringing back."

"Damn!" Scott sat back in his chair. "He must've known that."

"The perfect shield, we shoot him, we die. Stand down, Colonel."

Seconds later, PLR Two was destroyed.

"Now what?" Scott asked.

"I'm gonna kill the bastard."

"He's on approach," the radio operator reported.

Brigham drew his Colt. "Let's go."

By the time he got outside, a white streak blazed across the sky as the shuttle reentered the atmosphere at well over 18,000 miles per hour. "It'll take him twenty minutes to get on the ground," he told Colonel Scott. "I want every healthy man we've got out here to unload the salt."

"Yes, sir." Scott sprinted off.

The twin suns beat down on Brigham like the fires of hell. Twenty minutes seemed like an eternity. Though his legs felt weak, and his mouth dry, he held the Colt in his hand with every intention of using it.

***

The teleportation machine repairs were nearly

~410~

completed. Sangrean watched his technicians install the last panel in the control room wall. Two men were sweeping the floor. After all the damage the human scientists had done, the machine was now at full function, capable of teleporting thirty vehicles into orbit at once. Now all he had to do was convince General Brigham to use it.

"Good work, men." He headed for the door.

Outside, the humans stood together looking skyward. His curiosity spiked, and looking up, he saw the telltale streak of a returning shuttle. He swallowed hard. The final battle was about to begin.

A truck rumbled across the compound to where the men were standing. Behind them, several parked shuttles glistened under the intense shine of two suns. Curious Beltzans emerged from surrounding buildings. A murmur began to rise from the growing crowd.

Verrilla and Sashi rushed to his side. They were still wearing the new dresses Brigham had supplied them, though they'd become heavily soiled from working in the kitchens. "Is it Luthes?" Verrilla asked.

Sangrean swallowed. "If Brigham has kept his word, yes."

"Daddy," Sashi said, smiling brightly.

"He's home." Verrilla hugged her daughter as they watched the long white streak fade to nothing.

BOOM!

***

Aboard *Whiskey-Xray*, Luthes gripped the armrests of his seat and strained against the pressure on his chest caused by the decelerating shuttle. Out the side viewport, he saw the green seas of his home planet shimmering below him. It was a sight he thought he'd never see again. Finally, he was home. He'd never felt such joy.

Remsfield sat to his left, monitoring the computer

systems that controlled the shuttle's landing attitude, the sharp S turns and steep nose angle. Luthes remembered landing *Questnar* in *Latearian's* docking bay and how that maneuver seemed simple compared to this fiery return to Beltzee.

The shuttle slowed considerably and leveled off.

"Welcome home, Luthes," Remsfield said.

"All of Beltzee owes you a debt of gratitude, Major, for destroying the death beam satellites."

"Ah, yes." Remsfield opened a compartment on the console, moved a gun aside, and retracted a book. "I stowed this away for you."

Luthes took it, flipped through the pages, which appeared to be technical drawings of some kind. "What is it?"

"Compliments of Stan Burton," he said. "The blueprints for the death beams, as you call them. It's about time your people had the means to defend yourselves. You can't live in peace without the ability to wage war."

"This I have come to learn," Luthes said. "Sometimes violence is necessary."

"We'll be landing soon. You'll find your maroon flight uniforms in the C deck lockers. You and your men should get out of those white monkey suits and into something more comfortable."

"Yes. Thank you." Luthes unfastened the safety harness, got up, and worked his way down through the hatch to C deck. The route was familiar to him, as he'd traversed the shuttle before, just after his capture. It seemed different now. This time he was a free Beltzan instead of a prisoner of war.

The other crewmen had already begun changing clothes. Regarius handed Luthes his uniform. It had been cleaned and pressed. "You must look your best, Luthes...for your wife and daughter."

"Finally." He retrieved from a pocket the figurine

Peterson had given him, an object he would always treasure. "Do you think we'll ever see Agent Peterson again?"

The shuttle pitched a little, rolled into a gentle turn.

"We talked of a meeting..." Regarius held on to a handrail. "Under peaceful conditions. He plans to approach his superiors with the idea of sending a scientific delegation here some day."

"How will we know when?"

"We won't."

"Maybe he will bring Janis and Tracy."

"I hate to think what our fate would have been without them."

Luthes shuddered. "Cada was looking after us."

"Yes." Regarius inspected his buttons, brushed his sleeves. "Hurry. We are landing."

Done changing, Luthes ran a comb through his hair and returned to the flight deck. Safety harness in place, he saw the familiar layout of Fleet Base ahead. The towering repulsor cannons had been reduced to mounds of charred rubble. He imagined how fiercely Sangrean must have fought to save Beltzee, how futile that had been.

The shuttle pitched into a steep descent toward the granitite plain. He hoped Verrilla and Sashi were waiting for him this time.

***

"There they are," someone shouted from the crowd.

Brigham saw sunlight glint off the shuttle's fuselage, pictured Major Remsfield at the controls, totally unaware that he was about to die.

Smoke swirled from the tires as the shuttle's main gear touched down. Twin drag chutes deployed. The nose gear settled to the ground. Two miles away, the shuttle turned around and taxied to the tarmac, pulse light engines whining.

As it stopped, Brigham stood in front of the nosecone, feet spread and gun in hand. He hoped Remsfield could see the fire in his eyes.

The hatch opened. Armed soldiers gathered around. A ladder came down. Then boots appeared and maroon pant legs.

Brigham frowned as a Beltzan crewman deplaned, followed by another and another and another. That son of a bitch. Against a direct order, Remsfield brought back the prisoners. That made two good reasons to kill him.

Before long, twelve aliens lined up on the tarmac. Brigham recognized Regarius. A cheer rose from the gathering crowd of Beltzans. Let them have their moment of glory. He waited for Remsfield to show his face.

The radio officer approached with a handheld. "Sir. You'd better take this."

"What the hell?"

"It's Remsfield."

"The bastard." Brigham grabbed the radio, pressed the talk button. "Get your ass out here and get what's coming to you."

"I've brought back one day's supply of salt," Remsfield said. *"You may kill me for it, but that won't change anything, sir."*

Brigham's guts twisted. "Are you out of your mind?" he spat into the radio. "One day?"

"Yes, sir."

"Deplane. That's an order." Now Brigham had three good reasons to kill him.

"Be forewarned, sir, there's a court martial waiting for you back on earth. You'll pay for what you have done to these Beltzans."

"It's a goddamned war!"

"The war is over, General, and Sangrean has won without firing a single shot."

"You guys aren't so smart. I have *not* lost this war." Brigham felt a sudden rush of nausea, staggered with dizziness. The sun beat down on him. He desperately needed that salt. "It's not over until I say it's over."

***

It appeared to Sangrean, standing with Verrilla and Sashi some distance from the humans, that Brigham was losing his mind, yelling as he was. Sangrean's experience with this type of behavior was limited, but he feared the general was becoming more dangerous.

"Where's Luthes?" Verrilla whispered. "I don't see him."

Sangrean wondered the same thing. He looked down at Sashi, saw tears welling in her eyes.

Suddenly, Verrilla shrieked. "Sangrean. Look out."

He turned into the barrel of Colonel Scott's gun.

"I've had enough of you, old man," Scott growled.

Verrilla jumped on his back, pounded on his shoulders. "Leave him alone."

Scott tossed her to the ground like a bothersome child. "Get moving."

With a gun pressed to the back of his head, Sangrean complied, heart beating hard and fearing the same fate as his communications officer.

Scott forced him toward the clutch of humans and General Brigham, who stood in front of the landed shuttle still holding the gun and screaming into a handheld communications link. "Get out here, Major."

"Is there a problem?" Sangrean asked Brigham.

He turned around, gun held up, straight-armed. Sweat poured from his face and neck, his lips taught; a Tarreeda evil glared from his squinting eyes. "You will give me the technical plans for your teleportation system right now."

Sangrean glanced around, a fear he'd never known

pumping through his body. Oddly, he saw the same fear in the Tarreeda soldiers' eyes as they backed away from their enraged leader.

"Right now." Brigham turned the gun on the line of Beltzans who'd just deplaned. "Or I'm going to start shooting them one at a time, your precious survivors of *Questnar*."

"You'd better agree," Scott growled into Sangrean's ear. "A desperate enemy is a dangerous enemy. We've got nothing left to lose."

Sangrean knew that if he backed down now, everything the fleet stood for, all the Beltzans who'd lost their lives would have been wasted. "Nothing has changed. I will not give you what you have come to steal."

The gun came back around. "Your hand," Brigham shouted. "Show me your hand."

Confused, Sangrean offered his right hand, palm up in a gesture of good will.

"Hold it out."

"Why?"

"Hold it out!"

He extended his hand to the side. "This—"

Brigham's gun exploded.

Flesh ripped off Sangrean's hand, bone splintered, blood spewed. He grabbed the meaty stub of his palm, pulled it in to his stomach protectively. A scream lodged in his throat, not from pain but from shock.

Colonel Scott shoved him to the ground.

"No!" Verrilla screamed. She landed on her knees, hovered over Sangrean. "Leave him alone."

"S-stay out of this," Sangrean groaned.

Brigham bent down, grabbed Verrilla's arm and yanked her to her feet. "Sangrean, you stubborn bastard. You won't do it for your men. You won't do it for yourself. Perhaps you'll do it for her." He jabbed the gun into Verrilla's throat. "Give me those plans."

Sangrean prayed to Cada, *give me strength.* "My answer is the same. No."

BANG!

A gasp went through the crowd.

Sangrean's heart seized. He squinted against a bright sky, saw Verrilla's silhouette fall, Brigham's gun hand drop to his side. "No," Sangrean cried out. "No, Cada, no."

Colonel Scott stepped back, dropped his gun and raised his hands.

Verrilla knelt next to Sangrean, whimpering, clutching his shoulders. Cada had saved her. His eyes shifted to Brigham, still standing there but no longer cursing. Then his knees buckled. He keeled over and hit the ground with a thud.

Amazed, Sangrean looked toward the shuttle, saw someone on the ladder, pointing a gun at Colonel Scott.

"Luthes?"

***

"Stay where you are." Luthes stood at the top of the ladder, showing Remsfield's gun to everyone. Scanning the stilled crowd, a sickly feeling rose in his stomach. He'd just killed a Tarreeda, something he thought he could never do. But seeing Verrilla in mortal danger had propelled him to take the Major's gun from the compartment and scramble to the open hatch. Now, he could barely remember doing it, just going through the motions, his mind fighting panic, the scene before him surreal.

Brigham lay in a pool of blood. Wide-eyed human soldiers and Beltzans stared at him in disbelief. Lying on the ground, Sangrean moaned.

"Medic," someone shouted.

A Beltzan officer wrenched Colonel Scott's arms behind his back. Another picked up his dropped gun. He didn't resist, just stared down at his dead commander.

More Fleet officers converged on the scene with stun-wands and headgear. Soldiers dropped their weapons. The Tarreeda threat was quickly subdued.

Luthes saw Verrilla bent over Sangrean and looking up at him, her face morphing from terrified to joyful. "Luthes."

"Daddy." Sashi ran toward him, her long white hair streaming behind her.

Verrilla started running too, her dress swishing. "Luthes."

Finally he had found them.

"Give me the gun," Remsfield said. "It's over."

He tossed it to the Major then jumped down from the ladder to the granitite surface, arms outstretched for his approaching family.

"Finally," he whispered, holding Verrilla tightly, inhaling the scent of her skin, and kissing her neck. It seemed like a million years since that fateful day he'd brought *Questnar* to *Latearian* and the Tarreeda Cruiser appeared. "I thought you were dead."

"Me too, Daddy, me too," Sashi cried.

"Yes, you too." He lifted his daughter and hugged her with one arm. She'd grown in his absence. "I've missed you both."

Sangrean got to his feet. The medic had bandaged his hand. "Send Brigham home with the others," he told his officers. "His ashes will not defile Beltzan soil."

"You killed him," Verrilla said, looking at the general lying on a stretcher, one arm hanging over the side, dripping blood as they carted him away.

"Point and shoot," Luthes explained. "The Tarreeda have made killing easy. I feel sad for having done it, though."

"You saved my life."

"Sometimes violence is the only way to survive. I learned that on earth."

"I cannot imagine you imprisoned in that horrible place." She shivered. "To Cada, you have returned safely."

"To Cada." He hugged his wife and daughter. In the back of his mind, he thanked Lisa for the personal sacrifice she'd made so that he could be reunited with his family. "I'll never leave you again."

"I know."

"Quickly, everyone," Sangrean said. "We must ready the shuttles for teleportation. The Tarreeda will depart our planet at once."

A cheer rose from the victorious Beltzans.

***

NINE MONTHS LATER:

In a dimly lit hospital room, the miracle of birth had just taken place. Lisa coddled her newborn. This wasn't just any ordinary miracle, but the birth of a child who could change human destiny.

"Look, Dad."

Ray leaned over her shoulder, his misty gaze on the infant. "You did a great job, Lisa. I'm proud of you."

"Isn't she beautiful?" The pain of childbirth forgotten, she focused on the face of her daughter, pink and yawning, her small body, so light and frail, wrapped in a white blanket. She had five normal fingers, unlike her father's.

Luthes had given Lisa a gift. He had given her someone to love.

"What's her name?" Ray asked.

"Lilith. She's going to start a whole new human genome." Lisa rocked the child.

Lilith had a good chance of not possessing the Tarreeda's defective gene: mankind's only hope to end the violence.

Terry Wright

About the Author

There's nothing mundane in the writing world of **Terry Wright**. Tension, conflict, and suspense propel his readers through the pages as if they were on fire. Published in Science Fiction, Horror, and Supernatural, his mastery of the action thriller has won him International acclaim as an accomplished screenplay writer. When he's not writing, editing, or judging contests, he's an avid Harley Davidson Motorcycle enthusiast and rides with the Denver Chapter HOGs. He lives in Centennial, Colorado, with his wife and their four dogs.

He invites you to visit his website at
www.terrywrightbooks.com where you'll find more
information on his short stories, novels, and screenplays.

Enjoy other novels and short stories by Terry Wright

The 13th Power Quest, Book 1
https://www.twbpress.com/the13thpowerquest.html

The 13th Power Journey, Book 2
https://www.twbpress.com/the13thpowerjourney.html

The Pearl of Death
https://www.twbpress.com/thepearlofdeath.html

Black Jack
https://www.twbpress.com/blackjack.html

The Grief Syndrome
https://www.twbpress.com/thegriefsyndrome.html

The Duplication Factor
https://www.twbpress.com/duplicationfactor.html

Justin Graves
https://www.twbpress.com/justingraves.html

Z-motors, The Job From Hell
https://www.twbpress.com/zmotors.html

Street Beat
https://www.twbpress.com/streetbeat.html

Return me to Mistwillow
https://www.twbpress.com/returnmetomistwillow.html

Wilderness Rampage
https://www.twbpress.com/wildernessrampage.html

Discover more sci-fi, horror, supernatural, and thriller
works by authors from around the world at

https://www.twbpress.com